A BLIND GODDESS

Billy Boyle
The First Wave
Blood Alone
Evil for Evil
Rag and Bone
A Mortal Terror
Death's Door

A BLIND GODDESS

A Billy Boyle World War II Mystery

James R. Benn

Published by Soho Press, Inc.
853 Broadway
New York, NY 10003

Library of Congress Cataloging-in-Publication Data

Benn, James R.
A blind goddess / James R. Benn.
p. cm — (A Billy Boyle World War II mystery)
ISBN 978-1-61695-192-4
eISBN 978-1-61695-193-1
1. Boyle, Billy (Fictitious character)—Fiction.
2. World War,1939–1945—England—Fiction. 3. Murder—Investigation—
Fiction. I. Title.
PS3602.E6644B65 2013
813'.6—dc23   2013004268

Printed in the United States of America

10 9 8 7 6 5 4 3 2 1

For
Jeff and Ben Ross
Lively boys, strong men, fine fathers.

That Justice is a blind goddess
Is a thing to which we black are wise:
Her bandage hides two festering sores
That once perhaps were eyes.

—Langston Hughes, 1923

A BLIND GODDESS

A BLIND GODDESS

CHAPTER ONE

HUNGERFORD, ENGLAND
March 1944

TREE DIDN'T SPEAK. He'd look up and meet my eyes for a split second, then lower his gaze and shake his head, as if wondering if this was such a good idea. Given our past, I couldn't blame him. The pub owner worked his broom, muttering to himself as he swept shards of broken glass across the floor and looked at me with suspicion. I couldn't fault the barkeep either.

A fire burned low in the grate, but not enough to ward off the chill in the air. The Three Crowns Pub was empty except for us and the publican. Me, Kaz, and Tree. Sergeant Eugene "Tree" Jackson, to be precise. I'd brought Kaz along for moral support, so I might as well be precise about his full name as well: Lieutenant Baron Piotr Augustus Kazimierz of the Polish Army in Exile and my good friend.

Tree had once been a friend, the kind you get the hard way, by starting off as enemies. Over time we had changed, and found common ground. But then things turned sour, and somehow we ended up back where we started. That was a long time ago, but not the kind of time that heals any wounds.

We sat at the table nearest the fire. The pub wasn't much to begin with and was even less impressive with smashed glassware decorating every surface. Heavy mugs, pint glasses, whiskey tumblers, all reduced to sharp edges and reflected light. Tree didn't help by playing mute, even though he'd asked for this visit. When we met out front, he'd saluted, since both Kaz and I wore lieutenant's bars and he had sergeant's stripes on his sleeves. Tree addressed me by rank, and thanked us for coming, very stiff and formal. He reminded me of his old man, whom I'd never thought of as anyone but Mr. Jackson. I wondered what he saw in the grown-up Billy Boyle and told myself it didn't matter.

When we entered the Three Crowns, Tree didn't comment on the destruction. He nodded a greeting to the owner, appearing to be on friendly terms. The publican shook his head sadly, much as Tree was doing, and bent to his broom. There was a lot of glass to be swept.

Tree dug a pack of Chesterfields out of his pocket and offered us the smokes. We waved them off and watched as he flipped open a Zippo and lit up. It had been seven years since I'd last seen him, but his hands still looked like a kid's. Long and slim, just as he was, and graceful too, every move easy and assured. At six feet tall, with hands that could handle a basketball or a football like a pro, he suited the nickname well enough. Having Eugene for a first name didn't hurt either. He always thought it sounded like a girl's name, while Tree was unmistakably male. He inhaled the smoke, looking at us both with his dark brown eyes as he exhaled, holding his gaze this time. His skin was a shade lighter than his eyes. The color of polished walnut, I had always thought.

"Bet you're surprised to see me, Billy," Tree said, finally breaking his silence. He didn't smile, but one eyebrow arched slightly, a gesture of friendship, perhaps.

"Surprised you're still in the army," I said, wary of Tree's intent. Kaz kept silent, his eyes watching the publican as he went about his business, then drifting in Tree's direction.

"You're Polish," Tree said to Kaz. He was making small talk that seemed ridiculous in the circumstances. I figured since he wanted to see me, I'd wait until he was ready to spill. Meanwhile, I watched the two of them size each other up.

"Yes," said Kaz. "And I understand you were a colleague of Billy's in Boston."

"Colleague? I guess you could call it that, Lieutenant. You a colleague of Billy's over here now?" There was a challenge in Tree's words, no matter how lightly he spoke them. Or a warning.

"We work together, yes," Kaz said, with an air of studied indifference. The two of them were a world apart in all things, except for me. Tree was a Negro; tall and good-looking in a Josh Gibson sort of way. Gibson was a six-foot-plus player for the Homestead Grays, and once I'd called him the black Babe Ruth for his incredible hitting. Tree had then called the Babe the white Josh Gibson, and we'd laughed about it. We'd laughed about a lot of things back then. The foolishness of the adult world, mainly. And now here we were smack in the middle of it.

My friendship with Kaz was different in many ways. He and I'd had a few laughs, sure, and I'd call him my best friend in a heartbeat, but life these days wasn't all chuckles and mischief. It was about staying alive, and Kaz and I had helped each other out in that department too many times already. With Tree it had been out-and-out sidesplitting guffaws. With Kaz, it was more likely to be a lopsided grin, a few drinks, and then on to the next mission. Over here, you set aside foolishness pretty damn quick.

Small and wiry, sporting steel-rimmed spectacles, Kaz was a good-looking guy himself, if you only looked at one side of his face. On the other side he carried a scar from eye to jawbone, a souvenir from our first case together, and a daily reminder of all he'd lost. I caught Tree staring at it for a second, but he didn't ask questions.

Tree was poor. Kaz was rich. His British Army uniform was tailor-made, and he wore it well. Tree was wearing a Parsons jacket, outdated since the new M-1943 field jackets replaced them months ago. Probably the way things went in the colored units. A lot like life back in Boston.

"I thought we might have a drink," Tree said, drumming his fingers on the tabletop and glancing at the floor. "But there's a shortage of glasses."

"Listen, Tree," I said, giving up on waiting for him to explain himself. "I got your message yesterday, and came as soon as I could. I started a five-day leave today and spent my first morning packed into a train from London to come out here and talk to you. I don't know what the problem is, but you didn't invite me for drinks. And what the hell happened here anyway?"

"You Yanks happened, that's what," the owner said, emptying a dustpan filled with glass shards.

"That's not fair, Horace," Tree said. "I'm a Yank too."

"Don't mean your lot," Horace said. "You know that."

"So there was a brawl or something here," I said. "Let's find another pub and have a drink, okay? Maybe that'll loosen your tongue."

"Don't bother yourself," Horace said, and disappeared behind the bar.

"What does he mean?" Kaz said.

"He means that every damn glass in every damn pub in Hungerford is in the same condition. It wasn't a brawl. It was a deliberate attack, pure and simple."

"By Americans?" Kaz said.

"Yeah," Tree said. "White Americans."

"I don't understand," I said. I could imagine, but I wanted the details.

"You know how the army keeps things segregated," Tree said. "But I'll explain for your Polish pal here. Uncle Sam's got colored units, like mine, but that means they have to double up on everything else, to make sure white folks don't have to share the same building, transportation, food, or anything with us. Trains, ships, trucks, you name it. Even towns. Hungerford was designated an off-duty town for colored troops back in forty-two."

"Why?" Kaz asked.

"Women, liquor, politics, it all comes together over here," Tree said. "Plenty of my fellow American GIs don't like the idea of seeing us walking out with white girls. Given the lack of female Negroes in England, that's the only choice we have. And the ladies don't seem to mind one bit since they weren't raised to despise my race."

"There would be fights," Kaz said.

"Fights and killing, for certain. You see, over here a white man doesn't have the automatic right to kill a Negro, not like they do in the Deep South. Military justice ain't much, but it's better than Alabama justice. So to avoid unpleasantness, the army designates certain towns for whites and others for colored troops. Nothing official, of course. But no white GI has ever had a pass to spend time in Hungerford." Tree spat out the words, and I saw the humiliation beneath his anger.

"But your unit did?"

"Yeah. First colored troops in the area was a Quartermaster truck company, a few miles west. Then we came along. We're based outside Hungerford." Tree lifted his chin as he spoke of his unit, pride evident in how he held himself. No humiliation there.

"Let's get back to what happened here," I said, anxious to get to the bottom of this. My leave was ticking away, and I had places to go.

"Well, the army decided that with so many white troops moving into the area, they needed this town for their leaves. Orders came down yesterday. We get Kintbury, a few miles from here. Real small town, not much to do. White troops get Hungerford, starting midnight tonight."

"Did the colored soldiers break up the pubs because they were angry?" Kaz asked.

"Nope. We like the people here. Not a man among us would cause them harm. At noon today three truckloads of white boys drove into town, made for the three pubs, and took baseball bats to the drinking glasses. All of them. Didn't touch anything else."

"Why?" Kaz asked, wrinkling his brow as he tried to work out the logic of it. This was new territory to him, but all too familiar to me.

"So they wouldn't have to drink from the same glasses as Negroes had," I said.

CHAPTER TWO

WE MOVED OUTSIDE. I needed air, to get away from the broken glass and the downcast look on Horace's face. I wanted to keep going and leave Tree and his miseries behind, but it was too late for that. Seven years too late.

"Have a seat," Tree said, pointing to a rough wooden bench set against the whitewashed stone of the Three Crowns Pub. Kaz took the end, hitching up his tailored trousers as he sat. Tree stuffed his hands in his pockets against the chill and leaned forward, elbows at his side. He never liked the cold much. I had a trench coat on over my new Ike jacket, the M-44 service jacket with the short waist, designed by General Eisenhower himself. Nothing but the best for the boys from Supreme Headquarters, Allied Expeditionary Force. Kaz, with his Savile Row bespoke dress uniform, looked like the aristocrat he was as he checked his polished shoes. Tree looked like a kid from Beacon Hill's North Slope. Tough, and braving the cold in a hand-me-down coat. It was odd seeing him here in an English village, outside of a pub that had probably been there a hundred years before the house was built in Boston. Shops lined the street, white-washed low buildings with slate roofs and colorful signs. Solid brick homes and stately elm trees lined the road, springtime buds showing on the branches. A picture-book English village.

"Why am I here, Tree?" I said as I settled onto the bench, eyes forward to the road. "Is it because of what those GIs did?"

"No. If I called you every time a white man gave me trouble, I'd have run out of nickels long ago. I didn't even know about that until ten minutes before you showed up. I feel bad for Horace; he's a decent guy."

"Anyone report it?"

"No. The local police wouldn't be able to question anyone on base, and the army doesn't want any publicity. My guess is that when word reaches the right officer, guys will show up with a wad of cash for each of the pubs. A lot of guys will be happy to chip in for glasses untouched by Negroes."

"Yeah," I said. He was right. It would be taken care of quietly, and the insult would go unanswered. "Which base were they from?"

"Take your pick. There's an air force base over at Greenham Common. More fighter squadrons coming in every day, plus troop transports. The Hundred-and-First Airborne is spread all across Berkshire. One of their regiments is headquartered at Littlecote House, not far out of town," Tree said, shrugging at the uselessness of conjecture. "Plus other units I don't even know about. Could have been any of them."

"What's your unit?" I asked, curiosity getting the best of me. "Quartermaster?"

"Hell no, Billy," Tree said. "We're the Six-Seventeenth Tank Destroyer Battalion. Combat outfit. Used to be an anti-tank battalion with towed thirty-seven millimeter pieces, but now we're training on the M-Ten. I command a five-man crew, the best in Baker Company, if not the whole damn battalion." He sat up a little straighter when he said that, and I knew it meant a lot to Tree. Any Negro soldier who rose to the rank of sergeant and got himself into a combat unit had walked a hard road.

"I knew there were Negro units fighting in Italy," I said, "but I didn't know there were any tank outfits in England."

"They got us loading and unloading every damn thing under the sun," Tree said. "From Liberty ships to deuce-and-a-half trucks. They got us cooking and cleaning, everything but fighting. I've been in the army too long to sit out the shooting war humping supplies."

"If that's what you want, Tree, I'm glad for you. But what am I doing here? Are you in trouble?"

"If I was in trouble, I'd think twice about you helping me again, Billy. But I know you mean well, and there is someone who needs help."

"Who?"

"Abraham Smith, my gunner. They got him locked up in Shepton Mallet."

"For doing what?" I didn't know where Shepton Mallet was, but the most important thing was to understand what Tree was asking of me. I had the feeling it wasn't going to be easy.

"For murder. But he didn't do it." I looked askance at Tree, unable to disguise my cop's suspicious nature. "Really, he didn't."

"Okay, who didn't he murder?"

"A constable."

"They have him for killing an English cop? Then they must have evidence, Tree. What do you think I can do?"

"You're the one in the justice business, Billy, you tell me," Tree said. "How about allowing that he's innocent until proven guilty? How about trusting that I wouldn't ask if he wasn't innocent?"

"You know? For certain?"

"I saw him on base that night. And the next morning. He seemed fine, wasn't acting like he was upset or anything."

"When and where was the constable killed?"

"Around midnight, they think, three days ago. It was in a village called Chilton Foliat, a couple of miles north."

"Where's your base in relation to that?"

"Just south of here," Tree said, pointing down the main road. "We're bivouacked in Hungerford Park, some sort of nature reserve."

"So your gunner could have left after you saw him, and made it up to Chilton Foliat and back, right?"

"True, we're camped out in the open. But he didn't. Angry keeps to himself a lot. He's never skipped out without a pass."

"Angry?" I said.

"That's his nickname. Everyone calls him Angry. He's got a

reputation for a short fuse. Been in a few fights, nothing serious, though."

"So you want me to investigate the charges against your gunner, whose nickname is *Angry*, who could have gone up to Chilton Foliat unnoticed to murder a constable, and who happens to have a reputation for using his fists. Anything else while I'm at it?" I stood up and stared down at Tree, arms folded across my chest, hoping for just one more good reason to walk away. I glanced at Kaz, hoping for some support. He studied his fingernails with great care.

"What proof did you have that I didn't steal that cash?" Tree stretched his arms out and leaned back on the bench, his long legs crossed as if he were lounging out in front of the Boylston Street station where we used to hang out.

"I knew you didn't," I said, letting out a sigh and stuffing my hands in my pockets.

"Like I know Angry didn't murder anyone. I trust him. Like you trusted me."

"Billy, there's one thing you should be aware of," Kaz said. I'd been conscious of him watching us, trying to figure out what was going on. I hadn't told him much about Tree, except that I wanted company when I went to see him.

"What's that?" I said.

"Shepton Mallet," he said. "I saw mention of it in a report from the Judge Advocate General's office on the legal background to the Visiting Forces Act."

"Yeah, I must have missed that one. What did it say?"

"Shepton Mallet is an old, disused British prison that has been turned over to the American government as a military prison and place of execution for servicemen convicted of capital offenses. Five soldiers to date have been hanged at Shepton Mallet."

"Makes sense that there'd be a few bad apples among the thousands of GIs in England," I said.

"Yes, but I found it odd that of those five, three were Negro. Are there more Negro bad apples than Caucasian bad apples?"

"All depends on who you ask," Tree said, rising to face me. "I remember one Boston cop who was sure of it. Heard he came to a bad end, Billy."

"Basher," I said, before I could stop myself. "But let's stick with Angry Smith. Okay, I'll ask around, see what I can do."

"That's it? Ask around?"

"Listen, Tree, I started leave today. I have plans, but I will look into it. The case is only three days old, they're not going to hang him anytime soon."

"You're on leave, that's perfect. It'll give you time to talk to folks around here," he said. For a guy who didn't like me much, he sure wanted me to stick around. Angry Smith must be one damn good gunner.

"I have to be back in London for tomorrow morning. I'll talk to people there and see what I can find out. I promise."

"Got a girl, Billy? A hot date?"

"I'm getting promoted. General Eisenhower is pinning my captain's bars on me."

"The general himself!" Tree said. "I heard he's your uncle. That true?"

"True enough," I said. I had a girl, too, but I didn't want to get into that right now.

"Nice," Tree said. "Always good to have a relation looking out for you." He looked away, his lips tight in resentment. This was an old argument with us.

"Listen, Tree," I said, barely keeping my voice steady. "I've already been in the shooting war, so don't think I'm some desk warrior hitting the clubs in London every night. And as far as relations go, you couldn't even make it to your own father's funeral, so don't lecture me on the subject." We were nose to nose now, fists clenched, years of unresolved rage aching to get out.

"There's two reasons I wasn't there," Tree said, showing more restraint than I had by stepping back and addressing Kaz. "When I got the message my father had died, I was at Fort Polk, Louisiana. The army gave me compassionate leave, and I was on a train in a matter of hours. Only problem was, the Southern Railways route took me dead across the Deep South. You know what that means, Lieutenant Kazimierz?"

"Yes. The part of the United States that held slaves."

"Right," Tree said. "And some down there wish things never changed. I had to change trains in Birmingham, and by the time I got my duffle hoisted aboard and found a seat, I'd misplaced my ticket. In the confusion I must've forgotten where I was, because when the conductor came through and I couldn't find it, I said something like, *hold on buddy, it's here somewhere.* Big mistake. He pulled a revolver out of his jacket and placed the barrel right between my eyes. Said if I spoke another word, he'd put a bullet in my brain and toss me off the moving train. This was in the colored car, in front of fifty witnesses. You could have heard a pin drop. One white man with a gun in Alabama, that's all it took. Threw me off the train at the next stop, left me at some two-bit whistle stop where the colored waiting room was behind the outhouse. Not a train going in my direction for ten hours. By the time I made it back, I was a day late. *That's* why I missed my father's funeral." Tree's eyes were damp, but he locked onto mine. I should have known he hadn't missed it on purpose. I couldn't bear his gaze and looked away.

"You mentioned two reasons," Kaz said.

"The other one is right here," he said, pointing at me, his finger trembling and his voice choked with anger. "If it weren't for Billy, I never would have been in the army in the first place."

"You could have been in jail, Tree," I said.

"Maybe not. Would have been my choice, though," he said. I took a lesson from him and stepped away. It was an old argument, no reason to start it up again. I watched the traffic, what there was of it. A couple of horse carts, the occasional truck, and a number of shoppers at a bakery across the street. Hungerford was a lively town, a river cutting through it, spanned by a graceful bridge. Cottages close to the road were well kept, like the shops that dotted the roadway. A constable rode his bicycle across the bridge, his blue uniform bright in the sunny March air, his helmet bobbing along on the cobblestone street. I wondered if he was a pal of the dead cop as I watched him pass by.

"Sorry I wanted to help," I said. I knew I sounded like a sarcastic schoolboy, but I couldn't help myself.

"What you don't understand, Billy, is that a Negro down South might as well be in jail. Nobody was on our side. Not the army, not the law. They could do anything they wanted to us, and no one backed us up. You know we had to step off the sidewalk in some towns whenever a white passed by? Me, wearing the uniform of the United States Army, with sergeant's stripes on my sleeve, I had to stand in the gutter for no-account white trash. That's prison, my friend."

Somehow we'd come head to head again. Kaz stepped between us.

"It is interesting, you know," Kaz said, in a casual conversational tone. "The Germans have the same rule in Poland. Poles have to step aside when any German walks by, upon pain of death."

"Yeah, but there's one big difference," Tree said. "I'm going over there to kill those goddamn Nazis who make you step off the sidewalk. But when I go home, white men will still want me in the gutter."

CHAPTER THREE

WE HAD TWO hours before the next train to London, so I asked Tree to show us where the constable had been killed.

"But take us from your bivouac," I said. "I want to get a sense of distance and time."

"Okay, let's go," Tree said. "Jeep's around the corner."

"You off duty? I don't want you to get in trouble with your commanding officer," I said as we followed him to the vehicle.

"Don't worry, Billy. The captain doesn't pay much attention to who's around, unless it's a drill or maneuvers. As for my platoon lieutenant, well, in my experience lieutenants are pretty easy to fool. Hope you're an exception, both of you." Tree laughed as he pulled away from the curb, and I hung on to my hat.

"Are your officers Negroes?" Kaz asked, raising his voice from the back seat.

"Only one, a lieutenant on the battalion staff. The rest are white. Some hate being in a colored outfit, and pull every string they can to get out. A few are okay. All the non-coms stick together though. We'll have no trouble getting on or off base, long as we don't run into any MPs."

"White MPs?" Kaz asked. We were crossing the arched brickwork span, water flowing languidly beneath us. Tree waved to an older couple walking along the road, and got a cheery greeting. A marker on the bridge said this was the Kennet and Avon Canal.

A pathway graced one bank, and it looked like a pleasant spot for a summer stroll. But this was March in England: bleak, wet, and cold in spite of the clear sky.

"MPs are MPs," Tree said. "Negro MPs are as glad to crack your skull as the white ones. More so, maybe, since they can only go after other colored troops. White MPs can spread their batons around, know what I mean?"

The jeep rumbled over train tracks and through a more bustling part of town. We passed the town hall with its tall clock tower, and once again Tree waved a greeting to a small knot of men gathered beneath it. He got nods and smiles back.

"Are you running for mayor?" I asked. He turned left after the Three Swans Inn, a two-story white stucco building close to the road. The door was painted a glossy black, and an old gent on a bench out front lifted his pipe in recognition of Tree.

"It's something you can't understand, Billy," Tree said. "After going through camps in Louisiana and Georgia, Hungerford was like finding the Promised Land. Folks here never learned to hate Negroes. The first time I walked into a shop here and got a friendly greeting, I nearly cried, and that's the truth. No one telling me to go 'round back, or to get the hell out. Instead, they say, 'Good morning, Sergeant.' You got any idea what that means, especially after what we went through down South?"

I wanted to say it would be like my Irish great-grandfather being asked to tea by an Ulsterman, but I'm not so thick that I didn't know it wasn't time for comparing ancestral agonies. "Probably not. It must have been tough."

"Tough was on a good day," Tree said as we passed more houses made of brick with roofs of thick, grey thatch, like a postcard of a typical English village. "I'm happy here, can you believe that? I like the people, I like walking down the street and chatting with the old fellows. And now the army wants to take this town away from us to spare white GIs the sight of us walking out with English girls."

Tree sped up, the anger in his voice playing out in his driving. His hands flexed on the steering wheel as houses thinned out to reveal fields and pastures. It was cold in the open jeep, and we pulled up our collars and tucked our heads down as the wind whipped around us. I'd thought about Tree a lot over the past years, wondering what had become of him, and why he hadn't shown up for his father's funeral. I'd heard he'd been in town for a few days after, but never ran into him. Not that I tried. Now I knew why he wasn't there, and why he liked it so much here in England, a place where calling a conductor "buddy" wouldn't get you thrown off a train at gunpoint.

We drove along a dirt road lined with trees. Ahead, on a slight rise, were lines of canvas, rows and rows of six-man pyramidal tents. Sentries stood outside a hut by the road and waved Tree through as he slowed down. They looked sharp and gave us a quick once-over, but it was obvious they knew Tree. There was no fence, no real security.

"It appears you are well known here as well," Kaz said from the backseat.

"We're only four companies, plus battalion headquarters," Tree said. "Not hard for guys to know every non-com in the outfit." That was true enough, especially in an independent battalion like this one. But it was also true that Tree was the kind of guy who kept his ear to the ground, and made sure he had pals everywhere. Like any kid from the hard back streets of Boston.

"Here we are," he said, parking the jeep at the end of a row of tents. "This is our platoon area. Each crew has a tent, plus a couple for supplies." Stovepipes stuck out from the tent tops and wood planks had been laid between them, creating a rough walkway inches above the ground.

"Can we look at his gear?" I asked.

"Sure, come on in," Tree said, holding the tent flap open for us. "The boys are working on the engine, so no one's home. This is maintenance day, so they'll be busy for a while."

Inside were five bunks, five footlockers, and several empty crates used for tables. There was a wood plank floor, which at least kept everything from sinking into the damp earth. Tree pointed out Angry's spot, and I went through his meager belongings. Everything was army-issue except for a half-empty bottle of whiskey, a straight-edge razor, and a packet of letters tied with string.

"Nice that you're holding his whiskey for him," I said. "Is the straight-edge for protection?"

"Yeah, almost everyone carries something. I got a switchblade in my back pocket. Man has to have an advantage if he gets himself surrounded."

"Angry didn't have it on him when he was arrested?"

"No, he was on duty here. No need."

"Have you looked through the letters?" I asked.

"No, that's his personal stuff. Have some respect, Billy."

"Nothing's personal when it comes to murder. One man is dead and another falsely charged, right? That trumps privacy, and the army doesn't care about privacy anyway. I'll get them back to you after I've looked through them."

"How long have you been here?" Kaz said, distracting Tree while I pocketed the letters.

"Me? Six months. I was a last-minute replacement in the States. They were short a radio operator, and I'd finished communications school, top of my class. I came here a corporal, made sergeant, and got my own TD last month. Tank Destroyer," he added, for our benefit.

"Seven years and you only made corporal?" I said.

"Got my buck sergeant stripes after two years. Lost them when I tried to stop some MPs from cracking my buddy's skull down at Fort Huachuca. Didn't care much about getting them back for a while. Then the war came along and that changed things."

"How?" I asked as we left the tent and walked back to the jeep.

"The draft brought in a lot of new guys and at first we had some lousy redneck officers. I figured the men deserved non-coms who believed in them. So I kept my mouth shut and played by the rules. Now I got my stripes and my own crew. And we need Angry back."

We followed Tree out of the tent, and I was aware of men watching us. Strange white officers wandering around a Negro unit might mean trouble. I could sense things relaxing when it became evident we weren't taking Tree away in cuffs.

"Were you in tanks from the beginning?" Kaz asked.

"We don't call them tanks," Tree said. "We destroy tanks. They're TDs." He started up the jeep and we headed out of the camp. "I was in a service company at first, which meant I loaded and unloaded trucks all day. Then I got a transfer to an anti-aircraft unit, then radio school, then here. I asked for a transfer to a combat outfit right after Pearl Harbor, and it finally came through. Angry Smith is the best damn gunner in the company, so when we head over to France, I want him back in my crew."

"Can't blame you," I said, glancing at my watch. "What time did you say you last saw Angry the night of the murder?"

"Around twenty-one hundred hours. I had a pass to go into town and saw him as I was driving out with two other guys from my crew."

"He didn't have a pass?"

"No. He had guard duty until twenty-two hundred hours, patrolling the vehicle park."

Tree drove us through Hungerford again, over the canal and out past the pub where we'd met. In ten minutes we crossed a small bridge, this one spanning a marshy river, and found ourselves in the one-lane village of Chilton Foliat. Gently rolling hills of farmland and pasture rose up from the roadway and the river. The houses were made of the same brick as in Hungerford, as well as the dark, thick thatch for roofs. We passed a few shops and The Wheatsheaf, a small pub that seemed to be the center of things in this tiny village. Tree pulled over in front of a church, one of those typical English types, all grey stone and short steeple. He nodded in the direction of the graveyard.

"He was found in there," Tree said. "The constable."

"What was his name?" Kaz asked.

"I'll show you," Tree said. "Come on." I thought Tree had mis-understood when Kaz asked for the name of the constable, unless he'd been buried in the same graveyard where he was found. We passed weathered gravestones covered in lichen, dates fading back centuries.

"His name was Thomas Eastman, and he was found right here,"

Tree said, pointing to a grave marker. It read Samuel Eastman, 1888-1937. Next to it was Samuel's wife, Mary. The whole row was Eastmans, generations of them.

"Is this a joke?" I asked.

"Nope," Tree said. "Police Constable Thomas Eastman was found right here, at the foot of his pappy's grave. Head bashed in."

"Why?" I said, and Tree shrugged. I wasn't really asking him anyway. This was odd. Beyond odd. "Did Angry and Eastman know each other?"

"They had words, a couple of weeks back."

"Tree, now's the time to tell me everything. Did they fight?"

"No," Tree said as Kaz wandered off to the edge of the cemetery. "Eastman told him to stay away from his sister."

"He didn't want a Negro walking out with her?"

"He did call him a damned darkie, but that wasn't what it was about. His sister is married. Her husband came home wounded from Burma a few days ago. Eastman didn't want Angry around her."

"But he had been around her, right?"

"Yeah. The first word they got was that her husband had been killed. I got the impression he was a real bastard, and no one was shedding any tears. That's when Angry began spending more time with her."

"But then they find out he was only wounded, and is on his way home. Is that when Eastman and Angry had words?"

"Yeah. I think he was afraid for his sister if Malcolm found out. Malcolm Adams, he's the husband."

"Angry could've made it up here after he was off duty. I've seen how loose security is at your bivouac. Maybe he arranged to meet Constable Eastman here, to try and work things out. Maybe it didn't go well. Eastman might have called him names, got him to live up to his reputation."

"I don't believe it," Tree said, shaking his head. "Why here? Why would anyone meet at their family plot in a graveyard in the dead of night? It's crazy."

"It made sense to someone," I said, looking back to the road. A column of GIs in full packs trotted by, the insignia of the Hundred-and-First Airborne visible on their shoulders. "They from around here?"

"The Hundred-and-First is spread out in every direction. They have a Jump School here in Chilton Foliat and one of their regiments is headquartered about a mile down the road, at Littlecote House. Big mansion, where they got their brass bunked."

The stomp of boots on pavement faded as the unit passed by. No shortage of combat-trained men around here. But who did Constable Eastman in, and why did they leave him on his father's grave?

"What evidence did they have against Angry? Anyone see him with Eastman?"

"Sure they did. Eastman lived here but was on duty in Hungerford most days. MPs from the Criminal Investigations Division came nosing around the next morning, after Eastman's body was found. We'd all come in late and not entirely sober, so none of us could say we'd seen Angry. I think someone must've tipped them off about the argument."

"Malcolm Adams? Could he have done this and blamed it on Angry?"

"Maybe. But he was shot up pretty bad in the legs. Not sure he could've managed it. From what I hear, he prefers beating up on women."

"What did Angry say when they came for him?"

"Said he'd been in camp all night, and hadn't seen Eastman since they last had words."

"Jesus, what a mess," I said, as I heard Kaz call us from the stone wall near the woods.

"Look," Kaz said. He pointed to a trail that came up to a gate in the wall. It was wide enough for a vehicle, barely. "Where does this lead?"

"I think that would take you to the Jump School," Tree said. "There's a lane up that hill that takes you to a horse farm where they have a parachute training school. I hear it's for training medics, doctors, chaplains, and any other non-combat support personnel joining the Hundred-and-First."

"So anyone could have brought a body in, unseen, and dumped it here," Kaz said.

"Goddamn, you're right," Tree said. "Think CID looked at this?"

"I'll find out," I said. "It doesn't get Angry off the hook, but it opens up a range of possibilities."

"You'll investigate, then?" Tree said. I saw the hope in his eyes, and I thought for a second that this might patch things up between us. But I didn't know if I could.

"Tree, I'm on leave, remember? After today I have only four days left. I have to be at SHAEF in the morning, then I'm catching a train north for a few days of rest."

"Billy has been in Italy," Kaz said, leaving so much unsaid.

"So you won't," Tree said, and walked back toward the jeep.

"It's not that," I said, trying to convince myself as I followed him. "There's a dozen things to do; talk to CID, talk to the local cops, talk to the girl, and then move on to whatever that brings up. I'm not even on duty, I won't have any resources."

"Okay, I get it," Tree said. "You're getting a promotion and then you're going off with your girl. Can't blame a man for that. What about when you get back?"

"I'll make inquiries to CID before I leave. When I return, I'll see what I can do. Unless we get an assignment."

"What kind of assignments do you get?" Tree asked, obviously thinking his pal's troubles should come first.

"Kaz and I are part of General Eisenhower's Office of Special Investigations. We look into things for the general. Quietly."

"You're still a cop then. Still in the Boyle family business," Tree said, as if that might be a curse. I couldn't really blame him if he thought that. Which told me that Tree was damn certain Angry Smith wasn't a murderer. He'd never ask me for a favor without being a hundred percent certain he was right. He was too damn proud to take a chance on being wrong.

"Yes, I am. And based on what you've told us, I know two things for certain."

"What are they?" Tree said, starting up the jeep.

"That Angry Smith is innocent, and that you're both damned lucky I am still a cop. Now if you don't mind, we have a train to catch."

CHAPTER FOUR

IT WAS A quiet ride to the train station. My head was awash with memories and murder. I didn't know if Tree and I were friends again, or if this was simply a truce so he could get his gunner back. I didn't know if I wanted to be his friend again. Sometimes there's no going back. We were both older now, old enough to understand that those years when we yearned to grow into adults and leave our youthfulness behind may have been the best years of our lives. The passage of time, and the war, had conspired to dull the sense of anticipation we had felt before everything fell apart. Tree today wasn't the Tree I had known. I wasn't the same guy he'd hung around with either.

"Thanks for coming, Billy," Tree said as we stood on the station platform. "You too, Lieutenant Kazimierz." He gave Kaz a snappy salute.

"It was good to meet you, Sergeant," Kaz said, returning the salute and extending his hand. "We will do what we can."

"That's all I can ask," Tree said as they shook hands. A group of GIs moved around us, one of them muttering "goddamn nigger" as he brushed by Tree, throwing him off balance.

"Hey, Private!" I shouted, but he was lost in the crowd of GIs changing trains.

"It's not worth it, Billy," Tree said. "You dress him down, then the MPs come, and I get beat up for causing a disturbance. That's how it goes. Just help Angry, and don't fight my battles. Okay?"

"Okay," I said. I knew he was right, but I didn't like giving in. Then again, I wouldn't be the one paying the price. I'd seen it all before, back in Boston, but that didn't mean it sat well with me. Maybe I just felt guilty about how things had fallen apart with Tree, and wanted to make it up to him. We didn't salute or shake hands. I turned and boarded the train without a word, just as Tree had done a lifetime ago.

Kaz and I squeezed past squads of British soldiers with their tin-pot helmets and rifles slung over their shoulders. American swabbies in their pea coats were crammed into one corner of the car and GIs on leave slouched in the other corner, garrison caps pulled down over their eyes, recovering from last night's bash or resting up for tonight's.

We grabbed the last two seats and watched as more servicemen boarded the train until it seemed that it might not be able to bear the weight. Air force personnel and paratroopers from the 101st added to the train's burden, until finally, with a blast of the whistle and a release of steam, it slowly departed the station.

"Which do you want to explain first?" Kaz said. "What happened between you and Tree—marvelous nickname—or why you are certain Angry Smith is innocent?"

"I'll start with the easy one," I said, trying to get comfortable on the narrow seat. The track took us close to the canal, and I could see the tents of the 617th Tank Destroyer Battalion spread out beyond it. "There was something very methodical about the murder of Constable Eastman, which hints at a premeditated act."

"And according to his nickname, Abraham Smith is prone to sudden acts," Kaz said.

"Yes. If Eastman had been found outside a pub, near his sister's house, anywhere like that, it would point to Smith. But that grave-yard scene means Eastman was there for a reason. Either brought there already dead, likely on that trail you spotted, or lured there alive by his killer."

"Or, he arranged a meeting there, or simply strolled to that spot with someone he trusted."

"Would he have trusted Angry Smith? At night? In a graveyard? After they had argued and he'd called him a damned darkie? I don't think so."

"You're right, Billy," Kaz said as the coach lurched forward, taking a small rise. Smoke from dozens of cigarettes turned the air grey as voices rose, laughter and banter turning louder as bottles were passed around. The Americans were all on leave, while the British Tommies were under orders, carrying their gear and weapons with them, no leave passes in their pockets. They looked resentful, maybe scared. "Perhaps someone took advantage of the fact that Angry would be a suspect."

"Or it could have nothing to do with him. A family feud, maybe. Or a warning."

"The killer might go after other members of the Eastman family," Kaz said, thinking it through. "If they don't get what they want."

"Be nice to know what that was," I said.

"What are you going to do?" Kaz said.

"Should be easy to get a look at the CID report. See how serious this is. I'd like to talk to the local police, too."

"But they have no jurisdiction. The Visiting Forces Act, you know." I knew. The act gave the army the right to arrest and try our servicemen for crimes committed on English territory. It made a lot of sense, and took a lot of pressure off the English justice system. But I also knew that no police force in the world would look kindly upon outsiders taking over a case that involved the killing of one of their own.

"They'll still have information, and maybe a few leads that CID overlooked in their rush to close the case. Angry Smith is the most convenient suspect you could imagine," I said.

"But your leave," Kaz said. "You and Diana are going to Seaton Manor tomorrow, are you not?"

"Sure we are," I said. "It's all planned out. We're heading up there on the three o'clock train from King's Cross Station. I can't wait for some peace and quiet." There hadn't been much peace in Italy, and the Anzio Beachhead was definitely not the quietest spot around. I had been looking forward to this leave, but thoughts of Angry Smith in prison mingling with memories of Tree Jackson in Boston didn't put me in a happy mood.

"I can make inquiries while you are away," Kaz said. "You and Diana deserve the time together." He was right, especially about Diana. She'd been arrested in Rome by the Gestapo and spent some unpleasant days in a prison there. Diana Seaton worked for the Special Operations Executive, and had been on an assignment within the Vatican in German-occupied Rome. Disguised as a nun, she'd been arrested on black market charges. Luckily, the Gestapo and the Italian secret police hadn't uncovered her real identity.

"Thanks, Kaz. If you have time, pay a visit to the Berkshire Constabulary and see what the local office has to say."

"I will have time," Kaz said, and turned his head to stare out the window. Kaz had been granted leave as well, but his dance card was empty. He'd been invited to Seaton Manor along with me, but the memories there were still too painful for him. When I first arrived in England, Kaz was head over heels in love with Daphne Seaton, Diana's younger sister. Daphne had felt the same way about Kaz. They were my first friends over here, and they both became involved in my first case for the general. Kaz lived through it. Daphne hadn't. Things were rough for Kaz after that, and I know at one point he thought about killing himself. But he was tough, and curious, and the investigation business kept him getting up each morning.

Kaz was a real bookworm who could speak half a dozen languages fluently. He was also rich. Beacon Hill rich. Unfortunately it was because his father had seen the writing on the wall and transferred the family wealth from Polish to Swiss banks shortly before the Nazi invasion. Kaz had been attending school in England, and his father was planning to move the entire family there. But his prescience did not extend to the exact date of the invasion, and on September 1st, 1939 the Kazimierz family was still in Poland. They were all killed, exterminated as part of the

Polish upper class. Kaz was alone in the world, with memories, a big fat bank account, and me.

"Tell me the story of you and Tree," Kaz said, drawing his gaze from the countryside flowing by outside the window.

"It was years ago. We were just kids."

"You didn't want to talk about it on the way down from London," Kaz said. "That was fine; it allowed me to meet Tree without preconceptions. But now that we are involved, you must open up. Besides, it will ease the boredom of this locomotive ride."

Kaz hated being bored. I think some of his interest in keeping himself alive had to do with the hot water I often managed to get myself into. It amused him.

"Okay," I said, leaning in closer to Kaz and trying to block out the conversations going on around us. There were three GIs opposite our seats and one next to me, but they were deep into a discussion about the kind of girl they'd like to meet in London, a topic that could last a good long time.

"It was nineteen thirty-six," I began.

I'D DELIVERED NEWSPAPERS, shoveled sidewalks, done all the odd jobs kids do since I was old enough to cross the street by myself. That summer, with my sixteenth birthday a month behind me, I was ready for a real job. Meaning regular pay, greenbacks doled out in small manila envelopes every Friday. I wasn't greedy, but there was something I wanted—no, needed—to have. It was a 1922 Indian Scout. It needed a new oil pump, and the brakes were bad, but it was still a beautiful motorcycle. Low slung, red, with a 606 cc engine. And best of all, old man Warner, who'd last ridden it the year the market crashed, was willing to let it sit in his garage until I came up with the dough. And not say anything to my folks about it.

Mom had put the kibosh on the idea of a motorcycle half a dozen times. Dad would shake his head and tell me to listen to my mother, which I interpreted as practically a green light to proceed as long as I didn't get caught. So that was my plan: get a job, pay old man Warner, fix up the Scout in secret, and then show it off to my friends. Not the most well-thought-out plan, but remember, I was sixteen years old.

"I bought the Chief model," a corporal sitting next to me said, cutting into my story. "Got it up to one hundred on a flat stretch of road in Kansas once. But then I got drafted and left it with my girl. Some 4-F is probably out riding it now. Sorry, Lieutenant, go on."

"No problem, Soldier. I did stop to take a breath, after all."

"Don't mind him, Lieutenant," one of his pals said. "What happened next?" I hadn't realized I had an audience. The GIs seated with us had ceased their conversation and were leaning in, nodding at me to continue. I did.

What happened next is that I kept asking my dad to get me a summer job at the police department. There weren't a lot of them to go around, but police work in Boston was largely a family affair. When Dad and Uncle Dan joined in 1919, fresh from the war, they were filling in the ranks after the police strike, which Governor Coolidge broke up. Best thing that ever happened to the Boston Irish. After years of *No Irish Need Apply*, there was finally a place to get a job, and better yet, a place to get jobs for your relatives. Everyone else had their cut of the American pie, so why not us?

Dad and Uncle Dan were both homicide detectives, and both had connections. Uncle Dan's were more along the lines of the Irish Republican Army, but Dad was friendly with politicians and the unions. When he finally gave in, it took one phone call. At dinner that night, he told me to report to work at headquarters the next morning, and to wear my old clothes. I was to report to Mr. Jackson, and Dad said it was important to do what I was told and not embarrass the family. That was pretty much what he said about most things. I asked what the job was, and he told me to be thankful I had one, and to stop bothering him.

That night I thought about the possibilities, too excited to fall asleep. I was hoping it might have something to do with cars or even motorcycles. The Boston PD had plenty of both, and they all needed maintenance and cleaning. There was a shooting range and armory, too. Didn't they need all those weapons cleaned? I briefly entertained the notion that they'd want a kid for undercover work, and finally fell asleep imagining myself on a Hardy Boys adventure.

It wasn't any of those. When I got to headquarters, lunch pail in hand, I was told to go down into the basement and see Jackson. The desk sergeant didn't even look up, just crooked a thumb in the direction of the stairs. A sign above the stairwell did say PUBLIC NOT ALLOWED, and that bucked me up. I was going where the public could not go. I was practically a rookie policeman.

Not even close. At the end of a dark, narrow hallway, I saw a sign over the door. H. JACKSON, CUSTODIAL SERVICES. Mr. Jackson was the janitor, and I was going to spend my summer mopping floors. I was lucky to have a job, as my dad said. But back then, it was the greatest disappointment of my life, and I hadn't even opened the door.

When I recovered enough to pull myself together and enter, I got my first look at Mr. Jackson. He was a Negro. Not that I didn't see Negroes in Boston, but I had assumed my boss would be a white man. Hell, every boss I'd ever seen was white. The surprise must've showed on my face, because Mr. Jackson frowned and shook his head, the kind of slow, deliberate head-shaking you save up for the profoundly stupid.

"You don't like the idea of working for me, son, you turn around go home. Won't miss you none," he said. Mr. Jackson was about average height, but wide in the shoulders and thick at the waist. Not fat, but built like a fireplug. He was dark, too, the kind of skin that makes you think of pictures in the *National Geographic*. His curly hair was shot through with grey, and he wore blue overalls and a dark blue shirt with his name stitched over the pocket.

"Sorry, Mr. Jackson," I said. "It's just that I didn't know . . . I didn't expect . . . you know . . ." I sort of let it trail off and stared at the floor, then let my eyes drift around the room. There was a big sink in the corner and a drain in the floor. Shelves held cleaning supplies, tools, dusty boxes, and heaps of broken fans, radios, and other appliances. Above all that was a single narrow barred basement window with a parade of feet passing by, mostly heavy cop shoes and blue trousers, the busy men oblivious to Mr. Jackson's domain below.

"There's a lot you don't know," Mr. Jackson said. "But your daddy's a decent man, and I'm sure he meant no harm. Doesn't mean I want you around if you can't take orders and get the job done."

"I can do the job, Mr. Jackson," I said, remembering my father's injunction. "You can count on me."

"Not looking forward to it," he said, pointing to a broom. "Start sweeping."

"Where?" He was silent. "I mean, where, Mr. Jackson?"

"Start at the top, work your way down. That's six floors. Don't leave a speck of dust."

"PADDINGTON STATION," THE conductor proclaimed. "Next stop, Paddington Station."

"Wait, Lieutenant, that's our stop," the corporal said. "Why was he so sore?"

"Yeah," another GI with a southern accent said. "No colored boy oughta talk like that."

"Aw shuddup," responded a guy with a New York accent. "Come on, Lieutenant, wrap it up, huh?"

"There's still a lot of story to go," I said. "But the reason he was upset is that his son was supposed to get the job. Had it, actually, until my old man made that call. As soon as he did, Tree Jackson lost it and young Billy Boyle had it handed to him."

"Ain't right, if you don't mind me saying so, Lieutenant," the corporal said. "Colored folk got it hard enough." The southern fellow shook his head at this misplaced sympathy.

"Didn't sit well with me either," I said, rising from my seat. "But by the time I found out, it was too late. When I got to know Mr. Jackson a little better, he told me how things were. *If you're black, get back. If you're white, you're all right.* It was his son Tree who had to get back. Enjoy your leave, fellas."

"Is that what Tree is still upset about?" Kaz said as we walked out of the train station to hail a taxi.

"That ain't the half of it," I said. "But it's all for today."

CHAPTER FIVE

"NOT HUNGRY, BILLY?" Diana Seaton asked, not waiting for an answer as she snatched a warm roll from my plate and soaked up the rest of her soup with it. She was enjoying her SOE recuperation leave, determined to get her strength back after time spent in that Gestapo prison.

"Go ahead," I said, delighting in the sight of her by candlelight. Diana had a way of dealing with the curves life threw at her that I envied. She'd had her share of tragedy, but fought her way through each one, confronting them directly and then leaving them behind. I was more of a brooder, I decided. Which was pretty much what I was doing right now. As opposed to Diana, who settled back into her chair, sighed, and finished the wine in her glass.

"More wine?" Kaz asked, filling her glass from the bottle in the ice bucket. The three of us were dining at the Dorchester Hotel. It was elegant, and the food was terrific, even with wartime rationing. The Ministry of Food had decreed that no restaurant meal could cost more than five shillings, and meals were limited to three courses, to prevent rich folks from eating out to circumvent the strict rationing of groceries. Even with these limitations, the Dorchester kitchens managed to put on a fine feed. And wisely, booze was not rationed.

Kaz topped me off, not needing to ask. We knew each other pretty well. I'd bunked here with Kaz since I first arrived in England,

back in '42. Well, bunked might not be the right word. Kaz kept a
suite at the Dorchester, and had invited me to use one of the bed-
rooms. Kaz needed the company of the living. His family had visited
him here before the war, while he was at school, and spent the last
peacetime Christmas in that suite. Daphne, Diana's sister, had lived
with him there before she was killed. Scandalous, yeah, but there
was a war on, so who cared? Not the staff of the Dorchester, that's
for sure. Kaz was a big tipper with a heart of gold, and everyone from
the dishwashers to the concierge treated him like royalty. Not
because he was a minor baron from central Europe, but because of
his loyalty to his family's memory, and to the Dorchester, his home
for the duration.

"I'm sorry your visit didn't go well, Billy," Diana said. "People
change, don't they? It can be disappointing." She raised an eyebrow
in my direction, inviting a response. I'd caught her up on the story
I'd told Kaz on the train, and left it there. They'd both been trying,
in a nonchalant sort of way, to drag more out of me.

"Whoever said you can't go home again knew what he was
talking about," I said.

"Thomas Wolfe," Kaz said. Kaz knew everything.

"But it wasn't home Tree was asking about," Diana said. "It was
a favor over here. Far from home. Wasn't it?" Again that eyebrow. I
was saved by the arrival of the Dover sole. Kaz ordered another bottle
of wine.

"Our cellars will be empty of Bordeaux blanc by summer," the
wine steward said as he popped the cork. "But the invasion should
take care of that, unless the Germans carry everything off with them,
don't you think, Baron?"

"I am sure every soldier in the Allied armies will be diligently
searching for French wines. Do you know the date of the invasion,
Charles?" Kaz asked with a grin as the bottle settled into its ice
bucket.

"One hears things, Baron. One does not repeat them. I can tell
you we have some delightful Italian wines now, but they must sit for
a time after their long voyage. Enjoy," he said, and was gone.

"He probably knows more than we do," I said between mouth-fuls of buttery sole. "Wouldn't be a bad spot for a German spy, with all the brass talking shop at dinner." Looking around the dining room, it was packed with senior officers and the much younger ladies that accompanied them. Another good opportunity for a spy.

"England is so different now," Diana said. "In only a few months, it's become crowded with Americans. They're everywhere. Between the tanks, trucks, and jeeps, it's a miracle anyone can travel anywhere. I'm amazed this island can hold all of them."

"And the majority are here in the south of England, grouped all around London," Kaz said. "But that is the extent of our knowledge."

"Really?" Diana said in a low voice, inviting our confidence.

"Really," I said. "Kaz and I have been close enough to the shooting war that we can't be trusted with secrets. No one who might be captured by the Germans is let in on much of anything these days. It's understandable, but frustrating. There are three kinds of people in England right now, those who are going, those who are planning, and those who are left out in the cold."

"Yes," Kaz said with a grin. "Billy would certainly like to lead the charge from the first landing craft, wherever that may be."

"Let's not get carried away," I said. "I just don't like being side-lined."

"Then why not look into the murder Tree told you about?" Diana said, spearing another potato. "It will give you something to focus on."

"I have my leave," I said. "We might not get another chance to get away. Either of us might get an assignment."

"I have a month's leave," Diana said. "Perhaps you can get yours changed."

"I thought we had everything planned out," I said. "You were eager to visit your father at Seaton Manor." A day ago, she'd been excited at the prospect. Her father had recently been made an earl, and was now known as the Earl of Seaton, a step up, I guess, from Sir Seaton. The honor had been given for unspecified service to the Crown, which I knew to mean something to do with naval intelligence. Whatever the reason, Diana had been excited about it. Now, her eyes told a different story. I looked at her, then Kaz, who busied himself looking around the room. Then I recalled Diana had set up this dinner with the three of us. Not unusual, but now it looked like she wanted company when she delivered the bad news.

"I'm sorry, Billy," she said. "I know you probably cannot get your leave rescheduled at this late date, but something's come up. I have finally got an appointment with someone at the Foreign Office."

"About the camps," I said.

"Yes, the camps," Diana said. "The extermination camps." Diana's undercover mission in Rome had brought her into contact with both Germans and Italians who had witnessed the death camps in Eastern Europe. We knew there were concentration camps, where Jews from Germany and the occupied nations had been sent. We also knew the Nazis were beating, shooting, and working to death Jews and others they judged to be undesirable in forced labor camps. But the extermination centers existed for a single purpose. Wholesale industrialized death. It was mind-boggling, difficult to fathom, hard to believe. Which was the problem.

"You've been debriefed by the SOE, right? I know you told Kim Philby about what you learned," I said. Kim Philby was an SOE spymaster, and Diana's boss.

"Yes, of course. But I don't know what Kim did with the information, if anything. He seemed more interested in military and political data. So I asked my father to arrange for an off-the-record meeting with someone at the Foreign Office."

"With whom are you meeting?" Kaz said.

"Roger Allen," Diana said. "He is apparently close to Anthony Eden, the Foreign Secretary. Allen works for a group called the Joint Intelligence Committee."

"What do you hope to accomplish?" Kaz said.

"I'm not sure," Diana said, setting down her fork. "I don't know what can be done, but I am certain we can and should do more."

"There are a lot of men getting ready to do more," I said.

"And in the meantime, how many thousands die each day? There must be something that can be done now. Moral outrage expressed by our leaders, perhaps."

"Good luck," I said, holding my tongue. If Diana was counting on morality from politicians, she was going to need all the luck she could get.

"Moral outrage has done little for the Poles, what there has been of it," Kaz said.

"I know, Piotr, I know," Diana said, taking his hand in hers. "But I must try. You understand, don't you?"

"All too well, my dear. Do not let them break your heart."

"Hearts may be beyond mending, those that survive," she said. We sat in silence, remembering crushing sadness and empty places.

"Well now, my friends, how about dessert?" our waiter intoned, oblivious to the sudden depression that had settled over the table. "Something sweet?"

Surprised by his sudden appearance, we stared at each other, waiting for someone to speak.

"Yes," Diana said, slamming her palm on the table as if making a momentous decision. "The sweeter the better!" We laughed, the riotous laughter of those at the end of the world.

Later, as we left our table, Diana stopped to chat with a friend who was dining with an RAF pilot. Kaz and I walked to the lobby and waited.

"Did you know about this?" I asked.

"Diana's meeting? Yes, she told me yesterday. She was quite worried you would be upset. Are you?"

"I don't know, Kaz. It's important, what she's trying to do. What's a few days in the country compared to that?"

"She must try, but I fear nothing will come of it."

"Why do you say that?"

"Because Roger Allen is a notorious anti-Semite. He is more worried about keeping Jews from emigrating to the British Mandate for Palestine than anything else, including what is happening in the death camps."

"How do you know that?" I said. Kaz shrugged and turned away. Then I remembered. Kaz knows everything.

CHAPTER SIX

UNCLE IKE GAVE me his trademark smile as he pinned the silver captain's bars on my uniform. "Long overdue, William," he said, as the small group applauded. "I'm proud of you, son," he said in a whisper, as he gripped my shoulder.

"Thank you, General," was all I could get out before the well-wishers crowded in. Diana was there, along with Kaz, of course, chatting with Kay Summersby, Uncle Ike's driver and companion. Kay and I had been pals since North Africa. Back then she'd been afraid she wouldn't be taken to England when Uncle Ike got the Supreme Commander post, but here she was, right by his side. Mattie Pinette and a few other WAC secretaries gathered around the cake, which was probably more of a draw than the general's nephew getting a promotion, no matter how long he'd been a lieutenant.

"Well deserved, Boyle," Colonel Samuel Harding said, extending his hand. Harding worked for Uncle Ike in G-2—that's what the army calls intelligence—and is my boss if the general doesn't have anything for me to do. Like now.

"Thanks, Colonel," I said, giving a wave to Big Mike, who stood in the doorway, taking up most of the space. Staff Sergeant Mike Miecznikowski had been with us since Sicily, and had become Colonel Harding's right-hand man in the Office of Special Investigations. Everyone called him Big Mike because the army didn't make uniforms large enough for his wide shoulders and bulging biceps. Big Mike had been a Detroit cop, and still carried his shield in his coat pocket.

"Hey, congratulations, Billy," Big Mike said. "I mean Captain Boyle."

"Don't start with military courtesies now, Big Mike, you'll only hurt yourself," Harding said. Big Mike had a way with officers, at least the decent ones. He could have them eating out of his hand in ten minutes and on a first-name basis for life. Big Mike was the kind of guy who could get anything done for you if he liked you, and not much if he didn't. And who doesn't want a big, strong, friendly, proficient scrounger and former bluecoat for a pal?

"William, you should be honored that Big Mike remembered your rank at all," Uncle Ike said.

"General, I'm strictly here for the cake," Big Mike said. "And to see Estelle, of course."

"Nice to know where I stand," Estelle Gordon said, her voice drifting up from somewhere behind Big Mike's shoulders. Estelle was a WAC sergeant who worked at SHAEF. She and Big Mike were an item, about as head over heels as they were mismatched in size. She handed Big Mike a plate with a massive slab of cake and asked the general if she could get him one. He shook his head and lit up a cigarette.

"I'm glad you're back in England, William," Uncle Ike said. "And glad Miss Seaton made it back as well. I talked to her father yesterday and he said you might visit them soon."

"Sir Richard is in town? That probably explains it."

"Explains what?" Uncle Ike said.

"Diana has to stay in London," I said. "She has a meeting with someone at the Foreign Office, to talk about the death camps. Sir Richard probably pulled a few strings to get her in."

"From the reports I've seen, there's much to be concerned about, William. All we can do here is work as hard as we can to end this war as soon as possible. I'll leave the rest up to the politicians."

"You mean the guys who got us into this mess?"

"You're a captain now, William," Uncle Ike said with a wink. "Time to exercise diplomatic restraint."

"Then please don't ever make me a major, Uncle Ike," I whispered. I didn't call him that unless we were alone. He laughed, and it felt good to lift his spirits a bit. "How do you like the new headquarters?"

"I like it fine," he said. "But I think some of the staff think otherwise."

"It is kind of off the beaten path." Bushy Park was a royal park west of London. It was the new home to the Supreme Headquarters, Allied Expeditionary Force. Hundreds of officers and a few thousand enlisted men kept the place humming around the clock in rows of camouflaged huts, barracks, underground bunkers, and even tents.

"That is the whole point, William. The center of London had too many distractions. Clubs, dances, shows, and fine restaurants. I want my staff at work full-time, instead of going their separate ways in the evening. They can get to know each other here. We've got people from half a dozen nationalities and services, and they have to work together, and work hard."

"Makes sense, General. But what about me? I'm still posted at Norfolk House in London."

"Don't complain too loudly, William. There are officers who would kill to be sleeping at the Dorchester instead of in a tent."

"All right, General. There is one other thing I'd like to ask you. A favor."

"I can't deny my own nephew a favor the day I promote him, so ask away."

"I visited a friend today, a guy I knew back in Boston. He's with one of the colored tank destroyer battalions, over by Hungerford."

"Does he want a transfer to a white outfit?" Uncle Ike lit a cigarette and looked at me with a hint of recrimination. He thought my friend was a white guy looking to get out of duty with a Negro unit.

"No, that's not the case, not at all. He's a Negro, and proud to be in a combat unit. They've been training outside of Hungerford for some time now, and they've gotten to know the locals. The people in town seem to like them too."

"I know, I've heard it often enough. A lot of the English say our Negro troops are the most polite of the lot," said Uncle Ike, releasing a plume of blue smoke.

"Yes, sir. It's just that they got word that Hungerford is going to be restricted to white troops on leave only. My friend's unit won't be able to go into town at all."

"William, this seems like a minor affair, are you sure you want me to get involved?"

"General, when we met my friend yesterday, the pubs in town had been raided by white GIs. They smashed every glass in the place so when they went on leave in Hungerford they wouldn't have to drink from the same glass a Negro had."

"Damn it," Uncle Ike said, crushing out his cigarette. "Hungerford, you say? What's the unit?"

"The Six-Sevententh Tank Destroyer Battalion."

"Consider it done, William. I have a war to win, and I can't afford to get distracted by the rights and wrongs of race issues, but some things just aren't right. Hell's bells!" He signaled Mattie, who made a quick note and went to a telephone. Sometimes being the nephew of the Supreme Commander was a very useful thing.

Well, "nephew" wasn't exactly the right word. We were cousins of a sort, related through my mother's side and Mamie Doud's family, but I'd hardly known him before the war. It was my mom who had come up with the idea to get me assigned to his staff in Washington, DC. That was back before anyone else had even heard of Dwight David Eisenhower, when he was working in the War Plans Department in the nation's capital. Just the right assignment for a young Irish-American ex-policeman to sit out the war, or so my mother thought. We'd all thought it was a grand idea, having given up one Boyle in the previous war for the British Empire, as it was viewed in my household. Not to mention a lot of others in South Boston, where the Irish Republican Army and the fight against the British rule in our homeland was the one true faith.

As senior detectives on the force, my dad and his brother Dan had done enough favors for politicians to get me a spot on Uncle Ike's staff. But what we hadn't planned on was that our unknown and distant relative would be tapped to head up US Army forces in Europe in early 1942. And that he liked the idea of a police detective who was a relative to handle sensitive assignments. Assignments that tended to involve bullets and very loud explosions.

I didn't start off this war the gung-ho type. What I really wanted was to end it in one piece. But when Uncle Ike needed something done, I couldn't say no. Partly because he was a general and could order me to do whatever he wanted, but mainly because he was family, and he carried a heavy burden. So I hadn't minded asking him for one small favor this time.

"What do you say we celebrate tonight, Billy?" Diana said as she took me by the arm. "Let's go dancing at the Rhythm Club. Big Mike and Estelle fixed Kaz up with a nurse from the infirmary. It will be loads of fun, I promise."

"Sure," I said. I knew Diana was working hard at making up for the lost leave, and that a night out on the town might be just the ticket. I'd been down since seeing Tree again, and being sidelined by both SHAEF and my own girlfriend. So what the hell. "Kaz said he'd go?"

"Yes. Although he and Nini have been writing almost every day. It is quite touching. I'm so glad for him." Nini was an Italian princess, holed up within Vatican City in occupied Rome. Long story. Diana went off to tell Estelle, leaving me with not much to do.

"William," Uncle Ike said, as an officer beckoned him from the doorway. "You remember to write your folks and give them my regards."

I promised I would and watched him leave, trailing a bevy of aides carrying files and map cases. Planning an invasion while I ate cake. Really not a bad deal, I reminded myself. The WACs drifted back to their desks as the party wound down. Estelle left for her office in Air Force Operations while Harding took a telephone call.

"Kaz," I said. "Let's get over to the Provost Marshal General's office and see what they've got on the Smith case. We still have time before we hit the fleshpots of London tonight."

"Good. It will give us something to do," Kaz said.

"I'll drive you as long as Sam don't need me," Big Mike said. "We might have to drop him off at Norfolk House."

"You're staying put," Harding said, slamming down the telephone. "All of you. Major Cosgrove is on his way over. We have a case. You'd best cancel your reservations tonight."

So much for the Rhythm Club. And my leave. I wrote a note to Diana and gave it to Mattie to deliver. I told her I was sorry, and that it might be no more than a couple of days. I felt bad about standing her up, but we both understood wartime demands. I felt worse about letting Tree down and not getting into the Angry Smith arrest, but I have to say, an official case was just what the doctor ordered. Nothing like a cold corpse to make you feel needed.

CHAPTER SEVEN

"GLAD YOU'RE HERE, Boyle," Major Charles Cosgrove said, sitting down at the conference table and puffing his cheeks as he let out a deep breath, wiping away beads of sweat on his forehead with a handkerchief. "Congratulations on your captaincy, by the way."

"Thanks, Major," I said. "But what's the rush?"

"We have a bit of a problem, and it seems you are the perfect solution, Captain Boyle." It was odd to hear the word captain in front of my name. To me, a captain is a high-ranking cop, not a soldier one step above dime-a-dozen lieutenants. It was also odd hearing Cosgrove say I was perfect for anything.

Major Cosgrove worked for MI5, the British security service charged with counterintelligence. He was an older gent, the kind of guy who would have been long retired if it hadn't been for another war coming around. He was grey-haired and portly, with a white mustache that gave him a grandfatherly look that was at odds with his deadly, steel-blue eyes.

Cosgrove and Harding sat on one side of the table in the conference room just a few doors down from Uncle Ike's office. Kaz and Big Mike flanked me on either side. We eyed the manila folder with MOST SECRET stamped in red.

"I've asked Colonel Harding for help in this case," Cosgrove went on. "For reasons I cannot let on, it will be better for an American team to investigate this murder."

"Who's been killed, and where?" I asked. I'd only been back in England for less than a week, and I liked the idea of staying put for a while.

"A chap named Stuart Neville. He was found at his rooming house in Newbury—west of London—this morning."

"Newbury is close to Hungerford," Kaz said. "We passed through it yesterday." The look he gave me said it all. Close enough to look into Angry Smith while we were at it.

"Are the police investigating, or is this a hushed-up MI5 case?" I said.

"The Berkshire Constabulary are on the scene now. We want this treated as a normal criminal investigation," Cosgrove said. "Publicly."

"It won't be normal once we show up," I said. "What's our role?"

"There is an American involved. He discovered the body, actually. Sergeant Jerome Sullivan, stationed at the nearby US Air Force base at Greenham Common. That will explain your presence. It is a joint investigation with the local police. Inspector John Payne is expecting you and will cooperate fully. He has primary jurisdiction, of course."

"What is MI5's involvement?" Kaz asked, not unreasonably.

"For reasons of security, I can only say we have an official interest that must be kept quiet."

"Do you have an official interest in the killer being apprehended, or not apprehended?" I asked. Having dealt with Major Cosgrove before, I knew enough not to assume either.

"I am confident that you and Inspector Payne will ensure that justice is served, Captain Boyle. I cannot say more without prejudicing your investigation and military security. I have prepared some basic information for you which you can review on your way there. If you leave immediately you will be able to inspect the crime scene with the inspector before the body is removed." Cosgrove slid a folded piece of paper across the table. I handed it to Kaz.

"Hold on," I said. "Newbury is about fifty miles away. You're telling me that you found out about the murder this morning, had time to contact Colonel Harding, come out to Bushy Park to brief me, and I can still get to Newbury before they move the body?"

"There are telephones, you know," Cosgrove said.

"Who called you?" I wondered if it had been the killer.

"That is not germane. One thing I can tell you is that the owner of the rooming house, George Miller, emigrated here from Germany. He and his wife were active in the Social Democratic Party and had to flee after Hitler took power. He was originally Georg Mueller, but changed his name for obvious reasons."

"Is that common knowledge?" I asked.

"Yes. He keeps to himself these days, but his background is not a secret. He and his wife, Carla, have had some trouble since the war began—they have slight but noticeable German accents—but are reasonably well accepted in Newbury. Lots of foreigners on our shores these days, people have got used to it."

"By trouble, do you mean violence?" Kaz asked.

"Not that I know of. More along the lines of taunts in the street, that sort of thing. Inspector Payne can fill you in."

"And you know of Miller how?" I asked.

"It is my business to know of the Millers in our midst, Captain Boyle."

"I assume they've been investigated, since they are interned."

"Quite. Although technically enemy aliens, the Millers were defined as Category C, which means they present no security risk, especially since they were vocal opponents of the Nazi regime. Their son serves in the Royal Navy, actually. Now I suggest you leave promptly for Newbury, if that is all right with you, Colonel Harding?" Cosgrove glanced at Harding as if he really needed his permission. Cosgrove wore a major's uniform, but I'd always thought that was to blend into the scenery. Dollars to donuts, he ranked a lot higher in the secret world of MI5.

"Of course," Harding said. "Big Mike can drive you. Good luck."

"One final item," Cosgrove said as we all stood up to leave. "Be sure to report to me as soon as you learn anything. There is a telephone number on the paper I left you. Call that number when you have something. Under no circumstances are you, or Inspector Payne, to take any action before contacting me. Understood?"

"I get it, Major. But will Inspector Payne?"

"Consider that part of your brief, Captain. Make sure he understands. And the Millers are not under suspicion. Leave them out of the investigation, other than a basic interview about Neville." With that, Cosgrove patted his brow with his handkerchief and stalked out of the room. When we'd first met, Cosgrove and I hadn't seen eye to eye. He thought I was a useless Yank with political connections and not much more. I thought he was a stuffed-shirt imperialist of the old school. Neither of us had been far off the mark, but as time passed and we worked together, sometimes not without danger to us both, we'd come to understand and respect each other, to some degree. But this performance today was the old Cosgrove, vintage bluster and orders handed down to the stumblebum colonials.

"What's up, Colonel?" I asked Harding as soon as Cosgrove cleared the door.

"All I know is orders came down direct from General Whiteley, SHAEF G-2, to cooperate fully and without question with Major Cosgrove. That's what I'm doing and that's what I expect you to do, Captain, so shake a leg."

In other words, Harding was in the dark as well, and probably didn't like it much, but was too professional to let on. I also knew Whiteley was a British officer, and Cosgrove probably had an easy time getting him to cooperate. But I was smart enough to leave that unsaid. Uncle Ike didn't like Brits or Yanks criticizing each other based purely on nationality, so I let it slide.

"I'll bring the jeep around," Big Mike said, adding in a whisper, "and I'll tip off Estelle that we got called away."

Kaz and I retrieved our trench coats and walked outside to wait for Big Mike. It was a cold morning, and a thin layer of late spring snow lay across the park. Ice crinkled beneath our feet, the last gasp of winter's grip. Spring had come ahead of schedule, a rare treat for England in March. Camouflage netting was draped over the buildings, lending the scene a graceful, almost festive look. A bit like circus

tents under the winter sun, shading the hastily built wooden structures housing SHAEF personnel from the elements. And German
reconnaissance aircraft.

On the gravel drive, Major Cosgrove stood talking with a man
in civilian clothes. The guy was middle-aged, tall, and slim, with
angular cheekbones. He looked as if he'd been an athlete in his youth,
his easy stance and smooth gestures beneath the topcoat hinting at
strength and agility. He and Cosgrove could have been about the
same age, but Cosgrove, with his weight and worry, appeared stooped
and defeated in his presence.

All I could see was Cosgrove nodding yes, yes. The civilian got
into the rear seat of the automobile, which then pulled away, leaving
the major standing alone, patting his brow over and over.

"That," said Kaz, "is as public a demonstration of a crisis within
MI5 as you are ever likely to see."

"Any idea who that was?"

"The man who makes Major Cosgrove sweat," he said.

CHAPTER EIGHT

WE MADE GOOD time to Newbury. The roadway was shut down to London-bound traffic so army convoys could use both lanes heading south to the invasion ports. We moved along at a good clip, surrounded by British and American trucks carrying Tommies and GIs, flatbeds with tanks, towed artillery, and staff cars with their general's pennants flying. Everyone was headed for the Channel, men and the machinery of war flowing like lethal rivers to the sea. At roundabouts, MPs directed traffic and the few travelers headed in the wrong direction stood by their vehicles and watched forlornly as the heavy stream rumbled by.

"What do we have?" I said to Kaz from the back seat of the jeep. Kaz reached his gloved hand into his coat pocket and produced the sheet of paper Cosgrove had given us. The jeep's canvas top was up, but it was still damn cold inside.

"We are going to the Kennet Arms on Swan Court in Newbury, off Bridge Street, which is the main route across the Kennet and Avon Canal," Kaz said. "Owners are George and Carla Miller. They have a seventeen-year-old daughter, Eva, who lives at home and works at the canteen at the air base. Which is apparently where she met Sergeant Jerome Sullivan, who reported finding the body."

"Anything there on the victim?" Big Mike said from the driver's seat.

"One Stuart Neville, a long-term roomer, apparently. No other information on him. The Millers also have an older son, Walter, who is in the Royal Navy, currently in the Mediterranean. Nothing else."

"Cosgrove is well informed about the family situation," I said. "Enough so that he's convinced the Millers had no part in the murder. Bit soon to tell for sure, if you ask me."

"It makes some sense," Kaz said, leaning back in his seat. "MI5 would have a file on any German expatriates, especially those with political leanings."

"He never answered your question, Billy," Big Mike said. "About who called him. That doesn't make sense."

"It could have been Inspector Payne," Kaz said.

"Then he woulda said so," Big Mike said. "It's the easiest answer. But he changed the subject, talking about the Millers being Krauts and all, which of course got our attention."

"We'll ask Payne," I said, trying to sound confident. But Big Mike was right. Cosgrove got tipped off by someone else. Who and why would be nice to know. Cosgrove was a man of secrets, and maybe he had his reasons, but I didn't like going into an investigation blind.

"By the way, did you find anything in Private Smith's letters?" Kaz asked.

"They were all from his family. It sounded like he'd written them that he was thinking about staying on in England after the war. His mother was upset, but his older brother told him it might be a good idea. Said if he came home there was bound to be trouble with white folks."

"He must have earned his nickname before the army," Big Mike said. "Hell, if I was colored, I'd stay here too."

We entered Newbury, greeted by a statue of Queen Victoria, four lions at her feet. She wasn't saying anything either. We found Bridge Street, and then Swan Court, which was a quiet little street close to the canal, separated from it by a thick stand of trees, their budding branches shivering in the cold breeze. The houses were all red brick, with tall chimneys and set apart by waist-high brick walls. A path led along the riverbank behind the buildings. Small wooden boats were moored by the path, many of them covered in tarpaulins.

"Easy enough to get to these houses on all sides," Big Mike said, casing the neighborhood expertly. He parked the jeep near a black sedan, where a constable in the distinctive helmet and blue serge uniform stood on the sidewalk.

"You the Yanks we're waiting on?"

"That's us," I said to the constable. He nodded toward the front door of number eight Swan Court. A small sign proclaimed it to be the Kennet Arms, but it looked like any decent-sized house, three floors under a steep-sloped black slate roof.

"There you are," a man with a pipe clenched between his teeth said from the open door. "Come around the back and take a look at the body. Detective Inspector John Payne," he said, extending a hand. I did the introductions and we followed him around the side of the house. Payne was tall and lanky, a brown unbuttoned topcoat billowing behind him as he walked.

"Meet Mr. Stuart Neville," he said, working his pipe and blowing a stream of smoke to the sky. A constable who had been standing guard stood aside, revealing a set of stone steps leading down to a cellar door at the rear of the house. At the base of the steps was a crumpled form that a civilian might have mistaken for a pile of discarded clothes, if not for the pale white face with the startled look. Wisps of longish hair had fallen over one eye, but the other was staring up at us, or the sky beyond. You might expect him to hop up, dust himself off, and call himself a clumsy sod, if not for the odd angle of his neck.

"May I?" I said, gesturing toward the body.

"Oh, sure," Payne said. "We've had more than enough time to take fingerprints, waiting for you."

"Sorry," I said.

"Don't you worry, Captain Boyle. We're happy to cooperate. Two heads better than one, eh? Mr. Neville could have used another, that's plain to see. Go ahead."

I descended the stairs, which were steep and narrow, tailor-made for an accident. Maybe Neville slipped and broke his neck. Case closed. There was barely room to stand at the bottom, which was a square about four feet on either side in front of a cellar door. Neville wore a tweed jacket, a rumpled shirt, his tie askew, and wool pants that had seen better days. With clothes being strictly rationed, that didn't mean much. The soles of his shoes were well worn, the shoes themselves mud-splattered. I felt them; shoes and socks were wet. Maybe he had slipped and fallen after all?

But then I turned the head, and I realized what Payne had meant about a second one coming in handy. The back of Neville's skull was a bloody pulp. Someone had whacked him hard and sent him flying down the stairs. Maybe the blow had broken his neck or it happened when he hit the bottom. Either way, he was probably dead on impact.

"Any blood trail?" I asked as I came up the steps.

"None that we found," Payne said. "Seems like he took a blow to the head right here and tumbled down the steps."

"He was found early this morning, right?"

"Yes, by Sergeant Jerome Sullivan, who is still inside. He came to the house for breakfast. Apparently the sergeant is a fan of Mrs. Miller's cooking as well as being smitten with young Eva Miller, and is quite welcome at the house, especially when bearing the gift of coffee. He walked up the river path and was about to knock at the back door when he caught sight of the body."

"All right, I'll talk to him."

"He's the reason we're to say you're here, so I understand," Payne said.

"Same here, Inspector. And if I knew the real reason, I'd tell you straight out. But I don't, other than I was a cop myself in civilian life."

"Then we're both in the dark about this. Standard fare in our profession, isn't it? You're welcome to speak to the family, and I'll share what I know with you, but let's keep this friendly, Captain Boyle, shall we? Make no mistake, this is a Berkshire Constabulary investigation."

"This is your turf, Inspector." What else could I say?

"Fine. I'll be glad to brief you on the Millers' statements. First, I need to call the coroner to come and fetch the body."

"I'd rather speak to them myself, before you tell me what they said. Is that all right?"

"It's the way I'd prefer it, should I ever find myself getting in the way of a murder investigation in America. Go on in, you'll find them in the kitchen."

"Have you canvassed the neighborhood yet?" I asked.

"No, I planned to do that next. We're shorthanded here, and with a man out front waiting for you and one in the back standing over the body, I had no one to send."

"Sergeant Miecznikowski—you can call him Big Mike—was also a cop back in the States. He can help out with that."

"I believe I will use the nickname," Payne said, giving Big Mike a wink. "Constable Higgins, take the sergeant along and check the neighbors. Ask about anything unusual during the night or early morning."

"And ask them if they were used to seeing Neville out at odd hours, and if he went boating," I said. "His feet are wet."

"There are puddles on the path along the canal," Payne said. "Could have come from there. The ground is hardpacked, though, no footprints. So, off with you, Higgins. Lieutenant Kazimierz, perhaps you should wait outside, to keep up the appearance of a purely American involvement."

"Excellent idea, Inspector," Kaz said. His British uniform with the *Poland* shoulder patch would only raise questions we couldn't answer. "I will wait for the coroner and search Neville's pockets, if you don't mind."

"Have at him," Payne said. "Give whatever you find to Constable Gilbert."

"When you're done, Kaz, take a walk along the canal and check things out. Neville and his assailant probably came from that direction."

I followed the inspector inside. The aroma of coffee and cigarette smoke hung in the air. I entered the kitchen as Payne tromped down the hall to use the telephone.

"Sir!" A US Army Air Force buck sergeant stood to attention.

His eyes were wide, his expression fearful, but his posture was good. He looked nineteen, twenty tops.

"Relax, soldier," I said, focusing on the Millers, who sat at the kitchen table, eyeing me. "I'm Captain Billy Boyle. Would you mind answering a few more questions?"

"Yes, certainly," George Miller said, nodding in excessive agreement. His English was good but the accent was perceptible, the same as the potbelly stretching the buttons on his vest. "Anything we can do to help. This is a terrible business."

"Please, sit down, Captain. May I offer you coffee?" Carla Miller looked at me expectantly. Her English was also good, clipped with a British accent, either picked up here or from the person who taught her. She had a healthy look about her, ruddy cheeks, fair skin, and blonde hair shot through with strands of grey.

"Thank you, Mrs. Miller, that would be nice." I sat, and motioned for my fellow Yank to sit as well. I wanted them at ease, and the best way to do that was to make this a social call. Coffee and chitchat about the dead guy outside.

"A terrible business," Carla Miller said, busying herself with a cup and saucer. "Who could do such a thing to poor Mr. Neville?"

"And why, that's what I wonder," George Miller said. "There must be a lunatic loose. It makes no sense." George lit a cigarette, after offering me one. A Lucky Strike. I said no, and made a mental note that Sergeant Jerome Sullivan was no dummy, bringing gifts of scarce smokes and java to his girlfriend's parents. George shook his head sadly, blowing blue smoke in every direction.

"He was a boarder here?" I asked as Carla set a cup of steaming coffee in front of me. It would be impolite to ask for sugar with wartime rationing, unless that luxury was included among Jerome's gifts.

"Yes. Mr. Neville has been with us over a year now," Carla said, her accent almost musical in its cadence. "Or was."

"Where was he employed?"

"At the Newbury Building Society, over on Bartholomew Street," George said. "He handled mortgages and construction loans. This caused him to travel fairly often, never for long, but with little notice. It was why he liked keeping a room here."

"You have other boarders?"

"Just one at the moment. A fellow named Nigel Morris. He is traveling on business out Bristol way, I think. He works for a firm that manufactures radios. He's been with us only a few weeks."

"George is fixing up our only other room, Captain," Carla said. "He is always making improvements to the house."

"Was Neville in his room last night?" I asked.

"His bed was not slept in, no," Carla said. "We did not see him yesterday evening, but that was not unusual with his schedule. He would normally let us know when he expected to be here for dinner, and when we did not hear from him, we naturally thought he was away on business."

"What about you, Sergeant Sullivan? Were you acquainted with Neville?"

"Yes, sir, I was. Can I leave now, Captain? I just came over for a quick visit, I can't be away all day." Sullivan looked worried, but not about a murder charge.

"Not quite yet, Sergeant. No pass?"

"No. We were supposed to have flight training this morning, but it got canceled due to cloud cover, so I came over for a quick visit. I should be back by now."

"How much coffee did you bring? Or should I say steal?" It was time to shake things up. A man was dead and everyone was too polite for the circumstances.

"It was just a little gift," Sullivan said. "I traded for it at the base, honest."

"The sergeant has done nothing wrong," Carla said. "He is a good boy."

"Good boys don't trade in black market cigarettes and coffee. I don't think things would go well for a nice German couple to be accused of trafficking in the black market."

"Hey, hold on, Captain," Sullivan said.

"No, no, Jerome. Do not get yourself in trouble," George said.

"It is true, Captain Boyle, that I have a weakness for the Lucky Strike cigarettes. Jerome does not smoke, so he shares his with me. As for the coffee, on occasion he does bring some. Very often he eats with us, and brings food. Many American soldiers do so, given the rationing. You Americans have so much of everything, don't you?" George Miller was not a man to rattle easily. Maybe opposing and then escaping the Nazis had something to do with that.

"What I have so much of right now is an American soldier at the scene of a murder. As long as he had nothing to do with it, I don't care if he carries sacks of coffee under each arm when he comes here. So tell me now, Sergeant Sullivan. Did you and Stuart Neville ever argue about anything? Did he ask about supplies from the base, ask you to bring him anything on the side?" I fired off my questions with a practiced hard stare, looking for any sign of nervousness. A twitch or blink, any show of fear.

"No, nothing like that, Captain, really," Sullivan said, wide-eyed with naïve innocence. "He asked me a lot about America, but then everyone does. I'm from Kansas, and he wanted to know about our farm, that sort of thing. He never asked me for anything, and we never had a beef."

"Beef?" Carla said.

"They never argued," I said. "Did Neville have any visitors? Did he have a girlfriend?"

"No, he was a quiet man," she said. "He worked with numbers, financial numbers. He was quite busy with loans for all the repairs and rebuilding from the bombings. He worked long hours, and was gone two or three nights during the week."

"He wasn't in the service? He looked young enough."

"Punctured eardrum, he told me," Sullivan said.

"How do people here treat you?" I asked the Millers. "I imagine some folks don't like having Germans in the neighborhood, no matter what your politics were."

"It is not bad, especially after what we endured in Germany. Once the brownshirts have assaulted you, a few comments in the street are nothing. We came here before the war, you see, and that allowed us to get to know people. And they us."

"So there's no one with a serious grudge against you?"

"No. Do you mean I might have been the target, not poor Mr. Neville?" George looked astounded at the idea, Carla frightened.

"It's something to think about. It was dark, he was at the rear of your house. Any idea what he was doing out there?"

"No. Perhaps he took the path along the canal and was returning from work."

"Or from the pub," Sullivan said. "He stopped at the Hog's Head once in a while. I mentioned that to the inspector."

"I'm sure he'll check that out. Mrs. Miller, I assume Neville had given you his ration book, since he took his meals here."

"Yes, of course. He enjoyed my cooking very much. He said it was nice to have a home-cooked meal after traveling as he did." He was the perfect roomer. The Millers got use of his ration coupons but he ate many of his meals away.

"What about your daughter, Mr. Miller? Is she in the house?"

"Yes. The inspector spoke to her and told her she could go about her duties. She helps us with the rooms, keeping them clean. She's tidying up Mr. Neville's room now."

"Show me, please," I said, standing up. "Have the police checked his room?"

"This way," Carla said, taking the stairs at the back of the house. "Yes, the police went through it already. I thought we should organize things in case a relative wants his possessions."

I bit back a comment about overly efficient Germans and followed her up to the third floor. Payne likely gave the room a thorough search, but I'd feel better if I had my own shot at it. One of my dad's favorite sayings—and he had a lot of them—was if you wanted something done right, don't wait for someone else to do it. And since he'd taught me everything I knew about being a cop and a homicide detective, I thought I ought to follow what advice I could remember.

"Eva, this is Captain Boyle, he'd like to look at the room," Carla said, standing with her hand on the doorknob.

"Yes, Mother," Eva said, bundling up sheets stripped from the bed in her arms. She was fair-haired, with a spread of freckles across her face. A bit on the short side, with an intelligent look in her eyes, even as they avoided my gaze. And her mother's. She stared down at the floor, in sadness or obedience, perhaps.

"Hello, Eva," I said, trying to ease the tension.

"Hello, Captain. Are you going to find who killed Mr. Neville?"

"I hope so. I'm sure Inspector Payne is working as hard as he can on it. I'm here to help."

"The police can use the help," Eva said. "There's some girl gone missing and most of them are out looking for her. I think they'd rather find her than look for whoever murdered Mr. Neville."

"Eva, don't say such a thing," her mother said.

"It's true, isn't it?" Eva had no trace of a German accent. Her voice was pure English schoolgirl. "If there's a chance of finding that poor girl alive, why wouldn't they send all their men out to look for her? Mr. Neville is dead already."

"Finding whoever killed him is important too," I said, although I liked her logic. "Especially if we can stop him from killing again. Do you know the missing girl?"

"No, I only heard about it at school yesterday. She's one of the evacuees living in that manor house outside Kintbury."

"There are several large houses in the area where the children were put up," Carla said. "They were evacuated from London when the Blitz was at its worst. Some have gone back to the city now that the bombing has lessened. Perhaps the poor dear tried to find her way home."

"Oh no, she wasn't from London," Eva said. "She was with that group from Guernsey. She had no place to go back to." Guernsey was one of the Channel Islands occupied by the Germans. When the war began, many of the children were brought to the mainland in case the Germans took the islands, which they had done with ease.

"Be that as it may," Carla said firmly, "take the washing down and let Captain Boyle look at what he wants."

"Has anything else been removed?" I asked.

"No, I just hung up a shirt that was on the chair, and cleaned up a bit. In case any relatives come for his things, I wanted it to look nice," Eva said.

"Was Mr. Neville a nice man? I mean the friendly sort."

"A bit reserved, wouldn't you say, dear?" Carla said. "Like most of the English."

"Perhaps," Eva said. "But he didn't talk to me like most adults. Treating me like a little kid, I mean. I am eighteen years old, you know."

"Just last week, you were," her mother said with a smile, ushering her daughter out. "Don't rush things, Eva."

They left me alone in Neville's room. Searching a dead man's place was never a favorite pastime. It didn't bother some guys, but the little things people left behind always got to me. Change on the dresser. An unfinished book. All the possessions we think will be waiting when we return but only point to the uncertainty of life and the sureness of death.

The room was long and narrow, with a dresser on the wall to the left of the door. Next to it was an armchair, a bit worse for wear, but well placed. It faced the double windows on the opposite wall, which had an excellent view of the canal and the town beyond it. A church steeple crept above the rooftops, barely above the chimneys spouting grimy coal smoke. I watched a rowboat in the canal, the rower paddling idly as the current took him. A bed stood by the other wall, with a nightstand and lamp. Past the bed was a closet, and I opened the door to find a pair of shoes, slippers, and old boots. Neville had two suits hanging neatly, next to a few shirts and a couple of pairs of older trousers. A raincoat and a heavy winter overcoat filled out his wardrobe. After several years of strict clothes rationing, most Englishmen were making do as Neville obviously was. The suits were well-worn, a few faint stains and patches showing their age. I went through the pockets and found nothing but lint and a ticket stub for the Great Western Railway, Newbury to Cheltenham. Made sense, from what I knew of his job.

The book on his nightstand was *Pied Piper*, by Nevil Shute. Kaz
had a copy in his suite at the Dorchester, and I'd started it myself a
few days ago. It was about an English gent stuck in France at the
beginning of the war, trying to get himself and a bunch of kids safely
to England. Neville had gotten farther than I had, but I had a better
shot at finishing it. I hoped.

I sat in his chair. I looked out the window, then at the one
picture on the wall, a standard country scene. The wood floors were
polished and clean, no dust anywhere. It looked like it would take
about ten minutes to move Neville's stuff out and get the place
ready for a new tenant. I got up and checked the dresser drawers.
Nothing but clothing. Stuart Neville appeared to be a man with
few needs. He had a job, a room with a pleasant view, and friendly
housekeepers. No pictures of family, no smokes, none of the debris
of everyday life a working man might pick up and leave behind.
I wondered what his office was like, and what he kept there. I
checked the closet one more time, and noticed a clothes hanger
had fallen on the floor. It seemed oddly out of place, which made
me think.

I took the stairs quietly and darted into the scullery, which
opened onto the backyard. Eva was pouring hot water into a dolly
tub, a big metal-rimmed tub for doing laundry. The bed sheets were
in the tub, but hanging from a peg was a blue serge suit.

"Oh, Captain," Eva said, stepping in front of the clothing as if I
might not notice.

"Did you take anything else?" I asked. "I don't care about the suit,
although his relatives may."

"No," she said, her eyes downcast. "Just this. I thought I might
take it out a bit and it would fit Father nicely. He's had nothing
new since the rationing, and Mr. Neville told me he had no close
relatives. I was worried the police would take everything away. I'm
sorry." That last bit was drawn out as if she was talking to an idiot,
which meant she wasn't sorry at all, and that I should stop being
so mean.

"Don't worry," I said, going through the pockets and coming up empty. "Did Mr. Neville tell you anything else that you forgot to mention?"

"Yes. To be careful and not go out at night alone. He said the world was a dangerous place, and that I should watch out for myself. He was very serious about it. I didn't want to say anything in front of Mama, it would only worry her."

"He was right about the world," I said. "It was good advice."

"What should I do with the suit?"

"I'm not your conscience, kid. Do whatever you can live with."

CHAPTER NINE

IT WASN'T LIKE I was a stranger to valuables vanishing from a crime scene. I'd never take a treasured family possession, but I do recall nicking a smoked ham once, from the house of a guy who'd taken two slugs to the back of the head. He was a mobster, lived alone, and I figured no one would mind since he had about a dozen of them hanging down in the cellar. Depending on the circumstances, I could live with certain small appliances, foodstuff, clothing and whatnot walking away. One suit from a guy who either had no family or didn't care about them was a long way from crossing my line. I'd admired Eva's initiative, but felt like I had to play the tough guy.

I wasn't feeling so tough as I looked for Sergeant Sullivan, given that I was investigating a murder and had instead uncovered a kid pinching a dead man's suit for her paunchy old man. I found Sullivan in the parlor, leafing through a copy of a film magazine with David Niven on the cover.

"It's Eva's," he said, tossing it aside. "She loves the moving pictures. We're supposed to see *The Way Ahead*, the new David Niven film, tonight. But I'll be in Dutch with my CO for not getting back on time."

"Yeah, you got it rough, Sullivan. Tell me, how'd you get along with Neville?"

"Everyone calls me Sully, Captain."

"Okay, Sully. What did Neville call you?"

"We hardly exchanged a dozen words. I'm here to see Eva, so I stay in the kitchen most times. I had dinner with the family once when he was here, but he mainly talked with Mr. Miller. He was okay, I guess."

"He ever give Eva a hard time?"

"You mean come on to her? Hell, Captain, he was an older guy. Forty, maybe."

"Wouldn't be the first time. Eva's a pretty gal. You certain she never said anything?"

"No, she didn't. What, do you think he pulled a fast one and she . . . oh, wait, I get it. You think I clobbered him, huh?"

"You'd have every right to be mad about a guy making a move on your girl. Him living under the same roof and all."

"No, he didn't pull anything. And you got a suspicious mind, Captain."

"Goes with the territory. Anything out of the ordinary happen around here lately? Break-ins, strangers prowling around?"

"No, just that missing girl they're all looking for. It's the talk of the town."

"Did Neville ever go out boating on the canal?"

"Jeez, Captain, I don't know. I wasn't keeping tabs on the guy."

Big Mike came in and sat down on the couch next to me. I felt the springs sag. "Anything?" I asked.

"Sore feet and wasted time," he said. "No one saw anything, and most don't remember ever seeing Stuart Neville around. Nothing unusual to report, but everyone is keeping their kids close by until they find that girl. It's all they wanted to talk about."

"Okay. Big Mike, why don't you run Sully here back to his base. Shouldn't take too long. Put in a good word for him and let his CO know he discovered the body and was assisting the investigation."

"Thanks, Captain," Sully said. "You're all right. I'll say so long to Eva."

"One more thing, Sully. You have any Negro units on the air base?"

"Yeah, there's a Quartermaster truck company. Why?"

"Is there much trouble between the white and colored boys? Fights, that sort of thing?"

"Hasn't been any I know of, Captain. Might be because it's only one company, and they do a good job, no complaints there. When I was stationed in Northern Ireland, there were lots of Negro GIs around, and there was trouble, especially over girls. A lot of the Southern boys especially didn't like seeing those girls arm in arm with Negroes."

"What about you, Sully?"

"Well, it was pretty strange. Not something you'd expect to see back in the States. Can't say I got used to it, but no one forced those girls to go out with them. I heard it said more than once that the Negro troops were polite and well behaved, and the locals liked that. But some fellows really took offense. There was real trouble there, believe me."

"But not at Greenham Common?"

"No. We even got a baseball game coming up, our squadron against the QM company. I'm playing shortstop."

"Okay, take off. Meet Big Mike at the jeep in five."

"I'll pump him, non-com to non-com," Big Mike said after Sully cleared the door. "You think he's hiding anything?"

"No, he seems genuine. But I'm wondering about what Eva said Neville told her. That the world is a dangerous place."

"You think Neville had something to do with the missing girl?" Big Mike said, with a born cop's instinct and innate suspicion of everyone.

"All I know is he was pretty much a cipher except for that warning. I wonder why he said it. See what Sully thinks. Meet us at the Hog's Head pub, it should be within walking distance; it's where Neville drank."

"Okay, Billy. That stuff about the Negroes, that wasn't about this case, was it?" Big Mike gave me a skeptical glare. I'd filled him in about Angry Smith and he was playing mother hen, making sure I didn't wander too far afield.

"No. Just trying to get a feel for the attitudes around here.

Hungerford is the next town over. I might make some time to check in with Tree while we're here."

Big Mike left with Sully and I walked out the back door, standing in front of the now-empty cellar stairs. The body was gone, the air was quiet, and the day was winding down. Faint sounds of traffic came from Bridge Street, and water in the canal gurgled as an oarsman worked against the current. A line of trees separated the houses from the path and the narrow watercraft moored along the bank. The deck of one boat was uncovered, and leaves floated on a thin patch of water from the recent rains. Is this where Neville got his feet wet? I went aboard, and the vessel rocked in the water. It was decrepit, with faded, peeling paint and rusty metal fixtures. The bow deck was open, with a small enclosed cabin aft. I knocked and the cabin door swung open, sending the odor of mildew and rot wafting up. It was deserted, as was the tiny engine room with its ancient diesel engine, which was the best-kept part of the boat. My shoes squished as I crossed the water logged floor, and I realized Neville was not quite a cipher after all. He'd warned Eva and his shoes and socks were soaked. Two things out of the ordinary in a very ordinary life. I caught movement out of the corner of my eye, and glanced to the path.

"You may as well give up," Kaz said, grinning as I stood in fetid, pooled water. "There are half a dozen of these boats within a ten-minute walk of the house."

"You mean boats filled with water."

"Yes. There are half-sunken wrecks all along the canal. Much of it is in disrepair or overgrown with weeds. But the war has helped bring the water traffic back. Some materials are cheaper to move by water, especially if the delivery goes with the current. This saves petrol."

"Okay," I said, jumping ashore. "Have you become an expert on canals since I left you?"

"No, but the proprietor of the Hog's Head is. A former riverman, he used to run a barge between London and Bristol. The Kennet and Avon Canal connects the Avon River to the west with the

Kennet River here. It runs directly between Hungerford and Newbury, then follows the river to Reading, where it connects with the Thames. Quite a thing in its day, the entire waterway cut right across England."

"You've learned more than I have."

"There was not much to do once the body was removed, so I took a walk. Very pleasant by the canal. It is a short stretch to Bridge Street, and of course the bridge. The Hog's Head pub is close by. Before he left, Inspector Payne said he would meet us there in about one hour, when he is through with the coroner."

"Good. Big Mike is meeting us there too." I went over what I'd found, or hadn't found, and mentioned the warning to Eva. "Did you find anything when you searched Neville's body?"

"Nothing. Not a wallet or a scrap of paper. His pants pockets were actually turned out, as if someone had searched his body."

"So maybe he was killed somewhere else, and dumped down the stairs to avoid discovery," I said, but it didn't sound right.

"I do not think so, Billy. He could have been thrown in the river and might have drifted downstream some distance. Or put in one of these boats. He would have been undetected for days."

"So what did Neville see or do that made him a target? And what did he have on him that the killer wanted? Money?" We walked slowly along the path as the sky darkened. Clouds obscured what light there was from the sun, which was dropping behind the buildings across the river. My feet were cold.

"Perhaps the killer wanted it to look like a random theft. As if he took a cosh to the head a bit too hard."

"It could have been exactly that. Or someone who hated Neville and waited until he had his chance, then turned out his pockets, either looking for something specific, or as a red herring."

"Did you find out where he was employed?" Kaz asked.

"Yeah. He worked at the Newbury Building Society. Handled mortgages."

"That could get someone quite angry. Or in trouble, if they were embezzling funds."

"We should pay a visit tomorrow. Meanwhile, there's one important thing I need to do."

"What is that?" Kaz said as we knocked on the Millers' kitchen door.

"Steal a pair of dead man's socks."

CHAPTER TEN

I WAS WEARING dry socks, courtesy of the late Mr. Neville, while my shoes dried in front of the coal fire in the Hog's Head pub. Coal was rationed too, so it was banked low, but there was enough to give off a warm glow. Big Mike, Kaz and I finished our first round of Newbury Ale, delivered to the table by Kaz's new pal.

"Jack Monk's the name, fellows," he'd said. "Riverman most of me life. Now I run this place and watch the water flow by. That's the way of it. The baron told me all about what yer up to. Good luck, I say, but I wish you'd go on out and look for that lass who's lost."

That was the prevailing opinion. I planned on asking Payne what that was all about when he arrived. We ordered rabbit stew, Jack Monk having promised the meat was fresh and his wife the best cook in all of Newbury, now that his dear mother had passed on.

"Did you get anything new out of Sergeant Sullivan?" I asked Big Mike.

"He wouldn't stop talking about his girl," Big Mike said, setting down his empty pint glass and licking his lips. "He admitted to taking a fair bit of food to give mom and dad, but that only goes to show he's a smart kid. I did get this, though." Big Mike took a photograph from his pocket and tossed it on the table. Sully and Eva standing outside the front door of the Kennet Arms, smiling—no, laughing—as the camera caught them. It was a good picture of Eva, especially. She looked happy, mischievous, and young.

Sully's face was turned in her direction, his gaze admiring. The only thing that marred the picture was Stuart Neville, emerging from the door, a startled look on his face. He was obviously dressed for work, with his topcoat, hat, and briefcase.

"She's quite pretty," Kaz said.

"I had to promise to get this back to him," Big Mike said. "But I figured we needed a good photograph of Neville. Sully said he'd been all apologetic about stumbling into the shot, but it turned out it was the nicest one of Eva, so he picked it when Mrs. Miller offered."

"Room for a tired copper?" Inspector Payne said as he entered the room. Big Mike did his best to shove over in the booth, but with his shoulders it wasn't easy. "Wouldn't mind a constable or two your size on the Berkshire force, I'll tell you that."

"Any news?" I asked.

"Just came from the postmortem. Death was instantaneous, from a single strong blow to the back of the head. Your classic blunt instrument, probably tossed into the muddy bottom of the canal. No defensive wounds. There were bruises on his torso, likely from that tumble down the steps. We didn't find any drag marks in the vicinity, and his shoe heels gave no indication of being pulled over any surface." He puffed out a long breath.

"Time of death?" I asked.

"Anywhere from ten last night to two o'clock this morning."

"So we know he was killed on the spot, from behind."

"Nothing like a Yank detective on the job," Payne said. "Sorry, it's been a long day. What's that you've got there?"

"A picture of the victim," Big Mike said. "Courtesy of another Yank cop."

"Looks like this round is my shout," Payne said, signaling to Jack Monk at the bar. "Glad I didn't say anything about Polish coppers."

"There is something odd in this picture," Kaz said, tapping his finger on it. I could tell he was pleased at being included in the police banter, even though he disguised it well. "Where is the briefcase?"

"Right," Payne said. "This looks like he was headed out, and had his briefcase with him."

"Maybe at his office. Have you been there yet?" I asked Payne.

"No, first thing tomorrow. You're welcome to come along if you want. I've been busy with the coroner and coordinating the search."

"For the little girl," I said.

"Aye, it's all anybody asks about. Sophia Edwards, fourteen years old. Missing two days and nights now." Payne's face showed his weariness, and from the bags under his eyes I figured he'd been awake for most of that time.

"Runaway?" Big Mike asked.

"That was my first thought too, but she's from Guernsey, one of the Channel Islands. Forty or so girls came to this area when they were evacuated. As soon as France fell, it was obvious the Germans would take the islands, even though they are of no military value. There's simply nowhere for her to run off to. She's no family except back on Guernsey."

"Where's her home here?" I asked.

"A place was set up in Kintbury, a small village midway between Newbury and Hungerford. The girls live there, in a manor house that doubles as their school. By all accounts, Sophia was happy there. Content might be a better word. All the kids are worried about their parents, of course. But children are resilient and adaptable, and they seem to be getting on well. Not since her disappearance, of course."

"Any theories?

"There's always the canal. The girl's house is on the Hungerford Road, not far from the canal. She could have fallen in. The girls often walk into Kintbury—there's a sweet shop on High Street—but they seldom go alone. She simply vanished in the afternoon. Classes were over, and the girls were on their own until teatime. Several of them walked to the sweet shop. Sophia was with them, and they stopped along the canal on their way back. No one remembers seeing her leave, or seeing anything unusual."

"Here you go, gents," Jack Monk said, breaking the dour mood a bit as he set down four freshly drawn pints. "Mind the photograph there. Oh, it's Miss Eva and Sully. And what a nice snap it is."

"You know Sergeant Sullivan?" I asked.

"Sure, he comes in a few times a week, after the Millers put out the lights. He'll have a pint or two and gab on about his plans for Miss Eva. Head over heels that lad is."

"How about George Miller? Is he a regular?" Payne asked.

"No, not him," Monk said, shaking his head. "I hold nothing against him, mind you. He stuck his neck out against Hitler, and that must've taken guts back then. Got to admire the man, I say. But feelings run hard, you know."

"Whose?" I asked.

"Well, it was a month or so ago. One of the few times Miller came in. Old Tim Pettigrew, he'd just lost a son who'd gone down in a Wellington over Germany. Miller tried to give his condolences, in a neighborly way. He and Pettigrew hardly knew each other, but everyone knows about the Millers, of course. So George says he's sorry for the loss, or something close to that, and Pettigrew fair spits in his face, calls him a dirty Kraut, and says he hopes his boy killed plenty of Muellers before he bought it himself. Tim would've hit him, the rage was in his face, plain to see. But his pals sat him down, and Miller left without a word. Never saw him in here again."

"Is Pettigrew in tonight, Jack?" Payne asked.

"Aye, that's him," Monk said, nodding to a figure across the room. "Grey hair, brown cardigan." He squinted and tapped his finger on the snapshot. "I see poor Stuart got himself in that picture. That why you have it?"

"Yes," Kaz said. "Did you know him?"

"He was a customer. Not every night, but often enough to introduce himself. Seemed like a nice chap, don't know why anyone would want to do him in."

"Was he here the night Pettigrew went after Miller?" Payne asked.

"No, I think I would have remembered that. No, I'm certain he wasn't. I'll go and fetch your stew, it should be ready."

"Captain, care to join me for a word with Mr. Pettigrew?" Payne said. I put on my shoes, which were nearly dry, and followed him to the bar. Pettigrew was busy puffing on his pipe and nursing a half-empty pint. "Timothy Pettigrew? May we have a word?" Payne introduced himself, showed his warrant card, and nodded to a quiet corner of the pub.

"What's this about?" Pettigrew said as he stepped away from the bar. He looked to be near fifty, stooped, with greying, stiff hair and jowls beginning to form. He wore two sweaters and worn corduroy pants, and his hands were callused and rough. "And what's the Yank for?"

"Captain Boyle is assisting with an investigation that involves an American serviceman, to some degree. I understand you and George Miller had an argument recently. Almost came to blows."

"So? Almost is a crime now, is it?"

"No, it isn't," Payne said. "And I'm very sorry for the loss of your son. It must have hit you hard."

"Hard enough, not that it's any business of yours."

"I take it you did not appreciate Miller's comment to you."

"Mueller, you mean," Pettigrew said, stretching out the German pronunciation and looking like he wanted to spit. "I had enough of that lot back in the Great War, don't need them moving in here and drinking with decent folk. And I sure don't need that bastard telling me he's sorry my boy is dead!" Pettigrew looked away, rubbing his hand over his unshaven jaw. His pain was fresh, as if he'd just heard the news, and I wondered if Miller had been the one person he could rage at with righteous justification.

"What do you do for a living, Mr. Pettigrew?" I asked.

"What's that got to do with anything?"

"Please answer the question, Mr. Pettigrew," Payne said.

"I'm a pipe fitter, down at the Fawcett Plant. They make aircraft engines. Now what else do you want to know?"

"Did you have any other run-ins with Miller?" Payne asked.

"No. Saw him once on the street, but I ignored him. Truth be told, I didn't like to lose my temper that way. I don't like Miller or his kind, but I don't like folks thinking I'm a madman either." Pettigrew spoke quietly, and I had the notion he was ashamed of how he had acted, but too proud to admit it.

"Thank you, Mr. Pettigrew," Payne said. "That will be all for now."

"One thing," I said, as Pettigrew turned to leave. I showed him the photograph. "Do you know this man?"

"That's Miller's place, isn't it? The Kennet Arms he calls it, as if he's something special." Pettigrew squinted and studied the snapshot. "I've seen the Yank in here, aye. And the other fellow too, the one who was killed. That must be Miller's daughter, then."

"That's right. Thanks," I said, and Payne and I returned to the booth. Kaz and Big Mike were already at work on the rabbit stew.

"Good question about where he worked," Payne said, finishing off his ale. "A wrench or a pipe would be tailor-made for the wound on Neville's head."

"And he knew the house," I said. "It's one thing to know about the Millers in a small town like Newbury. It's another to know the exact house. Swan Court is a swankier place than Pettigrew's neighborhood, I'll bet."

"You're thinking he attacked Neville by mistake, thinking he was Miller?" Big Mike asked, spooning up the last of his stew. "You ought to try some of this, Inspector."

"Mrs. Monk runs a good kitchen, but so does my Mrs. Payne, and I ought to attend to her," the inspector said. "It's early days for such theories, my friend, but we best keep an eye on Pettigrew. I shall be at the Newbury Building Society nine o'clock tomorrow, Captain Boyle. Then I must leave to continue the search for Sophia Edwards. I've asked an American unit stationed near Kintbury to assist. The commander agreed, and tomorrow we'll work a sweep along both sides of the canal, Hungerford to Newbury. It'll be a long day."

"Which unit, Inspector?" I asked.

"Those colored chaps, the Six-Seventeenth battalion. Tank destroyers, I think they call themselves."

CHAPTER ELEVEN

"SO, WHAT DO we know?" I put the question to Kaz and Big Mike after Payne had left and I'd filled them in on the conversation with Pettigrew.

"Stuart Neville is dead, which seems not much different from Stuart Neville being alive," Kaz said. "Except from the perspective of Mr. Neville. He appears to be one of those men who leave little trace of his existence. We also know a twelve-year-old girl has gone missing. Timothy Pettigrew is in great emotional pain, and can easily put his hands on a blunt object, which puts him in the same position as any number of Englishmen who have managed without murdering a single person. And Mrs. Monk is indeed a good cook. Rosemary and shallots for seasoning, I think."

"And red-currant jam too, that's her secret," Monk said, appearing from nowhere and setting a fresh bowl in front of Big Mike.

"Mr. Monk, do you have lodgings?" I asked.

"Yes, but only one room vacant, it won't fit all of you. It would hardly fit the sergeant alone!" He had a good laugh at his own joke.

"It'll just be me," I said.

"What are we doing?" Big Mike said, his eyes closed as he savored the aroma.

"Sorry, guys, but I need to keep the jeep. I'll take you to the station and you can catch the next train to London. Big Mike, I want you to check with Army CID headquarters. Get me some details on the Angry Smith case. Find out if they had other suspects or any actual evidence against him."

"Billy, you know Sam wants us on this case," Big Mike said, around a mouthful of stew.

"Tomorrow the Six-Seventeenth is going to be part of this case. I want to be sure they're not harboring a dangerous murderer as they search for Sophia."

"Billy, you know Sophia Edwards is not part of this case," Big Mike said. "But I'll go and come up with a story if Sam finds out."

"Neville did give Eva a warning," I said. "And he was found near the canal, which is where Payne is focusing the search. It's a connection. Not much of one, but it bothers me."

"Why?" Kaz said.

"It's as if Neville came out of his shell to say that to Eva. What made him warn her? Had he seen something, or someone, that put him on his guard?"

"What guy needs a reason to talk to a pretty girl?" Big Mike said with perfect logic, before returning his full attention to the stew.

"Kaz, will you give Cosgrove an update first thing tomorrow? He wanted a call tonight, but let him sweat it out. Press him on what he isn't telling us, maybe you can get him to loosen up. And then maybe swing by the Dorchester and grab some gear? I could use a change of clothes and my thirty-eight Police Special. Boots, too." I'd started the day dressed in my Class A uniform, and I hadn't expected to be doing field work.

"I will call Walter and have him pack bags for both of us," Kaz said. Walter worked the front desk at the Dorchester and could be counted on to get things done. Everything from vintage champagne to firearms. "But before we leave, you need to tell the rest of the story."

"What story?" By that time I was pretty interested in the stew myself.

"About you and Tree in Boston. If we're going to work that case on the side, you owe us the truth," Kaz said. Big Mike nodded in agreement. I sighed, and thought back to the summer of 1936 once again.

= = =

I GOT REALLY good at sweeping that first week, not to mention mopping and scrubbing. Dad had told me to expect some ribbing from the guys at headquarters and not to let it get to me. It did, but I'm getting ahead of myself.

"You didn't tell me I'd be working for a colored man," I said to my father when he got home that night.

"You work for Mr. Jackson, Billy," he said, hands on his hips and his jaw clenched. "Don't you forget it. He's a man, not a color." I knew right away I'd made a mistake. I should have let Dad settle in to his easy chair and talked to him when he was more relaxed. It never was a good idea to talk to Dad at home when he still had his tie knotted around his neck. Even my little kid brother Danny knew that. I could tell he was angry, so I stepped aside and followed as he went into his den.

"You could have told me," I said. "About Mr. Jackson," I added, trailing in his wake.

"Better for you to learn how to deal with people on your own. How you act when confronted by the unexpected says a lot about a man," Dad said, turning to face me. "I hope I hear a good report tomorrow." He took a deep breath and put his hand on my shoulder, gave me a pat, and smiled. Then I knew I'd be all right, as long as that good report came to him tomorrow.

"Do you know Mr. Jackson?" I asked as Dad sat in his chair. He pulled his tie off and threw it on the floor. He tossed his head back and I noticed, for the first time, a line of grey hairs at his temples.

"Not well. He's a proud man in a tough spot. He has a decent city job, but things aren't easy for him."

"Why? I mean, beyond the obvious," I said.

"He wanted to be a police officer. He's a veteran, fought with the 366th Infantry Regiment in France. It was one of the colored units attached to the French army, so they saw real combat. I met him the day your Uncle Dan and I applied for jobs with the force, after the strike. We got to talking as we stood on line, and he was hopeful that the city would be hiring

Negro officers. He'd been a sergeant in the army, and seemed like he'd do okay."

"What happened?"

"They told him they had enough colored cops, but they needed a janitor. The next time I saw him, I was in my patrolman's blues and he was pushing a mop. I told him it wasn't right, and you know what he said?"

"I can guess. If you're black, get back. If you're white, you're all right."

"It's a hard truth, but he was right. Just the way things are. He was starting a family, so he grabbed the job that was offered. We've been friendly, but I can't say we're friends. When I told him I'd gotten you this summer job, he didn't seem thrilled. Probably worried you wouldn't work out and he'd be stuck with you. Hard to fire the son of a detective."

"Yeah," I said. I got it that my father didn't know about Tree, or at least that Mr. Jackson had hoped for him to have the job. I didn't say anything. I told myself I didn't want Dad to feel bad. I had a selfish motive too. If he knew, he might make me quit, and at the age of sixteen nothing was more important to me than getting that Indian Scout. Today, I feel ashamed to say it, but back then I couldn't see beyond my own desires, which now seem pretty foolish and shallow.

I also didn't tell my dad about the taunts that began the next day. It seemed a lot of guys didn't want a white boy taking orders from a Negro, even if the kid was only sixteen and the Negro was a combat veteran of the Great War.

It began with Basher McGee. If Basher ever had a real first name, no one remembered it, or how he got his nickname. That it was deserved was not in doubt.

"That's a nigger mop, ain't it?" Basher said that morning, twirling his nightstick as he stood in front of me, grinning. I'd just finished the entryway to the Berkeley Street headquarters, and was wringing out the mop between the rollers on the bucket.

"It's a City of Boston mop," I said, avoiding the yes or no question, not to mention his eyes.

"Then use it," Basher said, and gave the bucket a swift kick, sending dirty water cascading over the tiles. He gave one sharp laugh and sauntered off. It was as if Basher sent a message that I was fair game. The story about young Billy and his nigger mop made the rounds, and plenty of guys found it hilarious. Some lectured me on how to deal with coloreds, and that it was wrong to take orders from them. Others spilled full cups of coffee on floors I'd just cleaned, and then complained to Mr. Jackson. Garbage cans in the rear of the building were overturned each night and ugly wads of chewing tobacco stained the hallway in front of the chief's office. They wanted me gone, and it was getting to me.

"You fixing on doing what they want?" Mr. Jackson said at the end of the fourth day.

"Might be easier," I said. "For all of us."

"Running is the easy part," he said. "I learned that over in France. Living with yourself afterwards, that's the hard part. I ran once, fast as my legs would carry me. Still bothers me. But if you want to go, go."

"Could your son take over? If I quit?" I wasn't trying to do the right thing or anything like that, I just wanted a good story to tell my father if I did quit. Things weren't working out like I'd planned, and for the first time I began to think I could do without that motorcycle.

"I had a chat with your daddy this morning. You talk with him tonight, then you decide. It's up to you, Billy. You ain't a bad kid, you're just in the middle, that's all. Whatever you want to do, it'll be fine with me."

I didn't like what I heard. All week, Mr. Jackson had ridden me hard, snapping orders and checking my work. Now he seemed weary. I didn't know what was wrong. I didn't know a lot of things.

Dad had to work late that night. There was a murder out on Revere Beach, and it was past ten by the time he got home. He draped his suit jacket on the back of a kitchen chair, poured himself a whiskey, and motioned for me to sit down.

"I talked with Mr. Jackson today," he said, and then took a good belt. "He told me what's been going on."

"It's not my fault, Dad, honest."

"I know, Billy. Basher's always had it in for me, and he doesn't like colored folk. This is his doing. I tried to stay out of it, but things have gone too far."

"You knew they were giving me the treatment?"

"I expected something, but not this. Good-natured ribbing is one thing, but disrespect and threats are another."

"What are we going to do? Can you talk to Basher? Or should I quit?" I still didn't know if Dad knew about Tree, but he pretty much knew everything sooner or later.

"Billy, there's more going on here than meets the eye. You can't quit, and I can't do anything with Basher. He's beyond words."

"Sure I can quit," I said, indignant. "I know you'll be mad, but you don't know what it's like!"

"I know exactly what it's like," Dad said. "It's not about you. Basher is trying to get Mr. Jackson fired. That's why he and his pals are riding you. They want to prove he's an incompetent supervisor. As soon as you overreact, it will go to the chief. If you quit, it will be more evidence that a Negro can't be expected to supervise a white. Either way, they'll lay the blame on Mr. Jackson. I'm sorry, Billy."

"Oh," was all I could say. "You mean Mr. Jackson could lose his job, unless I knuckle under and take it?"

"That's about it, Billy. I'm sorry, I had no idea it would come to this. I never would have gotten the job for you if I had any notion it would get you in the middle of things. Or that it would cost young Jackson his chance."

"You know about Tree?"

"Mr. Jackson told me today. He said it would be best for everything to be out in the open. I knew he had a son, but didn't give it much thought. That was my fault, and I told him so. Why didn't you tell me that first day?"

"I don't know," I said, squirming in the kitchen chair and finding the linoleum suddenly fascinating. "I felt bad about it, but I wanted the job. And I didn't want you to feel bad either, after setting everything up."

"Sometimes things don't work out as we planned, Billy. What really matters is what we do when faced with the consequences." He finished off the whiskey in his glass and waited.

"I guess I'm going to work tomorrow."

"Good boy."

I LOOKED AT my watch. It was late, time to get Kaz and Big Mike to the railroad station.

"What happened?" Big Mike said. "Did you go back to work?"

"Too involved to get into now," I said. "More of the same at first, and then it got worse."

"But when did you meet Tree?" Kaz said. "You must tell us the rest."

"Later," I said as I settled the bill with Jack Monk. Truth was, I wanted the story to end right there, with my father's approval settling over me in the kitchen, the aroma of whiskey and his aftershave lingering as he left, the sound of his heavy shoes on the stairs as clear and true as the pub door closing behind me.

CHAPTER TWELVE

THE SMALL ROOM and lumpy bed at the Hog's Head was more than made up for by Mrs. Monk's breakfast. Warm bread, fresh preserves, and strong tea put things into perspective. I hadn't slept well, but the bed was only partly to blame. I was worried about Diana and her quest to report the truth about the extermination camps far above her place in the chain of command. In my experience, truth and warfare made for a volatile combination, and there were plenty of politicians who only let the truth see the light of day if it reflected well on them.

I'd wanted to talk to her about that, to help prepare her for what I knew would be a disappointment. But all I'd left her with was a few lines scribbled on paper.

Memories of that summer in 1936 had run through my mind all night as well. Funny, it wasn't all the crap I had to take from Basher and his buddies that stayed with me. It was Tree, and how for a short time we became best buddies, until the harsh world of grown men and their hatreds turned our way and ruined everything. Well, ruined Tree's life. I was white, and all right, so it was a bump in the road for me. He had to get back, way back.

I forced the thoughts and worries out of my mind as I buttoned my trench coat up tight and stepped out into the misty rain. The day was a refreshing change from yesterday's chill. It was warm and damp, the kind of early spring morning that holds the promise of growth to come. I stood on the bridge overlooking the canal and watched the path that led along the embankment, toward the Millers' house. An old man in a rain slicker walked his dog, and waved to a woman with a terrier on the other side.

They looked like regulars. Dog walkers who went out the same time each day, rain or shine. Dogs needed walking at night too. I left the bridge and walked down Bartholomew Street, with its brick buildings close to the narrow road and shoppers lining up beneath umbrellas at a butcher's shop. There must have been rumors of meat. There was a police car outside of the Newbury Building Society, where Inspector Payne and I were to meet.

"Captain Boyle," Payne said as soon as I entered. "This is Michael Flowers, manager of the society."

"The Newbury, as we like to call it," Flowers said, extending his hand. "Terrible news about Neville. Hard to believe, isn't it? Well, not in your line of work, perhaps." Michael Flowers was middle-aged, short, balding, and obviously nervous about detectives on his turf. He wore a pencil-thin mustache and an insincere smile.

"We do encounter it upon occasion," Inspector Payne said. "We'd like a look at Mr. Neville's office, if you don't mind."

"Certainly, certainly," Flowers said, nearly pushing us out of the lobby. "Please follow me."

"Is this a bank?" I asked him as he led us up two flights of stairs. "I'm not sure what a building society is."

"Not exactly a bank, more like a credit union, which I believe you have in America. Building societies were originally organized by a small group of people who wanted to save for a mortgage. A cooperative financial institution, owned by the members, operated for their own benefit. So not like a bank, if you take my meaning."

"What was Stuart Neville's job?" I asked, as Flowers unlocked the door to a small office. Small and nearly empty.

"He evaluated building plans, mortgage applications, that sort of thing. He was often on the road, making visits. He'd come in to write up his reports, but he didn't spend a lot of time here." I could see why. One wooden desk and chair. One sidetable holding a typewriter. A filing cabinet, a hat rack, and a bookshelf crammed with directories, atlases, annual reports of the Newbury Building Society, and some really fascinating reading on building regulations.

Payne sat at the desk and looked through the files and papers scattered in no particular order. "What was Neville working on before he died?"

"He'd finalized two applications, one for a shopkeeper in Kintbury, and another for a couple in Hungerford. The couple's was approved, but the shopkeeper's application was not," Flowers said. "Although I'm certain that could have had nothing to do with the murder." He nearly giggled as he contemplated death by mortgage.

"I thought you said he traveled quite a bit. Those two are certainly close by," I said.

"Oh, it all depends on our members and where they're from. We've expanded a great deal. In the old days, when all the original members of a building society received their mortgages, the society would disband. Job done, you see? But the Newbury has been so successful that we've stayed in business and grown. Still a cooperative venture, though."

"So Neville wouldn't travel to meet with a stranger, then?" Payne said.

"No, he only worked on applications from existing members," Flowers said. "And marketing was not his department, so there would be little reason for him to do business with anyone not known to us."

I opened the top drawer of the file cabinet. Folders were neatly arranged and labeled by name and date. "These are all from 1940. Where are his current files?"

"They've been distributed to other staff. I didn't think the police would want to look at them. I'm not even sure I should let you. I may need to ask the chairman of the board about that." Flowers didn't seem thrilled at the prospect.

"We don't need to look at the files themselves," Payne said. "I don't care about your members' finances, but I do want a list of names and addresses."

"I will have to ask Lord Mayhew," Flowers said, his smile disappearing.

"Reginald Mayhew?" Payne asked, looking up from his inspection of the desk.

"Exactly," Flowers said. "He has held the chair since the beginning of the war. Now if there is nothing else, I will leave you gentlemen to it. Please call upon me if you need any other assistance. You are not a member, Inspector Payne, are you?"

"No need, thank you." Flowers left, probably to telephone his boss and call down the wrath of His Lordship on Inspector Payne.

"Anything in the drawers?" I asked Payne.

"Erasers, pencils, application forms, and several other reasons I am quite happy to be a policeman, dead bodies and all. Nothing of interest."

"I can't help feeling that's the biggest clue we've found."

"What the devil do you mean, Boyle? We haven't found a single clue."

"Right. No clues, no evidence of anything other than a boring life and a boring job. He did have a nice view, though." I parted the curtains and looked through the wide window. From up here, he had a clear view over the rooftops, along the canal, and to the back door of the Kennet Arms. Where he'd been murdered.

"Your point, then, about the clues?" Payne said.

"It's like that Sherlock Holmes story. The one about the dog in the nighttime."

"Ah, the curious incident of the dog in the nighttime. The dog that did not bark, which was the clue Holmes observed. 'Silver Blaze,' I think it was."

"Yes, that one. Inspector, think about it. We've turned over Neville's home and office, and we've not found anything. Not a liquor bottle hidden in a desk drawer, no French postcards, not the slightest embarrassment. How many guys could pull that off?"

"Interesting speculation, Boyle. Put your time to better use and leaf through those books, will you? He may have hidden his dirty pictures in there." Payne gave a chuckle as he went through the last drawer, piling stacks of paper on the desk. I pawed through books and found one stamped rail ticket to Hastings from 1941. Hardly useful.

"Have you seen a briefcase?" I said. "He was carrying one in the photograph."

"No. Perhaps it was stolen when he was killed."

"Maybe," I said, although Neville had been dressed in an old tweed jacket, nothing suitable for the office. It seemed the briefcase could only be in his room or this office, and it was in neither place.

"Nothing here, Boyle," Payne said finally. "Let's go. I have a girl to search for. Sadly, we will more likely find a corpse at this point."

"Okay," I said, tossing the last of the books into the pile. I glanced around the room one more time. "Wait, there's one thing we missed."

"What's that?"

"The typewriter ribbon. If it hasn't been typed over, we might be able to read what he last typed out." The machine was a sturdy black Imperial, with two reels for the ribbon set on top. But there was no ribbon. It was gone.

"Someone beat us to it," I said.

"Let's go and see Flowers," Payne said.

We found Flowers in his office. It was a lot nicer than Neville's. His secretary was sputtering on about not interrupting him, but she quickly retreated when Payne showed his warrant card. Flowers was on the telephone and quickly put his hand over the receiver.

"Who else has been here?" Inspector Payne said, his voice grim and authoritative.

"Please, I am speaking with Lord Mayhew," Flowers said, his hand pressed tightly over the receiver. I guessed Mayhew wasn't used to being interrupted.

"Go on, then," Payne said, taking a seat in front of Flowers' desk and crossing his legs. "Tell His Lordship you are about to be detained for impeding a murder investigation."

"And destroying evidence," I said, standing close to Flowers, close enough that I could make out Mayhew's voice. He wasn't in a good mood.

"Yes, thank you, Captain Boyle, I nearly forgot. Unpleasant business for the Newbury, but there you have it," Payne said, a malicious grin on his face.

"Excuse me, Lord Mayhew," Flowers said, beads of sweat showing on his forehead. "The police wish to speak with me. Yes, I will ring you." He hung the telephone in its cradle and took a deep breath, but it didn't seem to relax him. I wondered who made him more nervous, the police or his boss.

"You've removed his files," Payne said. "Which I can understand, since business has to proceed. But what I can't figure out is why you'd take the ribbon out of his typewriter. Run short on office supplies, have you?" Payne had that look in his eye, the look a detective gets when he knows he's got the upper hand. Predatory, hungry. He was almost smiling at the prospect of an actual clue.

"What? I have no idea what you mean," Flowers said, confusion replacing his nervousness. "We have plenty of typewriter ribbons, there's no reason for it to be stolen."

"I didn't say it was stolen, I said it was removed. Now why would you do that?"

"I wouldn't, and I didn't," Flowers said. He pressed an intercom button and called for his secretary. I watched his hands. No telltale smudges. "Ah, Miss Gardner. Please tell the inspector if anyone has been given access to Mr. Neville's office."

"Why no, Mr. Flowers," she said.

"And was it locked when you and I went up yesterday for the files?"

"Yes, it was. Is something missing?" Her face showed concern. Was she worried she'd be accused of theft? She was on the far side of thirty, thin and pale, with wispy brown hair.

"Nothing of importance. Inspector, do you have any further questions?"

"How many keys are there to that office, and who has them?"

"Two, I believe. I have a full set, and Miss Gardner does as well. Both are kept in locked desk drawers." Flowers looked smug while Miss Gardner twisted a handkerchief in her hands.

"Miss Gardner," I said, as calmly as I could. "We're just trying to determine if any unauthorized person had access to that office. Is that possible?"

"No, I should say not. Mr. Flowers locked it as he left, I saw him. And I know my keys are accounted for."

"Fine," I said. "That's all we need to hear." I could see her face relax, and she looked to Flowers to see if she was dismissed. "Too bad about Mr. Neville. Was he popular with the staff?"

"He did his job well, which is all I was concerned with," she said, jutting out her chin and giving a brisk nod to Flowers as she left, shutting the door behind her. Brisk, efficient, and a bad liar.

"There will be an inquest," Payne said, standing with his hands on his hips, staring down at Flowers. "And you will be placed under oath. I shall ask you again if anyone else has been in that office. If your answer should prove to be untrue, I will arrest you on a charge of perjury. Is that understood?"

"All because of a typewriter ribbon?" Flowers stammered. "I don't understand what all the fuss is. Perhaps you should talk directly with Lord Mayhew. There's nothing else I can say."

I gave Miss Gardner my best smile as we left, and she returned it with pinched lips. In the hallway, I tapped Payne on the shoulder and motioned him to follow me. We went upstairs, back to Neville's office. I knelt at the door and studied the lock.

"I had the same thought," Payne said, glancing down the hallway. He produced a folding magnifying glass in a brass case and nudged me aside. "There, at the bottom of the keyway. A small gouge from the tension wrench. See?" He handed me the glass.

"Yes. This lock has been picked."

"Where does that leave us?" Inspector Payne said. I wished I had an answer for him. Finding nothing else of interest, we left.

Outside, steam rose from the pavement as the sun broke through the clouds. I told Payne about the dog walkers along the canal and he agreed to have two constables patrol the area that night and ask people if they'd seen anything.

"Might turn something up. The constables won't be happy after trudging through fields and woods all day, but there's not much to be done about that. Are you still staying at the Hog's Head?"

"No. Kaz and Big Mike should be back from London today, so we'll have to find another place. Kintbury is halfway between Newbury and Hungerford, right?"

"It is. We're starting the search from there, on either side of the canal, and going toward each town. If you want to stay in Kintbury, try the Prince of Wales Inn. You have business there as well?"

"I have a friend with the Six-Seventeenth," I said. "Thought I'd pay a visit. Do you know anything about the constable who was killed in Hungerford?"

"Tom Eastman, you mean? That was in the village of Chilton Foliat, to be precise. I know Tom had a quick temper," Payne said, "but was otherwise a good man. Odd that his body was found on his father's grave, isn't it? Strange place for a Yank soldier to dump it. Wait, he was from the Six-Seventeenth as well. Is your friend involved?"

"He's the accused's sergeant. He asked me to look into it for him. Nothing official."

"Hmm. You're a copper yourself, Boyle, so you know what it's like to have someone snooping around your patch once a case has been closed. You'll not make many friends."

"But the Berkshire Constabulary didn't close it, did they? It was the US Army, Criminal Investigation Division."

"They'll not like it, and Tom's friends may not be pleased if they think you're working to turn a murderer loose."

"I promised to look into it. I don't even know what evidence CID has."

"Circumstantial is what I hear. A weak case, made strong by a quick arrest and the fact that the killer is a Negro. I understand that carries a lot of weight in some parts of America."

"Alleged killer, Inspector."

"Fair enough. This is nothing I care to interfere with, but I'll ask a few questions of the right people and let you know what I find."

"Thanks. It could be that there's still a killer out there."

"Let's worry about the Neville case first, Captain, if you don't mind. I've put out calls to the surrounding constabularies to see if they can find any living relatives. So far, no luck."

"He has to have relatives, some place where he kept things. Personal possessions, important papers, letters and photographs."

"Perhaps he was glad to leave that all behind. Don't you ever feel like chucking it all, Captain Boyle? I'll be at the Dundas Arms, in Kintbury. It's right by the bridge over the canal. That's where we're starting the search." With that, he got into his automobile, without waiting for my answer.

CHAPTER THIRTEEN

KAZ AND I had agreed to meet at the Miller place, so I headed there. Another jeep was parked in the driveway, and I found Kaz in the kitchen, drinking coffee and chatting with the Millers. It would have been cozy except for the fact that they were all speaking German, which made it creepy.

"Please excuse us, Captain Boyle," George Miller said as his wife poured coffee. Doubtless American army coffee, since she gave me a full cup. "Baron Kazimierz wished to practice his German, and we do not get to speak it very often. He is quite fluent."

"In many languages," I said. "You and your wife must speak German at home."

"No," Carla Miller said. "We forced ourselves to speak English only when we arrived in England, to learn it better. Then, with the war, we did not wish to stand out. You understand."

"Of course," I said, sipping my coffee. "Feelings can be heightened in wartime. Like Pettigrew's."

"You met him, at the pub, I suppose?" Miller said.

"Yes. Was his response typical of how you are treated here?"

"No, not at all. The poor man was grief-stricken, and then I, a German, was standing right in front of him. His reaction was understandable."

"That is gracious of you," Kaz said. "Another man might have been angry at the slight."

"I was upset, but we passed on the street some days later and nothing was said. I thought he might have been somewhat embarrassed," Miller said, which fit in with what Pettigrew had said.

"Were there any other encounters like that?" I asked.

"When war first came, yes, there was some name-calling in the street, but that stopped quickly. Especially once Walter joined the Royal Navy. We are very proud of him. He wants to make a career of the navy, and become an officer. Do you think Mr. Neville was attacked accidentally?"

"I'm not certain of anything at this point. Just asking questions, like any police officer would."

"Are you still working with Inspector Payne?" Carla asked. "I do hope Sergeant Sullivan is not in any trouble."

"No, none at all," I said. "This is a joint investigation, so we are cooperating with the local police. As a matter of fact, an American unit is helping with the search for the missing girl today."

"Ah, the colored soldiers," George said. "So I heard. It must be very hard for them, yes? With the discrimination in America. The Ku Klux Klan, do I have the name right?"

"You do," I said. I damn well knew it was hard for Negroes, and I knew George and Carla Miller were anti-Nazi refugees, but I still felt uncomfortable talking about it. I hadn't liked the comparison Kaz and Tree had made about Poles having to walk in the gutter when Germans passed or Negroes doing the same when southern whites had the sidewalk. It was like airing dirty linen in public.

"I hope they find the poor girl, one way or the other. It must be so hard on the parents," Carla said. "Oh dear, I forgot. She is a refugee also." The table went silent, and I wondered what degree of guilt the Millers felt, and how that affected their relations with the townspeople.

I set aside my own guilt at coming from the land of lynching and the KKK. "Are there any adults from the Channel Islands here?"

"No, I don't think so," George said. "A large number of children were taken off the islands, shortly before they were occupied. They were sent to different towns, where they could be cared for, but I never heard of parents with them."

"That is right," Carla said. "There was an article in the newspaper recently, about their headmistress. Laurianne Ross, I think. She volunteered to work as their governess and teacher."

"So she would know if any of the children had relatives here?"

"I would think so, yes," Carla said, concern etched on her face. "But why do you ask about that?"

"It could be as simple as a relative coming to take Sophia away," I said. "Perhaps she's not missing at all. A message could have been misplaced." It had been known to happen, but what I wondered more about was the possibility of mistaken identity. With nothing to go on with Neville as a victim, it was tempting to focus on the Millers. But there were other possibilities. I could see a Channel Islander, perhaps someone who had recently escaped, taking out his frustration on the nearest German when he found Sophia missing. He cracks Neville on the skull in a case of mistaken identity and rolls him down the cellar stairs. It wasn't much of a theory, but it gave me a good reason to head into Kintbury, and I had no clues to pursue.

Kaz and I waited until we were outside to compare notes. I filled him in on what we'd found at Neville's office, and he recounted his conversation with Cosgrove.

"He refused to tell me how he came to know of the murder," Kaz said.

"Let me guess: he said it was his business to know."

"Precisely. I gave him what details we had, and the theory that the target may have been Miller instead of Neville, as well as the few details from the postmortem. He said to remind you to be sure Inspector Payne made no arrest without informing him first."

"Anything helpful?"

"You know Major Cosgrove better than that. He does not tip his hand."

"Neville's office caper bothers me," I said, leaning against the jeep. "Who broke in, and why? What else besides a typewriter ribbon did they take away in that briefcase?"

"Could Neville have been a spy?" Kaz asked. "It fits with the lack of personal items. Perhaps a German spy would feel more comfortable rooming with fellow Germans, even anti-Nazis."

"Or maybe he was here to eliminate them."

"And Miller found out, and killed him first?"

"I don't know," I said. "The Germans might have sent an assassin before the war, to send a message to any dissidents at home, but it seems far-fetched at this point."

"I have to agree. What next?"

I told Kaz about the search and where Payne was running it from. We'd meet there after Kaz found a telephone and left a message for Big Mike, telling him to meet us that night at the Prince of Wales Inn. Hopefully we could find Tree among the searchers and give him an update on what Big Mike picked up at CID.

"I'll meet you there after I have lunch with a young lady," I said. "Miss Gardner knows more than she's saying." I grabbed my bags and drove to Bartholomew Street. I parked a few doors down from the Newbury and hoped Miss Gardner didn't eat at her desk.

Half an hour later, she appeared on the sidewalk, buttoning her utility coat. I followed her, trying not to lose her in the crowd of shoppers and lunch-goers, most of whom were dressed in the same drab, featureless coat. Part of the rationing scheme, utility garments were designed to save fabric. Simple lines, no wasted material. Hard to tail one person when everybody is dressed alike.

"Miss Gardner," I said when I caught up to her. "Captain Boyle. I was wondering if I could buy you lunch. I have a few questions, and I might as well ask them over a meal."

"If you like," she said, searching my eyes as we stood on the sidewalk. She still looked afraid, and I wondered what she was hiding or if she was frightened by what had happened to Neville. "There's a teashop round the corner that will do." She led the way as a flight of C-47s roared overhead, taking off from Greenham Common on the other side of town. I looked up, but few others did. It was a routine occurrence.

We found a table by the window and both ordered the special, mashed potatoes with carrots and meat sauce. "As long as you're not curious as to what kind of meat," Miss Gardner had said. "But don't worry, there won't be much of it."

"I'm sorry about barging in on Mr. Flowers this morning, but we needed some straight answers. Would Neville have been typing anything confidential? Something that would be valuable?"

"Member records are all confidential, of course," she said. "But that's not what you mean, is it?"

"No. Did Neville have access to any member accounts?"

"Absolutely not! How dare you? Stuart would never . . . never have . . ." Her hand covered her mouth and tears welled in her eyes. Regaining her composure, she went on. "No, he didn't, and he struck me as a very honest man."

"A kind man?"

"Oh, please, Captain Boyle. Isn't it obvious? You are some sort of investigator, aren't you? I'm a sad spinster, pining for the eligible bachelor who on occasion showed a kindness. But I shan't know if it was anything but common courtesy now, will I?" She leaned forward, the question hanging in the air between us, unanswerable. The unexpected burst of emotion brought a glistening to her eyes, and transformed her for a moment from that sad spinster to a passionate woman.

"I'm sorry. I could tell his death had affected you even more than the sudden death of a co-worker. Is there anything you can tell me about him? Where he came from? Family?"

"Up north is all he ever said. I asked him why he didn't have pictures of his family in his office, like many of the gentlemen do. Of course I was wondering if there would be a picture of a wife, and I think he saw through me. All he said was that he and his family weren't close, and he preferred to have no distractions at work. Except for a visit from me, he went on to say. He was nice like that, always with a friendly comment and a chuckle."

"But no more than that?"

"No. He was a bit aloof, if you know what I mean. He went out with a few of the men after work every now and then, but not often. I think they resented him."

"Why?"

"His accent, for one. It wasn't Northern. More like London, and they thought he was putting on airs. His workload wasn't particularly onerous either. He often got the plum jobs, a few days' travel and expenses. All the chaps like those. Or the ones close by, easy to get to. Stuart always had the pick of the lot. One of the men asked Mr. Flowers if Stuart had Lord Mayhew looking out for him. There was a rumor that Stuart was his illegitimate son."

"What did Flowers say?"

"He laughed it off. But he did have me connect him with Lord Mayhew that very day. It's not often the manager calls the president of the board. Usually it's the other way round."

The waitress brought our plates. A mound of mashed potatoes was covered in a grey sauce with bits of meat scattered throughout. The only color was the bright orange of boiled carrots.

"It smells good," I said, trying to sound believable.

"Potatoes and carrots," Miss Gardner sighed. "After the war, I may never eat them again." The two root vegetables were easily grown in any backyard garden, and were among the few foodstuffs not rationed. British civilians had put up with four years of strict rationing so far, and I could see how it could get depressing.

"It must make the black market tempting," I said.

"Oh, everyone is tempted," Miss Gardner said. "And a few corners cut here or there gives people a sense they can make it through. But if you mean criminal profiteering, that's something else altogether."

"Did Stuart ever bring gifts to work?"

"He did give me a small tin of coffee once, as a thank-you for staying late one night. He needed to finish his reports before leaving on a business trip. He said an American sergeant brought all sorts of things to his rooming house."

"Mainly to impress the father, I'd say. Do you know the Millers?"

"No, although I do know they're German. I wonder if it's difficult for them." She inclined her head, thinking about that. "Yes, it must be, mustn't it?" She was smart, I could see that. I understood why she was good at her job.

"It can't be easy. Have you heard of anyone with a real grudge against them?"

"No, not at all. Wait, do you mean what I think? A case of mistaken identity?"

"I'm just guessing, Miss Gardner. I have no reason to believe that's the case."

"Tell me, please, Captain Boyle," Miss Gardner said in a low voice, almost a whisper. "Did Stuart suffer?"

"No. I doubt he even knew what happened. It was over instantly." It was true, but it was what I always said, true or not. Easier on everyone that way.

"Thank you," she said, her head bowed as if in prayer. "Do you think you will catch who did it?"

"I will do my best," I said.

"You may need help. From what I heard, Mr. Flowers is unwilling to give you the information you requested. He spoke with Lord Mayhew again after you left, and I took it that you were not to be given any details."

"The police may be able to get what they need through official channels," I said.

"It's a bit like the black market, isn't it? A bit of a corner cut once in a while helps us all get by." She took a pencil and a piece of paper from her handbag, jotted a few lines, and slid it across the table to me. "The last two mortgages Stuart worked on. If you need more, we can have lunch again."

I walked Miss Gardner back to work, impressed by her willingness to help. She played the role of the spinster secretary well, but there was some depth to her, and I was glad to have someone to count on within the Newbury Building Society.

I drove straight to the Prince of Wales in Kintbury, booked our rooms, and changed out of the dress uniform I'd been wearing since yesterday. The bag had been packed by Walter with his customary Dorchester thoroughness. Boots and a Mackinaw coat topped with a soft garrison cap were a lot more comfortable, not to mention suited for a search in soggy terrain. I put on a new dark-brown wool shirt, knotted my khaki field scarf, and admired myself in the mirror. With the addition of a shoulder holster and my .38 revolver, I looked like George Raft. The innkeeper gave me directions to Hungerford Road, on the other side of town, and the manor house serving as home and school to dozens of Channel Island youngsters. Minus one missing girl.

CHAPTER FOURTEEN

I TOOK THE Bath Road out of Newbury, heading west on the north side of the canal. Military traffic was heavy, and there were formations of paratroopers on the road with full packs and weapons. It was slow going. To my left, fields sloped down to the canal, and as I neared the turnoff for Kintbury, I could see a line of GIs on either side of the water, moving across the fields, searching. I knew that what Payne was looking for was a clue, or maybe a body. There was little hope of the girl simply being lost.

Heading toward the bridge spanning the canal before Kintbury, I had to halt and pull over as a line of trucks jammed with helmeted GIs came up the road. Units were conducting field exercises, and I wondered if the white commander of the 617th Tank Destroyer Battalion volunteered them for the search because he wanted to help out, or if he figured they'd never make it into combat and this was all they were good for.

The trucks on my right slowed to a crawl and then stopped, a traffic jam at the intersection behind us screwing everything up. I tried to get by on the shoulder of the narrow road, but the ground was wet and muddy, so I decided to wait. The GIs on the truck next to me broke out smokes and started to chatter.

"Hey," one of them yelled. "Lookit Mrs. Roosevelt's niggers over there! Don't them boys know there's no cotton in them fields!" More catcalls and insults followed, some of the men turning away and shaking their heads. The men of the 617th were too far away to know what was being said, but I saw them look in our direction. They didn't need to hear the words; they knew what a truckload of whites screaming at them meant. There might have been a time when I would have ignored taunts like these, or thought of them as nothing but ignorant, but seeing Tree again reminded me of how hurtful they were, and how ashamed I felt, deep inside, when I heard them and did nothing.

"Can it!" I yelled as loudly as I could. "They're helping to search for a missing girl. Which is a lot more than you're doing right now."

"Well, Captain, if there's a missing white girl, the last thing I'd do is send a pack of niggers to look for her. They probably took her in the first place." The loudmouth looked around for someone to join him, but an officer and a missing girl took the wind out of their sails.

"Sorry, Captain," one of the men, a PFC who had been quiet, spoke up. "Some of us are still fighting the Civil War over here. Right, Bobby Lee?" Laughter broke the tension, and one of the men leaned over the side of the truck.

"Captain, is that the Tank Destroyer outfit, the one bivouacked in Hungerford?"

"Yeah, the Six-Seventeenth."

"I'll tell ya, if we run up against any Tiger tanks over in France, and we got one of them battalions backing us up, I won't care much what color skin those gunners have, long as they stand their ground," the PFC said.

"Niggers can't fight," the loudmouth said. "Everyone knows that."

"I knew a guy in Boston," I said. "A Negro who fought in the last war. You should tell the Frenchman who awarded him the Legion of Merit about that. Or maybe all the Germans he killed."

The truck lurched ahead, taking their laughter, hatreds, and fears away. The line of men in the fields kept moving too, until they disappeared into the woods. Of the 617th, the paratroopers on the road, the GIs in the trucks, how many would be alive after we went into France? How many of them would even care about their petty prejudices and beliefs once bullets and steel flew in their direction? And afterwards, if the 617th and other colored units did get into the fight, would anything be different? The world had changed so much in the last few years, it seemed impossible for everything to go back to how it was. But what would it be like five or ten years from now? I had no idea. Finding Stuart Neville's killer was hard enough.

Crossing the bridge, I saw the Dundas Arms where Payne was coordinating the search. Police vehicles and US Army trucks were parked in the field where men with walkie-talkies barked commands. Kintbury itself was nice enough, narrow streets with red brick structures built close to the road, a few shops and pubs, but that was it. I could see why Tree hadn't wanted to trade Hungerford for this village when it came time for off-duty entertainment. I took a right on Hungerford Road, where a sparse run of shops and homes gave way to countryside. Fields with stubble from the autumn harvest stretched out on either side, and it was easy to spot the manor house the Channel Island girls called home. Trees lined the gravel drive, overgrown with weeds, but once likely spotless. The three-story house sported tall chimneys at the sides, high windows, and shrubs that had been halfheartedly trimmed. Unlike most of the buildings in Berkshire, this wasn't built with brick, but rather granite reflecting a pinkish hue in the sunlight. A plaque on the wall read AVINGTON SCHOOL FOR GIRLS. I knocked at the front door, and was greeted by a girl of maybe nine or ten.

"Good day. May I help you, sir?" The words were obviously rehearsed.

"Yes, I'd like to speak to the headmistress, please."

"All right," she said, leading me down a hallway. "My name's Nancy. Are you one of the Americans out looking for Sophia? Have you found her yet?"

"Not yet, Nancy. But an awful lot of soldiers are searching for her right now."

"Good," she said, and knocked on a door before opening it. "Miss Ross, there's a Yank here to see you."

"Thank you, Nancy. Would you run and tell Miss Jacobs that I will be with her shortly?"

"Captain Billy Boyle," I said as Nancy raced off on her errand.

"Laurianne Ross," she said, extending her hand. "Have you any news about Sophia?"

"No, I'm sorry. Only more questions."

"Please, have a seat," she said, returning to her desk. She was in her thirties, small, with longish dark hair and a look that said she was disappointed I didn't bring good news.

"I wish I had something to tell you, Miss Ross, besides that the search is still going on."

"It's Mrs. Ross, actually. Miss Ross is just what the girls call me. My husband is in Burma. Or so he was two months ago when I last heard. Tell me, Captain Boyle, why are you here? I know the American army is helping with the search today, but is that your connection?"

I could tell I wasn't about to pull the wool over this lady's eyes. I decided to try something different and tell the truth. "I am working with Inspector Payne, but on another case. Did you hear about the murder in Newbury yesterday? Two days ago, to be precise."

"No. Who was killed? Is the school involved in any way?"

"I don't think so. A man named Stuart Neville, who worked at the Newbury Building Society. Are you familiar with it?"

"Of course I am, and so is anyone else who grew up in this area, as I did. Ask your question, Captain, I have my girls to look after."

"Okay. In the past month or so, have any of the girls had a visit from a relative? Perhaps someone who escaped from the Channel Islands?"

"Captain, these girls are here precisely because they have no close relatives in England, none that would take them in. Their families are all trapped on Guernsey. There's most of the English Channel to deal with, not to mention the Germans."

"But some have escaped. A small boat could make the trip. You haven't heard of such a thing?"

"No, sad to say. If I had, I might not tell you, since there could be reprisals if word got out. Better for the Germans to think a man was lost at sea, don't you think?"

"Yes. But no one has come around?"

"No," she said as she pulled her cardigan sweater tight. "I do wish the council chap would come by though. He promised more coal. Is there anything else?"

"No. Thank you for your time. Caring for the girls must be demanding," I said as I rose to leave. I wished she had given me some hope for my theory of a relative from Guernsey. I wondered at her admission that she might have lied to me if it were true. It was honest, at least, but it led me to question everything else she had said.

"It keeps me busy. We have a teacher in during the day and a cook who lives here. But so many girls can be a handful, no matter how delightful they are." She walked me to the front door, as a great sadness washed across her face.

"Sophia. Was she one of the delightful ones?" I winced at my use of the past tense, but it was too late.

"Yes. And one of the oldest. She was quite a help, actually. Then one day she was gone. She and some of the other girls had walked together to the sweet shop in town. They decided to take the long way back, along the canal path. There's a lane off the main road that leads to a small stone bridge. It was a warm day, and they like playing by the bunkers."

"Bunkers?"

"You'll find them all along the canal, on the north side. This was to be the main defense line in case of invasion. They're all abandoned now, of course. Inspector Payne searched them first, thinking Sophia might have fallen and been hurt, but there was no sign of her. She'd simply vanished while the girls were playing. They thought she'd come back here ahead of them, and thought nothing about it. Do you think they will find her? Alive, I mean."

"If she is alive," I said, deciding to stick with the truth, "she's far away from this search."

"Then someone took her. Either alternative is horrible. But tell

me, Captain Boyle, why did you ask only about relatives in connection with your murder? I understand you would want to know about
any suspicious strangers in town, but couldn't a friend of the family
have taken Sophia away? Perhaps someone who didn't have legal
guardianship, but who had her best interests at heart?" She looked
at me with raised eyes, almost pleading for me to agree.

"Sure, that's possible. It was one of the first things I thought
about. Thanks again."

She shut the door behind me, and I think we were both glad to
end on that fantasy. I left, having accomplished nothing but the
raising of false hope.

CHAPTER FIFTEEN

I DROVE SLOWLY along the Hungerford Road, and took a wide, unpaved lane toward the canal, figuring this was the lane Mrs. Ross had mentioned. It did lead to an ancient brick bridge, probably built to accommodate horse and cart traffic a century or more ago. I parked the jeep and walked across, and sure enough, on the north side, past the railroad tracks, stood a squat concrete bunker, hexagonal in shape, with firing slits on each side. The door at the rear had once been padlocked, but the latch now hung open. Inside was nothing but cobwebs, trash, and cigarette butts. Not a child's playground. This wasn't what had attracted the girls. It was the quaint bridge, arching over the canal. Perhaps those narrow riverboats had passed by, the canalman greeting the girls on the bridge. The spring grasses were soft and abundant along the bank, and I could imagine the girls dangling their feet in the water. I knelt and stuck my hand in the current. It was cold. Too cold for dangling.

I wondered about the boats. Could Sophia have been grabbed, or gotten onto one willingly? Tempted aboard, perhaps, as the canal-boat slowed to a stop, and then gagged and thrown below while no one was watching? It was a connection, at least, to Neville's wet feet. Tenuous, but a connection. I scanned the bank one last time. A small plain paper bag was caught up in the grasses. It had been balled up and tossed away. I opened it and there was a distant, faint sweetish smell. The candy store. Or sweet shop, as they called it in England. Might as well make another stop.

I drove back down Hungerford Road to High Street, where Payne had said the shop was. It didn't take long to spot Hedley's Sweet Shop, with its bright red and yellow sign. I went in, a tinkling bell over the door announcing me. It was a small place, two large glass cases taking up much of the room. They were less than half full. A man emerged from the back room, wearing a blue apron and drying his hands.

"May I help you?"

"Are you Mr. Hedley?"

"No, the name's Bone. Ernest Bone. Bought the shop from old Mr. Hedley, and didn't think Bone was a good name for a sweet shop. Besides, folks around here know the old name, it's familiar to them. How can I help you?" Bone looked inquiringly at me, his thick eyebrows raised. He was balding, a bit stooped, but with a friendly face. A bit chubby in the cheeks. Just right for a candy store owner.

"I'm working with the police and the American troops who are looking for that girl," I said, introducing myself.

"Oh, such a sad business. Poor Sophia. She was in the shop the day she went missing. But that must be why you're here, isn't it?"

"Yes. I wanted to ask if you've heard anything at all about strangers in the area, or saw anything that day that was suspicious."

"Well, Captain Boyle, the only strangers hereabouts are you Yanks. And the colored soldiers, I must say, are all very polite and courteous. But that doesn't count for much, does it? I mean to say, a murderer could be quite pleasant, couldn't he?"

"Yes, charming in fact. I wonder about the canal," I said, picking up a syrupy-sweet smell wafting in from the back room. "Could she have been taken away on a boat? I heard the girls often go down to the little bridge, by the bunker."

"On a nice day, I'm sure they do. The village lads as well, to play at soldiers in the bunkers. Perhaps someone on a boat took her, although the police would have a better idea of that. There is more traffic on the canal these days, moving goods. It's very difficult with the petrol rationing, you know. Canalboats don't use much fuel going with the current."

"So I've been told. They don't travel by night, do they?"

"I doubt it, but I'm not from these parts. Moved here from Sheffield, up north. Don't know much about canals," he said. "But I do know a man was found dead by the canal in Newbury two nights ago. Is that why you're asking?"

"You don't miss much, Mr. Bone."

"Don't need to be a wizard to put two and two together. And folks like to chat, you know, when they stop in for their little sweets. Village gossip can be very informative."

"What do people have to say about the Millers in Newbury?"

"The Germans? Some don't like them at all, but I have to say many give them credit for going against Hitler when many of our own were going along with him. And for keeping a low profile, as well. They try to blend in, and not appear too foreign in their manners. People like that, they do." Bone nodded his approval of the foreigners who worked not to appear foreign, which was a compliment coming from an Englishman.

"So there's no strong feelings? No one who'd want to do them harm?"

"Not that I've heard, but remember Kintbury is a small village. We don't know everything that goes on in Newbury. But when a family loses a lad to the Boche, I can imagine they'd want to strike out at the closest German, and George Miller fits that bill. It isn't pleasant to say, but there it is. So it was the Miller place where the man was killed, eh?"

"Yes. Stuart Neville was his name. Sound familiar?"

"No. Can't say it does. Sorry I'm of little help, Captain."

"It was a long shot. One last thing. Did Sophia say anything when she was buying her candy?"

"I'm sure, but it was all about what I had on offer. I make my own, you see, working on a batch now, as a matter of fact. Boiled sweets the old-fashioned way, over open copper pans. Cough sweets, humbugs, that sort of thing. The children love them, but they can only get three ounces a week with their ration book, so you can imagine the excitement when they come in."

"It must be tough for business," I said.

"You don't know the half of it. I have to cut the coupons out of the ration book, then thread them on a string, and turn them in for my own supplies. I'm sure the government knows what they're doing, but they make it difficult enough. Sugar and flavorings are rare too, which is quite a hardship."

"I'd like to buy some, for the girls back at the manor house," I said. "But I have no coupons." I looked at the display cases with rows of colorful sweets, jars of peppermints, bowls of licorices, hand candies, and candied fruit jellies. The sights and smells made me feel like a kid again.

"I'd dearly like to sell them, but they'd shut me down as a black marketer if they found out. Can't have Yanks with cash buying out what's meant for civilians, now can we? Not that they would. Americans have more chocolate in their pockets than we've seen for years. Still, I don't begrudge them. I fought in the last war, and I know a soldier has to take what he can when he can. But here, I can give you one humbug as a gift. Don't tell Lord Woolton." Bone grinned and winked as he handed me a red and white candy.

The peppermint candy was refreshing. The Minister of Food would never hear from me.

I drove back through Kintbury to the search headquarters at the Dundas Arms. I found Inspector Payne hunched over a table in the dining room, marking a large-scale map of the area, and I asked him how the search was going.

"Nothing so far, and we're almost to the army bivouac area to the west of Hungerford, and two-thirds of the way to Newbury. Still, there's a lot of ground to cover. Either we find something or we rule out this entire area. If it's the latter, then we know she was taken away forcibly."

"I understand there's a lot more canal traffic these days. It would have been easy for someone on a boat to grab her," I said.

"If that's the case, then we'll never find her. She could be anywhere between Bristol and London." Payne stared at the map, but I knew he wasn't looking at the roads, rivers, and towns.

"Inspector?" A constable entered, followed by an American lieutenant. "The men on the north side of the canal have reached Bridge Street in Hungerford. Nothing to report."

"The south side?"

"Slower going," the constable said. "It's quite wooded."

"I'll have the men march back to camp, if you don't need them anymore, Inspector," the lieutenant said. Payne nodded his head, his eyes still glued to the map.

"Lieutenant," I said. "Where's Baker Company?"

"Most of them are on the south side, heading toward Hungerford," he said. "Lieutenant Binghamton, Captain. Can I help you?"

"Boyle's the name. You're with the Six-Seventeenth?"

"Yes, sir. Executive officer." Binghamton was white, fair-skinned with the ghosts of freckles across his cheeks.

"Okay, Binghamton. Do you know where I can find Sergeant Jackson? Eugene Jackson?"

"Tree? He's not in trouble, is he?"

"No. Why would you say that?"

"Can we step outside, Captain?" He didn't wait for an answer, and I followed. We stood in front of the whitewashed stone building, the water flowing and gurgling at our feet. "It's been my experience that whenever a white officer shows up asking about one of my men, it's because he's taking the fall. And it's usually not his fault. What do you want with Sergeant Jackson?"

"Relax, Lieutenant. I'm a friend of his from Boston. I've been detailed by SHAEF to assist the local police, and I only want to say hello to Tree. Purely a social call."

"I have to say, Captain, you're the first white officer ever to pay a social call on a Negro GI in this outfit."

"Tree and I knew each other as kids. Our fathers were friends, of a sort. They both fought in the last war."

"You're the ex-cop, right?"

"Yeah. What did Tree tell you?"

"Off the record, that he thought you might be able to help Private Smith. On the record, nothing. I don't want Sergeant Jackson getting in hot water for interfering with an investigation."

"Do you think Smith is guilty?"

"Well, he didn't get the nickname Angry singing in the choir. He's a fighter, and he's got no love for the white race. I'm sure he's capable of it, but the whole thing doesn't make sense to me. I think he's been set up, and if we ever get into combat, we're going to miss him. Have you learned anything yet?"

"No, we're still gathering information. Officially I'm here to look into a murder in Newbury. This is close enough that I thought I could get away and speak to Tree."

"Come on, Captain, I'll run you out there. He's on the end of the line, at the canal."

Binghamton gunned the jeep, turning onto a farm track that led through the fields. We passed the small bridge, cutting across the road I'd taken. Binghamton pointed to a line of men as they left a wooded knoll and descended to the farmland below. He cut across the field, spitting out mud and leaving deep tracks. He was enjoying himself.

"Lieutenant, do you mind being in a colored outfit?" I said, holding on to my hat.

"I did at first," he said. "Mainly because my father pulled strings to get me assigned to one. He figured that would keep me out of the fighting."

"And you didn't like that idea?"

"Hell no. But then they turned us into a Tank Destroyer outfit, and I figured we'd get into the fight sooner or later. Here we go," he said, slowing the jeep to a stop and sending up a spray of mud. We'd caught up to the end of the line, near the canal bank. Men were walking a few yards apart, searching for anything that might provide a clue. Along the bank of the canal, a line of GIs with long sticks pushed the weeds down, checking every inch along the waterline.

"Tree," I yelled out as I jogged up to the line of men. They turned and saluted. "As you were, men," I said, tossing back a salute.

"Billy," Tree said, and then with a glance at Binghamton, added "sir."

"Don't worry, Sergeant," the lieutenant said. "Captain Boyle told me you know each other from back home. Take a break and you can catch up." Binghamton went off with the rest of the men.

"Any news?" Tree said.

"Not yet. I have a man checking with CID in London. He should be back tonight. I've been sent to look into a killing in Newbury. That should give me a good reason to stick around and look into this. We're staying at the Prince of Wales Inn in Kintbury."

"Some English guy got killed, right? Funny that the army sends you to investigate that but won't help Angry."

"I'm here to help Angry. And if you think you can do better, then go find someone else, Tree."

"Sorry, Billy. Never mind, it's not your fault. We've been out beating the bushes all day long and haven't found a thing. I know you're trying to help."

"So how's Horace at the Three Crowns?" I asked.

"Okay," Tree said, and then the light bulb went off. "Wait, you know about that? We got to keep Hungerford."

"I was there when General Eisenhower gave the order. So maybe we can have a drink together after all." I didn't want to claim credit. Better for Tree to think it came direct from Ike. My interfering with his life was a sore point between us, and even this small gesture might be misunderstood.

"Let's hope you can solve the murder as quick as that," Tree said. "We can have that drink at the Prince of Wales Inn, too. Kintbury is too small a village to be allocated to anyone. Guys don't bother going there much."

"Can't blame them," I said, and then was distracted by yelling from the searchers. Tree and I broke into a run, heading down the path. A knot of men stood at the edge of the bank, Binghamton and another GI standing in the waist-deep water.

"Call the inspector!" Binghamton screamed, a look of horror on his face. "We found her! There's a walkie-talkie in the jeep. Go!"

Tree sprinted to the vehicle as I watched them lift the thin, pale body out of the water. A girl. Her dress was ripped, her skin mottled and wrinkled. Her arms hung limp and helpless, strands of vegetation wound about them like ribbons.

"Sweet Jesus," one of the GIs murmured. They laid her out on the path, and Binghamton arranged what was left of the torn dress to cover her decently. I knelt for a closer look. Her eyes had been eaten away, the soft tissue that fish and other creatures go for first. It was a blessing not to have to look into her eyes, but those dark, empty sockets held the promise of nightmares. They were gruesome, but not so terrible as to distract me from her neck. Dark bruises turning to yellow decorated her delicate throat.

"Help me turn her over," I said. No one moved. I looked to Tree, who handed the walkie-talkie to a GI and knelt. We gently rolled her over and I unhooked the last button that was holding her dress together. I told myself her modesty no longer mattered, she was beyond caring, but it still felt wrong and I tamped down the surge of emotion churning in my gut. Shame, horror, grief, sadness, and anger all tried to claw their way out as I took a deep breath and studied the body. Sophia's body. Her shoulder blades were bruised, a sickly color at each sharp angle of bone. We rolled her back and I picked up one leg, bending it at the knee. As I expected, bruises along her inner thighs. Setting her leg down, we rose, and I was grateful for a glimpse of blue sky overhead. She could not have been more than fourteen, still a child. Painfully thin, but then there were few chubby English children these days.

"The inspector's here," Binghamton said, his voice quivering. The water was cold, I knew. So was the feel of dead, waterlogged flesh. Inspector Payne hurried along the path and stared down at the body.

"Strangled," I said. "He held her down and choked her. The shoulder blades are bruised from being pressed against a hard surface. Raped as well."

"My God," Payne said. "That's as may be, but this poor girl is not our Sophia Edwards."

CHAPTER SIXTEEN

TREE DROVE THE shivering Lieutenant Binghamton to the 617th bivouac area as the search finished up. No Sophia, no other clues, and we were left with more questions than answers. We followed the coroner's wagon into Hungerford, skirting the Tank Destroyer encampment outside of town before arriving at the local police station.

"We'll wait here for the coroner," Inspector Payne said. "Doctor Brisbane's office is across the road. He'll give us an initial report as soon as he's through. Meanwhile I could use a cup of hot tea and some time to think." We had a lot to think about. I followed Payne into the small station, about the size of a house, built of brick, like most of the structures around here, and covered in ivy.

"Captain Boyle, this is Police Constable Peter Cook," Payne said, introducing me to the man on duty. He explained that I was working with him on the Neville case, and that I was a fellow officer.

"It was a bad turn, finding that girl," Cook said. "A missing girl is one thing. A missing girl and a corpse is another. I'll put the kettle on, Inspector. After a day in the fields it will go down well."

"You read my mind," Payne said. "Boyle?"

"Sure," I said. I wasn't a big tea drinker, but I knew enough about the English by now not to turn down a cuppa. Cook's office had that lived-in look of any small-town station. One wall was taken up with photographs of previous constables, the oldest a picture of a stern

Victorian with bushy sideburns. A worn couch that he'd probably spent the night on more than once and an easy chair next to a radio. An interior door opened into what looked like a squad room anywhere in the world. A table full of papers, empty cups and full ashtrays.

"Cook's a widower," Payne said, noticing my observations. "He puts in a fair amount of time here. Gets on well with everyone, and knows their business as well."

"That reminds me," I said. "Speaking of business, Miss Gardner did give me the names of Neville's last customers."

"Did you go through official channels, or charm the information out of her?"

"I bought her lunch, and she's willing to help if we need it. Here." I handed the slip of paper to Payne, glancing at the names as I did so. I hadn't had the time to look before, and I figured the names wouldn't mean anything to me anyway. I'd been wrong.

"One of these is Ernest Bone," I said.

"The sweet shop fellow?" Payne said.

"Yes. I stopped by today, and asked him if he'd heard of Stuart Neville. He said he hadn't."

"And what brought you to interview Mr. Bone? Or do you have a sweet tooth?"

"I get all the Hershey bars I need at the PX," I said. "It was a long shot, but I thought there might be some connection to the missing girl. A stranger in the area, either known to her or not."

"A stranger who might have bashed in Neville's skull, you mean?"

"I know it sounds farfetched, but I keep thinking about the canal. It's a quiet getaway route, for either a killer or a kidnapper."

"Or both," Payne said. "These are small towns, Hungerford and Newbury. Kintbury is merely a village. We don't have gangsters running about. There's some logic to one villain as opposed to several. But no evidence, more's the pity."

"Do you know the other name Miss Gardner gave us?" I asked.

"Stanley Fraser, Atherton Street," Payne said, reading the other name. "Yes, Fraser is a solicitor, does quite well for himself. Not surprising he's getting himself a new place."

"Ernest Bone seems to be barely hanging on," I said. "I wonder what he's up to. And why he said he didn't know Neville."

"You know, I believe he did mention something about renovating his shop," Payne said. "I've been in there a few times; the missus likes her sweets well enough. We got to chatting. He lives upstairs, and said he needed the room. He's quite keen on making the sweets himself, the old-fashioned way. I have the impression he has some money, and the store is more of a hobby. Not a bad business, if he can hang on. Once the war is over and rationing is a memory, sweets will be an affordable luxury. Tell me, did you show him the picture, or give him Neville's name?"

"I didn't show it to him. It was more of an offhand remark."

"We'll have to ask him again, but perhaps he simply forgot. Chap from the bank comes around with paperwork about your mortgage application, you might not pay much attention to his name," Payne said.

"Unless you don't get the mortgage," I said.

"Right. Then you go and bash the bloke's head in. Nice try, Boyle. Ah, tea."

Constable Cook set a tray on his desk and we poured ourselves tea. He had sugar out, but knowing how hard it was to come by, I passed. We drank in silence for a few minutes, and I was glad of the warmth of the cup, if not the taste of the milky brew.

"I got the report back from Broadmoor," Constable Cook said to the inspector. "No escapes."

"What's Broadmoor?" I asked. "A prison?"

"More or less," Payne said. "The Broadmoor Criminal Lunatic Asylum is about thirty miles east of here, in Crowthorne. I thought it worth checking to see if any of the inmates had broken out."

"It's good to know I'm not the only one with a weakness for long shots," I said.

"The inspector's been known to go the long way around to solve a case or two," Cook said with a grin. "But no pleasure men have gone over the wall."

"Pleasure men?" I didn't know what that meant, but it wasn't uncommon for me to not understand plain English spoken by a Brit.

"Many of the inmates are charged under the Criminal Lunatics Act, which sentences them to incarceration until His Majesty's pleasure is known, as the law states. Hence, pleasure men. And women, as well. It is effectively a life sentence."

"A nutcase on the loose is the last thing we need," I said.

"Hard enough finding one body while looking for another," Cook said. "But an escapee would at least give us something to go on. We've caught runaways before, and sent a few there as well."

"Any ideas?" I asked. They both shook their heads.

"We haven't had any other reports of missing girls," Payne said.

"Not from the Berkshire force," Cook said. "But she could have been a runaway. From Oxford, Bath, even London. We'd not hear a word of her."

"Wouldn't it be more likely for a young girl to run away to those places, not from them to Hungerford? No offense, but this place isn't exactly bright lights and big city."

"No offense taken, Boyle," Payne said. "We like it that way, don't we, Constable?"

"Aye. And not to offend you, Captain, but she could have been following a boyfriend around. Mainly Yanks on our patch here, so that's who comes to mind. And remember the current; it could have carried her from Newbury or beyond."

"True," Payne said, sipping his tea. "She could have been put in last night east of Newbury and gone unnoticed in the dark. Tangled in the weeds as she was, we could have missed her for days."

"The question is, did Sophia suffer the same fate?" I said.

"As soon as word gets out, every family hereabouts will keep their daughters close," Cook said. "From your description, the two girls are about the same age. Not a good sign."

"No," Payne said. Silence slipped into the room as we considered what that meant, for Sophia and possibly other girls.

"Inspector Payne said you were interested in the Tom Eastman murder." Cook spoke quietly, as if not wanting to intrude on our thoughts about the girls.

"Yes. I'm looking into it for a friend. Unofficially. Anything you can tell me would be appreciated. I don't mean any disrespect to Constable Eastman. I know I'd be suspicious of anyone snooping around a closed case back home."

"I'll tell you this," Cook said, leaning forward. "Your chaps from CID were plain lazy, if you don't mind my saying so. Once they got Private Smith on the brain, that was all they wanted to hear."

"You know his nickname," I said.

"Indeed. Any man called Angry bears watching, I decided, when I first heard of him."

"Did he cause any trouble for you?"

"Not really. His friends stopped a fight outside the Three Crowns once. I was told it took three of them, and Private Smith wasn't all that riled up. But the occasional fisticuffs among soldiers is to be expected."

"The fight was between two Negro soldiers?"

"So I heard. Can't say who it was, the talk was more about the effort it took to restrain Private Smith. I've seen him a few times. Strong fellow, he is."

"Do you think he killed Tom Eastman?"

"It's possible," Cook said, considering the question. "From what circumstantial evidence I saw, and knowing his temper, he could have done it. And there was bad blood between Tom and him as well. You know about Rosemary Adams?"

"Tom Eastman's sister, and wife of Malcolm Adams," I said, pulling the names out of my mental notebook.

"Yes. Tom was very protective of Rosemary. Had to be, with a brute like Malcolm for a husband. I can think of no man who was grieved less when we thought he'd been killed."

"Eastman didn't like a Negro keeping company with his sister?"

"Tom Eastman was a fine man," Cook said, his voice firm and his eyes on mine. "Finer than many Americans I've seen who treat these colored boys like dirt. He may have called Private Smith a few choice names, but that didn't mean he objected to his entire race. When Rosemary thought Malcolm might have been killed, Tom told Smith to stay away until they got official word from the army. He was protecting his sister, and rightly so."

"But Rosemary and Angry didn't listen to him."

"No, except that they kept things quiet. Tom knew, of course, and when word came that Malcolm had been wounded, not killed, he became quite upset. He knew that Malcolm would make life horrible for poor Rosemary. He blamed Private Smith, when he should have blamed both equally. But that's a brother's love, isn't it?"

"How did they meet?"

"His company was on a march and passed by the Adams place, so I heard," Cook said. I got the impression the constable heard everything that went on around here. "She has a little garden and a coop with some chickens. The fence was down and the chickens were wandering out into the road. They gathered them up, and Rosemary brought out water from the well. Smith offered to come back and repair the fence, which he did. Not the first time one of these chaps offered to help out the locals. Farm boys miss the soil, don't they?"

"Well, I miss the sidewalks in Boston, Constable, but I'm not offering to walk your beat."

"Different with country fellows. Anyhow, that's how they got to know each other, and things were proper like until word came that Malcolm was dead. Rosemary did her best to put on a show of grief, but everyone knew what a blighter her husband was. Truth be told, most were glad to see a kind man around the house."

"So you don't think he's guilty."

"As I said, he could have done it. But no, I don't think he did."

"But Angry Smith didn't get along with white people, as I understand. He could have turned that rage onto Eastman."

"Ah," said Cook. "It's your lot he doesn't like. American white people, that is. He told me Hungerford was the friendliest town with white people in it he'd ever been to." Cook grinned at the memory. He seemed to have taken a liking to the man named Angry.

"He was thinking of staying on, after the war," I said, remembering his letters, and what Tree had told me about being accepted as a human being, and what a novel experience that was.

"We could use men like him," Payne said. "With all the losses from the last war, and those already dead in this one, we have too few men about. The Royal Berkshire Regiment took heavy losses at Dunkirk, you know. And with the invasion coming any time soon, there'll be more mourning done before the end."

"You don't think a Negro and a white woman would have a hard time?" I asked. I knew they would back home.

"We have our faults, to be sure," Payne said. "But we weren't brought up to believe these sons of Africa are the devil's spawn like so many of you Yanks. The smashing of glasses in the pubs, that said more about the white soldiers than it did the Negroes. Thank goodness someone saw the light and rescinded that order. No one was looking forward to the louts who did that coming here on leave."

"Have you seen the sign Horace put up at the Three Crowns?" Cook asked. We hadn't. "It says, 'This place for the exclusive use of Englishmen and American Negro soldiers.' That about sums up the feelings in town."

"Okay, I get it. But back to Tom Eastman. If Angry Smith didn't kill him, who did?" I thought there had to be a more personal connection with Tom, but I wanted to see what the cop on the scene thought.

"There's got to be something about where the body was left. That points to a local person who knows the family," Payne said.

"Any candidates?"

"I would have looked at Malcolm Adams, if it weren't for his legs," Cook said. "He can move about, but he has to use a cane. If Tom had been left where he fell, Malcolm would be on my list. But the coroner said he'd been killed elsewhere, and brought to the gravesite."

"And Malcolm couldn't manage that?" I asked.

"No, not without help. And Malcolm isn't the type to have friends who would do such a favor."

"What do we know about the father? Samuel, wasn't it?"

"Sam Eastman was a decent man and fine a police officer," Payne said as Cook nodded his head in agreement. "Taught me the ropes, he did."

"What?"

"Sergeant Sam Eastman," Cook said. "He ran this very nick for more than ten years. Started as constable after the Great War. That's his photograph, behind you."

"Tom Eastman's old man was a cop?" I stood to study his picture. The elder Eastman was square-jawed with mutton-chop sideburns and a look that said he might arrest the photographer if he didn't get on with it. He had the hardy look of a cop who had to handle things by himself. "And Tom was found dead on his father's grave?"

"That's right," Payne said. "And before you get hot under the collar, of course we looked at the old files. Sam passed away in nineteen thirty-nine. Heart attack, in this very room. We went back to when he joined the force, and every villain he sent away on serious charges was accounted for. Dead or still in prison, every one."

"What about that track, from the rear of the cemetery? Where does that lead?"

"To the parachute training school at Chilton Foliat. Your Hundred-and-First Airborne has a facility there, qualifying soldiers for their parachute wings," Payne said.

"Mostly non-combat types, I think. Chaplains, physicians, that sort of thing," I said, recalling what Tree had told me. "Could that have been the route the killer took? It would be hidden from view."

"Partially, yes. But it does go directly through the training facility at one point. It would be hard to carry a dead body and not be noticed."

"I don't suppose the CID agents looked at that?"

"No," Cook said, shaking his head. "I showed them, but they weren't inclined. They already had their eyewitness to Private Smith being in the area without a pass."

"Who was that?"

"Rosemary Adams herself," Cook said. "That night, her husband

Malcolm had gone down to the local pub, the Wheatsheaf. He took
his bicycle, which he had handled well enough once or twice since
he'd been back. He came home late, his face bloodied and one leg
badly bruised. He refused to say what had happened, and was in a
foul mood the next day as I heard. Rosemary was afraid Smith had
confronted him that night. So when the CID men came around
asking about him, she said he'd been with her."

"To protect him."

"Aye. Malcolm had blackened her eye two days before, and that's
what she thought he and Smith had fought over," Cook said.

"But it was all for naught," Payne said. "We found Malcolm's
bicycle in a ditch. He'd taken a fall and hurt himself, and was too
damned obstinate to admit it. That much I can understand. It's only
a short stroll to the Wheatsheaf, really. It must have been a blow to
his pride."

"The one thing he has too much of," Cook added.

"Constable Cook, if there's no one else to consider, I'll get going.
Thanks for the tea," I said, hoisting myself out of the comfortable
chair, wondering if the elder Eastman had breathed his last in it. "I
wish we had more to go on, but thanks for the background. I'll wait
until the morning to hear what the coroner has to say."

"Drop by if you need anything," Cook said. "I'll likely be here."

PAYNE DROVE ME back to my jeep, which was still at the
Dundas Arms. It wasn't far from the Prince of Wales Inn, where Big
Mike, Kaz, and I were supposed to rendezvous tonight. I was tired
and hungry, and in a few minutes I could have been sitting with
friends in a warm pub, hashing things over. But I was restless, worked
up by the lack of clues, the unexpected body, and the eerie image of
a dead son on his father's grave. I found myself back in Newbury,
drawn to the canal again. I parked on Bridge Street and walked along
the embankment. It was dark, but a half-moon cast its distant light
on the water, giving me a clear path. The blackout was still in effect,
so that was the only illumination to be had, but it was enough. I

strolled past the rear of the Miller place and heard laughter from inside. Maybe Sully was there with Lucky Strikes and coffee. The muted sounds of a family in their kitchen struck me as unattainable, a sad reminder of how far away my own family was. I glanced at my wristwatch and began to calculate what time it was back home, but I never finished.

Something exploded at the side of my head and I heard a noise. I was cold, very cold, and I realized the sound was my body hitting the water. I struggled to get out of my Mackinaw before its sodden weight pulled me under. I saw the moon, floating above me, and then the pain went away, and so did the moon.

CHAPTER SEVENTEEN

I WAS COLD. My bones shook with it, my teeth clattered, and my hands were blocks of ice. I heard voices, splashes, then felt my body roll and sink, as if a giant had shoved me beneath the surface. Something grabbed at me, lost me, then pulled and pulled again until I was somewhere else where it was even colder. My whole body quivered as I tried to gulp air but couldn't. Panic assaulted me, even as hands pulled at me, turned me over, and I felt foul dirty water gushing out my throat until I could drink in heaving gasps of air.

I saw the moon again, then it faded away, and the shivering seemed to go on for a long time, in some distant place, far away from dark and dangerous canals. I saw an eyeless body drift by, and prayed I had dreamed everything, but I hadn't. I had a glimpse of my room back in Boston, and heard my mother's voice. I knew that wasn't real either, and began to worry that I was dead, which didn't worry me as much as it should have. The shivering receded, until all that remained was a cold, certain calmness broken by an occasional tremor.

"Billy," I heard a voice, insistent and alarmed. I didn't know what the fuss was all about, and couldn't open my eyes to see, so I let sleep take me away.

"Billy," the voice said again. I recognized it this time. It was Diana. Worth opening my eyes for.

"Hey," I said. It wasn't much, and it took a lot of effort.

"Billy, you almost drowned," Diana said, cradling my face in her hands.

"Where am I?" All I could see was Diana, her wide eyes, light brown hair, and red-rimmed eyes.

"At the Prince of Wales Inn. The doctor said you were fine, that you just needed warmth and rest, but I've been so worried, Billy. What happened? Did you fall into the canal?"

"I don't know," I said, trying to recall. "Something hit me, I think. Or someone." I felt the back of my head, and found a bump. A sore bump.

"The doctor thought you might have fallen and hit your head, then gone off the embankment. He said the bruise was nothing serious. How do you feel?"

"Confused," I said. I saw light streaming through the window. A coal fire burned in the grate, and the room was warm and cozy. "What time is it?"

"Three o'clock in the afternoon. They found you last night."

"Who?" I tried to sit up, which was easier said than done. Quilts and blankets smothered the bed, and I threw back a couple of layers.

"A constable. Inspector Payne said you saved your own life. It was one of the men he put on duty to watch for dog walkers who might have seen something the night of the murder. The constable heard you go into the water and jumped in after you. He said he almost lost you in the current."

"Wait," I said as the cobwebs cleared. "What are you doing here?"

"I saw Big Mike at Bushy Park," Diana said. "He told me you were all meeting here last night. There was nothing else to do in London, so I came to see if you needed help."

"How was your meeting with the Joint Intelligence Committee? What was that guy's name?"

Diana looked away, as if the question was painful. She wasn't in her usual First Aid Nursing Yeomanry uniform either. Today she wore a wool jacket over a white silk blouse and a blue skirt. It was nice, but she was proud of her tailored FANY uniform and usually wore it.

"Roger Allen," she said finally. "I'll tell you about it later, Billy. You rest now. I'll go and get you some food." Diana's face turned hard as she said Allen's name, and I knew things had gone badly for her before she'd left the room.

She had taken it as her personal mission to convince those in a position to take action that the extermination camps had to be stopped. But they were far away from the front lines, and the people being exterminated in those distant places were Jews, gypsies, and others who had no voice in Whitehall. I wasn't surprised she hadn't had any luck with Allen.

Me, I was lucky my eyes weren't fish food right now. I was in a soft bed by a warm fire to cheer me up. I'd awakened to Diana at my side. I should be happy, I told myself. But that's tough after being a victim of attempted murder. I knew I didn't fall. Someone hit me; not a killing blow, but hard enough to knock me off balance and send me into the drink. That much I knew for certain, as well as the fact that it didn't add up. No one knew I was headed to the Miller place. Hell, I didn't know it until I was in the jeep heading back there. So who was there, and why did they smack me one?

"Billy!" Big Mike had to stoop to enter the room, barely squeezing through the door as he did. "Diana said you woke up. How you doin'?"

"I'm all right. I'd like to know who hit me though."

"Yeah, I knew you didn't fall in," Big Mike said, taking a seat in a straight-backed chair that groaned under his weight. "You remember anything?"

"I recall being struck on the side of the head. Then the water, I guess. It was cold." I didn't bother trying to describe how cold.

"The sawbones said you might have slipped and hit your head."

"No," I said, feeling the tenderness above my ear. "I was up, then hit, then in the water. It wasn't a blunt object, like whatever was used against Neville. More like a two-by-four, maybe lighter."

"I spoke to the Millers. They said they didn't know you were out there."

"No one did, that's the strange part. It was a whim. I wanted to walk the ground again, get a feel for what it's like at night."

"Well, you got that, Billy." I couldn't argue.

Diana came in with a tray. Hot tea, cakes, and jam. It tasted great. Being alive probably had something to do with it. Big Mike filled me in on what had been going on while I was sacked out. Kaz had gone off to help Inspector Payne with a more extensive search of the pathway behind the Millers' house. Big Mike and Diana had stayed to watch over me in case anyone else wanted to have a go at cracking my skull. My clothes were being cleaned and ironed, Berlin had been bombed, and the Detroit Tigers had signed Boom-Boom Beck as a pitcher, with great prospects for the upcoming season. That last bit was of interest only to Big Mike, who thought everyone else cared as much about Detroit baseball as he did. I freshened up, shaved, put on a new uniform, and promptly fell into the easy chair by the window.

"Okay, Big Mike," I said. "What did you find out at CID?"

"Plenty of nothing," he said. "I told Diana on the ride out here that those guys are the laziest investigators I ever saw. They got no real evidence, other than Private Smith's nickname is Angry and his skin is black."

"That's what Constable Cook thought, too," I said, and filled Big Mike and Diana in on the story he'd told me.

"It was Rosemary Adams's statement that they hung their hat on," he said. "Even though she admitted she lied."

"Why didn't your Criminal Investigations Division turn over the case to the local police, if Private Smith's guilt was in doubt?" Diana asked.

"They want convictions as much as any police force," I said. "To be fair, if they thought a GI was a suspect, they had to investigate. Once they turn it over, there's no going back. It's all because of the Visiting Forces Act."

"You'd think common sense would win out," Diana said. "There's a killer on the loose now, and no one is looking for him."

"We are," Big Mike said.

"Yes, we are," she agreed. I was about to ask what had happened with Roger Allen when footsteps sounded in the hall and the door opened.

"Glad to see you up and about," Inspector Payne said. "I have news. Bit crowded in here, isn't it?"

"Join the party," I said. "What do you have?"

"This," he said, setting a small worn suitcase on the bed. "We found it in one of the boats not far from the Millers'. Likely it belongs to the girl in the canal. Margaret Hibberd." He held up a tag tied to the handle. "Her name, with an address in Great Shefford crossed out and an address in London added."

"Where's Great Shefford?" I asked.

"About ten miles north of Hungerford. They have a school for children evacuated from London during the Blitz. We have a constable headed there now to see if this girl is missing, ask for a photograph, and break the news if it's the same one. Lieutenant Kazimierz is accompanying him. The clothing points to a girl the same size." Children had been evacuated not only from the Channel Islands, but from all the major cities in England within range of German bombers.

"Terrible," Diana said, picking through the threadbare garments.

"It is," Payne said. "What's worse is that the girl's street in Shoreditch was bombed back in January. I called Scotland Yard and they checked the records. Her father's body was found, but not her mother's. Missing, most likely incinerated. They already had her listed as a runaway to watch for."

"So this poor girl takes it upon herself to travel to London, only to be killed before her journey is barely begun," Diana said.

"How would she get from Great Shefford to London?" I asked.

"Most direct route would be south on the road to Hungerford, then by train to London," Payne said. "I'd wager she left on foot from Great Shefford, someone offered her a lift, and she never made it to the station."

"Could be," Big Mike said. "Question is, why was the suitcase found near the Miller place?"

"Does Miller have an automobile?" I asked.

"No," Payne said. "And if he did there's no petrol to be had. It's rationed for official use only, and for businesses that require it."

"He could have met the girl in Hungerford easily enough," Diana said. "Offered to help her, perhaps."

"I think we might be asking the wrong question," I said. "The real question is why was I attacked, at that time and place?"

"Perhaps it was Miller," Payne said, stroking his chin. "He sees you snooping about, figures you'll find the suitcase, and Bob's your uncle, you're in the canal."

"What you're suggesting is that George Miller has committed one murder and one attempted murder, all to keep the suitcase from being found. If he's the guy who took Margaret Hibberd, why didn't he put rocks in the suitcase and toss it in the canal? Or bury or burn it?"

"So why *were* you attacked, Billy?" Diana asked.

"Because somewhere along the line, I got somebody nervous. My guess is the girl's killer had the suitcase and needed to get rid of it. What better place than near the scene of a recent murder? Maybe we'd start looking at Neville or Miller as suspects. He waits until dark to plant the suitcase, and then sees me walking down the path. He might think I followed him, and he can eliminate me as a threat and divert suspicion at the same time."

"Or he didn't try to kill you," Big Mike said. "You told me you weren't hit that hard. Maybe he figured by attacking you, he'd ensure a search of the area."

"I'm not sure I see the same connection you do," Payne said. "You're assuming the disappearance of Sophia and the murder of Margaret are tied to the Neville case. Why?"

"Because of the warning Neville gave to Eva Miller. He told her to be careful."

"It's not much," Payne said.

"What else do we have?"

"There's a sad truth," he said. "Perhaps it is time to press our German friend Miller a bit harder."

"Why not? It may serve to get some things out into the open."

"Where MI5 are concerned," Payne said, "they may be better left hidden. But we've little else, so I will invite Miller to come to the station for a bit of a chat. Would you like to attend, Captain?"

"No, I'm still a bit wobbly. How about Big Mike?"

"Indeed! We shall put the fear of God into the man, and see what happens."

After Payne and Big Mike left the room was quiet, and I enjoyed the silence with Diana in the chair beside me. No talk of dead girls or drowning. After ten minutes of peace came a knock at the door.

"Tree," I said, surprised at the visit. "Come in."

"There's been trouble, Billy. Oh, sorry, ma'am, I didn't mean to interrupt," Tree said as soon as he noticed Diana. But he was worked up, and halfway into the room.

"It's okay," I said. "This is Diana Seaton, the woman I told you about."

"You're Billy's friend, aren't you?" Diana said, extending her hand. "Sergeant Jackson?"

"Yes, Miss Seaton. Call me Tree if you like, everyone does."

"You must call me Diana," she said. "Come and sit down, tell us what has happened."

"Billy, what's the matter?" Tree asked as we sat. "You don't look so good." I filled him in on the events of the night before, and the discovery of Margaret Hibberd's suitcase.

"I'm still a bit shaky, but I'm fine," I said. "Now what kind of trouble?"

"There's rumors flying all around about the girl we found. Two of our guys were changing a tire on their jeep when four white GIs jumped them. They beat them up pretty bad, told them there'd be a lynching if any more white girls were raped and murdered. We had a supply truck headed to Greenham Common today and they had to turn back when their windshield was smashed."

"Same story?" I asked.

"Worse. GIs at the base said they heard we had a white girl held prisoner in camp, and a bunch of rednecks were going to head out tonight to rescue her. I hope they come, they'll see how Negroes can fight, you better believe it." I believed. I knew Tree would stand up for what he knew was right, but in this situation it was likely to get him killed.

"Jesus. Did you go to the MPs?"

"Billy, have you heard anything I've been telling you? I go to the MPs and I'll get my head busted for making trouble. Just like going to the cops in Boston. A waste of time at best, dangerous most likely."

"Yeah, you're right," I said, knowing it all too well.

Diana shot me a questioning look.

"I'm sorry, Miss Seaton—Diana," Tree said. "But it's the truth. Seems we can't get away from prejudice and hatred even when we're fighting the same enemy."

"What can you do, then?"

"I was hoping Billy was about to apprehend the real killer. That would help."

"Not even close," I said. "Not to who killed Neville, the guy I was sent here to investigate. Or to who killed this girl, or Constable Eastman, for that matter."

"You're close enough for someone to try and do you in," Tree said.

"Yeah. A few more clues like that and I'll wake up at the bottom of the canal. But I do know for sure that CID doesn't have much of a case against Angry. The local constable doesn't think it was him either. Did you know about Rosemary Adams saying she saw him that night?"

"I heard that, but didn't believe it." I filled Tree in on the details, and the fact that Tom Eastman's father had been a policeman as well.

"If I have time tomorrow, I'm going to pay a visit to Rosemary and Malcolm Adams, see what they have to say. Then I want to visit that jump school at Chilton Foliat. That track to the cemetery is interesting. I'd like to know how often it's used."

"Tell you what, Billy. You go see the Adamses if you can. I can go to Chilton Foliat and look around. We need to map out a route for a field exercise. I can swing it as official business."

"Okay, that'll help. If you don't need to get back, stay and have dinner with us. Kaz is on his way back from the boarding school in

Great Shefford, where Margaret was coming from. He's confirming it was her. And Big Mike—you haven't met him yet—might be back from an interrogation with Inspector Payne."

"Okay. Anything hopeful?"

"Long shot. I don't expect much." I was getting pretty tired of long shots. I was ready for a close shot, right to the heart of whoever tried to kill me.

CHAPTER EIGHTEEN

FIVE OF US sat around the table in the dining room downstairs. It was odd having a friend from my Boston past here with my new friends from three nations. They were all so different. Diana, with her beauty, aristocratic airs, and passion for the truth; Kaz, with his studied nonchalance and languid manner masking an iron fierceness; Big Mike, with his working-stiff wit and dogged loyalty; Tree, with his determination to fight, his rage right beneath the surface at how hard it all had been.

And me. The parsley and potato soup came before I could figure out what I brought to the party, other than an affinity for people I could count on. I wasn't sure what I could count on Tree for, except that something always happened with him around.

"This is the late Margaret Hibberd," Kaz said, passing a photograph around. "Her school picture. The headmistress had notified the local police that she'd gone missing, and they had in turn called Scotland Yard. Her friends said she often talked about going home, that she missed her mother especially." I took the photograph and studied it. It was the girl from the canal. Thin, dark hair, lost.

"Did she have anyone local she knew, might have gone to?" I asked.

"No one. She was worried that she hadn't had a letter from her parents in quite a while. The police in Great Shefford knew about her father being killed in the bombing, but kept it from her until the mother's death could be confirmed. They hoped she might be found in one of the hospitals."

"It is pure chaos in some of them," Diana said. "Records are destroyed along with buildings, patients moved about. It was worth hoping for."

"Margaret slipped away one night," Kaz said. "She could have walked to the Hungerford railroad station easily enough for the morning train to London."

"We found her just east of Hungerford," Tree said. "So she must have made it to town. The current flows east to west. She could have been dumped in Kintbury, anywhere along the canal."

"Inspector Payne finally heard from the coroner," Big Mike said. "She didn't drown, but that much was obvious from the marks on her neck. The doc said she could've been in the water three to five days; it was cold enough to slow down decomposition."

"I can attest to that," I said, glad of the warm soup in my belly. "How did it go with Miller?"

"I had my suspicions when Payne asked him to come down to the station for a chat," Big Mike said. "Mrs. Miller looked like she was about to faint."

"Do you think she knew something?" Diana asked.

"Suspected, or was afraid maybe. But Miller himself was calm and said he'd be glad to help. We took him down to the station and went over Neville's killing, where he was last night, and pressed him on any connection to Sophia Edwards. Came up with nothing."

"How did he react?" I asked.

"Cooperative at first," Big Mike reported. "Then started looking at his watch. Then he wanted to know how long it would take. Finally he asked if he was a suspect. Then he got upset. Completely normal for an innocent man or a practiced liar."

"You certainly have a difficult profession," Diana said. "How can you tell the two apart?"

"Keep pressing them until they break," Big Mike said. "Kinda hard if they're innocent, right, Billy?"

"Billy knows all about that," Tree said. An awkward silence

followed as the soup bowls were cleared. "I can tell by their faces you've already told your friends about how we met, Billy."

"Part of the story, anyway," I said. "They're a nosy bunch."

"We know Billy took your job," Big Mike said. "That was a raw deal."

"Billy did not get to the part yet where you two actually met," Kaz said. "Tell us your side of the story."

"Yes, do tell us, Tree," Diana said with enthusiasm, as if it were a parlor game. "What was Billy like as a schoolboy?" All eyes were on Tree. I shrugged and glanced away, pretending it didn't matter, even though I wanted to hear his version as much as anyone. No, more. I waited as Tree settled back, took a deep breath, and began.

IT WASN'T THE first time a white boy took a job from me. Pop got me a job stocking shelves in a grocery store that winter. He'd heard one of the cops say his brother-in-law needed a kid to work after school, so Pop sent me down there right away. The owner hadn't even put a sign up yet. I worked three days before a customer made a comment about that nigger boy being in the way. The problem was I didn't say "yes ma'am" fast enough and look at the floor while I did so. I told my boss what had happened, and got docked one day's pay for talking back. That was my first lesson in working with white people. You don't complain, unless you're ready for things to get a whole lot worse. Works the same in the army, except you don't lose your pay, you get a billy club across your head. Anyway, I found out later that the woman who complained about me happened to have a son who could take my spot, so things worked out exactly the way she'd wanted.

I wasn't surprised when Pop told me not to bother showing up for work at the station. Even though I'd put in my application a month before and had been approved, it didn't mean a damn thing, not when a white man, and a detective at that, wanted the job for his kid. No way a Negro janitor could match that pull. I was mad, real mad. And things got worse when I heard that some of the cops didn't like the idea of a Negro man bossing around a white boy. Pop had worked for years at police headquarters, and had a good record. I don't think Basher—Billy must have mentioned Basher McGee—minded a colored janitor one bit, but he hated the idea of a white kid working for one.

At first, I thought the kid would quit, once I heard about the tricks Basher and his pals were pulling. Dumping coffee on a floor, grinding out cigar butts outside the commissioner's office, that sort of thing. But Pop knew what all that meant. Either he'd get blamed for not supervising Billy properly, or it would prove that a Negro man wasn't up to the job of bossing a white boy. He'd be in trouble either way. That was the thing about Basher. He enjoyed putting the squeeze on you and watching while you figured out which was the least awful alternative.

So I wore out shoe leather looking for work. I wanted to save up for college. I had good grades, and I figured if I could get started at any college I'd find a way to finish. I had my eye on a state teacher's college in Bridgewater, figured I could afford that and still keep close to home. I finally got a job working nights at a gas station, out on Boylston Street. I'd always kept Pop's jalopy running, and repairing engines came easy, so I was able to talk them into taking me on as a mechanic's assistant, at half the pay a white man would get, of course. But I counted myself lucky to get any job, and I went right to headquarters to tell Pop all about it.

That's when I first ran into Billy. He was pushing a broom in the main hallway, outside the detectives' squad room. At that moment, Basher came out and I saw his eyes flash between Billy and me, and I knew we were both in trouble.

"You come for your job, boy?" Basher said to me. I remember Billy looking startled for a moment as he figured out what was what.

"Detective McGee," I said, not meeting his eyes.

"Ain't neither one of you worth shit," he said, spitting on the clean floor. "One can't sweep a floor and the other don't show no respect. You answer my question, boy."

"I have a job, Detective," I said. "I work down at Earl's Gas Station now. Don't need to push a broom."

"Well now, Billy, what do you think of that?" Basher said. "Eugene here doesn't need to push a broom anymore, not like you do, you goddamn shanty Irish."

"Maybe I'll steal that job from him too," Billy said. This threw Basher off his stride. I caught a quick glimpse from Billy and knew what he was up to.

"You could try, but they had a sign in the window. No Irishmen need apply." I threw it right back at him. Basher, being an Irishman one step above shanty, didn't have much to say to that, and went sputtering back into the squad room. We thought it was funny, and for a minute I forgot about this kid swiping my job. We went down to Pop's office and told him about the encounter, but he didn't think it was funny at all. Said Basher always found a way to get back at you, and never forgot a slight. But we were kids, and thought it was all fun.

I'd come to visit Pop on my way to work at Earl's most days, and kid around with Billy for a while. Pop said Billy's old man had gotten the job for him without knowing I'd been in line for it, and since he was a decent sort for a white man, and his kid was a good worker, I should go easy on him. I was a couple of years older than Billy, so naturally he looked up to me. Especially when he found out about my job at the garage. He started dropping by after he was done at headquarters, and we got along okay.

One day I came to the station early to bring Pop his lunch. I took the back stairs, to avoid running into Basher, but that one backfired on me. He and one of his cronies had Billy cornered on a stairwell above me, and were giving him a hard time, pushing him around. I yelled something, I don't remember what, and they spotted me below. Basher said something about a dirty nigger needing a bath, and kicked Billy's mop bucket over. I got a good drenching with filthy mop water, but what none of us knew was that the deputy superintendent was not far behind me. He saw everything, and took a good soaking himself.

The look on Basher's face was priceless. His cigar dropped right out of his mouth, and it stayed open as he tried to yammer out an excuse. But Deputy Superintendent Emmons wasn't having any of it, and he bawled out Basher and his buddy right in front of us, a dressing-down like I haven't ever heard again, not even in the army. Of course, Billy and me being kids, we thought it was hilarious. We're standing behind Emmons with big smirks on our faces, while Basher is saying *yessir* and *nosir* as fast as he can. But the whole time he's got one eye on us, and I should have known he'd never forgive us witnessing his disgrace. Him being white, my presence was especially humiliating.

"LET'S GIVE TREE a chance to eat," I said as the landlord delivered plates to the table. I couldn't help smiling at the memory of Basher getting chewed out, even though I knew what had come of it.

"Nice of you to watch out for Tree," Big Mike said, "since you look up to him and all." A ripple of laughter went around the table.

"I'd call some parts of his version a slight exaggeration," I said. "But not the part about Emmons standing there in his wet trousers, yelling at Basher."

"Remember how his shoes squished, every time he shifted his feet? That only got him madder," Tree said. We both broke up over that. It felt good.

"What are we eating?" Kaz asked, investigating the food on his plate.

"Looks like there's chicken and carrots swimming in some kind of sauce," Big Mike said, shoveling a load onto his fork. "Potatoes and parsnips on the side."

"Root vegetables aren't rationed," Diana said. "They at least are plentiful, especially here in the countryside. It does wear one down, I must say, parsnips day after day." She moved the food around on her plate, her voice trailing off as the chatter around the table picked up.

"It didn't go well, did it?" I asked.

"No." She set her silverware down. "Not at all."

"The Joint Intelligence Committee?" Kaz asked, in a low voice.

"Yes," Diana said, her eyes downcast. Big Mike and Tree halted their conversation and looked to me.

"Maybe we should talk about something else," I said.

"That's exactly what Roger Allen said." She clenched and unclenched her hand, and brought her eyes up to look at everyone around the table. "I imagine it is what many in America say about Negroes and the injustices visited upon them. An unpleasant topic brought up by unpleasant people." She brought her hand to her mouth for a second, and I thought she might burst into tears. But that wasn't Diana's style, not the English way at all. When she lowered her hand, her expression was still angry, but controlled.

"Who is this Allen character?" Tree asked.

"A powerful man from the Foreign Office who sits on a powerful committee. A man who sees no reason to be moved by the extermination of Jews throughout Europe," Diana answered. "He said that the Poles and Jews were deliberately exaggerating reports of atrocities simply to stiffen British resolve."

"Any chance that might be true?" Tree asked.

"About as true as lynching being an invention of your Negro newspapers," Diana said, her voice hard. "Even with the eyewitness reports we brought out of Italy, our leaders still refuse to do or say anything."

"All sounds pretty familiar to me," Tree said. "Europeans don't have colored folk, so they go for the Jews instead."

"Is that an apt comparison?" Kaz asked, perhaps feeling slighted as a European.

"Yes, and I think Tree has a point," Diana said. "My father told me that the Americans had asked Anthony Eden of the Foreign Office to help get about sixty thousand Jews out of Bulgaria. Their government has yet to turn them over to the Germans, but no one knows how long they can last. I asked Allen about that, and he said they recommended that the British government do nothing."

"Why?" Kaz asked.

"Because then Hitler might want to negotiate for all the Jews in

Europe. 'And that wouldn't do at all,' Allen told me. When I asked why, all he said was, 'Whatever would we do with them, my dear?'"

Diana twisted her napkin, her lower lip quivering. I reached out my hand to take hers, but she pulled away.

"Whatever would we do with them?" she whispered, and left the table.

CHAPTER NINETEEN

"I HAVE FAILED, Billy." Diana curled up against me in bed, twisting her hair between her fingers in a childlike gesture. "And I was a fool to think I wouldn't."

"It's not your fault that the rich and powerful of the world don't give a hoot about mass murder at a comfortable distance. To them, it's like reading about a flood or an earthquake half a world away. Terribly unfortunate, but what can one do?" I spoke the last sentence in a snotty Beacon Hill drawl, trying for a laugh. I got a smile.

"No, it isn't my fault. I know that," she said, sitting up straight and clutching a pillow to her breast. "What really bothers me is the bravery and sacrifice of those who worked to get the truth out: Poles, Jews, Italians, even Germans. What will they think? Are we worthy of them? And the deaths, Billy. All the people dying in the camps every day, while we do nothing."

"I feel the same way about Margaret Hibberd and Stuart Neville," I said, understanding there was no real answer to the question Diana had posed. Some might argue that fighting men were dying every day to end this war, and that was the best we could do for those in the camps. But that wasn't what she needed to hear right now, or what I necessarily believed. "My dad always said to remember that every murder victim deserved to be alive all the days we were investigating the crime, and more beyond. And that our police work had to be worthy of the days we had and they lost."

"I would like to meet your father, Billy. He seems like an interesting man."

"He'd like you," I said. "Your spirit." I kissed her. "But you'd have to lose the accent, and none of this lady stuff. Wouldn't go over well in Southie." Diana punched me in the chest. Hard. I tickled her, and then we forgot about the sorrows of the world for a while.

Inspector Payne came by in the morning, as we'd arranged. We planned to interview Ernest Bone and the other guy Neville had visited before he was killed. It was doubtful they'd be able to help, but we had damn little else.

"First, we drop in on Stanley Fraser, the solicitor," Payne said, as a constable drove us into Hungerford. It was a warm day, the sun bright and the ground smelling sweet with the promise of spring. "I'm sure I've heard the name, but I can't recall where. I do know most of the solicitors hereabouts, but I don't think I've seen him in court."

"I thought only barristers appeared in court," I said. "Or do I have that backward?"

"No, you're right that barristers argue before the bench, but a solicitor may view the proceedings, and I've got to know quite a few by sight over the years. But not this Fraser chap."

"Any news on Sophia or the girl we found?"

"Nothing new, no. There is a panic rising, though, and I'm not surprised. It would be worth his life if anyone witnessed a man approach a young girl today. I'm worried about some innocent traveler being drawn and quartered for saying a simple good morning to a schoolgirl."

"I've asked Kaz to drive Diana out to the Avington School for the Channel Island girls this morning, to see if she can get any information out of them," I said, watching as we drove by a farmer plowing his field.

"Woman's touch, that sort of thing?" Payne asked, raising an eyebrow.

"That, and the fact that she's a Special Operations Executive agent," I said. "She might pick up on something."

"When our girls were young," Payne said, leaning back and closing his eyes, as if visualizing the memories, "they could keep any secret from us. But perhaps Miss Seaton can wring the truth out of them. Nothing like an SOE interrogation to break a pack of twelve-year-olds, I imagine."

"If there's a truth to be told," I said.

"Girls and secrets go together. You may learn that yourself one day, Captain. Perhaps you and Miss Seaton are headed in that direction?"

"Perhaps," I said. "But we're more often going in separate directions. Maybe when the war's over."

"Hmm," Payne said. "Peace. I wonder what that will be like? Ah, here we are."

We'd gone from fields and farms to a residential street on the outskirts of Hungerford. Atherton Street, where Stanley Fraser lived, contained rows of modern semi-detached brick houses with neat gardens and lace curtains in every window. Two women were walking back from the market in Hungerford, bags heavy in their hands and jackets open to the warming air. An elderly gentleman pedaled his bicycle slowly past us. The neighborhood was quiet, the few people subdued, as if not to disturb the tranquil setting.

Payne told the constable to wait. Fraser inhabited both sides of the semi-detached, a brass plaque marking the right half as his office with the left side apparently his home. In the reception area we were greeted by a young woman who was busy putting away her nail polish, and with little else.

"One minute, please," she said, without asking our names. She walked to an inner door, swiveling her hips all the way, and stuck her head in the room. Payne raised his eyebrows at the view and looked away guiltily. Me, I kept looking in case there was a clue in that general direction.

"Go in, gentlemen," she said, returning wearily to her chair. It looked like a tough job.

"Inspector Payne, Berkshire Constabulary," Payne said, holding up his warrant card. "This is Captain Boyle. We have a few questions for you, if you don't mind."

"What do the police and the American army want with me?" Fraser said, leaning back in his chair and studying us, pointedly not inviting us to sit in the two comfortable armchairs fronting his desk. He had a paunch restrained by a tight-fitting vest and a disappearing hairline that had left a glossy sheen in its wake, as if the crown of his head had been polished. He tapped a fountain pen on his desk, flashing his manicured nails.

"Now I remember you," Payne said, snapping his fingers. "Razor Fraser, they called you for a while, didn't they?"

"I don't know to whom you are referring, Inspector, nor am I responsible for what names I am called by. I am not aware of any matters pending with the police, so please state your business."

"How does murder sound as a pending matter?" Payne said, seating himself and crossing his legs. "Didn't know you'd set up shop in Hungerford, Razor."

"First of all, I find that name offensive," Fraser said. "Secondly, what murder?"

"How'd you get it?" I asked, following Payne's lead and sitting. "The nickname, I mean."

"I don't have time for this," Fraser said, tossing the pen onto his desk.

"Then you should get a real receptionist instead of your girlfriend out there," Payne said. "Bit young for you, eh Razor?"

"Miss Swinson is not my girlfriend. She is my employee."

"As I said," Payne continued. "It was up at the Oxford Crown Court, if I recall. There was a case of an enforcer from the Noonan Mob who had slit the throat of a rival criminal and was clumsy enough to have gotten caught. You prepared the brief for the barrister, which included testimony from witnesses who were threatened with the same treatment if they didn't cooperate."

"That was never proven," Fraser said. "It's nothing but a pack of lies." He worked at staying calm, but his face was getting beet red.

"Proven and known to be true are two different things, I grant you," Payne said, nodding sagely. "So you and your barrister get the villain off, and then guess what happens? He himself turns up dead, his own throat slit for the trouble he caused the Noonan boys. That, Captain Boyle, is how our friend here came by the nickname Razor Fraser. Nice sound to it, eh?"

"Interesting coincidence too," I said. "Us being here on a murder investigation."

"Do you need representation, Captain?" Fraser said, trying to gain control of the conversation. "It was so nice of the inspector to think of me."

"Actually it was the Newbury Building Society who thought of you," I said.

"What? About the loan, do you mean? I thought that was all settled."

"Do you recall the representative from the society who visited you?" Payne asked.

"From the Newbury, you mean," Fraser said. "They prefer that name, you know."

"Yes," Payne said. "The Newbury. I can understand how sensitive you are to the matter of names. Do you recall that visit?"

"Of course," Fraser said, leaning back in his chair and making a show of remembering, wrinkling his brow and rubbing his chin. The guy was a pro. "We went over the paperwork and I showed him the plans for the place. We want to put a passageway between the office and the house, and to add a morning room and a small greenhouse for my wife. She so enjoys puttering about her flowers and all that. Any law against the enjoyment of flowers, Inspector?"

"What was his name?" I asked, thinking back to Ernest Bone not mentioning he'd been visited by Stuart Neville.

"Can't recall, really. It was strictly pro forma as far as I was concerned. Ah, I almost have it. Chamberlain? Something like that."

"You've got it turned around. Neville was his last name. Stuart Neville," Payne said.

"If you say so," Fraser said with a small shrug. "Has he done something wrong?"

"Got himself killed," Payne said. "Head bashed in three nights ago in Newbury. Did you happen to be out that night yourself, Razor?"

"Please, Inspector. Why would I kill a chap from the Newbury when they have just agreed to give me a loan? And if you suspect me of nefarious dealings with criminal figures, why do you suspect I would wield the weapon myself? I'd be more apt to hire one of those Noonan fellows you spoke of."

"Would your wife, or perhaps Miss Swinson, know where you were that night? Late, I mean."

"Three nights ago?" Fraser made a show of counting on his fingers. "Yes, three nights ago it would have been my wife."

"Was there anything unusual about Neville when he was here? Something he might have mentioned?" I asked.

"I hardly remember what he looked like," Fraser said. "He seemed perfectly ordinary. We discussed the terms of the loan, hardly stimulating conversation. What I do find interesting, though, is why you are here, Captain."

"Captain Boyle is assisting us," Payne said. "He helped coordinate the search for that missing girl from the Avington School, and is working with us on the Neville case, it being a matter of mutual concern."

"Why?" Fraser asked, allowing a smirk to show. "Do the Americans need a loan? I thought they were swimming in money."

"We ask the questions here, Razor," Payne said. "So is there nothing you remember about Neville's visit? Nothing you noticed?"

"Well, now that you mention it, I'd have thought he'd have been more interested in reviewing the plans," Fraser said, gesturing at drawings unrolled on a nearby table. "We had an architect draw them up, all ready for inspection, but he gave them only the slightest attention. He is supposed to determine whether we have everything planned out properly, after all." He sounded offended, as if he wished the dead man alive again only so he could berate him for his shortcomings.

"You haven't heard anything about a kidnapping gang around here, have you?" Payne asked. "I know you've defended some dicey characters in your time, but crimes against children were never among the charges. Sexual crimes. If you've heard anything, it might save a young girl's life."

"I've heard about the drowned girl, it's all over town," Fraser said quietly. "Speaking in the hypothetical, I may have had certain contacts with people you'd not consider on the up and up. But every last man of them would draw the line at children. If I knew anything that would help apprehend the fiend who put that poor girl in the canal, I'd tell you and be glad I'd done my duty. Sadly, I cannot."

"Thanks for your time, Mr. Fraser," Payne said, ending on a cordial note. He rose and studied the drawings. "A greenhouse, eh? My wife'd fancy that herself."

"I trust this incident will not hold up the loan, Inspector," Fraser said, opening the door for us to leave.

"No, it should not," Payne said, squinting at the printed legend on the plans. "You can tell the firm of Harrison Joinery not to worry. They should be on the job in no time."

We left the office, and quickly confirmed with Mrs. Fraser that her husband was home the night of the murder. I wanted to ask about the other evenings, but bit my tongue. Instead, I asked Payne what his comment about the carpentry firm was all about as soon as we were out of earshot.

"Just a hunch," he said. "Razor Fraser has likely accumulated income he cannot properly account for. I wouldn't be surprised if the business doing the renovations is owned by him. Then he has the work end up over budget, and pays himself the difference from a stack of pound notes given to him by his criminal clients, so the illegal income gets washed clean. All sorts of ways 'round the taxman for a rogue like him."

"Do you believe him about his gang drawing the line at crimes against young girls?" I asked Payne.

"From what I know of Fraser, I'd guess he believes that. There is a code of sorts among most villains. But there's always a chance of one really rotten apple among all the merely bad."

Payne's driver took us out of Hungerford, taking the long way around to Kintbury, since the main road was closed off because of military traffic. We could hear the roar of engines in the distance, perhaps the start of the maneuvers Tree had mentioned. I wondered if he'd found out anything useful at the Chilton Foliat jump school. We planned to meet for lunch at the Three Crowns Pub and exchange information. He was as anxious for me to solve the case of the murdered and missing girls as he was to get Angry Smith out of the slammer, now that wild rumors were sweeping through every base and billet in the area. As we drove along back roads where farmers were plowing their fields, I thought about Tree and how nothing was ever easy between us. It was like we could never simply do one thing and not have it cascade into a dozen problems. There was no straight line between us, only the hard angles of race and distrust, softened by familiarity, then hardened again by betrayal.

I shook off the memories as the automobile gained the main road and we made for the outskirts of Kintbury, passing the Avington School, where Diana was paying her social call, or conducting an interrogation, depending on how you viewed things. The driver slowed as we approached Hedley's Sweet Shop, and I could see a horse cart halted at the side of the shop.

"That's our man," I said to Payne, pointing out Ernest Bone. He was unloading lumber from the cart and stacking it at the rear of the store. His shop adjoined a bakery on one side, but on the other there was nothing but a large shed, a fence, and open fields.

"Good morning, Mr. Bone," I said as we approached the store owner. He dropped the planks of lumber he'd carried on his shoulder from the cart onto sawhorses set up by the shed. For a paunchy older guy, he had some strength to him. A pony in traces whinnied as we walked by.

"Captain Boyle," he said. "Come back for more humbugs, have you?" He gave a nervous glance in Payne's direction, and then spotted the uniformed constable in the car. "Did I break a law giving them out like that?"

"As strict as the rationing laws are, Mr. Bone, I doubt a few humbugs would amount to a crime," Payne said, showing his warrant card to indicate the formality of the visit. "We wanted to ask you a few more questions about the gentleman from the Newbury Building Society who came to see you about your loan."

"My loan? What about it?"

"Does this man look familiar?" I said, holding out the picture of Stuart Neville at the Kennet Arms.

"Yes, indeed it does. That's the fellow from the Building Society. Wasn't very pleased with his report, I can tell you that."

"Really? Do you remember when I asked if you knew a man by the name of Stuart Neville? Well, this is Neville, murdered shortly after visiting with you."

"What?" Bone looked shocked, his eyes wide. "But I didn't recall his name, honestly. I had no idea it was the same man."

"Why weren't you pleased with his report?" Payne asked.

"Well, he didn't approve the loan," Bone said, "and I needed it for my kitchen and storage. There's hardly enough room to make my boiled sweets, and I need a cool place to keep them. I make them all here, the old-fashioned way, Inspector. Over copper pans, you know." Bone's face brightened up as he spoke of his candy, which evidently was his passion.

"Yes, you told me when I was last here. Did Neville tell you why he turned your application down?" Payne asked.

"Not in so many words, but I got the impression he thought that with the war and rationing, I couldn't make enough money to pay the loan back. He said that perhaps I should wait until peace had come, and people would have more time and money to buy sweets."

"Were you officially turned down?" I asked.

"Yes, the Building Society sent a letter saying it hadn't been approved."

"Did you ever see Neville again?" Payne asked.

"No, never." I watched for any sign of nervousness or deception, and saw only the gentle smile of a candy maker.

"Did you have building plans drawn up?" I asked.

"Nothing so fancy as that," Bone said. "The society didn't require it, and I figured why spend the money until I get the loan, right? But I wrote out everything I wanted to do and had a rough sketch I drew myself. The plan was to expand the kitchen, and build a storage area in the basement where it's cool."

"Are you going to do the work yourself?" I asked, pointing to the lumber.

"Oh, no, that's too big a project for me. Just a bit of fixing up to hold things together. I'm glad I have Sally here to fetch the lumber for me." He patted the pony and brushed her black mane. "A Dartmoor pony, she is. Children love her, which helps when we sell at fetes and the like. I put baskets of sweets in the cart and Sally draws them in, adults and kids alike. Everyone loves a pony, don't they?"

"Sounds like you have a good business for yourself, Mr. Bone," I said.

"Good enough. Someday better, I hope. Sorry I couldn't help you, gentlemen. Inspector, do stop by again when I'm open, won't you? There are all sorts of new temptations inside." He waved us off, smiling as he caressed the mane on his Dartmoor pony.

We left the temptations behind, driving to the Three Crowns to meet Tree.

"Interesting that the society doesn't require plans," Payne said. "It fits my theory that Razor is funneling his illegal gains into a legitimate business."

"He probably paid Harrison Joinery a pretty penny for those drawings," I said.

"Yes. I think I'll look into who does own that firm. Not that it will help us much, but at least it will make me feel like a policeman with a clue."

I knew the feeling.

CHAPTER TWENTY

WE WAITED FOR Tree for an hour at the Three Crowns. We'd eaten our rabbit-meat pasties and finished our pints. We went outside and took a seat on the bench—the same one that Tree, Kaz and I had sat on a few days ago—and let the warmth of the spring sun wash over us. The constable leaned against the automobile and lit a cigarette. It was quiet and peaceful, but I felt something was wrong. It wasn't like Tree to let anyone down. Not Angry, not me, not his unit.

"He probably couldn't get away," Payne said. "New orders or something. It is the army, after all."

"Maybe. But he said he was scouting sites for maneuvers this morning, and from what we saw today they're about to start up. He should be done by now."

"Well, I hope they don't ruin too many plowed fields," Payne said. "I know they have to train, but some of your chaps—and ours too—get carried away. Stone walls knocked down, crops ruined, and who gets a call? The police, that's who, and there's damn little we can do about it."

"How about you drop me back at the inn so I can take a ride up to Chilton Foliat?" I said, hardly listening to Payne's complaints. "I'll look around and then head to the bivouac if I don't find Tree there."

"If you'd like. I'll be at the station later today if you want to come round," Payne said. "Perhaps we should have another go with Flowers at the building society."

I agreed, and thirty minutes later I was negotiating the curves on my way into Chilton Foliat. I parked by the church, and walked through the graveyard where Constable Eastman's body had been found. I followed the wide path we'd spotted in the woods, figuring I might as well check it out as a potential route for bringing a corpse to the cemetery.

It would do fine. Wide, a bit rough in spots, but obviously a farm track a jeep could easily handle. Or a tractor, maybe a car, or a big strong guy carrying a body. I spotted Quonset huts through the trees, rows of them on a wide lawn sloping down from a large house with columns fronting it. The track merged with a paved lane that curved around a stand of fir trees and continued up to the house. Along the lane stood a row of sheds, a horse barn, and finally a thatched cottage, larger than my house back in Southie, probably originally lodgings for the manager of the estate. Whoever lived there now might have seen something that night, but it was hard to believe they would have stayed silent about it.

Horses neighed from inside the barn as I passed, and I remembered that Constable Tom Eastman's head had been bashed in. An accident, perhaps? A horse kicking and killing him, a nervous groom looking to hide his involvement? The cemetery was close, so why not leave Eastman on the family plot? Maybe, but maybes were as common as crows.

I left the lane with its centuries-old stone-and-thatch buildings and walked between rows of that ubiquitous invention of the twentieth, the Quonset hut. Curved galvanized steel roofs over ends of plywood, they housed tens of thousands of GIs all over this island. The paths between the huts were covered with wood planks, like the sidewalks in an old western movie. I heard the rumble of boots stomping on wood, and caught a glimpse of men running toward the road that went up to the main house. Agitated shouts came from the road, and I double-timed it to see what was going on.

It was a fight. A circle of GIs five deep were yelling and

whooping it up, clapping and waving their fists. It sounded like they were having fun, but I couldn't tell if it was a fair fight or not. If it was, I'd probably leave the enlisted men to their own devices. If not, I should act the officer and break it up. Then I heard it, loud and clear.

"Give it to the nigger! Give it to 'im, Charlie!" I felt a moment of panic, knowing somehow that it had to be Tree in trouble. I pushed my way through the frenetic crowd, and as guys noticed my captain's bars some faded away, suddenly needing to be somewhere else. Before I saw Tree, I saw Charlie. Charlie was huge, fists the size of hams and arms thick with muscle. He seemed to tower over Tree, but he had him by only a matter of inches in height. In terms of coiled power and weight, he had him beat six ways to Sunday.

Charlie moved like an ox. Tree danced around him, coming out of his shadow and trying to throw a punch but coming up short. He stumbled but regained his footing quickly, moving to the edge of the crowd. I didn't dare call his name and distract him, leaving him open to a roundhouse punch from a freight train.

Tree didn't look like he could last much longer. One eye was swollen shut, he was bleeding from his nose and a cut above the open eye, and he kept his left hand down, probably protecting a cracked rib. Aside from the vacant look in his eyes, which he'd probably been born with, Charlie didn't have a mark on him. Another GI in the circle had a black eye, and his knuckles were scraped and bleeding. Charlie wasn't Tree's first opponent in this rigged fight.

I shoved a corporal standing next to me. I tapped my bars for emphasis.

"Ten-hut!" he shouted, and snapped to attention like a good soldier. Most of the men followed his example, and saluted. I returned the salute, noting that more GIs slithered away from the rear of the crowd. Tree kept silent, swaying in the stillness as blood dripped on the ground in front of him. He turned his good eye toward me, his fists still raised. He spat blood.

"What's going on here?" I asked.

"Just a fight between friends, Captain," a sergeant said as he stepped forward. He wore an MP's white brassard.

"You're an MP and you let this fight continue?"

"Well, the boys were riled up a bit, and the only way to calm things down, sir, was to let them blow off some steam with a fair fight. This here nigger started it, anyway." He gestured to Tree with his thumb. I noticed another GI with a bloody nose behind him. I stepped forward and grabbed his hands. He flinched as I squeezed his swollen knuckles.

"You, Private," I said to Charlie. "Why did you fight this man?"

"I do a lot of fighting, Captain." Charlie's voice came out in a low rumble.

"Yeah, but why him, today?"

"I dunno. Sarge just said to put him down, so I stepped in. He's hard to hit, though."

"This sergeant?" I said, pointing to the MP.

"Yeah, that's Sarge." Charlie probably knew there were other sergeants in the army, but to his dim lightbulb of a brain, there was only one Sarge. His.

"How did this start, Sergeant?" I said, restraining myself from clocking him one.

"Somebody said there was a colored boy drivin' a jeep, and that it might be one of them who took that white girl. You know, the one that was found in the canal?" He shrugged, as if that was explanation enough for a beating.

"Yes, Sergeant. It was the Negro unit that found her, helping the police with their search."

"Well, there you go," he said, as if that confirmed all his preju-dices. "So a few of the boys went up to ask him, and I guess he back-talked, which a few of the fellas didn't take to. He sounded like one of them northern coloreds, you know? Acting better than he ought to. So I come along to be sure nothing got outta hand. Pulled 'em apart and made sure it was just one-on-one."

"So you're the ringmaster here, sending in three men to fight one?"

"Not at the same time, Captain. Now you ask that colored boy if he wants to complain about anything at all. Ask him if he didn't agree to it, too. Go ahead, it's a free country."

I looked to Tree. He shook his head, signaling to leave things alone. He was right. If he filed a complaint there'd be a dozen witnesses swearing he started the whole thing, and he'd be the one in the slammer. He buckled at the knees and fell into Charlie, who grabbed his collar and held him up easily with one hand.

"You got an infirmary here?" I asked.

"For white men, sure," the sergeant said.

"I'll take him, Sarge," Charlie said. "Wouldn't want Sobel to find out we didn't treat a man hurt after a fair fight." Charlie looked like a dumb ox, but he knew how to handle his sergeant.

"Okay, okay," the sergeant said. "Clear out, the bunch of ya, show's over!" The crowd dispersed, except for a civilian who might have been the caretaker. He wore a cloth cap, Wellington boots, old corduroys, and three-day stubble. He looked thirty or so, but the grin on his face made it hard to tell. A cigarette was crammed into the corner of his mouth, and he puffed and blew smoke without removing it. He stuck his hands in his pockets and walked away, throwing a last glance after us. He didn't look like the sociable type.

"Who's Sobel?" I asked as Charlie and I each took an arm and walked Tree to the infirmary.

"Captain Sobel, he's in charge of the jump school," Charlie said. "He goes by the book. Real strict."

"Charlie, did you hit Tree? It looks like you could break him in half with one hand."

"Tree? Is that what they call him?" Tree moaned at the mention of his name, and gripped my shoulder tighter.

"Yeah, because he's so tall. You didn't hit him, did you?"

"No, sir. Sarge wanted me to, but he'd already fought two guys and they got him good a few times. Didn't seem right. Not sure I could have, the way he moved so fast."

"Coupla . . . more minutes . . . you woulda," Tree croaked.

"Maybe," Charlie said. "Maybe not."

Charlie stayed with us while a medic patched Tree up. Other than commenting on how much blood was pouring out of him, he didn't mention color, so I figured the sergeant's comment about "whites only" was all bluster.

"Be best if I put a coupla stitches in that cut above your eye," the medic said. "You mind?"

"Not if you're quick," Tree managed to get out. "And if you've done it before."

"First guy didn't complain," he said, cleaning the wound. "But then he was unconscious." Tree gasped as the first stitch went through, and Charlie looked away. I had the feeling Charlie wasn't the tough guy his size led you to believe. "Get those out in three days, and keep it clean. Ice would be the best thing for the swelling, but this is England, so good luck."

"He going to be okay?" Charlie asked the medic.

"Yeah, Charlie. But he's lucky you didn't land one."

"I don't feel too lucky," Tree said, gasping as the medic wound a bandage around his ribs.

"You might have a cracked rib, but it looks like a bruise to me. Take it easy for a while and you'll be fine." We left and returned to Tree's jeep, Charlie supporting Tree by the arm.

"Sorry, Tree," Charlie said. "I wish this all never happened."

"Who started it, exactly?" I asked.

"Not sure," Charlie said. "I think I heard Crowley talking to some of the guys about it. He said something about the colored fellow in the jeep being one of the gang that took the girl. We'd all heard about that."

"Who's Crowley?" Tree asked, easing himself into the jeep.

"The English guy. He works in the stable."

"Was he at the fight?" I asked.

"Yeah, he was the civilian. He takes care of the horses. I tried to look at them, but he yelled at me to get out. This place used to be a horse farm, I heard." Charlie looked happy at the thought of horses, a lot happier than being forced to fistfight. I wondered if the

Eastmans had any connections to the former horse farm, so near the graveyard.

"Okay, Charlie. Stay out of trouble, will you?"

"Sure thing, Captain. You too, Tree," he said, grinning like a kid.

"Not the easiest thing, Charlie," Tree said.

CHAPTER TWENTY-ONE

THEY WERE WAITING for us at the bridge. Three British military police in their distinctive red caps. One waved me to the verge and approached.

"Are you Captain Boyle?" He was a sergeant, and should have added "sir" to that question. I didn't press the point, since I wasn't much for military courtesies myself, and the look on his face was the type a cop reserved for picking up a drunk and disorderly.

"Yes I am, Sergeant," I said, dropping a subtle hint. "What can I do for you?"

"You can follow me, Captain. Someone wants to see you, and he's not used to waiting, so he tells me." He nodded to his MP pals, and one of them mounted a motorcycle, pulling out in front, while the other started up his jeep.

"Wait, Sergeant," I said as he turned away. "I've got a hurt man here, I need to get him back to his unit." I pointed my thumb at Tree, his face bandaged and swollen.

"Are you bleeding to death then, soldier?" the MP asked.

"I'm fine," Tree said.

"Let's get this sorted first, and then the captain can take you wherever he needs to. Follow the motorcycle. We'll follow in the jeep."

"Sergeant, what's this all about?" I asked. "Where are we going?"

"Hungerford police station, where all will be answered."

They kept close, the motorcycle proceeding at a stately pace, the jeep riding our rear bumper. I could have broken free at a turn if I'd been inclined, but something about the sergeant's attitude told me not to show off.

"Can you hang on?" I asked Tree.

"I'm okay," he said. "Any idea why they're after you?"

"Hey, this is an escort, a sign of respect."

"Hell, Billy, looks like you pulled me out of the frying pan and now you got an escort to your own fire," Tree said, his laugh turning into a wince.

"Just like old times," I said.

"Except this time the cops are wearing brown. Looks like neither of us has learned very much." We slowed and pulled in behind the motorcycle as it parked in front of the police station.

"You mean you went into that fight willingly?" I asked.

"I didn't run," Tree said. "Decided I was sick of running when I was down South. It was the same on every damn base, every damn cracker town. Walk in the gutter, eyes down. Yessah, nosah, boss. Can't do it anymore, Billy. That's why I want to fight. This TD unit is the best thing that ever happened to me, and I want Angry along for the ride."

"Let's go, Captain," the MP said.

"As long as I walk out of here, Tree, I'll do my best," I said in a low voice. The MP sergeant looked like he wanted to prod me with his billy club, so I got out. Tree followed, and no one barred the way. I figured if he didn't have enough sense to stay out of a police station, that was his business.

Constable Cook stood in the hallway, arms folded and a frown on his face. "Glad they found you, Captain Boyle. Now get this over with so I can be rid of that windbag and back in my office!"

"Windbag? I think I know who you mean," I said.

Cook squinted at the figure following me. "Tree, is that you under those bandages? What happened?"

"A fight," Tree said. "I'm fine."

"Wait here," I said, making for the closed door.

"Nope," Tree said. "You came to my rescue, least I can do is explain where you been."

"This is none of your business, lad," Cook said. "Best leave it alone, is my advice."

"No, I need Billy to help Angry. I'll do what I can."

I didn't think there was much Tree could do, but I understood the value of a diversion, so I opened the door and let him follow me in.

"Boyle! About time!" As I'd suspected, the windbag was Major Charles Cosgrove. He was seated at Cook's desk, not wearing his usual uniform, but dressed in a tweed suit, the vest's buttons straining to keep his belly from bursting out. Inspector Payne sat across from him, a glazed look in his eyes. I felt sorry for the man; he must have had his fill of Cosgrove by now.

"The MPs were a bit drastic, Major," I said.

"They were obviously necessary," Cosgrove said, slapping a file closed on Cook's desk as he took notice of Tree. "Who is this soldier and why is he here?"

"Billy . . . I mean, Captain Boyle got me out of a jam, sir," Tree said. "He got a medic to patch me up and was taking me back to my unit. I guess that's why you couldn't find him. I wanted to explain, so he wouldn't be in hot water."

"Sergeant Eugene Jackson?" Cosgrove opened the file and pulled out a photograph. "Bit hard to tell with the bandages and that swollen eye, but I'd say you're the fellow they call Tree. Am I right?"

"Why am I in that file?" Tree asked. "Who are you anyway?"

"Is that a state secret today, Major?" I said, interrupting before Tree got himself in too deep.

"Major Charles Cosgrove," he said, introducing himself. "In mufti today so as not to draw undue attention to the flogging of Captain Boyle. Sergeant Jackson, please be so good as to wait outside with Constable Cook."

"Okay, Major Cosgrove," Tree said and shot me a wink on his way out. I knew he wanted to repay me for getting him out of that rigged fight, but he didn't know enough about Cosgrove to understand how dangerous he was. He'd made the same mistake years ago with Basher, and Cosgrove made Basher look like an amateur. I heard the door shut, and waited until Tree's footsteps faded away. He had enough problems without the gatekeeper for the British Empire on his back.

"Okay, Major," I said as I took a seat. "What's this all about?"

"It is *about*, Captain Boyle, your disobedience and willful misconduct in this investigation. What do you have to say for yourself?"

I glanced at Inspector Payne, who lifted his hands from his lap, palms up, signaling that he was lost as well. I didn't like the legalistic sound of those words, and I was sure they were mentioned somewhere in the Articles of War. Probably in the same paragraph as courts martial and hard labor. I went through the possibilities of what I might have done and came up empty. Then I recalled something about checking in with Cosgrove. Every day, was it? At least it gave me something to apologize for.

"I'm sorry, Major. I was supposed to call you, right? I know Kaz did, but I forgot last night, I know."

"Yes, you were supposed to check in each day, which you have yet to do. Consider yourself fortunate that I have my own means of following your progress, or lack of it. I'm sure you were too busy dining with your friends to place a simple telephone call."

"Major, my progress has led me to nearly being drowned. Someone clobbered me and pushed me into the canal. That means we're close to the killer."

"I am glad you survived, Boyle. But I am not concerned about your lack of communication. It is your disobedience of a direct order I am here to discuss. Do you recall that I told you the Millers were not under suspicion, and that other than an initial interview, neither you nor Inspector Payne were to further involve them in this investigation? Is that not correct, Captain Boyle?"

"You said that, Major, but you weren't on the scene. Neville was killed on their basement stairs. I couldn't ignore that." I figured that was all I needed to say on the subject.

"No, Captain Boyle, it is *you* who cannot ignore *me*, or the orders

I give you," Cosgrove said, his voice grim. "I have already instructed you once on this matter, but perhaps being an American you need more precise orders, not open to your own interpretation. The Millers are not suspect," he went on, pointing his finger in my direction. "Period. Do you understand?"

"Sure, Major, I get it."

"None of them are to be taken into custody or questioned officially," he said, obviously not believing I did get it. "If you need to talk to them, pay a social call and have a nice chat. Inspector Payne has heard much the same, so I hope there will be no further confusion upon this point. Have I made myself clear?"

"Yes, clear as rain on my parade, Major. But you can't tie our hands like this."

"We are not engaged in a debate. You either understand these orders, or require further clarification. Which is it?"

"Understood, Major. But I do have one question," I said.

"Go ahead."

"Why? Why are the Millers off limits?"

"They are not off limits. Feel free to visit them in their home in a cordial manner. Now, I've sent Big Mike back to London. You don't need an entourage to carry out this investigation. Having too many people about may have led you to dispatch Big Mike and Inspector Payne to take Miller to the police station in the first place."

"Now hold on," Payne said. "I've listened to this blather long enough. Captain Boyle did not dispatch me anywhere. We agreed Miller should be interrogated, like any sensible coppers would, here or in America. I've a mind to pay that social call to George Miller tonight, and find out what makes him so special."

"You do that, Inspector Payne," Cosgrove said in a low, threatening voice, "and I'll break you. I'll take your pension and put you in prison for the duration of the war. And don't think I can't. Or won't. Now please wait outside for Captain Boyle. I need a private word."

"Gladly," Payne said, lifting his lanky frame out of the chair and giving the door a good slam on the way out.

Cosgrove sat back and watched me, his face softening a bit. "Boyle," he said, weariness creeping into his voice. "Take everything I've said to heart. The stakes are enormous, and there is much I cannot reveal to you."

"But what's the game?"

"For now, the game has to be trust. The stakes are counted in lives, if not the direction of the war itself."

"That's a lot to swallow, Major. It would help to know more."

"I can't tell you more." Cosgrove rubbed his eyes, and I could see the strain he was under as he let out a heavy sigh. He hadn't shaved well; there was a cut on one cheek and stubble where he'd missed under his chin. He was dead tired. Something was keeping him up nights. Or someone.

"The man in civilian clothes, at Bushy Park. Tall and slim. We saw you have words. Is he calling the shots on this one?" I remembered that Kaz had pointed him out as the man who made Cosgrove sweat.

"He doesn't exist. You'd do well not to mention him again. And there is always someone calling the shots, as you say."

"Okay, forget I mentioned him. So what's the private word you wanted?"

"Miss Seaton," Cosgrove said, leaning forward and whispering.

"What?" I said, panic surging in my gut. "Is she all right?"

"Yes, yes," Cosgrove said, trying to calm me. "She is fine, still staying here at the inn. What I'm about to tell you is unofficial. Quite off the record, do you understand?" This wasn't a directive. I could see the concern in his eyes, sense it in his voice.

"I do."

"She's pressed the matter of the extermination camps at a high level. Her father facilitated access to some rather important people for her, but I fear he's done her no favors."

"Roger Allen, of the Joint Intelligence Committee," I said, recalling Diana's description of her meeting.

"A name that one does not bandy about," Cosgrove said. "He was not pleased to have his viewpoint questioned. There are those who feel more should be done about the camps, bombing them, that sort of thing. Others maintain that landing on the Continent and defeating Germany militarily is the best way to end their murderous regime."

"Which group is Allen in?"

"The third group. The group that does not care what happens to the Jews of Europe, as long as they do not become our responsibility. Especially not in Palestine, where an influx of Jews would upset the delicate balance of Arab politics and British rule. There are only a few of them, but they are powerful and secretive men. Please tell Miss Seaton to keep quiet about the camps, for a while at least. They have their eye on her."

"Like you have your eye on me," I said.

"No, Boyle. Not like that at all." Cosgrove slumped back into his chair and signaled for me to go. In that moment he was an exhausted old man, shooing away a bothersome child. I left, thinking how crazy this game really was. Diana went undercover in Nazi-occupied Italy and brought back information on the extermination camps. Now her own people were suspicious of her, and Major Charles Cosgrove, an English straight arrow if ever there was one, was whispering their names here in this remote village lockup, looking afraid for his own life. And me, asking the wrong questions of the wrong people, apparently. Or the right people, judging by the reaction.

I caught a glance of the photograph of Constable Sam Eastman before I closed the door quietly behind me. He looked impatient.

CHAPTER TWENTY-TWO

"WHAT THE HELL are you going on about, Boyle?" Payne demanded. "I had to sit through three versions of that intolerable man's tirade before you showed up. What I want is an explanation, not questions about madness."

"He's a big shot with MI5, likes to throw his weight around. I don't get why he cares so much about the Millers, but then I don't get a lot of what MI5 does. But tell me more about the pleasure men," I said to Inspector Payne, eager to get off the topic of Major Cosgrove and his motives.

"I'd say Cosgrove fits the bill," Cook said with a chuckle, lighting his pipe and leaning against the whitewashed wall of the station. He, Payne, and Tree had been waiting out front, soaking up the waning rays of the late afternoon sun. The weather had turned away from winter's last grasp, the skies were clear, and the ground damp and smelling of green.

"He's under a lot of pressure," I said, feeling the need to defend him. "There's a lot he can't tell us. I know he comes across as heavy-handed, but he can be a stand-up guy."

"From what these fellows tell me, he's not standing up much for your investigation," Tree said. "I hope he won't get in the way of proving Angry innocent."

"That's why I want to know about the pleasure men," I said. "Now." All I wanted to do was get back to Diana and pass on

Cosgrove's warning. I didn't like the look on his face; it wasn't the usual bluster, it was dead serious. Frightened.

"What are you talking about? Pimps?" Tree asked. Cook gave him the background about inmates serving at the pleasure of the King in the Broadmoor Criminal Lunatic Asylum.

"You said you checked all of Sam Eastman's arrests," I said to Cook.

"I did. All dead or in prison, the serious offenders anyway. Might be a poacher or the like we missed, but I doubt that sort would be a threat."

"Any in Broadmoor?"

"Yes, there were two sent there. One way back when Sam was new on the force, and another from nineteen thirty-five. One is still inside, and the other died there. Same with Tom Eastman: no recent releases."

"Why the sudden interest, Boyle?" Payne asked.

"I was thinking how crazy Cosgrove sounded myself, and then I looked at the elder Eastman's photograph. That made me wonder if we weren't being too logical about this case."

"You mean Tom Eastman being found on his father's grave," Tree said.

"Exactly. That's nothing Angry would have done if he were the killer. There's no point to it. It's as if someone was delusional enough to think Sam Eastman would know his son had been killed. We may well be looking for a lunatic."

"I'll inquire with Broadmoor again," Cook said. "Perhaps they overlooked someone. I'll go through the files and make sure none of the chaps who received lesser charges went on to more serious offenses. They might blame their first brush with the law for everything that followed."

"Maybe you should check up on anyone from the village who was sent to the asylum," Tree said. "Criminal or not. It could be any local nut case."

"Fair point," Cook said. "I'll talk with Doc Brisbane, the coroner. He'd likely know who has been committed over the years."

"Good thinking, Tree," Payne said. "Were you a detective your-self in the States?"

"Naw," Tree said, grinning mischievously. "I was a criminal, according to the judge."

"Hardly a criminal mastermind," I said. "But that's a good idea. I'll come by tomorrow, Constable, and see what you've found out. I've got to get Tree back to his unit."

"I will be back at the Newbury Building Society in the morning," Payne said. "I want to find out if Neville might have made any notes after his last visits. I still think finding Razor Fraser in the midst of all this is damned odd."

"He's kept his nose clean, that's all I can say," Cook offered. "The gossips say his wife craves the respectable country life. In a comfort-able sort of way, of course."

"You think he's reformed?" Payne asked.

"No, his type seldom do. But quieter than in his youth, I'll bet. Smarter maybe. I'd say the driving force behind his new image is the wife. She'd not like her reputation besmirched by the inconvenience of her husband going to prison. Certainly not over a bank loan."

"Still, there's something fishy there," Payne said, "even if it's not about Neville's murder."

"The missing girl?" Tree asked.

"No," Cook said. "Not Razor's area of interest. Well, good night, gentlemen. I'll go and see if I can reclaim my office."

Cook returned to the station, Payne walked to his car, and Tree and I got into the jeep. I buttoned up my coat against the cool eve-ning air, and was about to start the engine when Cook burst out of the front door.

"He's unconscious," Cook yelled. "Cosgrove. I'll get Doc Brisbane." As he raced across the street to the coroner's office, we rushed inside, Payne not far behind. I didn't know what we'd find, and I felt a surge of fear it would be a corpse.

Cosgrove was sprawled on the floor in front of Cook's desk, but he wasn't dead. Yet. His face was flushed and sweaty, his mouth agape as he tried to draw in air with ragged, wheezy gasps. One arm clutched the edge of the desk, as if it were a life raft floating upon the deepest sea. Papers were scattered around him, spilled out of the files he'd been carrying.

"The doctor's on his way," I said, kneeling next to Cosgrove. I took his hand from where he was grasping the desk and laid it on his chest. His skin was clammy. I loosened his tie and unbuttoned his shirt, the collar soaked with sweat. Tree took off his jacket, folded it, and slid it under Cosgrove's head. "Can you hear me?"

"Yes," came the answer, a hiss of air, no more. Cosgrove's eyes darted left and right, looking for something. I prayed for the doctor to hurry.

"What do you need?" I asked.

"Pa . . . papers," he whispered. The papers from the file he had on the desk. Secrets.

"I'll take care of them, Major," I said. "I promise. Relax and wait for the doctor, you'll be okay." He didn't really look like he'd be okay anytime soon. Payne entered the room with a stretcher and set it down next to Cosgrove.

"How's he look?" Payne whispered.

"Bad," I answered, in a low voice. "I think it's a heart attack."

"Boyle," Cosgrove said, his voice surprisingly strong.

"Yes," I said, my face close to his.

"Get . . . the papers. No sedative."

"Okay, the papers," I said. "But do you know what's wrong? Have you been ill?"

He thumped his chest, weakly. His heart.

"Out of the way, young man." Doctor Brisbane, at last.

"It's his heart," I said.

"Well, you don't need me then, do you?" Brisbane pulled open Cosgrove's shirt and listened with his stethoscope. I decided against further diagnosis as I gathered up the files on the floor. Brisbane checked his eyes, spoke to the major, and got the same insistent rejoinder about sedatives. He and the others got Cosgrove onto the stretcher, and we each took a corner to carry him across the street. He was a big guy.

"Boyle," he rasped out. "Call the number, the one I gave you. No sedatives, remember." His eyes went to the file tucked under my arm, and for the first time since we'd found him, he seemed to relax. "No sedative."

Doc Brisbane got Cosgrove settled in his examination room. I reminded the doc about Cosgrove's insistence on no sedation, and vaguely hinted at state secrets.

"If he rests quietly, there will be no need," Doc Brisbane said. "It does look like a heart attack, you were right. Not much we can do beyond bed rest. He could stand to lose some weight, though. I'll keep him here overnight and check his vital signs. You'll see about getting him picked up?"

I said I'd attend to it, then asked Inspector Payne to drop Tree off at his battalion, and to explain the situation to his CO, and to let me know if that wasn't enough.

"Thanks, Billy," Tree said before he got into the car. "I owe you."

"What are friends for?" I asked. "Take it easy, I'll let you know if we come up with anything." Payne and I made plans to meet at the building society at nine o'clock the next morning, and I went back to the station to make the call.

I sat at Constable Cook's desk and dialed the number on the piece of paper. It rang twice, and a female voice answered, repeating the number. I said I was calling for Major Charles Cosgrove.

"He is unavailable."

"No, I'm calling on his behalf. He's ill, probably had a heart attack." More questions about who I was, where I was calling from, and how I got this number. I promised to call with an update and the woman said someone would be in Hungerford by morning. Then she hung up, no goodbye, no "tell Charles to get better." Nice bunch he worked for.

I hadn't mentioned the file, and they hadn't asked. No one had told me not to look in it, but MOST SECRET stamped in red on the cover was a pretty strong warning. I'd had to look at the papers when I picked them up, I told myself, so another glance wouldn't hurt, would it?

They looked like personnel files. Sergeant Eugene Jackson, Inspector John Payne, and me. Photographs, service records, a local address for Payne. My photo was from my identification papers. Tree's wasn't so formal, a bit blurry, like it was taken with a telephoto lens. Was MI5 spying on Tree?

Carla and George Miller were there too, along with their son, in his naval uniform, and their daughter, Eva. Lots of details about their lives, but no conclusions, no assessment of their loyalty. Sergeant Jerome Sullivan was pictured arm in arm with Eva Miller.

There was Michael Flowers of the Newbury Building Society, along with Miss Gardner, the helpful secretary. Razor Fraser and Ernest Bone. Laurianne Ross and the missing Sophia Edwards. Jack Monk from the pub, and old Tim Pettigrew. Can't tell the players without a scorecard.

But what was the game?

CHAPTER TWENTY-THREE

IT WAS STILL light when I arrived back at the Prince of Wales Inn. The sun was down, but the clouds were backlit from the sunset, casting a soft golden glow over the landscape. It shouldn't be so pretty, I thought, with a young girl dead and another missing, the innocent behind bars, and a good man dying. I found Kaz, Diana, and Laurianne Ross from the school seated outside, the flagstones warm from the day's sunlight. I'd half forgotten that Diana and Kaz had paid a visit to the Avington School for Girls today. Diana was in her brown wool FANY uniform, which I guessed she'd worn to interest the kids, since her brass buttons and leather belt were polished to a gleam.

"Billy," Kaz said as I sat down on the wooden bench. "You remember Miss Ross?"

"Of course," I said. "What brings you here?" She looked nervous, twirling a half-empty glass of what looked to be brandy, the same as Kaz and Diana were drinking. It had to be serious.

"We brought her back with us, Billy," Diana said, patting her on the arm. "It was a bit of a shock. And we thought it best for you to hear it directly from Laurianne."

"Okay," I said, slowly, holding back my curiosity. "Tell me about it."

"When the baron and Lady Seaton came by today, I of course thought they were bringing news of Sophia," Laurianne said. Kaz used his title whenever he made restaurant reservations or needed to gain entry. Evidently it worked. "But they wanted to question the girls, as you know. We thought it best if we treated it as a visit, with the baron speaking about his native Poland and Lady Seaton talking about her experiences with the First Aid Nursing Yeomanry. The girls were thrilled, especially about the FANY. So many of them want to sign up as soon as they are old enough." She took a sip of the brandy, and I watched Diana nod encouragingly.

A roar of engines announced a low-flying pair of fighters, P-47 Thunderbolts by the sound of their growling radial engines. They swooped over the village, probably headed back to Greenham Common air base. It was a routine event, but Laurianne jumped in her seat.

"I'm sorry," she said. "Ever since I saw that picture, my nerves have been on edge. I can't help but feel guilty."

"Tell me about the picture," I said.

"Lady Seaton—" Laurianne began again, taking a deep breath.

"Diana, please call me Diana. That lady business is frightful, really."

"Thank you, Diana. Well, Captain Boyle, Diana asked the girls a few simple questions about Sophia, what she was like and so on. Then one of the girls said she looked like that girl who had come by asking for food. Similar hair, that sort of thing. Both were slender girls."

"Wait," I said, trying to understand. "What girl? Not one of yours?"

"No. She rode up on a bicycle one day and asked for food. She said she was traveling to Southampton and would work for a meal. She looked like a runaway so I invited her in and went to my office to call the constable. She must have overheard me on the telephone, because when I came out, she was gone."

"You didn't mention this before," I said.

"No, I hardly recalled it. I wasn't certain she was a runaway, but thought I should place the call just in case. Then she was gone, and there were a hundred other tasks to attend to. I quite forgot about it until the girls reminded me today."

"I showed her the picture of Margaret Hibberd," Kaz said, taking the photograph out of his pocket. "It was her."

"She'd be alive if I hadn't called the police," Laurianne said. Her chin quivered and she looked ready to fall apart.

"Whatever happened to Margaret easily could have happened after a good meal," I said. "We know she was making her way to London to search for her parents. She said Southampton to throw you off."

"I keep telling myself that," Laurianne said. "But if she had stayed, she might not have met up with whoever killed her. Isn't that right?" Her dark eyes were watery, tears about to cascade down her cheeks. I searched for the right thing to say, and came up empty. She had spoken the truth, and there was no dancing around it.

"What fates impose, that men must needs abide; It boots not to resist both wind and tide," Kaz said quietly.

"Shakespeare," Laurianne said. "*Romeo and Juliet*, wasn't it?"

"Yes," Kaz said. "A story of another doomed girl. Margaret was set upon a course to find her parents, only she could not know they were both dead. Fate led her to them, not you."

"Thank you, Baron," she said, and finished her brandy.

"Did she say anything at all, other than asking for a meal?"

"She had some story about working on a farm, but being called back to Southampton by her father. She did say he found a place in the country for her because Southampton was so heavily bombed, which is true enough."

"Anything else? Anything unusual?"

"No. She was friendly. She had confidence. It took some nerve to bicycle up and ask for a meal. I imagine she saw the girls and felt comfortable enough about it, but still, it would be hard for any girl her age to do that."

"She was trusting," Diana said.

"Yes. Open and trusting," Laurianne said, clasping her hands around her empty glass. "Now she's dead, isn't she? So much for confidence."

Kaz offered to drive Laurianne back to the school, and Diana and I stayed outside in the cool air under the feeble lamplight. I hadn't had a chance to tell her or Kaz about Cosgrove's heart attack, much less pass on his warning.

"Diana, I—" She held up her hand, watching as Kaz helped Laurianne into the jeep and started the engine.

"Wait, Billy," Diana said, "but there's something else. Before I left, I had a chance to speak to several of the girls alone. They all saw Margaret ride in on her bicycle. They were coming in from the playground when she knocked on the front door. But none of them actually saw her leave."

"Where were they? Could they have seen her?"

"They'd come in through a side door from the playground. The girls I spoke to were in a classroom at the front of the house with a clear view of the drive. They saw Margaret waiting in the foyer as they entered, and then never saw her again."

"Is there another road or path leading away from the house?" I asked, leaning back in my seat, trying to remember the layout of the place.

"I don't know," Diana said. "Laurianne escorted us throughout the building, so it seemed impolite to wander about. I thought it best to tell you. Perhaps Margaret hid herself there."

"I'll check it out," I said. "Good work."

In my experience, runaway girls don't end up tucked safely away in a girl's school, but no reason not to let that remote possibility stay with us. Chances were the girls missed seeing her leave, or she went out a different way. Miss Ross didn't seem the type to store bodies under the floorboards, but I knew I had to look into the possibility that Margaret had come to grief not far from the school. Or at the school, which was much more sinister. Laurianne Ross was in charge at the school, she had the run of the entire building. She could have brought Margaret wherever she wanted, and quietly disposed of the bicycle. But why? There was no motive I could think of. Still, it was odd that she had forgotten to mention Margaret Hibberd until one of her schoolgirls brought it up. With one child missing, why not report a runaway who showed up and then disappeared?

"Sorry, Billy, what were you about to say?"

"It's Major Cosgrove. He's had a heart attack," I said.

"How terrible," Diana said with a gasp of surprise. "How did you hear? Will he recover?"

"It happened this afternoon, at the Hungerford police station. He came to read me the riot act about the investigation." I gave Diana an account of our meeting, and how we'd found Cosgrove on the floor. "He's at the doctor's now. Luckily the surgery is right across the street from the station. Doc said he'd keep him there overnight."

"How bad is it?" she asked.

"I don't know. He was able to speak, but he looked terrible. He had a message for you."

"What was it?" Diana asked, worry furrowing her brow. Her hands clasped the empty glass in front of her as if it might give off warmth.

"It was off the record," I said. "He seemed very concerned about you. He said they have their eye on you, and that you should stop talking about the extermination camps."

"Who are *they*?"

"Roger Allen, for one. Cosgrove said that your father may have inadvertently gotten you involved with people who do not want the truth about the camps to come out."

"I know I ruffled his feathers," Diana said. "He certainly didn't like being confronted by a woman, much less a woman concerned about Jews. But what did poor Charles mean when he said they had their eye on me?"

"I asked him if it was the same as him keeping an eye on me. 'Not like that at all' was his answer. He was truly worried for you Diana, and now I am too." I didn't think Allen and his ilk would cause Diana harm, not directly. What I wouldn't put past them was a dangerous assignment, dangerous enough to silence her indirectly.

"Billy, we have both been in danger before. Just yesterday someone tried to kill you. That is the price we pay for being who we are and the times we live in. I'm not going to be told to be quiet like a schoolgirl because it's inconvenient for some politician. People are being murdered, Billy, by the thousands. We can't pretend it isn't happening."

"I know," I said, leaning over and taking Diana's hand. "But you also can't pretend these aren't powerful men, and you've offended them, challenged the way they look at the world. You went into the lion's den, Diana. Don't be surprised at how sharp their claws are."

"Well, perhaps this isn't the best time to tell you, Billy, but Father has got an appointment with Anthony Eden, the Foreign Secretary. We are both dining with him tomorrow night in London." She gave a rueful laugh.

"They have their eyes on you, Diana. Be careful."

"Don't worry, Billy. Father has known Eden since they served in Parliament together. It is more of a social occasion, really. I think Father is hoping this will put an end to my campaign."

"I don't want you to end it, Diana. Just let the dust settle."

"After this dinner, I shall take the remainder of my leave and lounge about Seaton Manor, drinking tea and eating biscuits, all the time thinking of you."

"Okay. If I wrap all this up in time, I'll come visit."

"That's settled then," Diana said, shivering as she tried to rub warmth into her arms. "Let's go inside. This may be our last night together for a while."

I had no argument with that. As we ascended the stairs to our room, I thought about what I'd read in reports smuggled out of Poland, where the extermination camps were working overtime, incinerating bodies in ovens and belching greasy smoke out over the countryside. I tried to clear the gruesome images from my mind and enjoy the rest of the night with Diana. But some dust never settles.

CHAPTER TWENTY-FOUR

THERE WAS A heavy rain the next morning when I dropped Diana off at the train station in Newbury. The downpour didn't leave much time for long goodbyes or lingering kisses on the platform. I ran by her side with an umbrella in one hand and her suitcase in the other. I handed both to her as she boarded, the locomotive releasing a gasp of steam as if it were straining to depart and carry Diana away.

We kissed quickly, and Diana smiled at me, her eyes latching onto mine. Then she laughed as a stream of water cascaded off the roof of the railcar, spattering the top of my service cap. Passengers surged around us, in a hurry to get out of the rain. Civilians, soldiers, and sailors pushed Diana back as they boarded, and all we could manage was a half-hearted wave before she vanished and I retreated to the jeep. The rain on the canvas sounded like a drumroll, and I shook the water off my trench coat like a shaggy dog, glad that I had on my rubber-soled combat boots.

I sat, watching the empty street, blurry and grey through the rain-streaked windshield. Pretty close to how I felt about this investigation. Nothing made sense. I had no idea why anyone would have killed Stuart Neville. No idea why Cosgrove was preaching hands-off the Millers. No idea who had killed Margaret Hibberd. Not a clue what happened to Sophia Edwards or who killed Tom Eastman.

So what did I know? That there was something weird about the

Neville murder, and Cosgrove's instructions to lay off the Millers. And why was Neville such a cipher? All I knew for sure was that along the line I'd gotten close to something important, important enough to warrant a smack on the head and a midnight try at the dead man's float. No, check that. No one could have known I was headed to that part of the canal. I was sure I wasn't followed. So it was a chance encounter, an attack of opportunity. What was important was the suitcase. Someone, probably the same person I spooked without knowing it, had planted it there. Why? To throw suspicion on Neville, or possibly Miller. Or maybe to distance himself from the scene of the crime.

As far as Angry Smith went, all I knew was that he was innocent, the victim of a perfunctory CID investigation. The agents had gone straight to the easiest answer, and the fact that Angry had been seeing a white girl certainly hadn't helped move the wheels of justice in the right direction. I liked the notion of the killing being linked to Sam Eastman's past. It made sense, in a warped sort of way. Sam arrests a guy who is sent to prison or the lunatic asylum. Time passes and that guy gets out, and he decides to take his revenge—no, make that a relative, someone close to the imprisoned guy. Sam is long dead, so this avenger kills his son Tom, and deposits his body on the grave. A final insult. Nice and neat, except for how much time had passed since the elder Eastman had been on the force. I couldn't see an old man coming out of the joint and carting Tom Eastman's corpse through that cemetery. I'd heard revenge was a dish best served cold, but this revenge had been in the ice box a damned long time. I needed to learn more about Sam Eastman. But first, it was time to meet Inspector Payne at the Newbury Building Society and bang our heads against that wall for a while.

When I arrived at the building society at nine o'clock, it was raining even harder, with rolls of distant thunder echoing off the buildings. I dashed in and found Payne shaking off his umbrella in the foyer.

"Damned rain," he said, stamping the wet off his feet. "Any word on Major Cosgrove?"

"No," I said. "I sent Kaz over to see how he's doing. I'll drop by after we're done here."

"Too bad," he said. "Not the most likable chap, but it's a pity to finish up like that. Had an uncle who had a heart attack and lived. Doctor told him to stay in bed, and so the fool did. For the next three years."

"What happened then?" I asked.

"Had another heart attack and died. Nothing the doctors can do about it, so they tell you to rest. Not the way to go out of this life, with nothing but bedsores to show for your last days. But that's neither here nor there." He leaned in and spoke in a low voice. "Follow my lead. I won't reveal it was Miss Gardner who put us onto Neville's last appointments."

It was quiet in the society offices, the hard rain keeping customers inside their homes and shops. We entered Miss Gardner's office, where she served as gatekeeper to the exalted Michael Flowers. I tried to think of a way to tell her that her secret was safe, but it wasn't necessary. Miss Gardner wasn't there. Not stepped out for a moment, but gone.

Her desk was clean, no papers, pens, not even a paperclip. The shelf to the rear of the desk, where there had been a couple of pictures and knickknacks, was empty. Her typewriter was covered and the wastepaper basket was empty.

"Gentlemen," Flowers called out from within his office. "How can I help you?"

Payne raised his eyebrows at me, noting the desk, and we went in.

"Short of help today?" Payne said, in the friendly tone cops use when they want information the easy way.

"Oh, Miss Gardner, you mean? We're looking for a replacement now. It's been quite difficult without her. I never realized all the things she took care of. Very efficient."

"What happened to her?" I settled down into one of the leather chairs facing Flowers, like a charter member of the society making small talk.

"She left," Flowers said.

"Suddenly, I take it," Payne said. "Since you're just now advertising for her position."

"Well, yes, it was very sudden. I came into work the other morning and found a note from her, saying she was sorry but a family matter had come up and she had to leave. She left instructions about her final paycheck and that was all. A bit mysterious, don't you think?"

"Where is the check being sent?" I asked.

"To a bank in Glasgow. Scotland, can you believe that? I had no idea she was Scottish."

"Do you have the note?" Payne asked.

"No, I threw it out after I gave the payroll department the information. Why are you asking about Miss Gardner, anyway?"

"Did you recognize it as her handwriting?" Payne asked, ignoring Flowers's question.

"Of course I did. I saw her handwriting every day for almost eight years. I expect I would, don't you?"

"When did you find the note?" I asked.

"Yesterday morning. Now, really, tell me what this is all about."

"As regards Miss Gardner," Payne said, "purely professional curiosity. You can't tell a policeman about a sudden and strange departure without encouraging questions, can you?" Payne laughed and smiled, putting Flowers at ease, he hoped. "Habit, that's all. What we came to see you about are the last two appointments Stuart Neville kept with customers. In the course of our inquiries, we learned he visited Ernest Bone, the fellow who runs the sweet shop, and Stanley Fraser, the solicitor. We would like to see any records of those visits, notes or anything that may provide information about his activities."

"You must be retracing his steps thoroughly," Flowers said. "I don't recall giving you names of our members."

"That's what the police do, Mr. Flowers," I said. "Do you have many members like Stanley Fraser?"

"What do you mean?" Flowers asked. He pushed back from his desk, putting more space between us.

"Members with nicknames like 'Razor' and known criminal associates," Payne said.

"Yeah, funny that you should turn down a loan to a guy with a little sweet shop, but give one to a gangster's shyster," I said. Flowers looked uncomfortable.

"I'm sure Mr. Flowers doesn't know anything about money laundering," Payne said to me.

"Probably not. But in the States, we'd let the prosecutor decide that."

"Arrest the lot of them, and let the Crown Prosecutor sort it out? That might work," Payne said, rubbing his chin and staring at the ceiling. "Mr. Flowers would likely be let go, but we'd have to arrest him here and keep him several nights in jail. Not good for business, but that's not my concern, is it?"

"Gentlemen, gentlemen," Flowers said, pulling his chair closer to his desk and turning on the charm. "I assure you, neither I nor the Newbury know the details of Stanley Fraser's sources of income. We're not the Inland Revenue, after all. Perhaps you should speak to them."

"Perhaps," Inspector Payne said, leaning toward Flowers but leaving all charm behind, "you should show us what we ask for and save yourself a pile of trouble."

"I should really call Lord Mayhew first," Flowers said, with such a lack of conviction that I knew he was waiting to be talked out of it.

"I don't think there's reason enough to bother His Lordship," Payne said. "Him being a busy man and all. Show us the paperwork, and we'll be out of here in no time." He clapped his hands on his thighs, grinning at the both of us. Flowers did his best to return the smile, but it was hard on him. He drummed his fingers on the desk, right next to the telephone. Lord Mayhew, who apparently called the shots around here, could be on the line in a minute, and then Flowers could explain what we wanted. Or, he could give it to us and get us out the door before Mayhew would be done hollering over the phone.

"Very well, gentlemen," he said, standing and smoothing back his pomaded black hair. "I'll not let it be said the Newbury stood in the way of justice. Follow me." We did, down a hallway to a room with a frosted glass door. Inside was a table, with several stacks of files arranged on it. Two chairs, nothing else. "Take your time," he said, and left.

"He's had a sudden change of heart," Payne said, taking off his raincoat and draping it over a chair. "Probably means he had time to go through the file and remove anything remotely embarrassing to the sainted Newbury."

"Embarrassing or incriminating," I said.

"Perhaps, although I can't understand what they'd be incriminated in," Payne said. "I don't peg Flowers as the killer type."

"No, I don't either," I said, taking a seat and reaching for a pile of file folders. "But there was something odd in his speech."

"Odd how?"

"It was only yesterday morning that he found out Miss Gardner was gone, right? But today he said *saw* her handwriting every day. He used the past tense without losing a beat. I don't know about you, but I find people stumble over that with the recently dead or missing, until they're used to the idea."

"Right you are," Payne said. "But he could have that kind of mind, adjusting to a new idea quickly."

"So you don't want to arrest him?" I asked.

"It would be preferable to sorting through this lot, but he'd be out in no time. Maybe you could shoot him, Captain Boyle," Payne said, gesturing to the bulge under my jacket. "I know I'd be tempted if I went about armed."

"Maybe," I said, patting the .38 Police Special. "But then I'd have to write a report. Let's try this first."

It wasn't just Stanley Fraser and Ernest Bone. There were files on dozens of applicants. None of them lived very far away. Lots of renovations and additions, but not much new construction or large-scale work. German bombing raids had devastated London, the ports to our south, and any city with large-scale industry. Newbury had been hit once, earlier in the year, with casualties and a number of houses destroyed. But it was nothing like the wholesale destruction in some cities. That rebuilding took all the available labor and materials, leaving little for small towns and villages. People fixed things up, houses, clothes, and automobiles alike, making do until the war was over and the boys came home.

We read for over an hour, pursuing one of the most boring aspects of police work: reading bank reports. Some folks, like Razor Fraser, had blueprints and plans drawn up. Most made do with a written description. The level of detail varied. There were specific measurements, giving the dimensions of a new room, and others that were sketchy on the details. None of that seemed to matter. Neville's notes spoke about income, business plans, funds in the bank, and potential earnings more than the building plans themselves.

"Do you get the feeling there wasn't much to Neville's job?" I asked.

"He had a nose for numbers, that's plain to see," Payne said.

"He did, but anyone here could have put all this together. Why did he visit the applicants? There's hardly a comment about the actual plans or buildings."

"He had to assess future earnings potentials, didn't he? Can't do that from an office."

"Right," I said, leaning back in my chair. That was why he turned Ernest Bone down, and it seemed logical. Why put money into a business that sold a rationed product? Hedley's Sweet Shop probably sold out every month on a regular basis. Once the ration coupons were used up, there was no way to increase sales. He couldn't even sell to me for cash.

"Why did Fraser want to build?" I asked, tossing down the file I had been pretending to read.

"To create an image of himself as an upstanding and successful man. And to please his wife," Payne said.

"That makes perfect sense," I said. "And why did Bone want to build?"

"To prepare for the future, I'd say," Payne answered. "He had adequate space for current business, according to Neville's notes."

"Right. But who knows how long the war will last? It could be over by Christmas if the invasion comes soon enough. Why wouldn't Neville approve the loan? It wasn't for that much."

"Perhaps you should advance Mr. Bone the loan yourself," Payne said with a laugh. "Then you'd have all the sweets you'd want."

"It seems odd."

"Well, the war could be over by Christmas, just no telling which Christmas. If we're still at it in 1946 or so, the Newbury would never get their money back. Bone can't make enough under rationing. It's too bad the man chose the profession he did, but he's got all his eggs in one basket, now, doesn't he?"

"All his sweets, you mean. Let me see his file."

Payne grunted and shoved it over. He returned to poring over Razor Fraser's application, looking for anything even slightly illegal.

Bone's proposal was fairly simple. He wanted to remove a wall and extend the kitchen. Build a larger storage area for his products in his basement, and remodel the façade. He mentioned expanding after the war, shipping his sweets to France from the Channel ports. All smart ideas, it seemed. Neville had scribbled notations in the margins.

> *Rationing? How long?*
> *Excavation unnecessary.*
> *Foreign markets?*

I looked at Neville's typewritten report. He didn't mention any of that, simply saying that economic circumstances due to the war did not favor the loan, and that the business and Bone's own savings might not be sufficient to cover any potential loss. It made sense.

"Did Neville have any handwritten notes on Fraser's papers?" I asked.

"He did," Payne said. "A bit hard to read, but here they are." He handed me a notepad. Neville had a list of questions written down.

Mrs. Fraser?

Harrison Joinery—who owns?

Source of income?

Room necessary?

"He had the same suspicions you had," I said. "But he approved the loan."

"Aye, but that's his job. Fraser has the money, and that's all Flowers and his high and mighty boss Lord Mayhew care about," Payne said.

"But if Neville looked into the source of the income, he may have found out that Fraser didn't need the loan at all. Not for the building project, anyway. He needed the loan to launder his illegal money."

"So, you're saying Neville took his role a bit too seriously and played detective. Found out about Fraser's scheme and had to be silenced?"

"It's possible. Have you found out about Harrison Joinery yet?" I asked.

"No, I haven't had the time. This afternoon, though, I'll make it a point to find out who really owns the firm. If things lead back to Razor, we may want to press the matter with him. At the station."

That was all we came up with. Other than the lady who wanted to build a special room for her cats. All thirty of them. Neville's handwritten note simply said *crazy*. On our way out, Flowers gave us a cheery wave, leaving us with the idea we were missing something at the Newbury Building Society, something bigger than both of us.

CHAPTER TWENTY-FIVE

PAYNE WENT OFF to follow up on Harrison Joinery while I took a walk. It wasn't far, over the bridge to the other side of the canal, following Stuart Neville's walk home from work. Time for a pleasant chat, a social call. I knocked on the front door, which was answered by a guy I didn't recognize. He wore a sweater and had a pipe clenched between his teeth.

"Yes?"

"I'm Captain Boyle," I said. "Here to see George Miller."

"Of course," he said, opening the door wider. "I'm Nigel Morris. George told me about you and Inspector Payne."

"You're the other boarder, right?"

He shut the door behind me and settled back into his chair, where he'd been reading the newspaper. "Yes. The only one at the moment. Awful news about poor Stuart. I was away and heard only when I came back yesterday." He fiddled with his pipe, banging out the ashes and filling it again, in the way pipe smokers do when they can't sit still. "Any progress?"

"We're following up leads," I said. "What kind of work do you do?"

"Plumbing fixtures. I make the rounds of builders and plumbers, showing the firm's new wares. Even in wartime, people need new faucets, that sort of thing. I'm off for several days now, then I do the northern route." Morris was skinny, around fifty or so, with thinning hair and a neatly trimmed mustache. His eyes were a clear blue, and they searched my face as he answered. "Well, when are you going to ask me?"

"Ask you what?" I said.

"If I killed Stuart," he said. "Isn't that why you've come?"

"The Millers said you weren't here," I said. "Should I doubt their word?"

"Not at all, Captain. Having some fun with you, that's all. Never been questioned by the police before. I was actually quite curious."

"Okay," I said, ready to oblige. "How did you and Neville get along?"

"Friendly ships in the night, I'd say." Morris blew a stream of smoke toward the ceiling, his pipe bowl giving off a red glow. "We'd chat now and then, the occasional visit to the pub, but many days I was traveling and didn't even see him. Or I'd be so knackered I'd go to my room right after dinner."

"Anybody on unfriendly terms with him?" I asked.

"Not that I knew of, but then again we didn't share confidences."

"What did you talk about?"

"Oh, the war. Rationing, all you Yanks everywhere. The same small talk as most, I'd wager."

"Did you kill Stuart Neville?" I asked.

"No, sir, I did not. But I'd rest easier if you caught who did it. Don't like glancing over my shoulder at night. Not one bit." He puffed away, one eye squinted against the smoke, the other on me.

"Do you get along with the Millers? No trouble with them being German?"

"Get along fine with George and Carla," Morris said. "The way I see it, we had our own English fascists before the war, and a lot of good folk never objected to them. But along come two anti-Nazi refugees and all of a sudden there's trouble. Makes no sense."

"I'd have to agree. Any special troublemakers in town?"

"Some chap gave George a mouthful, but his son had just been killed. Understandable."

"Did Neville ever mention the missing girl?"

"The girl from the school? No, why do you ask?" He looked up from his pipe, surprised at the question.

"He told Eva Miller to be careful, that's all. I wondered if there was any connection."

"Well," Morris said, lowering his voice. "We both took a paternal interest in young Eva. Poor girl, through no fault of her own, is uprooted from her native land and brought here. Never mind it was for the best of reasons, it was still hard on her. The other children teased her, of course, and called her names."

"Do they still?"

"No, she adapted well. She already knew English, and lost her accent quickly. And walking out with that American sergeant helped as well."

"Anything else you can think of that might shed some light on the killing?" He wasn't much help but he seemed a bit of a gossip, and those types usually pick up tidbits of information.

"No. But it's interesting you asked about the missing girl. Sophia something, if I recall. Do you think there's a link to the murder?"

"All I have are questions, not answers. Thanks for your help, Mr. Morris," I said, taking my leave.

"Not at all," he said, looking at me through the smoky haze. "I take it no arrest is imminent? And the girl is still missing?"

"For now," I said, and left in search of George Miller. I didn't need any reminders of how badly the investigation was going. No one was in the kitchen, but I followed the sounds coming from upstairs, and found him in Stuart Neville's old room, stripping wallpaper.

"Captain Boyle, how are you?" He held a brush in one hand and a scraper in the other. Pieces of torn wallpaper littered the floor.

"Fine. Sorry to interrupt your work."

"No problem, Captain, I am glad for a break. I thought while I had no boarder I would fix up this room and get rid of this ugly wallpaper."

"You're quite the handyman," I said. "Did you ever ask Stuart Neville about a bank loan to help you renovate?"

"Oh no." He laughed. "Why pay someone for such simple work? And I enjoy it. When I finish here I will get back to our other room. Hopefully we will have three boarders again soon. Is there anything I can do for you?"

"No, I just wanted to drop by to say hello. I met Nigel Morris downstairs. You said he was gone the day Neville was killed, right?"

"Oh yes, he left a day or so before. He is often gone for days at a time, taking the train to his customers."

"Did he seem upset when you told him about Neville's death?"

"Yes, I suppose so. It is hard to tell with the English, yes? They are not the most emotional people. But then again, neither are we Germans." He cast his eyes down to the floor, as if embarrassed to mention his nationality out loud. "And how are you, Captain, after your attack by the canal?"

"I'm fine," I said. "Thanks for asking. Anything else unusual going on in the neighborhood?"

"The police questioned me, of course. It was to be expected. Other than that, nothing. Eva is at school and Carla is at the market. You could ask them, but aside from Mr. Morris returning, it has been quiet."

"No need to bother them," I said. "I was curious about something though. You might know a friend of mine. Charles Cosgrove, a British major. I think he has something to do with refugees."

"No, the name is not familiar."

"Does anyone from the government come around and visit you? To see how you're getting on?" *To check up on you*, I meant. It seemed strange that Miller enjoyed the protection of MI5 but claimed not to know Cosgrove. Following instructions, or telling the truth?

"We get a letter from the Foreign Office every few months. We have to stay in touch and let them know if we move, but we have not seen anyone since we came here. They gave us a small stipend to live on for a while, to help get us settled. But no, the name Cosgrove means nothing to me."

"No matter, just thought I'd take a chance. I'll let you get back to work."

I left, passing Morris in the hallway, making for his room. I glanced in the third bedroom, where Miller had been working before. There was new molding cut and painted, ready to be nailed up. The guy was a real do-it-yourselfer.

He was also telling the truth about not knowing Cosgrove. There had been no quick widening of the eyes, no attempt at recovery. He was either a great liar or had never heard the name. I was no closer to understanding Cosgrove's interest in this murder, or solving it, for that matter.

I strolled to the Hog's Head pub for lunch and was greeted by Jack Monk.

"Been for a swim, I hear," he said.

"No worse for wear," I said, then ordered a pint and a cheese sandwich. "I bet you hear a lot, Jack. Anything new on Stuart Neville?"

"What, are you tired of folks asking you that question? Want to hear it out of your own mouth, do you?" Monk laughed as he wiped down the bar.

"Yeah, I thought maybe I'd get some answers that way."

"Well, not from me, more's the pity," Monk said as he pulled my pint. "Everyone's talking about the lass you all pulled from the canal, and wondering if Sophia will be next. Me, I'd say she's dead or gone far away."

"Why do you say that?"

"As with any kid her age, there's a chance she ran off on her own. She may have had her own reasons, not that we'd understand them, mind you. And there's also a fair chance she was taken by some fiend and then killed and buried, after he had his way with her. When you think about it, those are the two most likely ways for it to go." He set down the pint, foam cascading down the glass.

"Likely," I agreed. But likely didn't rule out everything else. "Here's another question for you, Jack. Neville's feet were wet. How would that happen on the canal path?"

"He could have stepped into one of the boats moored along the canal," Monk said, rubbing the stubble on his chin. "We had a heavy rain not long before he was killed, so some might be soaked. Or it could have been from the wake of a boat on the canal washing over. The Kennet River flows into the canal near here, and all that rain would have raised the water level. Take your choice." He shrugged and moved on, taking other lunchtime orders and gabbing with the regulars.

I knew about water in the boats; I'd gotten my own feet wet that way. But I hadn't known about the water levels. I wondered what boat might be out on the canal that late at night. And if it had been water from its wake that soaked Neville's shoes and socks, could the boatman have seen him? And his assailant? I tried to work the angles as I waited for my sandwich, wondering how much could be seen from a moving craft.

"Jack," I said when he put the plate down. "Are there many boats out on the canal between ten o'clock at night and two in the morning?"

"Ah, you mean when Neville was killed? It would be a rare thing. No lights with the blackout, so if you didn't know the canal like the back of your hand it would be dangerous."

"Rare, but not impossible for someone who knows the canal?"

"Aye. There's one man who comes to mind. Blackie Crane. He runs a steamboat up to Reading, selling coal. Brown coal, that is, what they call lignite. It's mined out by Pewsey. Not very good stuff, but he manages to sell a boatload between there and Reading every week."

"But can a coal barge go fast enough to make a wake?"

"Fully loaded? No. But on the return trip from Reading, heading west? Once Blackie gets up a head of steam, there's no stopping him. And it's not like a flat-bottomed barge. His is a riverboat, long and narrow, and he keeps it in prime shape. Signals with his steam whistle when he comes through. Reminds folks of the old days, when steam on the water was the way of the world. Around here, leastways."

"Was he on the river the night Neville was killed?"

"I'm sure he was. I saw him that morning, when he delivered my coal. Said he had one more stop near Reading and then would make the run back. That would put him here late, after closing time."

"When's the last time you saw him?"

"Yesterday, on his way up to Reading. Ought to be headed back this way in a day or so."

"Thanks, Jack. Keep this conversation between us, all right?" I wanted to be careful not to tip my hand about a possible witness.

"Whatever you say. Mum's the word."

I bit into the sandwich, wondering if there was such a thing as too careful. Big Mike had assisted in the investigation, but then was ordered back to London. Why? Miss Gardner pointed me to Bone and Fraser, then suddenly vanished. Why? I didn't want Blackie Crane to slip through my fingers as well. I was sure I could trust Payne, but no reason to broadcast the fact we might have a witness to anyone else.

The beer was sharp and bitter.

CHAPTER TWENTY-SIX

NEXT STOP WAS the Chilton Foliat Jump School, to continue the snooping around that had been cut short by Tree's fight. I passed the barns, outbuildings, and Quonset huts, and parked on the gravel drive in front of the main house. It was a solid three-story affair with elegant columns, seated on top of a hill with a commanding view of the countryside. In the distance I saw a platoon double-timing it along a road. Closer to the house, GIs were climbing a short wooden tower, then jumping onto a pile of hay, bending their knees and rolling, while an instructor barked at them to hurry up. A corporal threw me a salute on his way into the headquarters.

"Where can I find your commanding officer?" I asked as I returned the salute.

"Captain Sobel is inspecting the service company, sir. Take the path around the back."

I followed the path, marked by the white-painted stones the army loves so much. At the rear of the house, near a row of hedges that might once have bordered an elegant garden, lines of GIs stood four rows deep. I could make out a tall officer walking the ranks, a sergeant trailing him with a clipboard. I edged to the side of the group, waiting for the inspection to be over. Hearing the sound of shovels, I glanced to the rear and saw Charlie, the big fellow from the fight, and one other GI hacking away at the ground. They were both waist-deep in what looked like wide graves. Charlie saw me and looked quickly at the officer, who I figured for Sobel. Charlie looked scared. His eyes met mine and he shook his head, then bent back to his digging.

"Out of uniform," Sobel yelled at one man, who seemed dressed exactly like the others. "Confined to quarters." His voice was squeaky and grating at the same time. He walked with his hands clenched behind his back, swaggering between the rows of GIs as his sergeant followed along, writing on his clipboard. Sobel was tall and dark-haired. He had a face that reminded me of a half-moon: a high forehead, long nose, and receding chin.

"What's this? Dirty ears?" I was amazed to see him actually bend a man's ears back like a mother checking a little boy. "You want to get dirty, soldier? Then start digging." The GI dropped out and headed to the rear, picking up a shovel and a yardstick. He began measuring an area the same size as the hole Charlie was digging, and started in on it. There was a ready supply of shovels, and as I looked past Charlie, I could see the ground had been dug up and tamped down repeatedly. The inspection went on, Sobel continuing to find fault with most of the enlisted men, doling out punishments ranging from KP duty to loss of a weekend pass. Finally the company was dismissed, and I never saw men scatter so fast.

"Captain Sobel?" I said as I approached him.

"Yes, Captain, what can I do for you?" Sobel came close, his arms akimbo. He looked down at me, using his height to dominate the conversation.

"Captain Boyle," I said, holding out my hand. He didn't take the offered shake. "I'm investigating the murder of a local police officer. One of our men was arrested, and now there's some doubt as to his guilt."

"Our men? What unit are you from, Captain?"

"SHAEF. General Eisenhower is interested in seeing that justice is done." It was then that Sobel took notice of my shoulder patch with the Supreme Headquarters flaming sword badge, but if he was impressed he kept it to himself.

"Is anyone under my command a suspect?" Sobel asked.

"No, I just have a few questions—"

"Sergeant Evans," Sobel said, turning away from me and addressing his non-com, "assist this officer and then report to me once he is off the base."

"Yes, sir!" Evans said as Sobel walked away.

"Your commanding officer is a strange one, Sergeant," I said, watching Sobel's back.

"Nothing strange about doing a job right, Captain. How can I help you?" Evans had a southern drawl and the look of a long-haul non-com.

"First tell me about the holes. Why are those men digging them?"

"Captain Sobel trains the men to follow orders, and he does a damn good job. If they don't, they get extra duty digging a hole six by six by six."

"Six feet deep?" I couldn't believe my ears.

"Yes sir. And then they fill it in again. The captain says it's good training for digging in when we're in combat."

"That GI has to dig a hole that size for having dirty ears?"

"Captain Sobel likes his men to look sharp. If they don't, they reflect poorly on the unit. That man will probably wash his ears first thing every day after this."

"What about this man?" I said, pointing to Charlie.

"Out of uniform," Evans said. "He was missing a button. Now tell me what I can do for you, Captain. We're running a jump school here and we have thirty new field artillery observers to train."

I wasn't taking to Sergeant Evans any more than I had to Captain Sobel, but I bit my tongue and gave him the basics about the murder, the graveyard, and the track going through the jump school to the back of the cemetery. I needed a helpful non-com, not an uncooperative one. We walked away from the hole diggers and I pointed out the track I'd mentioned.

"What I need to know is if anyone here noticed a person who wasn't supposed to be on this post. A local, or maybe a colored GI."

"That's who they got for this, right?" Evans asked. "One of those tank destroyer guys."

"That's who CID arrested," I said. "They may have been wrong."

"Well, anyone can drive up here," Evans said. "Or walk in. We're not a secure area, although a colored boy coming through here would cause some comment. Not the usual thing, if you know what I mean. That path leads past the barns and the older civilian buildings we don't use. Too broken down. You could ask Crowley, he might remember something."

"Is he the Englishman?"

"Yeah, local caretaker. Came with the place, far as I know. I think the family who owns the property left him here to look after the horses. He's always around, so maybe he can help. If he's not in the barn check the mess tent. He doesn't have a place to cook, so we let him eat our chow. I'll take you there."

"I can find it, Sergeant," I said, eager to get rid of the disagreeable Evans.

"I'll take you," he said. "Captain Sobel doesn't like people wandering around."

"You said you weren't a secure area," I said, walking alongside Evans. "What's the concern?"

"We may not be top secret, but we are responsible for packing the parachutes for the entire division. That, plus the personnel we train, is enough to keep any CO on top of who comes through here."

"But you're saying no one noticed a Negro from a tank destroyer unit carrying a dead body?"

"I didn't, but I wasn't on the lookout for one neither." We came to the barn, and Evans pushed the wide doors open. It smelled of fresh hay and stale horse. Three stalls on each side, two of them empty. "Crowley takes the horses out for exercise every afternoon. Down that track you're so interested in."

"Where does he stay?" I asked.

"He's got a room off the barn, through that door," Evans said, pointing at the far end. "Not a real sociable guy, but he does his job. I doubt he's there this time of day but we can check." We walked the length of the barn, horses neighing after us, eager for attention and fresh air. Evans knocked, then opened the door. The room was as long as the barn, but only about ten feet wide. A coal stove stood in the corner next to a worn armchair. A narrow bed was shoved against the wall, blankets with US ARMY stenciled on them tossed over it. A small table littered with tools, a rickety desk, an old bureau, and shelves with a few tins of food completed the scene. It looked like temporary lodgings for a farmhand, not a caretaker's home. The only personal touch was a framed photograph on the wall by the bed. An unsmiling young man with dark eyes stared out of the frame, dressed in a stiff collar and black jacket, maybe from the turn of the century, judging by the hairstyle and cravat.

"What are you doing in my room?" We both jumped as Crowley spoke, standing not five feet behind us.

"Looking for you," Evans said. "This officer wants to ask you some questions."

"How long does it take you to figure out I ain't in there?" Crowley asked. "No place to hide, is there? May not be much, but it's my place, Yanks or not. You don't own the bleedin' place, not yet anyway." Crowley was stoop-shouldered, his body beaten down from manual labor. He had several days' worth of stubble on his face and his worn and dirty clothes looked like they hadn't been washed since the last time he was caught out in the rain. If Sobel ever inspected him, he'd be digging a hole to China.

"Sorry," I said. "I'm Captain Boyle and I need a few minutes of your time."

"I'm called Angus Crowley, and you can ask what you want, but I've got to get the horses in. Feels like rain, it does." We went outside, where Crowley had tethered the two horses. Evans retreated for a smoke, and I glanced at the sky. No sign of clouds.

"Angus, do you recall the murder that took place a few weeks ago?"

"You mean the constable?"

"Yes, Tom Eastman. He was found in the churchyard."

"So I heard," Crowley said, leading the first horse into the barn and brushing his coat.

"The track that runs by this barn leads to the cemetery. I was wondering if you saw anything the night of the murder."

"Can't recall the night, exact like. Be hard to see that darkie at night, wouldn't it?" He laughed at his joke, glancing at me to see if I'd join in.

"So you don't recall seeing anyone around who wasn't supposed to be here?"

"Not since that other colored fellow, the one you helped out of the fight," Crowley said, chuckling again to himself.

"No, I meant the night of the murder."

"What? Are you asking if I saw some bloke carrying Sam Eastman over his shoulder, plain as day? I'd have said something about that, wouldn't I?"

"It was Tom Eastman, not his father," I said. "Who said he was carried?"

"Right you are, Captain. Tom, the son. I knew the father well, just got the names mixed. And of course someone carried him into the cemetery. Not a place you'd go with a man who wants to kill you."

"So you didn't see anything suspicious, anything out of place."

"This is a busy place, with all you Yanks coming and going. But I can't say as I saw anything different than any other day. Mind you, that big colored fellow could have come through and not been noticed."

"One of the men said you did your best to start that fight yesterday. You don't like Negroes, is that it?"

"What's it to you if I do or don't? I got a right, don't I? I don't mind watching a good fistfight, no law against that. Bad enough we have to put up with you Yanks underfoot and scaring the horses. I wish you'd all go away, I do."

"Many of us feel the same way, Mr. Crowley. Thanks for your time." Crowley was a strange one, all right. Mean and surly, and intelligent even if prejudiced against Americans and Negroes. So would he have a problem with Angry Smith? A big enough problem to stage a frame-up?

"Not a lot of help," I said to Evans as he escorted me back to my jeep.

"Sometimes I think he's not all there," Evans said. "Talks to himself, always muttering about the horses. You done here, sir?"

"Done, Sergeant." I started up the jeep and drove down the hill, watching Evans go inside the big house. As I rounded the corner I stopped by the hedges bordering what had been the garden area. I checked to be sure Evans or Sobel weren't around, and trotted over to Charlie, now chest-deep in his hole. He was good with a shovel.

"Charlie," I said, squatting down between piles of dirt. "Is this a normal punishment for a missing button?"

"No, he went easy on me," Charlie said. Then he smiled. "Not much normal around here, Captain. They say Captain Sobel is good at what he does, but I can't make much sense of it. This is plain silly. Say, how's Tree?"

"He was okay when I last saw him. I just talked to Angus Crowley. He doesn't seem to like Negroes very much."

"I don't think he likes anybody much," Charlie said. "I know I don't like him."

"Why?"

"It seems like he talks to himself, which is strange enough," Charlie said, setting his shovel in the dirt and resting his hands on it. "But he's talking to someone else. Someone who isn't there. That's different, isn't it?"

"Yeah, it is," I said, checking again to see if anyone was coming. "You know who?"

"Naw," Charlie said. "Don't care either, I steer clear of him."

"Okay, Charlie, you take it easy. Don't lose any more buttons."

"You know what's strange, Captain?" He leaned forward, his voice conspiratorial.

"What?"

"I like digging holes. It's interesting to see what's down here. Layers and different colors, you know?"

"You sound like a detective, Charlie." He beamed.

CHAPTER TWENTY-SEVEN

I WANTED TO catch up with Kaz and find out how Cosgrove was doing, but there was one stop I needed to make first. I wasn't looking forward to it, however, it had to be done. I stopped at the only pub in the village of Chilton Foliat, the Wheatsheaf, and asked where Malcolm and Rosemary Adams lived. The gent I spoke to pointed up a side road and told me fourth house on the right, and wasn't it such a sad thing. I didn't know if he was talking about Malcolm's shot-up legs, how he used Rosemary as a punching bag, her brother being murdered, or her taking up with a Negro back when she thought Malcolm was dead. I would have been happy to order a pint and pursue the topic at leisure, but I was short on that last commodity.

The dirt road was rutted and followed a drainage ditch that ran from the fields above. Cows grazed in the fenced green pastures opposite a row of ancient houses. The Adams place was whitewashed stone with a thatched roof, set back from the road and surrounded by a kitchen garden and chicken coops. I knocked on the door and a young woman answered.

"Mrs. Adams?" I asked, not sure if I was talking to her or not. She was young, maybe just twenty.

"She's in the kitchen. Are you from the army?" I said I was, which was pretty clear from my uniform, but I didn't crack wise over it. I had the feeling I was missing something. "Come in, then."

Rosemary Adams sat in the kitchen, clutching a cup of tea. There was an immediate sense of wrongness in the room, a calamity I did not yet understand. She hardly looked at me as her friend guided me in front of her.

"Mrs. Adams," I said. "I'm Captain Boyle. Billy Boyle. I'd like to ask you some questions, if this isn't a bad time." Although it was obvious it was.

"Questions?" she asked, as if struggling to understand the concept.

"Aren't you here about the damages?" asked the other woman.

"I'm sorry, I'm confused," I admitted. "What damages?"

"For Malcolm, her husband," the young woman said. "Who was killed last night by one of your trucks."

"I don't know anything about that," I said, caught flat-footed by the news. "What happened?"

"Dorothy," Rosemary said to the young woman. "You can go home now. I'll be fine."

"You sure?" Rosemary nodded and Dorothy shrugged as she left.

"Please sit down, Captain Boyle," Rosemary Adams said. "Would you like some tea?"

"That would be great," I said. Back in Southie, it was more likely to be a shot and a beer at a time like this, but it was basically the same. A soothing ritual, the familiar in the midst of the horrible.

"Malcolm went to the pub last night. Like most nights," she said, putting the kettle on. "No, to be honest, like he did every night. Took his bicycle, since it hurt to walk that far. He'd taken a nasty fall once, but he still insisted, even though his legs pained him even with the bicycle. His wounds were terrible, just terrible."

"I heard about that," I said, filling in the sudden silence while she wept.

"Stayed until closing, they told me, and then left to come home. He fell again, and couldn't get up, from what the driver said. One of yours, a big truck. They had the headlamps taped over, for the blackout, you know. Only a slit of light showing, and one bulb was out, so they could hardly see. Ran poor Malcolm over in the road." The teacup rattled in her hand as she set it in a saucer. "But that's not why you're here, is it? I've heard your name, Captain Boyle. You're looking into the murder, aren't you?" She set down the tea in front of me. I took it with milk, but said no to the sugar.

"Yes, I am here about the murder. That's why I came by today. I'm sorry to intrude."

"I'm glad you've come," Rosemary said, sitting across from me. She wore a faded cotton dress, and her dark hair was pulled back and tied with a bright ribbon. Her eyes were red with tears, and traces of freckles from the sun stood out on her cheeks. She was a good-looking woman, worn hard around the edges by work and tragedy. "Do you have any news about Abraham?"

"No," I said, barely recalling Angry's given name. "But I don't think he's guilty, if that helps."

"Nothing helps," Rosemary said, as she slowly rubbed her hands. "First I thought Malcolm was dead, and God help me, I was glad of it. Even before I met Abraham, I was glad when I heard. Malcolm was a charmer when he and I were young, but there was a meanness in him that I didn't see then. It was a relief when he went off to war and an even greater relief when he didn't come home. Isn't that a terrible thing to say?"

"He used to beat you, I heard. That would make me glad to be rid of him."

"He would apologize when it was over. I hated that more. So when he was reported killed, I pretended to be sad, to join in with the other grieving widows. But when I was alone, I would dance. In this very kitchen, I would swirl around the table in absolute joy. And then I met Abraham. I know what they call him, but he was never that way with me. Never angry. Gentle and kind, he was. I must shock you terribly, Captain Boyle."

"I'm not shocked easily, Mrs. Adams. Whites and Negroes don't mix back home, so I do find it strange to think about. We have a lot of history in the way."

"But you're a friend of Tree's, aren't you? You'll help us?"

"Yes," I said. She relaxed, leaning back into her chair.

"I was happy for the first time in my life," she said. "And then I got the letter, saying that Malcolm had been found, wounded. He'd lost his identity disc and was unconscious for days. He'd had several surgeries on his legs. The hospital never contacted his unit, so they thought he was dead, left in the jungle to rot."

"What was he like when he came home?"

"You know, finding out about Abraham gave him something to live for. It gave him something to hate. It was all he had." She stood up, and I wondered if she would dance around the table after I left. "He hit me once, and fell over. Gave me a black eye, but never tried again. Not because he was kind or ashamed, but because he was embarrassed to have lost his balance in front of me."

"Do you think Malcolm or Abraham had anything to do with your brother's death?"

"No. Tom was a good brother, and he was trying to protect me. I know he said some awful things to Abraham, but it was to drive him away. I truly have no idea why anyone would want to hurt him. Or leave him on Dad's grave, for that matter."

"And Abraham?"

"He felt terrible about leaving me with Malcolm, and I knew Malcolm would have liked nothing more than to goad Abraham into striking him so he could press charges. That's why I lied about that night when Malcolm didn't come home. I told the police Abraham was with me; I thought he and Malcolm had fought, and that I was protecting him. As it turned out, all I was doing was placing Abraham close to Tom's body."

"Is there any reason you can think of that Tom was killed? Did he or your father have any enemies?"

"Tom never had the chance for any really big cases, like Dad did. Not enough time for that. Poor Tom," she said, and a sob burst from her lips. "All he ever wanted to be was a policeman. He followed Dad's investigations, badgered him something awful when we were kids. Dad would come home and want to put his feet up by the fire and read the evening newspaper, but Tom would pepper him with questions about what he did that day." She smiled at the memory as she wiped her tears.

"PC Cook is looking into his old cases," I said. "Your father's, I mean. To see if there's any possible connection. Perhaps someone released after a long prison sentence."

"Would you like to see the scrapbook?" Rosemary asked.

"What scrapbook?"

"The one Tom kept when we were kids. Newspaper articles and the like. The odd bit of police paperwork Dad left lying about. I still have it."

"May I borrow it? I'll have it back in a day or so." It was a long shot, but there might be some clue about a long-forgotten feud.

Rosemary left the room and returned with a thick scrapbook, browned paper showing at the edges.

"If it will help, keep it as long as you need," she said. I stood, and took the book from her. "Promise me you'll do your best."

"I will," I said. "Whatever it takes."

She walked me to the door and opened it, stepping out into the fresh air. "Good," she said. "I've already lost so much of my life. I want some of it back. Bring Abraham to me, Captain Boyle."

I left her standing there, eyes closed, letting the sunlight wash over her face. I hoped one day there would be real dancing in the house, two happy people arm in arm. It wasn't the easiest thing for me to imagine, a black hand on a woman's white skin. But I had a harder time imagining lingering sadness and a lifetime of loss, played out in a hardscrabble yard full of carrots, cabbages, and clucking chickens.

CHAPTER TWENTY-EIGHT

I SPOTTED KAZ and Tree sitting on the bench outside the Three Crowns, the same one where we had sat the day we met up. It seemed like a decade ago. Until then, my thoughts of Tree had been all about Boston, motorcycles, and scuffles with the law. Not to mention being upset that we'd parted on harsh terms. It seemed childish now. The war was waiting for us, and I had drowned and missing girls on my mind, along with the image of Neville crumpled at the bottom of his cellar stairs. Angry Smith sat in a prison cell, charged with murder. We had grown up, Tree and I, and the troubles of the world had come along for the ride.

"Tree, how are you feeling?" I asked as I approached. A bandage covered the cut above his eye, which was swollen about half shut, an improvement on yesterday.

"About as good as I look," Tree said, attempting a grin, which was hampered by his healing split lip. "Lieutenant Binghamton gave me the day off to rest up. Came in for a pint and Kaz kept me company."

"Tree has been telling me stories of what it was like in the southern states, where he trained," Kaz said.

"Where were you based down South?" I asked Tree.

"First it was Camp Claiborne, Louisiana. That place was bad for everyone, worse for Negroes. Then Fort Hood, Texas, which was a little better. Later Fort Benning, in Georgia, where a Negro soldier committed suicide. Funny thing was, his hands were tied behind his back. Didn't know a man could hang himself that way."

"I had heard of the lynchings, but I truly did not understand how bad things are for Negroes," Kaz said.

"Can't be good for white people either," Tree said. "It's a lot of work to carry around that much hate, and pass it on to the young ones. There's going to be an accounting one day, in this life or the next. Has to be."

"I'm going to focus on staying in this life for as long as possible," I said, squeezing in next to Kaz and stretching my legs out. "I just came from Chilton Foliat, to finish looking the place over. The CO there is a piece of work."

"Sobel, right?" Tree said. "I heard he's real strict. Like crazy strict."

"Yeah. Charlie was digging a hole six feet wide, deep, and long. For missing a button."

"That's crazy all right," Tree said, nodding.

"Apparently he thinks it will help train the men to dig foxholes in combat. I can't fault him on that logic. There's times when you need to get under cover, quick. Real quick."

"That time might come sooner rather than later," Tree said. "Rumor is that after the maneuvers, we're shipping out. Maybe Italy, maybe France. They say the invasion could be any day now."

"They say everything, Tree. Don't put too much score in scuttlebutt. In case it happens, though, and you ship out before we meet again, I'm sure you'll do fine. That's a good outfit you're in." The way the army worked, Tree could be gone by the morning, and it was important to tell him what I felt.

"Thanks, Billy. And you'll keep working on getting Angry out of jail?"

"I will. I talked to that caretaker today, Angus Crowley. Said he never saw anyone pass by that track leading to the cemetery. But he wasn't exactly the friendly type. I doubt he'd tell the truth unless it served his purposes."

"He looked plain mean to me," Tree said. "You find anything else?"

"Not there. But I stopped in to see Rosemary Adams. Her husband, Malcolm, was killed last night. Hit by a truck."

"Damn," Tree said. "Not that I can say I cared much for him, but Rosemary's had her share of trouble."

"It is unfortunate," Kaz said. "But from what I have heard of Malcolm Adams, his wife may be well rid of him. They say he was never the kindest man in the village, and that his wounds only made him worse."

"Plenty of men have been wounded; maimed and worse. They all don't take it out on their wives," I said. "Still, it's hard to be glad a man has died on a dark road, after surviving a Japanese machine gun." We didn't speak for a while. Maybe we were giving Malcolm some respect for his service, no matter what his personal shortcomings. Or maybe we were all embarrassed by how little he'd be missed. I studied my boots for a while.

"They took Major Cosgrove away," Kaz said finally.

"Who did?"

"Two rather large and very quiet men. In an ambulance, with a nurse to attend to him. They arrived as I did, spoke with the doctor, had him sign something, then put Cosgrove on a stretcher."

"But you saw him? He was alive?"

"Yes, he was. The men knew who I was by sight, and told me I could say goodbye. Cosgrove was pale, and his voice was weak, but he did say to remind you of what he said about being careful."

"Yeah, he did." What I didn't explain was that he meant Diana. "Did they say where they were taking him?"

"I asked, but they said that information was classified. When they loaded him into the ambulance, the nurse gave him an injection and the men hooked him up to an oxygen tank. While they were busy with that, I walked around to the front of the vehicle. One of the doors was open, and I got a quick look inside. A road map was folded open, and I noticed a familiar town. Saint Albans."

"What's there?" Tree asked.

"Saint Albans Rest Home," I said. "We've been there before on a case. It's a high-security hospital for people with too many secrets. High-ranking officers, commandos, spies, you name it. If you know too much and mumble in your sleep, Saint Albans is the place for you."

"What the hell is the big secret?" Tree said. "It can't be Angry or the missing girl, that stuff is all out in the open."

"And Neville seems to be a non-entity," Kaz said.

"So the question is, what was so important that Cosgrove was afraid of spilling the beans while under a sedative?"

"But who would even hear him? The doctor?"

"That's a good question, Kaz. Cosgrove risked his health, if not his life, to not be sedated. What could he have said that would have been so dangerous?"

"Something not even a respected doctor could hear," Tree offered. "Maybe some military secret."

"There's air bases, paratroopers, all sorts of military units around here that are going to be involved in the invasion," I said. "Even the Six-Seventeenth Tank Destroyer Battalion. Maybe your unit is the big secret, Tree."

"Hell, we tell everyone we see that the Nazis better watch out for us once we hit France," Tree said. "We're the worst-kept secret in England."

"Perhaps it is something as simple as the date of the invasion, or the exact location," Kaz said.

"That assumes he knows either of those," I said. "They're tightly held secrets, the biggest secrets of the war. Cosgrove might know bits and pieces of the plan, but I doubt he has the whole picture." The wind freshened and I stuffed my hands in my pockets against the chill.

"What do you know, Billy?" Tree asked me.

"Barely the time of day. They keep us pretty much in the dark. Need to know, ya know?"

"Yeah, I've heard that one plenty of times," Tree said, getting up from the bench and stretching his limbs. "I hope they put us up front in the invasion. I've been hearing that colored folk can't fight too damned long. I need to set that straight for my father's sake. The army's forgotten about how he and the others fought in France last time around. I aim to make sure they don't forget again after this war."

"Be sure to keep your head down," I said. "This isn't a fistfight you're headed for."

"All right, Billy," Tree said with an easy smile. "I know you're looking out for me. We got maneuvers coming up in a couple of days. We're Red Army, attacking Blue Army. You both oughta come out and watch. You can see us in action."

"I'd be proud to," I said, and Kaz agreed. Tree left with a bounce in his step, and I knew it would mean a lot to him if I had a front seat as he put his TD through its paces. Hell, it would mean a lot to me as well.

"Well, that at least gives us something to do," Kaz said. "We can watch the maneuvers and wonder where the killer is."

"Killers," I corrected him. "Maybe three of them. We have at least three victims: Stuart Neville, Tom Eastman, Margaret Hibberd, and perhaps Sophia Edwards. Why not three killers?"

"But you don't really think so," Kaz said.

"No. I have the nagging feeling there's a connection between Neville and Margaret. Maybe he knew her killer, or rather discovered who it was." I told Kaz about the canal man Blackie Crane, and how there was a chance he had seen something that night as he passed by the Miller residence.

"It will be good to pursue that lead," Kaz said. "But I think you're straining to find a connection. The fact that Neville told the Miller girl to be careful doesn't mean anything. It's the kind of thing any man might say to a young girl."

"It's just that Neville left no other trace of himself. It's like he wanted not to be noticed," I said. "Anything unusual stands out, and his mentioning that was out of character, which makes me think he had a specific reason for saying it."

"That's a fine straw you're grasping at, Billy. What is our next step?"

"Let's see if Constable Cook has come up with anything. He

was going to check further with Broadmoor and ask Doctor Brisbane if any villagers were committed there, voluntarily or otherwise."

"You think it might be a pleasure man we're after?"

"Might be. The whole thing is crazy, after all. Let's go. After we talk with Cook we'll get dinner. I'm hungry."

"Billy," Kaz said as we walked to our vehicles. "When are we going to hear what finally happened to you and Tree, in Boston?"

"When this thing is wrapped up, and Diana is back. She wouldn't want to miss it."

"Neither do I," Kaz said.

CHAPTER TWENTY-NINE

"EVENING, GENTLEMEN," CONSTABLE Cook said as we entered his office. He was puffing away on his pipe, his desk a mass of files and paperwork. "I see your Major Cosgrove was taken away by ambulance this morning. How is he?"

"We don't know," I said. "The people who came for him are a tight-lipped bunch."

"I could tell as much from Doc Brisbane," Cook said, blowing smoke toward the ceiling. "He's a good one for a story or two, but all he told me was that it was best to forget all about the incident. That's what he called it, the incident. Sounded like he was reading from a script." Cook raised his eyebrows, inviting us to tell him more.

"Major Cosgrove is involved with security matters," I said. "Probably normal procedure."

"Ah, well, perhaps. Not that there was much normal about our major. I suppose you're more interested in what I've found out about Broadmoor. The doc told me he knew of no one who had been committed there for purely medical reasons, so I reviewed the file of criminals from our jurisdiction who ended up serving their sentences there."

"Anything new?" I asked as he shuffled through his papers.

"Not much. Turns out the chap Sam Eastman arrested back in nineteen thirty-five died two years ago in Broadmoor."

"The arrest Sam was directly involved in?"

"Yes. Previously Sam helped arrest a vagrant who had assaulted a farmer. But Sam wasn't even listed on the arrest warrant, so I doubt that fellow even knew his name."

"The nineteen thirty-five arrest was different?" Kaz asked.

"Oh, yes. Quite. It was a local stonemason, Alan Wycks. He had a job at the Chilton Foliat manor house, back before the government took it over. The owner, Lawrence Brackmann, accused Wycks of stealing three shirts. Laundry drying on the line, I think it was. Sam found the shirts all right, hidden away at Wycks's cottage. He arrested him, and then it turned out that Wycks couldn't stand being in an enclosed space. Started banging his head against the walls, right here in our own lockup. Had to send him up to Berkshire Constabulary headquarters in Reading, where they had facilities for that sort of thing."

"What happened then?"

"Went stark raving mad in no time, I heard. You could ask Inspector Payne more about it. He picked up the case when Wycks got transferred to Reading. He was a detective sergeant at the time, if I recall. It was a solid case, and from what I heard Wycks was incoherent before the judge. Got himself sentenced to Broadmoor, at the King's pleasure."

"And that's where he died?" I asked.

"Yes. Just two years ago next month."

"Did he have any family?" Kaz asked.

"His wife had run off with their son the year before. After Wycks went mad, we worried he might have harmed them, but we never found a trace. Searched his garden for signs of recent digging, but found nothing. My thought was she began seeing signs that he was losing his mind and left him when she could."

"Sounds like a dead end," I said.

"It was worth looking into," Cook said. "Police work is the same all over, isn't it? Looking into people's lives, discovering more than you want to know, often for naught."

"It would help if you could forget what you didn't need to know," I said.

"There's a truth," Cook said. "You've heard about poor Malcolm, have you?"

"Yes, we were just discussing his death," Kaz said. "No one seems to really mourn his passing."

"No, I'd say not," Cook said, giving it some consideration. "No family hereabouts, and he never spared a kind word when a harsh one would do. Still, it's a pity for a wounded soldier to end up dead like that after going through so much. Not to mention Rosemary. She was always a sweet lass, full of life. She must have put that all away to make a life with Malcolm."

"What do you think she will do?" Kaz asked.

"Wait for you to exonerate Private Smith," Cook said. "I hadn't seen her so happy in years, back when Malcolm was thought dead and Smith was free."

"It doesn't bother you, Constable? A white woman and a Negro together?" I couldn't help but think what a scandal that would be in Boston, or anywhere else in the States for that matter.

"We're just country folk here, Captain. It takes us time to get used to anything new," Cook said, unbuttoning his uniform collar. "But that's all it is. Something new. Why, we might even look kindly upon an Irishman settling down among us." He smiled as he worked on his pipe, knocking out ashes and cleaning the stem.

"Point taken," I said. "And I do hope we can get Angry out of prison. Rosemary gave me the scrapbook she and Tom kept when they were kids, said there were pictures and clippings from her father's career. I'll look through that tonight and see if anything jumps out at me."

"I remember that book," Cook said. "When Tom was a pup he and his sister would race through here, and pinch anything not nailed down if they took a fancy to it for their scrapbook. There might be something in there, you never know."

"What was Tom like as a boy?" I asked, wondering if there was any connection we'd overlooked.

"Sam was a stern father, and Tom sought to stretch the limits now and then. Nothing serious, just the mischief of youth. Stealing

apples from an orchard on a summer's night, that sort of thing."
Cook's face softened at the memory.

"Do you have children, Constable?"

"I did," he said. "A fine wife and a handsome boy. She died three
years ago. The saving grace was she didn't have to hear of Teddy
being killed in Sicily. Teddy and Tom were a right pair, only a few
months between them. Played rugby together when they weren't
pinching apples. Nothing's the same anymore, is it?"

What could I do but agree? I nodded, and let the silence settle
for a moment before I asked, "Do you know a canal man by the name
of Blackie Crane?"

"Sure, everyone knows Blackie. Quite a character, he is."

"There's a slight chance he saw something on his last run
through here. If you see him, we'd like have a chat. Tell Inspector
Payne, but keep it quiet otherwise, okay?"

"Lots of secrets these days, Captain, aren't there?"

"Only until we figure them out, Constable."

We invited Cook to have dinner with us, but he declined, saying
he needed to walk his beat around Hungerford one more time. His
cot was made up in the corner of his office, and I think I knew why
he often spent nights here. There were no ghosts in the local nick,
only emptiness, or the occasional criminal, drunk, or rowdy GI. It
was better company.

Kaz and I drove back to the Prince of Wales Inn in Kintbury,
ready for our dinner, but we were stopped halfway there by a column
of GIs marching quick-step, coming up from the Kennet River and
crossing our path on the Bath Road. Their boots were muddy and
sweat streamed down their faces, even in the cool late-afternoon air.
There were hundreds of them, a battalion perhaps, on a forced march
to toughen them up for the invasion. The 101st Airborne, evidenced
by their screaming eagle shoulder patches. Some were probably
named Teddy.

The invasion of France—well, probably France—was on everyone's mind. Mostly a pent-up anxiety, like a bow pulled taut while
your hand quivers as you hold it, ready to release. I didn't know if I'd

be there on the big day, but I could feel myself pulled along by the current of nerves, fear and desire to get it over with. Right now, watching these men cross the road—these cherished boys, these Teddies, all I could think about was the heartache to come for their mothers, fathers, wives, and friends. It was good that we fought our wars so far from home, not so much because it saved our towns and cities from destruction, but because it put distance and time between death and mourning. How many folks back in the States on that day of invasion would wake up, pour a cup of coffee, and read the morning paper without knowing their son or husband was already dead?

The last of them crossed the road and I was glad to see them go.

CHAPTER THIRTY

AS WE PARKED next to the Prince of Wales Inn, I did a double-take. Sitting at a bench by the door were two men: Michael Flowers and Nigel Morris. Neville's boss and his fellow boarder. I pointed them out to Kaz and gave him the lowdown on each.

"It is a small town," Kaz said. "Perhaps Neville introduced them. Sometimes coincidences are just that." I doubted it.

Morris caught sight of me and gave Flowers a nudge. Flowers went inside as Morris nodded to someone at our backs. I heard car doors slam, and knew this was no coincidence. I turned sideways to keep my eye on Morris and check who was coming up on us. I pulled Kaz with me as I glanced around for an exit. No go. Coming through the gate from the road were two British MPs, big guys. Another filled the doorway to the inn. We were boxed in. My hand moved to my shoulder holster and the reassuring grip of the .38 Police Special. But I didn't draw. This was damned odd, but no ambush, not with a full complement of MPs surrounding the joint.

"Lieutenant Kazimierz?" said an MP sergeant as he took Kaz by the arm, not waiting for an answer. "Come with us, please. We have orders for you to return to London immediately."

"Whose orders?" Kaz asked.

"Not at liberty to say, sir," the polite MP said, not relaxing his grip. His hand took up most of Kaz's upper arm.

"Let go of me," Kaz said, digging in his heels. "I must pack my belongings if I am to go to London." Kaz and I looked at each other, neither of us understanding what was happening. Kaz looked stunned as the MP held his arm.

"No need, Lieutenant," the MP said as he pulled Kaz toward a waiting staff car. "Your suitcase is in the automobile. We are leaving immediately." With an MP on either arm, all Kaz could do was shrug helplessly as they led him away.

"You've got someone waiting inside, Captain Boyle," Morris said. His eyes flicked up and down the street, then settled on the automobile carrying Kaz back to London as it drove away. His hands were stuffed into his pockets, and I could make out the bulge of a revolver on his right. "Don't worry, lad, I won't shoot. A friendly visit inside, that's all."

"Who are you?" I asked. Not a traveling salesman, that was for sure.

"Whoever I need to be," Morris answered. "Now go inside and see Mr. Flowers. He'll direct you." I went to pass the MP, who was standing at parade rest like he was guarding a military headquarters. He put out his arm and asked for my weapon. Reluctantly, I handed it over and went inside. Flowers stood in the hallway, his hands stuffed in his pockets, showing the same telltale bulge. His face was stern, a far cry from the visage of the friendly banker. He nodded toward a small room off the dining area and bar, and I entered.

Inside, seated next to a coal fire burning low in the fireplace, was the man who had made Major Cosgrove sweat, sipping a glass of sherry.

"Ah, Captain Boyle," he said, in a quiet voice drenched in authority. "Please sit down."

"Not that I have a choice, with your goons outside the door," I said, sitting across from him. He had a strong chin, thin lips curved into a slight smile, and lively eyes that drilled into mine. He was well dressed in civvies, worn but with a faintly academic air, like a distracted professor who didn't quite pay attention while knotting his tie. He was trim, in good shape for a fellow with strands of grey in his close-cropped hair.

"Goons. I rather like that. Yes, I do have goons, Captain. They come in handy from time to time."

"Who are you, and why am I here?"

"We're in no rush, Captain Boyle. Let us take a moment and get to know each other."

"Names are a big help. See, you know mine, and isn't that useful for carrying on a conversation?"

"Not here," he said, waving his hand. "Not that names wouldn't be useful, but the walls have ears, as they say, and I keep my own secrets."

"Okay," I said, figuring my next move. "So we're talking about secrets. Whose?"

"His Majesty's, of course. The deepest and darkest secrets of the war, perhaps."

"There are a lot of dark secrets in this war, Professor," I said.

"Professor? Why do you say that? I am simply a government bureaucrat."

"You have the look, that's all. And most bureaucrats have a paunch by your age. You have a healthy look that doesn't come from sitting in a government office year-round. So a professor at some swank college, where maybe you played rugby when you were a student."

"Oxford, and mainly cricket," he said. "Charles said you were a smart one, but hard to control. Seems like he was right on both counts."

"Major Cosgrove? How is he?"

"Greatly weakened, I'm afraid. But resting comfortably."

"At Saint Albans," I said. I didn't have to reveal I knew where Cosgrove had been taken, courtesy of Kaz and his snooping, but I needed to get an edge on this guy. His eyes widened a fraction before he resumed his pose of bemusement.

"Smart and resourceful too," he said. "Reading your file, I am not surprised at your capabilities, Captain Boyle. But there is a streak of antagonism to authority, especially British authority, which troubles me."

"What's it to you?" I asked, getting impatient with this exchange. And then I realized, it *was* something big to him. Whatever he was leading up to, it was because he needed me. Otherwise, I'd be headed back to London between two oversized MPs right now. I didn't know what I'd done wrong, but I'd bet it was outweighed by what he needed me for.

"That's quite to the point," he said. He finished his sherry and set the glass down, then sat quietly, his fingers steepled in a thoughtful pose. Maybe for a minute, but it seemed like an hour. He was deciding on me, and I let him take his time. "Let's take a walk, Captain," he finally said, and I followed him out of the room. Flowers handed him his overcoat, and we took the path along the canal, Morris up front, Flowers to the rear, both out of earshot.

"Are they your bodyguards?" I asked. He ignored the question.

"My name is John Masterman," he said, glancing around to be sure there was no one nearby. The sun was right at the horizon and the wind was picking up, a chill breeze sliding along the canal. Anyone with any sense was indoors, waiting for the dark to descend. "What I am about to tell you is covered by the Official Secrets Act. You are aware of that document?"

"Sure. They had me read that my first day in England."

"It gives us extraordinary powers to imprison you for revealing anything I say. I am certain you do not need to be reminded, given your exemplary record, but I do so to stress the seriousness of what I am about to reveal."

"Understood, Professor Masterman," I said, wondering what kind of rabbit hole I had fallen into.

"Even given your powers of observation, Captain Boyle, I would be surprised if you have heard of our organization. The Twenty Committee." He spoke in a hushed voice, his head bent toward the ground. He wasn't a man who liked giving up his secrets.

"No, I haven't. Is Major Cosgrove a member?"

"He acts as a liaison with MI5," Masterman said. "He was in charge of this issue, until his attack. It was he who suggested your involvement."

"The murder of Stuart Neville, you mean." The presence of Flowers and Morris led to that obvious but strange conclusion.

"Yes. We wanted the killing looked into, and we wanted more resources than the local constabulary offered. But we couldn't reveal our interest in the case." Masterman turned up his collar and checked to see if Flowers was still close behind. The sky in that direction was streaked with sunset reds and yellows. Ahead it was the dark blue of coming night.

"So I was chosen, with the cover story of being brought in because an American sergeant was in the house."

"Correct," Masterman said. "It was a good plan, the only drawback being you couldn't be told the reason behind all the secrecy."

"You mean the reason for the hands-off policy with George Miller. Is that what you were talking to Cosgrove about at Bushy Park? It looked like you were laying down the law to him."

"Ah, the ever-observant Captain Boyle," Masterman said. "Yes, I was telling the major that you had to be controlled. I was worried about what steps you might take, and with good reason, evidently."

"Such as having Miller brought in for questioning?"

"That was the first thing. I sent Major Cosgrove here to make sure that did not happen again. I assume he spoke with you before he suffered the attack?"

"He did. He wasn't happy. Are you going to tell me why?"

"Bear with me, Captain. I don't have many opportunities these days for a stroll beside the water. It was the second breach that brought me here, by the way."

"What breach?"

"You asked George Miller if he knew Major Cosgrove. You dressed it up quite innocently, but it told me that you were still determined to go your own way. I wanted you off the case, but Charles convinced me you could be trusted, if you knew the truth. He said it was a common American failing, this need to understand why an order was being given."

"That sounds like him," I said, wondering if Masterman would actually ever get around to spilling the beans. We walked a few paces in silence as I imagined him working up to telling the actual truth.

"The reason we are called the Twenty Committee," he said, "is because the name was first written in roman numerals. Two Xs. For double cross."

"Okay," I said. "You're in the double-crossing business."

"The greatest double cross of the war," he said, "perhaps of all time. In a nutshell, Captain, we control all German spies who have been captured since the war began. Most we have turned against the Germans, using them to radio false information back to their masters."

"Most?" I asked.

"You might be surprised at how many of these spies were quick to take us up on our offer. Cooperation and life. The few who didn't were executed. It worked out well, after all, giving their spymasters in Berlin evidence that some of their number were captured, which they would expect."

"But what about the ones that you didn't catch?"

"That's just the thing, Captain," Masterman said, stopping to look me straight in the eyes. "We are fairly certain we have bagged them all. Each and every spy the Germans sent into Britain. Quite extraordinary, actually. We have Adolf's best spies working for us, sending their own reports back by Morse code, as dictated by the Twenty Committee."

"So what do you need me for?" I was still confused. This cloak-and-dagger stuff seemed right up Cosgrove's alley, but I didn't see how I fit in. We took a few steps along the canal, and Masterman took a deep breath.

"There is one thing we live in absolute fear of, Captain Boyle. That we could miss one enemy agent. If a German spy were to land on our shores now, as we prepare for the invasion, he could easily report back facts that do not coincide with the stories we have been feeding the enemy. Do you understand?"

"Sure," I said, seeing the problem. "You've created a web of lies, and all that the Germans would need would be one loose spy to crack it all wide open."

"Exactly," Masterman said. "One of the dangers of counter-espionage is that if the enemy determines that the information they've been given is false, they can draw certain conclusions about what is then actually true."

"You're giving them phony intelligence about the invasion site," I said. "Or the date. And if they find out that it's not the real McCoy—"

"Then they could deduce the real location and time, or close to it. A disaster."

"But what do you need me for? I don't get it."

"Really, Captain Boyle?" Masterman turned around and began walking back to the inn. "A man of your skills? Certainly you can work it out." He grinned as if coaching a backward pupil. I thought about it. Neville is killed. Cosgrove brings me in and tells me hands off George Miller. Cosgrove works with the Twenty Committee, which has corralled all the German agents who have landed in England. The Millers are German refugees.

"Jeez, of course!" I said as the pieces fell into place. "The Millers are spies. Real ones, I bet. You let them set up shop in case a new agent makes contact with them. And Neville was one of your agents, like Flowers and Morris."

"Quite right. We discovered the truth about the Millers from two captured Germans. We let them set up their house, even helped them with resettlement funds. And then we surrounded them with watchers. You've seen how George Miller keeps one room always under renovation? That way he has a spot open if an agent makes contact."

"So the Millers are not gathering information themselves?"

"No. Their role is to provide a safe house for arriving agents. They are under orders not to engage in suspicious activities them-selves. So we let them be, the perfect trap for any German spy who manages to slip through. The next few months are critical, Captain. We need them in place, our unsuspecting spiders, to draw in the flies. We need to be sure there is no threat to them. We need to know who killed Neville, and why."

"And if it was George Miller who killed him?" I wondered how big a mistake I'd made to mention Cosgrove's name to George. I didn't want to be taken off the case and sent to Broadmoor, so I didn't mention it.

"I don't believe it was. There was no indication that Miller had stumbled onto the fact Neville was anything but a quiet boarder. And Neville was a professional; he never would have let an argument or a petty squabble get out of hand. Our biggest worry is that it was a German agent, but we've no actual proof."

"But if it was Miller, you'd let him get away with it," I said.

"For now, of course. There are too many lives at stake. Justice will find the Millers for their crimes, of that you can be certain. When we are done with them."

"The wife and children as well?"

"Oh yes, Frau Miller is a full partner in this enterprise. We aren't sure about the children. The son Walter is kept busy on board a supply transport in the Mediterranean, and he hasn't made any moves. Eva is perhaps too young to have been recruited. We think she is likely innocent."

We were close to the inn, and I laid my hand on Masterman's arm to stop him. "You know about the missing girls?"

"Yes, I've heard."

"Neville had warned Eva to be careful. Now that makes more sense, given that he was a professional agent, trained to watch for anything unusual. I think he saw something that raised his suspicions, and told Eva to watch out. Maybe he was about to look into it further. Did he report anything to you?"

"Not about the girl, no. His reports went through Flowers, and he would have informed me of anything concrete. As you should do. Call this number if you have anything to report." He handed me a card with nothing but a London telephone number—the same one Cosgrove had given us.

"What happened to Miss Gardner?" I asked, remembering her sudden departure.

"She has been transferred elsewhere. She was told not to provide you with any information, and when she did we needed to remove her. Just as we had your sergeant and the baron taken off the case. We must be sure that you, and you alone, are working on this, since you know the stakes involved. There can be no missteps."

"What if it was George Miller who killed the girl we found in the canal?"

"As I said, justice will find him eventually. But for now, Captain Boyle, remember that many young girls are being killed in this war. We bomb cities at night and incinerate them all across Germany. French towns where there are military targets are bombed every day and many little French girls are blown apart. We are engaged in a ruthless, titanic struggle that consumes lives on a massive scale. One cannot worry about a single life without going mad. Find Neville's killer, Captain Boyle, and all this will end one day."

"You forgot the little girls in the extermination camps," I said. I watched his face, saw the quick eye movement again, and then the curtain closed.

"No, I haven't forgotten them," he said, and turned in the direction of the inn. "There are those who see them as a political problem that might be best solved for us by the Nazis. Your Miss Seaton has taken it upon herself to convince one of those men otherwise."

"You are well informed," I said, following Masterman.

"I soak up what information I can," he said. "I discard most, manipulate the rest, and send it on its way to create discord among our enemies. But this matter bothers me, I must say, and I wish Miss Seaton well." He sighed, and his pace slackened.

"But you doubt she'll succeed," I said.

"I know she won't," Masterman said. "She will receive orders in the morning to report to an SOE training camp. Exile in remote Scotland for a troublesome agent."

"Are you sure?" I asked. Masterman only smiled. "Can you do anything?" I was relieved at exile. Better than a parachute drop into occupied France.

"Not my department, Captain. It's the Foreign Office that decides these things, and it has been decided at the highest levels that too many Jews making their way to Palestine after the war will not be good for relations with the Arabs. Fellows like Victor Cavendish-Bentinck and Roger Allen have convinced Anthony Eden not to raise the war cry over the camps. They claim it would harm the war effort if the British public thought we were fighting for the Jews of Europe."

"Eden is who Diana is dining with tonight," I said. Eden was head of the Foreign Office, and Diana had told me her father had arranged the meeting.

"Yes, and she will be welcomed cordially, as a gesture of friendship to Lord Seaton. But the die is cast. Eden will listen, offer wine and promises to look into the matter, and promptly forget about it. I'm sorry to bring you such poor news, Captain. I wish it were otherwise. Now, get some rest and find this killer." Masterman extended his hand, and we shook. He walked away, Flowers and Morris on either side.

I was alone on the path, the faintest of lights lingering on the western horizon. To the east, the heavens were pitch black.

CHAPTER THIRTY-ONE

I ATE, HARDLY noticing what was on my plate. My pint glass was empty and I didn't remember drinking a drop of the ale. People and conversation flowed around me but I didn't hear a thing.

I had been told one of the greatest secrets of the war, and it was too enormous to even think about. Now I understood all of Cosgrove's cautions and warnings, and the worry he must have felt, with me nosing around and asking all the wrong questions. Tomorrow I'd visit Inspector Payne and get back on track, asking the right questions, the ones that didn't implicate the Millers.

And if Masterman's secret wasn't enough, I had Diana to worry about. From what he told me, her punishment for speaking out was benign, at least. But Diana wouldn't see it that way. She wasn't one to sit things out in a training camp. Would her superiors dress it up as an honor, or would she be told why she was being sent away? The former, I figured. The kind of Brits behind this weren't big on the honest truth when an artful lie would do.

One secret protected lives, and perhaps hastened the day when the Allies would liberate the extermination camps. The other kept the true face of the killings in those camps quiet. The news was full of Nazi atrocities, which was good for morale and the war effort. But now that I thought about it, the papers and the BBC would routinely mention the suffering of Poles, Danes, Czechs, and others under the ruthless German occupation, but never Jews as a group, even as they were being herded into gas chambers in ever-increasing numbers.

Politics. The British Empire keeping their own occupied peoples from revolt. There were millions of Arabs for them to govern, and damn few Jews in the Mideast. Why rock the boat? Especially with the Suez Canal and vast oil fields to worry about. I knew I'd take Masterman's secret to the grave, but Roger Allen's machinations were not worth the honor of secrecy.

I got another pint, took it back to my seat and wondered how Diana was doing at her dinner with Anthony Eden of the Foreign Office. Perhaps they were having soup, discussing mass murder intently, Eden nodding, seeming to agree with everything Diana said as he savored the hot broth. It didn't bear thinking, so I took a drink, remembering to taste it this time, and began to leaf through the scrapbook Rosemary Adams had given me. I'd barely remembered to take it from the jeep after my encounter with Masterman. The first few pages were from early in Sam Eastman's career: old, yellowed newspaper clippings and the occasional memo on police stationery. A childish hand soon grew into a graceful cursive, Rosemary's penmanship a marked improvement on that of her brother Tom, who was more given to underlines and exclamation points.

"May I join you, Billy?" I nearly jumped as Kaz dropped his bag on the floor and set his whiskey down, a grin of obvious pleasure lighting his face.

"What are you doing here?" I asked, surprised and happy as he slid in next to me.

"Ignoring a ridiculous order," he said, downing a healthy slug of whiskey. "Those MPs were foolish enough to think that simply putting me on a train in Newbury would stop me from getting off at the next station and taking the return train here. It serves them right."

"Glad you're back, Kaz," I said, raising my glass to him. "But remember it's not just those MPs you have to worry about. It's MI5. Cosgrove's bosses obviously want this handled their way."

"Which MI5 boss gave you that message?" Kaz asked.

"The guy we saw at Bushy Park," I said. "He laid down the law, pretty much the same story Cosgrove gave us. My guess is he wasn't sure if the major had given us the message before he had his attack."

"The fact that he came to be sure the message was delivered is interesting," Kaz said. "Did he have a name?"

"Yeah. Mr. Smith." We laughed, and I thought how easy it was to lie to a friend who trusted you.

"Did he say anything else?"

I filled Kaz in on what Masterman had told me about Diana, and my own observations about how the BBC never mentioned Jews specifically as victims of the Nazis. I figured the closer I stayed to the truth, the easier the lie would be. And Diana had nothing to do with the Millers, so there was really no reason to keep it from him.

"He told you all this for what reason?" Kaz said, suspicion edging his voice.

"I think people who keep secrets for a living like revealing those that they can," I said, steering damn close to my own truth. "Maybe Cosgrove told him about Diana. Maybe he's sympathetic to the truth about the camps. Who knows?"

"What you said about the BBC is certainly true. When I was with the Polish government-in-exile we obtained a classified government report. The BBC and the Foreign Office determined that saving the lives of Eastern European Jews would not be seen as a desirable war aim by the British public. Their public stance was to refer to Poles exclusively, not Polish Jews, for instance. The Foreign Office was wary of Jews exaggerating the extent of atrocities and using public opinion for their own ends."

"Like not being murdered by the hundred thousands," I said.

"Yes, but remember, in the First World War, there were fantastic stories of German atrocities in Belgium, which turned out to be fictitious. The British government was seen as untrustworthy, and their credibility suffered. Perhaps they now are too careful with stories of atrocities."

"Kaz, we don't even have the right words for what's happening in those camps. Atrocities happen when all self-control is lost, bloodlust is up, and men are crazed with violence. These camps are planned, industrial murder. You know that, you've seen the same eye witness reports I have. I don't think these Foreign Office diplomats understand what's really happening."

"Or worse yet, they do," Kaz said. That silenced both of us. Kaz toyed with his empty glass, then left to get another. I watched him melt into the crowd at the bar, mostly civilians among a smattering of uniforms. British Army, mostly, with a few American airmen and GIs for good measure. There were even two Negro soldiers throwing darts with the locals. One of the locals was Ernest Bone, from the sweet shop. He gave me a nod of greeting from across the room.

Kintbury was a small village, off the beaten track, too undistinguished to be allocated to any unit, black or white, for leave. I wondered if there'd be trouble, but everyone was going about their own business. Maybe these were guys who liked the quiet of a rural village, and the kind who left well enough alone. Whatever the reason, I appreciated the low murmur of voices, the agreeable laughter, and the sharp tang of the ale. Sometimes, you have to take what satisfaction you can get.

"What's all this?" Kaz asked when he returned, looking at the scrapbook.

"A scrapbook Rosemary and Tom Eastman put together when they were kids," I explained. "I thought there might be a clue as to anyone who had a grudge against their father, Sam. A long shot, at best."

"They must have been proud of their father," Kaz said. He took the book and began leafing through it from the beginning. "Did you ever keep a scrapbook of your father's cases?"

"No, it never occurred to me," I said. "He always told me not to believe what I read in the newspapers anyway. He said there was so much that couldn't be said and so much said wrong that the only things he trusted were the sports page and the funnies."

"That reminds me, Billy, when will you tell the end of your story about Tree?"

"That'll have to wait—hey, stop there," I said. Kaz had gone about halfway through and a headline jumped out at me. "This is about Alan Wycks, the local stonemason who was sent to Broadmoor after his arrest."

"Right," Kaz said. "The fellow Constable Cook told us about. The story here is much as he said. Wife and child gone missing, the theft of the shirts, his incarceration and subsequent sentencing at Broadmoor at the pleasure of the King. The tone of the story is one of pity, a once-prosperous villager and his descent into madness. Constable Samuel Eastman is mentioned as the arresting officer."

Kaz turned the page, reading to the end of the article. It contained a picture of Wycks, taken in court. His hair was disheveled, his collarless shirt grey and worn. What stood out were his eyes. Dark and deep, they stared into the camera from a sunken, lined face, aged by harsh sun, stone shards, and a crazed mind. I had seen those eyes before. On a younger face, a picture taken before hard times had come his way.

"I've seen this man," I said.

"Where?" Kaz asked, leaning in for a closer look.

"Angus Crowley's father. When I was in his room I saw a picture of a much younger man, but they're the same person, I'm sure of it. It was the only personal touch in the place."

"The eyes," Kaz noted. "They are quite intense."

"They were the same in the other photograph. It was a formal portrait, and he was probably around twenty or a little older. But the eyes held a hint of what was to come. Crowley has dark eyes too, set deep in his face, like this guy."

"And he lives in the barn on the track leading to the Chilton Foliat cemetery," Kaz said. "That alone makes him suspect. He must have returned to the village some time ago and taken on the job of caretaker. Perhaps his mother changed her name, or gave him her maiden name to distance them from the memory of his father. Or the shame of his insanity."

"He was just a kid when the mother disappeared. Fourteen years old, the paper said. Crowley seems older but he looks like he may have knocked about a bit before settling down here. A hard life working outdoors can age a man."

"He obviously wasn't called up for service," Kaz said. "Perhaps he did inherit his father's mental instability. But do you think he killed Tom Eastman after all these years? Why now?"

"That's a good question, Kaz. Maybe we can track down the owners of the Chilton Foliat manor house. They must have checked references when they hired Crowley. The Hundred-and-First moved into this area less than six months ago. It ought to be easy enough to find the owners."

"Why not put MI5 to work on it?" Kaz asked. "I will call the number Cosgrove gave us and tell them you need the information as part of your investigation. With their resources, we should know by morning."

"You're supposed to be on a train to London," I said. "Wait a while and then call. Tell them it's a loose end you're wrapping up and have them leave a message with Constable Cook when they have the skinny."

"I will use those exact words, Billy," Kaz grinned. He had a thing for American slang, the more obscure the better.

At that moment, a loud voice sounded off from the entrance to the bar. "What are them damned niggers doin' here?" A GI with corporal's stripes and a red neck stood in front of a pack of his pals, his jaw jutting forward in a show of aggression.

"You shut your mouth, soldier," the barkeep said, a middle-aged fellow with salt-and-pepper hair. "I'll have none of that talk in my establishment. Either turn about and walk out, or order your drinks and be peaceable. There's enough war waiting for you across the Channel, I can promise you that." He pulled his sleeve up over his elbow, and thrust his forearm toward the new arrivals. A twisted cord of scar tissue ran all along his arm. "Got that at the Somme, and counted myself lucky. So spend your time here in good cheer, gentlemen. There's pain and fight enough waiting in France."

The room was silent. The barkeep leaned forward, resting his ruined arm on the bar, watching the corporal, who looked stunned by the response. One of his pals whispered to him, and he shook him off roughly before he stalked out, muttering about niggers and Englishmen. His friends shuffled their feet, unsure of their welcome.

"What'll you have, boys?" boomed the barkeep, and that was that. They went up to the bar with sheepish grins, shillings jingling in their palms. Tension eased out of the air, and the hum of conversation and laughter returned. But it was only a fight postponed. This was neutral territory and the bar was manned by a guy who knew the ropes. It wasn't anything like that in the world outside.

"Not the best representative of the American type," a voice said from my side. It was Ernest Bone, from the sweet shop. I introduced him to Kaz, who agreed with his assessment of the departed corporal.

"You don't harbor any ill feelings toward the colored troops, Mr. Bone?" I asked.

"None at all. Those fellows behave themselves, and would never enter an establishment as that lout did. Pity your army doesn't treat them better."

"They got a combat unit not far down the road from your shop," I said. "Tank Destroyers."

"Indeed. They've got maneuvers laid on for tomorrow. The whole village is buzzing about it. Most want to watch and the rest are worried about the fields and fences being torn up. I'd like to chat, gentlemen," Bone said, draining his pint. "But I must excuse myself. It'll be an early morning tomorrow, getting the cart ready and all. It's a good chance to sell to the onlookers if the weather's decent. Good night." He touched his cap in the old-fashioned manner and we wished him luck. I secretly wished for some myself.

"He was one of Neville's customers, wasn't he?" Kaz asked.

"The one who was turned down for the loan. He's starting the renovations himself."

"Optimistic chap," Kaz said. "Rationing must make it difficult to sell delicacies in a small town like this."

"He's near the girls' school at Avington. People always want candy, don't they?"

"I prefer my sweets from the dessert cart at the Dorchester," Kaz said. "But it will be some time before we dine there again. Now let me find a telephone and make that call."

I stayed and had another pint. I watched the darts match, which the locals won. Their Negro opponents were from Greenham Common air base, and four of the biggest fellows in the bar walked them out to their vehicle in case of trouble. It wasn't in the cards tonight, but I wondered how much longer before this powder keg blew. I found myself hoping for the invasion to come around soon, just so we'd have a common enemy close at hand.

CHAPTER THIRTY-TWO

THE MORNING WAS crisp and bright, sunlight lifting the heavy dew off grasses and leaves, filling the air with the scents of springtime, a ripe dampness that carried the promise of life. It was invasion weather too, the season for returning young life to the soil, a morbid twist for our times. Kaz had made his telephone call to MI5 about Crowley the night before, and we stopped at the police station to see if a message had been left. The place was locked up tight. The street was deserted and quiet, except for the sound of a bicycle on cobblestones. I wondered where Diana was right now. On a train to Scotland? Or sitting in an SOE office in London, receiving an official reprimand.

"Everyone's over at the Common," Doc Brisbane said, slowing his bicycle to a halt. "It's the maneuvers. The army said people could watch from the roadside. I'd guess there's a crowd by now, and the constables will have their hands full. Thought it best to be there myself in case I'm needed. Plus I wouldn't mind seeing those Tank Destroyers tearing about."

"We may as well go watch ourselves," Kaz said as the doctor pedaled off.

"Sure," I said, starting the jeep. "We can swing by the Avington girls' school. Ever since Laurianne Ross told us about Margaret Hibberd showing up there, I've been curious about where she disappeared to."

"Right," Kaz said. "Diana told us none of the girls observed her bicycling away out the main drive."

"I'd like to know if there's another route away from the school, and where it leads. Maybe we'll bump into Constable Cook. We can ask him about Alan Wycks and let him know we're expecting a call."

"I also telephoned Big Mike last night," Kaz said as we headed out of Hungerford and into the countryside toward the Common, a large stretch of open land between Kintbury and Hungerford. "I asked him to try and find Diana. He said he would get Colonel Harding to ask some questions."

"Thanks, Kaz. But I doubt MI5 will admit to any Yank where they've sent her. But it's worth a shot." We had to take a few detours where roads were closed for the maneuvers, due to the large number of units involved in addition to the 617th Tank Destroyer Battalion. We finally got on the road to the Avington School, and as we came to the drive, Miss Ross was leading her charges out.

"We're going to watch the maneuvers, Captain," she said, the girls letting loose with a chorus of excited giggles. "Do you need to speak with me?"

"No, I just wanted to check around the back of the school, if that's all right. Seems like everyone is headed to watch the maneuvers today."

"It's like a parade," one of the girls said. "We hope it will be awfully loud!"

"Go ahead, Captain Boyle, look around all you wish," Laurianne said, busily organizing the girls into a single file. Walkers and bicyclists were flowing into the roadway, like people headed to a parade or a county fair.

"Guess there's not much entertainment in the wartime countryside," I said to Kaz, as we drove slowly up the drive to the school.

"Perhaps the locals like the Negro soldiers and want to see them in action. I am sure many of them have been told by your countrymen that Negroes are incapable of fighting. Seeing Tree and his unit driving their armored vehicles will make quite a statement."

"Could be," I said, still trying to get used to the idea of white people cheering on well-armed Negroes. I parked the jeep on the side of the school and we walked around back. There was a neatly laid-out vegetable garden, taking up much of what had once been a lawn. Chickens squawked in their coops and rabbits stared at us blankly from within the confines of their hutches.

"Here," Kaz said. A well-worn path led between rows of gooseberry bushes, flowers beginning to show between thorns. The path continued through a meadow, and along a fence marking a boundary between plowed fields.

"A shortcut to Kintbury," I said. From a slight rise, we could see the path descending through the fields, to the low-lying ground along the river. It petered out as it met with houses and shops along the main road. "It probably ends at High Street, down there." I pointed to a bright yellow and red sign. I couldn't make it out, but I remembered there had been a sign like that over Hedley's Sweet Shop.

"Should we continue?" Kaz asked.

"No. We can check it from the High Street end later. I doubt there will be any clues left after all this time."

"It is a well-used route," Kaz said. "The girls must use it as well as others from the village. It probably cuts through the school property. There are many such right-of-way paths in these English towns." He was right about that. The grass was trampled and the ground was hard-packed. Margaret could have met up with any number of people on this route. This was another thing to ask Inspector Payne or Constable Cook. The local police would certainly know about this pathway and have checked it out. We decided to head to the maneuvers, like all the other gawkers.

It looked like every constable for miles around was on duty, forming a cordon along the stretch of roadway open to the public. A switchback wound its way up a slope above the Common, which was on the lower ground along the canal. In the grassy area between the switchback, townspeople had laid out blankets and were sharing thermoses of tea and sandwiches from their picnic baskets. The scene reminded me of pictures from a book I'd read about the Civil War, all the civilians coming out in their carriages to watch the Battle of Bull Run. I hoped these maneuvers wouldn't end as badly.

We had no trouble driving the jeep onto the Common; the constables weren't there to keep US Army personnel out. We had a clear view across the canal and up the opposite slope. Pinpoints of smoke blossomed and were followed by the rolling sounds of the explosions from smoke rounds traveling across the valley. We sat in the jeep, watching swarms of GIs heading down to the canal, accompanied by Sherman tanks; the opposing force. From a wooded glen to our right came a roar of twin diesel engines, the unmistakable sound of the M-10 Tank Destroyer.

Four of them came out of the woods, trees cracking and snapping beneath their treads. As they cleared the foliage they accelerated, probably hitting thirty as they raced parallel to the road. In unison, they turned hard right, treads chewing at the ground and spitting it out until their gun barrels faced the opposite slope. The crowd cheered like they were the home team at a football game. It was a well-planned move, probably put on to impress the locals. Looking around I spotted Ernest Bone with his pony cart, set up to sell his sweets. Children gathered around the pony while parents took their precious ration coupons and handed them over for a rare treat on this festive occasion. Laurianne Ross led some of her charges to the cart as well, and I saw Bone wave off the offer of coupons. The girls squealed with joy. Was the candy bag found at the pillbox on the house as well? People say "it was like stealing candy from a baby," but giving candy to a child can be just as sinister. I decided to look into Ernest Bone's background a little deeper. He claimed to have served in the last war. What had he been doing since them? He'd only purchased the sweet shop in town recently.

I pointed out Angus Crowley to Kaz. He loitered at the edge of the gathering, watching the maneuvers closely, but moving a step or two away whenever someone came close. His eyes flitted about the crowd as if he were looking for someone, or perhaps avoiding them. Michael Flowers and Nigel Morris sauntered along the lane, chatting idly like old friends. I figured their appearance meant the Miller family was in attendance as well, but I couldn't find them in the sea of faces.

Further down the Common, other platoons of TDs took up position, opposing the force crossing the canal. One group fired smoke shells in their direction. Grey smoke wreathed the low-lying ground, cover for the other TDs, which crept closer, taking advantage of the terrain to keep their silhouettes low. A distant whistling heralded the overhead trajectory of artillery shells, causing the civilians to draw back, children clutching their mothers' skirts. But the explosions were far away, across the canal, hitting open land that the opposing forces had already traversed. It was live ammunition, but far from us or any troops. Still, the shriek of incoming shells and the geysers of good farmland being blown sky-high lent a realistic air to the exercise. It's one thing to watch fireworks; it's another to feel them striking near enough to pepper your helmet with falling debris and shrapnel.

An M8 six-wheeled armored car roared to a quick halt beside us, Lieutenant Binghamton in the turret, a broad grin on his face as he saluted. "Come to watch the show, Captain?"

"We did," I said, and introduced Kaz. I asked where Tree was and he pointed to the lead TD in the nearby platoon. He switched on his radio and a few seconds later Tree popped up from the open turret, waving me over.

"Thanks for coming out, Billy," Tree said as I clambered up the side. "I mean Captain Boyle," he added, with a glance at his men and a salute for me.

"Tree, first thing to learn in combat is not to salute. Unless you don't like your officers. It only points them out to snipers." That got a laugh from the other four crewmen.

"Fellas, this is the guy I told you about. He's working on getting Angry free." We were interrupted by another radio call, and the driver began to work his gears.

"I have a lead," I said, before jumping off. "I'll find you after the maneuver and tell you about it." Tree's response was lost in the sound of the four TDs moving off in unison, widening the space between them. I saw observers and umpires ahead, speeding around in jeeps, their armbands marking them as non-combatants. The Common quickly became a smoky confusion of fast vehicles, TDs, armored cars, and jeeps weaving between each other, darting from cover when they could, seeking out the folds in the land to settle into and fire simulated rounds directly at the foe, umpires barking into their radios.

Two TDs were flagged down by the umpires and declared destroyed, red smoke grenades marking their demise. In the woods by the canal, yellow smoke rose up from several spots, marking the enemy casualties, each one raising a cheer from the crowd. I returned to the jeep with Kaz, who was watching the progress through binoculars.

"Tree's platoon is still intact," he said, pointing to a small grove of pine trees where the TDs had hidden as much as they could. A dispatch rider on a motorcycle sped onto the scene, handing papers to Lieutenant Binghamton in his armored car.

"That's an Indian Scout," I said to Kaz, pointing at the motorcycle. "The model I bought as a kid." This was a new one, decked out in olive drab with leather saddlebags. I watched as the motorcycle raced from unit to unit, delivering orders. It looked like the driver was enjoying himself. We were so focused on the ebb and flow of the battle that we were both startled when a constable came up to us. "Inspector Payne would like a word, sir."

We left the jeep and followed him back to the roadway. I caught sight of Flowers, standing next to George Miller, like the best of friends. Bone was closing up his cart, sold out of humbugs and the like, I figured. Crowley was nowhere to be seen, but Razor Fraser raised a hand in a friendly greeting, or at least a reasonable imitation of one. Payne's car was on the side of the road, turned away from the crowd. The constable opened the door and we climbed in back. Payne was in the driver's seat and his passenger was watching the maneuvers intently.

"Gentlemen," Payne began, "let me introduce Blackie Crane. Constable Cook said you'd like a word."

"Thought I ought to see what's holding up traffic on the canal," Blackie said, without taking his eyes from the maneuvers. "Not a bad view, is it?" I could see where Blackie got his name. Coal dust coated his hands, clothes, and hair. From what I could see of his face, his pores were clogged with the stuff.

"I found him with his barge, tied up by the Hog's Head Pub," Payne said, turning in his seat to face us. "I thought it best to bring him along before opening time, otherwise we might not get much out of him."

"Not much else to do, Inspector, with the Yanks closing down the canal, now is there?" Blackie kept his eyes glued on the Common as vehicles raced about, churning up soil as they spun their treads. "Bloody good show, though." He interrupted his viewing long enough to light a cigarette, striking a wooden match with his thumbnail. I was relieved when we all didn't go up in an explosion of coal dust.

"Mr. Crane," Kaz said. "We understand you are one of the few canal men who run at night."

"Cor! What have we here, a foreigner? Not enough to have Yanks all about, is it?" Crane addressed this remark to the air, and I wondered if he'd started his drinking early.

"Polish, Mr. Crane. And unused to your damp climate, I must add. So I have enjoyed being warmed by your excellent coal at the Hog's Head."

"You have, have you?" Crane turned in his seat, giving Kaz his full attention. Everyone likes to be flattered. "Old Jack Monk buys from me. We used to pass each other on the canal, back when he was on the water. Now he likes to have a good supply on hand. Folks drink more when they don't have a chill going through their bones."

"Perhaps we will have a drink there when we are done here. You have worked the route from Pewsey to Reading a number of years," Kaz said, holding out the promise of free booze. "You must know the water well."

"Indeed I do. When I sell the last of my load, I turn back and try to make it home in one run. Nighttime is tricky with the blackout and all, but you've got the canal to yourself. Give me a bit of moon-light and I can be back in Pewsey in no time." He grinned, and the creases on his face showed in lines of coal dust.

"Did Inspector Payne tell you what we wanted to ask you?" I said. Blackie was the talkative type, too talkative. He was the kind of guy that might lead in whatever direction he thought you wanted to go, especially with the promise of a drink at the other end. Kaz was smart appealing to Blackie's vanity, but dangling that pint out in front of him was dangerous.

"No, only the night in question. I recall it well, perfect half-moon, brilliant light to guide me home. I'd made my last delivery and came through Newbury a bit after midnight. I remember hearing the churchbell toll from a ways out."

"Not many people out that time of night, I'd guess," I said. Outside the car, a few people were drifting by, the action having moved farther away.

"No, not many. So why don't we adjourn to the Hog's Head?" Blackie said. "So I can get underway when the canal's opened."

"Not many, you said. Does that mean no one?"

"Listen, Yank, if I meant no one I'd of said no one. You should have manners like your Polish friend here."

"Steady on, Blackie," Payne said. "He's got his job to do, just like you do."

"Was the water high that night?" Kaz asked, jumping in to keep Blackie calm.

"Aye, it was. There'd been a hard rain, and the river that feeds into the canal was at a rage, it was. But the canal is smooth, no matter how much water she carries."

"Do you remember who you saw out in Newbury that night?" Kaz asked. "Along the embankment."

"No, not really. I mean that I did see two men, not far from the Hog's Head, downstream. They were arguing, I could tell since one of them was pointing his finger hard at the other fellow's chest. But I didn't know them, by sight or by name."

"But would you recognize either one of them?" I asked.

"Oh sure, since one of them cursed me."

"Why?" Kaz asked.

"Oh, the water. Like I said, it was high, and I had a full head of steam up. Probably going faster than I should of, especially with an empty boat and it being the middle of town. But it was late, and I wanted to get home."

"What do you mean, the water?" I asked. I didn't want to give Blackie the answer, I wanted to hear it from him.

"The wake, man, are you daft or simple? The wake kicked up onto the embankment, right where they were standing. Gave their trousers a good soaking I did. Might have laughed at the sight of them, caught up in their argument and then splashed by old Blackie! One of them shook his fist and cursed at me, and the other walked off, none too happy himself."

"So you'd recognize one of them?" I asked.

"The one who raised his fist to me, sure I would. He had his collar up and wore a cloth cap, but I got a good look at his face. Walked a bit stooped over, as well. The other fellow, maybe not. He didn't look at me for very long."

"He walked back to the house," Payne said. Blackie nodded, and we all knew what he had witnessed. The last seconds of Stuart Neville's life.

"Can you describe the other man, the one who cursed at you? His face, I mean," Payne said.

"Close to your age, Inspector. Shorter, stooped over, like I said. Big cheeks, like he was well fed. Sort of like that gent," Blackie said, pointing to the crowd streaming by the car.

"Which one, man?" Payne demanded.

"Cor, if it ain't him! That one, with the pony! I'll swear to it." Blackie raised his hand, his coal smudged finger pointing straight at Ernest Bone.

CHAPTER THIRTY-THREE

BONE SAW BLACKIE Crane pointing directly at him. His eyes widened for a fraction of a second, and then he bolted, but not before he slapped his pony hard on the rump and sent him trotting into the crowd, the cart barreling along behind him as people stumbled out of the way, shouting and cursing, creating exactly the kind of confusion Bone wanted. He had betrayed no surprise, no shock of wonderment or bemusement at being singled out. It was a rapid, calculated decision to run. He had the look of a practiced criminal who knew the jig was up. A murderer. Worse. I should have tumbled to it sooner. Seeing him with the girls had started the wheels turning, but not soon enough for a nice quiet arrest.

Payne and I were out of the car immediately, our cop's sense sending us running before our brains caught up with what we'd seen. Kaz was behind us and for all I knew Blackie was still staring at his finger. The road was filled with people walking back to town. The pony cart had created enough chaos that the crowd was milling about, asking what had happened, what all the fuss was about, and why had Mr. Bone run away? Payne and I pushed people aside, trying to spot our quarry in the tumult.

I caught a glimpse of him, weaving through the throng, heads turning as he rushed past. His cloth cap blew off, his bald head with its low ring of dark hair now a clear marker. The noise of the crowd was pierced by a child's shriek, and we pushed through to find Miss

Ross on the ground, holding one of her students, luckily with no injuries other than badly skinned knees.

"He ran through the girls, knocked them over," Laurianne shouted, pointing down the lane with one hand and cradling the head of a dazed girl with the other. We followed her lead, and I was glad to see the crowd had thinned out, only a few stragglers left watching the distant maneuvers. I looked up to where the road switched back on itself as it ascended, expecting to see Bone making for the fields and woods beyond. There was no sight of him.

"There!" Payne shouted, and I saw a constable sent sprawling as he tried to keep Bone from leaving the road and entering the off-limits area, still jam-packed with tracked and wheeled vehicles driving in seemingly random patterns.

"He's heading for our jeep," I hollered, vaulting a low stone wall that bordered the road. I came down on a loose rock and pitched forward, hitting the ground hard. I rolled and got up, pulling my revolver from my shoulder holster and wincing from the sharp pain in my right knee. The inspector kept going, his legs churning as Bone jumped into the jeep and pressed the starter. I heard Payne yell, probably something about the name of the King, and saw Bone turn in panic at how close he was. But the panic turned to quick calcula-tion. Instead of driving away, he jammed the jeep's clutch into reverse and stepped on the accelerator. In a second the vehicle collided with Payne, sending him flying backward, landing with a crack and a thud in a tangle of limbs.

I left the inspector behind. I knew there were plenty of constables about and probably a medic nearby. I also knew that Bone was determined to get away, and by the look on his face he'd spare no one who got in his way. All around me shouts and frantic commands rose up in a confused crescendo. A jeep raced after Bone as I ran as fast as I could, the pain in my knee stab-bing me with each long pace. Binghamton's armored car joined in, and I could see him standing in the turret, one hand holding a radio and the other gripping the .50 machine gun for support as the six-wheeled vehicle careened over the open ground at top speed. No one else was nearby. Not until I heard the Indian Scout behind me.

"Stop!" I shouted, holding up my hand. He skidded to a halt and without explanation—a privilege of rank—I strong-armed him off the bike and took off after Bone, spitting mud and fighting mad. I caught a glimpse of him as I rounded a stand of trees and navigated through an opening in another stone wall. His shiny bald head was a fine beacon, but he was making for the canal where smoke still wreathed the ground as Sherman tanks and other vehicles crossed his path. GIs from the opposing force milled around, not sure what to make of this headlong rush in their direction.

I lost sight of Bone as I downshifted to take a small rise. I went over the top and the bike came down on damp grass, the rear tire fishtailing crazily until I got it under control. I couldn't spot Bone anywhere. The other jeep following him was dead ahead of me, kicking up dust and obscuring my vision. A Sherman tank burst out of the woods, flattening trees as it blindly crossed paths with the jeep. The jeep's driver slammed on his brakes and skidded sideways, smashing into the side of the tank as it swept by. He was thrown clear, but the tank treads chewed up the jeep, leaving shreds of metal and rubber behind. I swerved around the wreckage and behind the tank, the exhaust blinding me. I blinked away the blurriness and had to swerve again as GIs rushed out of the woods to gawk at some actual destruction.

I saw Bone ahead of me. He was making for the path along the canal, a nice flat stretch of hard-packed ground where he could make time and disappear. Or so he hoped. The path would make it easy for me, too, and I hoped that by now the constables were working to seal off the area. But no, I realized. Other than the bicycles they came in on, they only had one vehicle—Payne's car. Unless Binghamton was giving orders for his unit to block the roads, there was no one with the time, transportation, or sense to do it.

The Scout was giving me all it had, but Bone was flying along. On the hill above me, I spotted Binghamton in his armored car, the big wheels churning up ground as fast as I was. The M8 could make over fifty miles an hour, but not in this soft and undulating terrain. It could be tricky to handle cross-country, but Binghamton was going for the most direct route, a straight line to the open ground where Bone was heading. Once there, we had him pinned.

The armored car was speeding downhill at an angle, the slope of the land increasing as it approached a jumble of rocks. Binghamton had no choice but to go left and head straight down, losing his advantage and increasing the distance from Bone. Or so I thought.

I saw him slam his hand on the turret, shouting down to the driver, his words lost in the snarl of engines. The M8 picked up speed, its left wheels sinking into the soft ground, as it kept on course, narrowly avoiding the boulders, but tilting at a precarious angle, Binghamton hanging on, clutching the .50 caliber.

It looked like he'd make it. Even ground was about fifty yards away. But then gravity took over, and the tilt was too much for the eight tons of steel to sustain. I could tell the driver was trying to compensate, but it was too late. The M8 went over, sliding on its side as Binghamton ducked his head in, finally rolling over, once, twice, then plowing into the ground, coming to rest on the path we'd been making for.

I slowed, hesitant to give up the chase, hoping Binghamton and his crew weren't badly injured. I hadn't know him long, but he seemed like a decent guy, and a friend to Tree. I circled the vehicle as dust settled from the violent impact, gear and men rattling about inside. I slowed, rounding the car, one foot skittering along the ground. What I saw wasn't good. I stopped.

Binghamton was half in, half out of the turret, his back bent sideways at an impossible angle. Crewmen bolted from the hatches as Binghamton flailed with his arms, trying to get his useless legs to work, to pull himself out of the vehicle. I jumped up onto the M8, screaming for someone to get a medic.

It was pointless. He must have been tossed partway out as the armored car turned over. His spine was snapped, and the internal injuries had to be terrible. He was choking on blood as he frantically tried to get his body to move, his eyes fixed on some distant spot, still chasing Bone, still leading his men, dreaming of glory as he died.

"Hold steady," I said, trying to grip his arms. "You're only making it worse."

His eyes widened, and I thought he might actually see me. He struggled, still trying to move. He gagged on blood and I raised his head, cradling it in my lap.

"Medics are on the way," a GI said, and I heard the distant siren. Binghamton thrashed in my arms and I struggled to keep him immobile, even as I knew he was dying.

"Binghamton," I whispered. "Quiet, quiet. Say a prayer with me." I held his hand as I spoke into his ear, reciting that everyday prayer, the only thing that came to mind. "Our Father, who art in heaven."

By the time I got to "deliver us from evil" he was gone, and not for the first time in this war I was glad a man was dead, if only to put a halt to his suffering.

Your will be done. But His will didn't make much sense right now. Binghamton had missed his chance to lead his men and face the enemy, killed by a murdering child rapist.

CHAPTER THIRTY-FOUR

MARGARET HIBBERD. SHE'D bicycled up to the Avington School but no one saw her leave. Because she took the path in the gardens around back. She'd been spooked by Miss Ross calling the police, and darted off, out of sight. Which put her on a course straight to Ernest Bone and his sweet shop. Mr. Bone and his charming pony. Perhaps he'd been out back with the pony, and young Margaret had stopped to chat. Or had she gone into the shop?

That part didn't matter. Tears burned across my cheeks as the wind whipped my face. I drove along Hungerford Road, watching for the turnoff to High Street and Hedley's Sweet Shop. I had to beat Bone there, although I doubted any sane man would return to his own house after Blackie Crane's bony coal-black finger had pointed in his direction. Still, I swept the road with my eyes, looking for US Army green and a bald head. No sane man raped and killed young girls either.

High Street came up on my right and I took the turn fast, righting the Scout as it came out of the curve. If I was right, there was still a chance that Sophia Edwards was alive. For the moment. Pieces came together in my mind, not so much like a puzzle, but like the pieces of paper and photographs Dad used to mull over in his den, late into the evening, when a case was going nowhere. He'd look and look at the same thing, until something made sense. Like now.

It all fit. Bone was a killer and a child molester. He'd set up shop here to entice his targets with candy and charm. The way I figured it, when Margaret was killed he had to have another. Sophia's disappearance fit with the best estimate we had of the date of Margaret's death. I shuffled some more papers in my head, and there it was. Stuart Neville and Ernest Bone. Had Neville seen something at the sweet shop? Or recognized Bone when he was ditching Margaret's suitcase near the Millers'? George Miller would have made an excellent scapegoat.

But all that didn't matter right now. What did was the sign ahead, for Hedley's Sweet Shop. And the jeep parked next to it.

I cut the engine and coasted to a stop several houses away. The street was silent. The wail of a siren in the far distance echoed along the valley. No one was out. People were either at work or returning from the maneuvers, at a much slower pace than Bone or I had. I crouched low and scurried along the front of houses and shops until I came to the corner of Hedley's. I ran to the jeep and ducked behind it. Taking out my pocketknife, I slashed the front and rear tires on the passenger side. If Bone got by me, at least he wouldn't enjoy a high-speed getaway.

I circled the store, listening for any sign of movement. I heard a faint thud from inside, perhaps an inner door closing. It had a heavy sound, not like a thin bedroom door but more solid. Something that couldn't be broken down. His storeroom, maybe? I duck-walked under a window and raised my head to the corner of the glass. It was his kitchen. Large pots were arranged on the counter next to a black cast-iron stove. Hard candies were laid out on trays, ready to entice the innocent. There was no sign of Bone.

The rear entrance led directly into the kitchen. I tried the door but it was locked. Time was running out for Sophia, if she had any time left. The kitchen door was solid; there was no way to get at the lock. I went back to the casement window and worked on it, but it was shut tight. His toolbox was set up outside, next to a pile of lumber. I grabbed a hammer and went to work on the window.

It was loud and slow work. The glass was thick, and the metal frame around the panes was reluctant to give way. I reached inside and fumbled for the latch. As it gave I felt something warm on my hand. I pulled it open and squeezed through, blood dripping from my palm where the glass had sliced the soft flesh. I fell into the kitchen clumsily and got to my feet, looking for my next move.

I checked the storefront and found it empty. I darted down a hallway, opening doors with my good hand to a bedroom and a study, both empty of all but the most functional furniture. The pantry off the kitchen held shelves of jars and tins of sweets. It looked like enough inventory for the rest of the war. So where was the storeroom renovation Bone said he was working on?

I went back into the store, wanting to check the jeep and make sure Bone hadn't got out some other way. The counter and cash register were on my left. I moved quietly on the bare wood floor and peered over the counter. A narrow carpet was bunched up in the corner, revealing a latch set in the floor. A trapdoor. I pulled out my revolver and gripped it as best I could, blood oozing from my palm. With my good hand I took hold of the latch and pulled. The door swung up with surprising ease. A set of wide stairs led down into a well-lit cellar. I held the revolver ahead of me and took a step.

"Come down, Captain Boyle, by all means," I heard Bone say. "But leave your pistol behind, or I shall slit this poor girl's throat." He drew out the *poor girl* in a macabre imitation of pity.

"You're going to kill her anyway," I said, continuing down the stairs. It was what I needed to say to Bone, but as soon as I saw Sophia Edwards I regretted it. Bone held her bound hands at her back with one hand. The other hand had a knife at her throat. She was gagged, which only brought out the deep terror and anguish in her eyes, which stared straight at me.

"But now it will be because of you, Captain Boyle," Bone said, edging closer to me in the narrow space. Behind him was an open door, the room beyond which had been first Margaret's prison, then Sophia's. It was painted a cheery yellow, with a bed covered in a quilt, a nightstand with a lamp, and stuffed animals in the corner. It made me sick. "You and Inspector Payne, that is. It felt good to lay him out like that. I trust his injuries are serious?"

"Bone," I said, taking one step and lowering my pistol. "You can't get away, not in a US Army jeep with every constable in the valley looking for you." I didn't mention Sophia. It made sense that he was going to kill her, if only to not be encumbered by her.

"Certainly not," he said. "Now lay down that revolver and step aside."

"I'm not giving you my weapon," I said. He was using Sophia as cover. Even if my hand hadn't been sticky with blood, it would be tough aiming well enough to incapacitate him. If I put it down, he'd go for it. I didn't have many cards to play, but the pistol was an ace.

"Sensible of you," Bone said, moving around me with his back to the basement wall, Sophia tight in his grip. "Be my guest and remain here. The bedroom is quite cozy."

"I'll drive you," I said, holding up my hand. Bone tightened his grip and a muffled shriek escaped Sophia's lips beneath the gag as the blade pressed into her neck.

"I don't need you."

"With me driving the jeep, there'll be no questions, right? Isn't that better than taking your chances at the wheel?"

"Captain Boyle, I do not wish to harm this pretty face, but if you don't put that gun away, I shall. A nice scar along one cheek would do the trick."

Bone had something up his sleeve. He should have been more concerned, but he seemed calm for a pervert killer with no getaway vehicle. Which meant he had a plan.

"No," I said, backing up. I holstered the revolver, wincing as the pain got to me. There was really too much blood on the floor. I felt a bit dizzy. "How's that?" Keep 'em talking, that's what Dad always said. If they're talking they're not doing anything else, for the moment.

"Good enough to stay the blade," Bone said. "Move farther away from the stairs." There wasn't much room; it was a tight space. I could see the evidence of fresh-cut wood where Bone had built an interior wall for the bedroom prison. His own do-it-yourself project.

"I can still drive you," I said, shuffling to the side. "Your car or mine."

"That wasn't so hard to work out, now, was it? Leave nothing to chance, I say." Bone approached the stairs, turning so he'd pull Sophia up behind him. His eyes flitted upwards and then back to me. He was calculating the odds. If he left me in the basement and locked me in, how long would it be before I was discovered? Long enough? Probably not. He needed me silenced, preferably someplace away from here. I saw the hint of a smile and knew he'd decided. He was the kind of guy who thought he was smarter than everyone else, who saw other people as fools, who enjoyed thinking two steps ahead.

"I'll leave the revolver down here," I said. "I'll come up after you and we'll all leave together." It was too good a deal to turn down. My only prayer was to stick with Sophia and hope for a chance.

"Wait," he said, pulling Sophia up the stairs. When he was at the top, he peered down at me. The knife was still at her throat, but his grip was relaxed. He had the upper hand, after all. "Let me see you lay it down."

I withdrew the .38 from my shoulder holster. The butt was smeared with drying blood. I laid it on the floor and held up my hands for him to see. He nodded and I took the stairs. Bone stepped back as I came up and instructed me to close the door and put the carpet back over it.

"Now," he said. "Go ahead of me, out back through the kitchen. If you try anything at all, Sophia will suffer a scar that will haunt her for the rest of her life, if it doesn't kill her. Do you understand?"

"Sure," I said, grabbing a dish towel to wrap around my cut palm as I passed through the kitchen. It was obvious he wasn't going to kill her right away and lose his leverage. I went out the door and turned as Bone stayed in the doorway, looking around the backyard.

"Open the shed doors," he said. Sophia whimpered beneath her gag. The shed was about twenty feet away, and I had a view of the road. It was still quiet, except for the distant sound of engines echoing along the valley. I had hoped for a dozen constables and maybe a Tank Destroyer or two, but we were alone in the midday stillness. I opened the double doors.

The shed was small, and I never would have guessed a vehicle could fit inside, but this was an Austin Seven, a tiny, black two-door British car about as long as I was tall. Bone ordered me to get in and pull it forward. I folded myself into the driver's seat on the right and started it up. The engine sounded tinny and the frame shook. I drove it out of the shed and stopped. Bone whipped open the passenger door and dove in, pulling Sophia cruelly by her bound hands. She landed in a heap in the cramped back seat with him, moaning from an injury, fear, or both.

"Drive," Bone said. "Right on High Street and then the next right. Like a Sunday excursion, Captain Boyle, or else I'll have to put this knife to work. Now you, dear Sophia, you get down on the floor." I heard more muffled cries as he pushed her down, out of sight.

"Let me guess," I said, keeping my eyes on the road and the speed respectable. "You've done this before."

"There's much I've done before, Captain, but little that gave so much pleasure. Now be quiet." He tapped the blade against my head and laughed. He was enjoying himself. I wondered if the danger was as important as the girls in his twisted mind. I waited for a minute, which seemed to go on forever as I drove this madman down a quiet country road. We were headed away from the main road and the town, probably already outside of any cordon the police managed to throw up.

"You ever come this close to being caught before?" I figured he wouldn't mind bragging about his escapades. He didn't even hesitate.

"This is nothing," Bone said, as I caught a glimpse of him in the rearview mirror, checking the road behind us. It was clear. "Who was that in the police car anyway?"

"A canal man. He saw you that night, outside the Miller residence, arguing with Neville."

"Ah, the inquisitive banker. He became unduly suspicious when he inspected the shop. Said my plans were wrong for a storeroom and kept asking why I needed so much space. I didn't like it, I can tell you that much. There was something about him that said copper. So I removed the threat."

"While casting suspicion on the Millers by dumping the suit-case," I said. "Brilliant."

"No," Bone said. "The brilliant ones are those you never catch out. There are plenty, I promise you that. The canal man, now that is the kind of threat no one can plan for. Random. I remember the boat that night. Good moon, as I recall. He passed by just as Neville turned his back on me."

"Big mistake on his part," I said.

"I prefer to think of him as being maneuvered into position. Quite a difference, but not from his point of view, I admit. Here, take this left." Another tap on the shoulder with his knife, and he was back to talking. It had to be lonely being a criminal genius, after all. "But when I saw the fellow point me out, I knew it was all over. This chapter, that is."

"You acted quickly," I said, trying to keep some admiration in my voice. "Some guys would have tried to bluff it out, or act indignant."

"Yes. Those types are all in prison, or soon will be. That is not my desire. There, take that lane." We drove down a narrow lane, leafy branches hanging low overhead. The track took us to a small cottage nestled along the canal, and I realized the turns we'd taken had brought us back to the water. There were no other buildings in sight. The canal was wider here than in town, and the walking path along it was overgrown, thick lush grasses growing along the bank. The cottage stretched out along the waterfront, soft limestone topped with an old thatched roof. Weeds grew on the path to the door, and two canalboats were tied up in front of the house.

"You had this all set up," I said, taking in the isolated spot. "A bolt-hole."

"Switch off the motor," Bone said. "Notice how quiet it is here. No one about, except for the occasional traffic on the canal."

"So you're not really in the sweets business at all," I said, trying for admiration, anything to keep him talking and maybe distracted.

"Oh, I don't mind cooking them up. And the pony cart was an excellent prop. But as for business, I robbed two banks in my youth. All in the service of this. My life's work, you might call it. My girls."

"I bet you move around some," I said, buying time, keeping Bone talking, looking for an advantage. "Find a remote spot for a hideout, then set yourself up where you have access to girls the right age. What else have you been? A schoolteacher?"

"Never mind that. Listen to me, Captain. We are going to go inside, all three of us. The same rules apply. Make one wrong move and Sophia will be mutilated. Make a very wrong move and I'll slit her throat. Understand?"

"Once you do that, what do you think will stop me?"

"Your conscience will stop you before I slice into her. I love a good conscience. Such a great help to me. Now get out, open the door, and turn around." I did, stepping back and facing the cottage. It was run-down, a damp chalky odor rising up from the stone. It didn't look like a decent place to die, which I figured was what Bone had in mind for me. Maybe he had a weapon hidden inside. A pistol or a shotgun near the door. First me, and then when he was done with her, Sophia. A couple of bodies in the canal, and in a day or so he could head upstream towards London, and get lost in the city. I couldn't let that happen, but I was unarmed, and he had Sophia in his grasp.

"What now?" I asked, glancing at the boats. One looked decrepit, but the other was in fairly good shape, about twenty feet long, narrow, with a low, enclosed cabin. It looked like any other vessel along the canal. I imagined Bone puttering away, admiring the scenery, two more bodies discarded behind him.

"Walk to the door. There is a large, flat stone under the window on the left. You'll find the key there." I moved to the door, stepping on planks set up as a walkway from the cottage to the boats. I knew if I opened that door I'd never come out under my own power, and Sophia would endure horrors before her end as well. I glanced back, as if checking my instructions.

"That window?" I said, pointing. We were all on the walkway now, the boats behind them, moored a few yards apart. Sophia's eyes looked dead, the terror having exhausted her. Bone's eyes glinted with excitement, the anticipation of what was to come.

"Yes, yes. Get the key, open the door. Hurry, Captain, or I'll carve a new set of lips for this dear girl."

I bent down, lifted the rock, and got the key. I thought about throwing the rock, but it was too heavy to aim. I brought the key to the door. Bone stood clear, waiting at the edge of the water. Now or never, I told myself. I dropped the key, my fingers not working well with my dried blood between them. I bent to pick it up.

"Hurry, damn you!" Bone yelled.

I turned, mid-crouch, and launched my body at them both.

I hit them hard, my head down and my arms wide. I dove into them chest-high, hoping for my momentum to break Bone's grip on the knife without driving it into Sophia's neck.

It worked. Bone's hands flung wide and he lost his grip on Sophia. But he still held the knife tightly as his arms pinwheeled, trying to keep his balance while the force of my hit drove us all back, into the water, between the two boats.

The cold washed over me as we hit and I tried to roll to the side, giving Sophia what room I could. I had no idea if she could swim or even keep her wits about her, but I knew this was her only chance at survival. I could have simply run away, and gotten help in time to capture Bone. But that would have left Sophia a corpse.

Which she still could be in short order. Hands tied behind her back, she might only have seconds before she breathed water. I dove down, trying to see in the murky water. Legs thrashing—Sophia. She'd managed to get clear of the boats and into the middle of the canal. The water was soaking my wool uniform, my boots getting heavy, my legs aching from the cold and the effort to swim with all this added weight.

I saw Bone. Swimming the breaststroke, metal blade in one hand cutting through the water towards Sophia. I swam up, breaking the surface and gulping air.

"Bone!" I shouted, hoping he'd break away from Sophia to deal with me. She was churning in the water, the gag loose in her mouth.

She caught sight of Bone and turned her body away, arching her back and diving like a seal, her legs kicking ferociously. She disappeared and Bone came at me, less than two yards away, bringing the knife down in a slashing arc that missed my face by an inch. I dove for his knife hand, came up empty, and back-paddled away from him.

We both looked around for Sophia, but she was gone.

Bone swam closer, knife at the ready. I was breathing hard, the weight of my clothes dragging my limbs down. Holding my head above water took all my energy. Bone was dressed in lighter clothes, and his insane energy fueled each stroke. He slashed at me, not close enough to hit, but to drive me back, to tire me out in the middle of the canal.

I spotted a ripple of bubbles close to the shore. Sophia, alive, I hoped.

Another slash, this one catching on my arm, slicing through my jacket. I felt nothing, but I could tell the blade was sharp by the way it went through the fabric, and probably flesh. I kicked, trying to swim backward, to keep Bone away from Sophia and to escape his blows. I went down once and took a gulp of canal water, choking as I came up.

"Tired, Captain?" Bone shouted. "Let's put an end to this then." He was next to me in a second, treading water with one arm and raising the other to strike.

Sophia broke the surface several feet behind him. Her hands were in front of her, still bound, but holding a rock. She flung it at his head and it caught him in the back of the neck. Bone was stunned and turned to face this new threat, forgetting about me for a split second. I surged forward, reaching for the knife hand again. I got it this time, pulling him down, beneath the surface, the weight of my boots and clothes working with me now. I held his wrist with one hand and went for his throat with the other while he punched at my face, the blows cushioned underwater. He'd made a fatal mistake. I could take those hits for as long as he dished them out, but my grip on his neck was solid. His arm trembled as he tried to work free of me, but I had the advantage now.

I kicked upward, desperate for air, dragging Bone after me in a terrible imitation of how he had dragged Sophia. I got my head above water and drank in the air as Bone's face rose up with me, halting inches below the surface. I felt my hand tighten around his throat, crushing his windpipe as his eyes widened, staring at me in mute horror as I breathed in the precious oxygen he craved. He bared his teeth as his arms and legs kicked and thrashed, his neck muscles straining to get his head above the waterline. My arms ached as I kept him under, feeling his brute strength rising up, but not far enough. I watched him, and waited. Finally his mouth gaped open as his lungs gave out, a torrent of bubbles rising from his lips. His arm went limp and the knife slipped away. I pushed him down with both hands, a trail of small bubbles finally giving way to nothingness. I held him down until I felt my own strength give way, and then kicked my feet against his chest as he went further under and I made for land, hoping it wasn't as far away as it looked.

CHAPTER THIRTY-FIVE

I DON'T KNOW how I got ashore. Sophia was beside me, trying to break the cloth strips that bound her hands by rubbing them against the hard edge of the dock. She was crying. Who wouldn't be?

"Here," I croaked, rolling over and digging my pocketknife out. She shrieked and skittered away from me. I opened the knife and beckoned her closer, too exhausted for words. She came closer, offered her bound hands to me as if they were a gift, and I cut the wet fabric.

"Is he gone?" Sophia asked, her teeth chattering from the cold, the terror fading from her face.

"For good," I said. "For all time." I wanted to say you don't have to worry about him, but she might spend a lifetime doing just that. Remembering and wondering what she'd done to deserve that treatment.

"I'm cold," Sophia said. I got up and took off my sodden uniform jacket, then realized it would do her no good. Her schoolgirl cotton dress was soaked and torn, but there were no marks I could see.

"Let's see if there are blankets inside. Then we'll get you home." I held out my hand.

"That's his place. I can't go in there. I won't."

"Okay," I said. "Wait here." I retrieved the key and opened the door. Inside was damp and musty. Dust coated the few pieces of furniture in the sitting room. A shotgun rested against the wall by the doorway. I found a blanket in the kitchen, draped over a rocking chair by the stove. I was feeling dizzy, and made my way outside, unsteady on my feet.

Sophia was standing on the bank, looking out over the canal. Downstream, something dark floated in the water. It could have been Bone, or a tree branch.

"He's really dead?" she asked.

"Yes." I put the blanket over her shoulders and turned her away from the canal. "Are you injured?"

"No," she said in a small voice. She shook her head, a silent acknowledgment of the injuries that didn't show. "But you are." She pointed to my arm. Bone's blade had cut me across the bicep, on the same arm I'd cut breaking into his shop. I hadn't felt a thing before, probably from the cold water and a good dose of shock.

"Maybe I should get us both to the doctor," I said. "Just for a quick look. Okay?"

"Okay." She let me lead her to the car, but I could tell she didn't want to get in.

"It's all right," I said. "You'll be up front with me." I opened the door and she got in, after turning it over in her mind. Like she'd probably do for the rest of her life. I got in and watched her fidget with the cloth still tied around her wrists.

"Is it really over?" Sophia asked.

"Yes." Her small voice reminded me of another woman who'd gone through an ordeal with a madman. If I could find Diana, bring her back from her SOE exile, perhaps she'd be able to talk to Sophia. It might help both of them.

"What's your name? He called you captain, didn't he?"

"Billy Boyle. Yeah, I'm a captain in the army. But you can call me Billy if you want. I like it better anyway."

"Billy," she said, trying it out. "Were you looking for me?"

"Yes. A lot of people were."

"I wish you'd come sooner," she said, her face cast down to the floor. "But thank you."

I couldn't say you're welcome. I pressed the starter and drove to Hungerford, careful to avoid High Street and the sweet shop. My arm hurt like the devil, but that didn't matter. What mattered was Sophia, and the days and nights she'd been a prisoner. I'd been sure there was a connection between Stuart Neville and the kidnappings, but I hadn't been able to work it out in time. Neville saw something in the building plans or in the shop itself that raised his suspicions. It must have been churning in the back of his mind, which is probably what caused him to warn Eva Miller. Maybe he would have gone to the police the next morning. Bone had sensed it, his criminal smarts telling him Neville was onto him, or soon would be.

As an MI5 agent, Neville had been trained to observe and assess data all around him. That's what got him killed. Bone had been intelligent, that much I was sure of. I was curious as to what the police would find in the cottage. Money, identity papers? Maybe another corpse, but I doubted it. The cottage and the boat were his ticket out of here. He'd have been careful not to compromise them.

I took the turn into Hungerford, having detoured around High Street and the maneuver area. I hadn't seen a constable or a roadblock yet. Sophia was shivering under her blanket.

"You looked like a good swimmer," I said, making conversation.

"We swim all summer," she said. "At least we used to, my parents and I, back on Guernsey. When do you think the war will be over? So I can go home."

"I don't know, Sophia. Seems like it's been going on for a long time, doesn't it?"

"It does." We were silent for a while.

"How did you get that rock?" I asked.

"Oh, it was easy to slip my feet through my tied hands, especially underwater. Then I dove to the bottom. The hardest part was finding a rock big enough, but not too large."

"You can open your eyes underwater?" I asked, remembering what a big challenge that was when I was a kid. It took me a while to be able to do it.

"Yes, I can," Sophia said proudly.

"And you can throw pretty well too."

"Yes. And I'm glad I did. Are you all right, Billy?"

I'd swerved a bit as I rubbed my eyes to stay awake. I'd lost a fair bit of blood and was glad to see Doc Brisbane's office ahead, with the police station opposite. "Sure," I said, working up a smile for her sake. I pulled to the side of the road, and thought how sad it was that a young girl like Sophia had to be glad she'd helped save my life. And ended Bone's.

Life just isn't fair, I thought as I set the brake and promptly passed out.

I AWOKE TO a jab of pain in my arm, and my first thought was of Bone stabbing me. But it was only the doctor, pouring antiseptic over my wounds. The room seemed crowded, and it took me a few seconds to focus on who was who.

"Billy, did you get him?" That was Tree. "The guy who got Binghamton killed?"

"Yeah, I got him. We got him. Where's Sophia?"

"You settle down, Captain Boyle," Doc Brisbane said. "I need to finish bandaging that arm. You have a nasty cut. Sophia is in the back room with Miss Ross. She brought some clothes over for her."

"Inspector Payne?" I asked. I remembered Bone had run into him with the jeep. It seemed like years ago.

"Right over there," Brisbane said, nodding to a bed in the corner. "Just finished setting his cast when that girl came in soaked to the skin and said you were outside, unconscious. Haven't been this busy since the last time we were bombed."

"What happened, Boyle?" Payne said, trying to rise from his bed.

"You stay put, Inspector," the doctor growled. "I'll get crutches for you as soon as I finish here."

I saw Kaz come in with a bundle of clothing in his arms, and it was only then that I realized all my clothes had been stripped away. The doc had a sheet over me, but that was all I had, and it felt damned odd in a roomful of people. The feeling didn't last long, because I passed out again.

When I woke up the second time, I was in the bed and Inspector Payne was trying out his crutches. He had a cast on one leg, below the knee, and looked pretty banged up, but still alive. Kaz and Tree were leaning against the wall, and Sophia Edwards and Laurianne Ross sat on chairs by the bed.

"Sophia, how are you?" I asked. She was dressed in a white blouse and sweater with a grey skirt. She was cleaned up and her eyes had some life in them. Miss Ross held her hand.

"I'm fine, Captain Boyle. I want to thank you for rescuing me. It was very brave of you." She leaned over and kissed my cheek, blushed, and sat down, folding her hands in her lap. She was a girl brought up with good manners.

"Sophia refused to leave until you were awake, Captain," Laurianne said. "I'm so glad you found her in time." That point was debatable, but I let it pass. Alive was good enough for now.

"Thanks, Sophia," I said. "You should get some rest now. I'll visit you as soon as I can. Is that okay?" She smiled and nodded, and for the first time I saw her as a nice young girl, not simply a victim. I sent up a prayer for her, to Saint Agnes, the patron saint of young girls. Agnes was only thirteen when she was killed for her faith; I was glad Sophia would outlive her.

"Some food, then rest," Laurianne said. "Sophia, the baron is driving us back to the school. Will you go outside with him? I'll be there in a minute." Sophia smiled shyly at me and left.

"How is she?" I asked.

"The doctor says it could be worse," Laurianne said. "Like the dead girl you found. But he didn't have her for that long. Still, it's horrible for her. We'll do our best to keep her spirits up."

"Without being too explicit," Doc Brisbane said, "while she was abused, it was not with the brute force that was visited upon poor Margaret Hibberd. Perhaps with time, as he tired of her, that would have been the case. Quite bad enough though, I assure you. I'll come out to the school tonight to check on her. She may need a mild sedative."

"Thank you, Doctor. And thank you again, Captain." After she left, Tree brought over my uniform. Kaz had brought my other clothes to the inn to be washed and cleaned, and brought back this new set of duds.

"Up to going over a few things, Boyle?" Inspector Payne asked. "PC Cook is searching Bone's store now and should return soon. He needs to take a statement from both of us."

"What about Sophia?"

"That can wait until she's rested."

"Don't you need to rest?"

"I'll sleep when I'm dead," Payne said. "When you're dressed, join me at the nick." He hobbled out the door, cursing at the crutches with every step.

I made it across the street with Tree's help. Kaz and Cook returned and the constable went over what he'd found at the shop. He still had other constables out trying to trace my route to the cottage.

"We found the room, just as you described," Cook began. "Here's your revolver. I cleaned it for you."

"Thanks," I said as he handed me the .38 Special. "You sure you don't need it for evidence?"

"You sure Bone is dead?"

"Absolutely certain."

"Then no. We did find a diary, hidden under a floorboard in his bedroom. It would be more than enough to convict him if he were alive. Glad he's dead, from what I read."

"Was there any money?"

"What? Other than what was left in the till? No."

"Bone told me he'd robbed a couple of banks. Sounded like it was a while ago. It was to fund his work, he called it."

"Well, he's been at it for some time. This was the third town he'd set up shop in. There was a clothing store, a stationery shop, and a greengrocer's. If we can match the diary to missing girls and shop owners, we may close a few open cases."

"The money is likely hidden at the cottage," Payne said, his leg propped up on a chair. "We'll find it."

"Anything else unusual at the shop?"

"No, other than he'd recently installed acoustic tiles in the basement," Cook said, consulting his notes. "The kind of thing they use in music studios and radio stations, to dampen sound."

"I wonder if that's what Neville saw," I said. "Maybe a crate of those, and Bone saw him taking note of it."

"That's precious little to kill a man over," Cook said.

"It was a threat, and one Bone thought he could eliminate easily. From his perspective, why take a chance? Neville knew about building construction, and he'd come to the conclusion sooner or later that a sweet shop would have no need for soundproofing."

"Makes sense," Cook admitted. "Now let's go through this from the beginning." We spent the next hour going over my statement, detailing what Bone said and did while I was with him. Payne went over Blackie Crane's identification and his chase. Tree confirmed what he had seen of Lieutenant Binghamton and the crash of the armored car. As we finished, the telephone rang.

"It's for Captain Boyle," Cook said, handing the receiver to me.

"We've been waiting for a call from MI5," I explained, my hand over the receiver. They'd probably been calling all day with the answer from the owners of the manor house at Chilton Foliat, about Angus Crowley. I listened to what they had to say and hung up, not quite grasping what I'd been told.

"Well?" Kaz said.

"There are no owners of the Chilton Foliat manor," I said. "No private owners, that is. The last family member died and willed it to the government back in nineteen thirty-nine."

"Anyone in the village could have told you that," Cook said. "I even mentioned it to you, that the government took it over. What's this all about?"

"I thought you meant in the recent past, when the Hundred-and-First moved in," I said. "Angus Crowley told them he was sent by the owners, to look after the stables. But MI5 confirmed there are no private owners."

"Doesn't Crowley work for the army?" Cook asked. "I know I

saw him eating in their mess hall on two occasions when we investigated the Eastman murder."

"No," I said. "They let him eat there since he doesn't have a
kitchen, but he claimed he was sent by the owners to live and work
in the stable."

"Why would this fellow represent himself as employed by the
owners?" Payne asked. "Not for three meals a day, certainly."

"Perhaps this will answer the question," Kaz said, tossing the
scrapbook onto Cook's desk. It was open to the article about the trial
of Alan Wycks. "You all know this man did work for the actual
owner, prior to nineteen thirty-nine."

"Of course we do," Cook said with some irritation. "I told you
that story myself."

"Wycks?" Payne said, his brow furrowed as he dredged up the
memory from almost ten years ago. "Stonemason, wasn't he? A minor
theft, if I recall, but a clear case of insanity. But what's that got to do
with the Neville case?"

"Nothing. But when I was in Angus Crowley's room," I said, "he
had a picture of that man on his wall. A younger face, but I'm sure
it's Alan Wycks, and Crowley is his son. He killed Tom Eastman
and threw his body on Sam Eastman's grave. Revenge for Sam
arresting his father."

"After all this time?" Cook asked. "It makes no sense. That picture could have been left by Wycks himself years ago."

"No, it was hung in a prominent position, and there were no
other personal items in the room. It clearly wasn't someone's forgotten junk. Besides, Wycks worked there, but he lived at home with
his wife and child."

"It's a thin thread, Billy," Tree said. "You sure?"

"I wasn't sure of anything, but the call from MI5 clinched it.
Crowley deliberately misrepresented himself to the army personnel
at Chilton Foliat. He may have known about the horses in the stable
and decided that was his ticket. No one paid him much mind or
checked his story, so he moved right in. A US Army installation is
the perfect place to hide out in plain sight. Plus, it gave him easy

access to the graveyard where Sam Eastman was buried. He watched and bided his time. What I can't figure out is what the horses were doing there in the first place."

"There was a fellow from London who leased it out for a time," Cook said. "Never met him, but I heard he kept horses there. I always thought your army had hired him to look after the grounds."

"What's important now is that we find out where he came from, and if he's known under any other name," Payne said. "Boyle, you call your MI5 chaps and I'll have my superintendent contact Scotland Yard. Between them we should learn something. I'm not sure I put much stock in your theory, Captain."

"Should we pick Crowley up in any case?" Cook asked.

"Not yet," I suggested, knowing Payne probably wouldn't go along with it anyway. "Let's wait until we're certain. This could get Angry Smith off the hook for Tom Eastman's murder. I want to get our ducks in a row."

"Damn straight," Tree said.

"Ducks?" Kaz said.

CHAPTER THIRTY-SIX

TREE PICKED US up the next morning. He'd been given a jeep and a pass to help us. His CO wanted Angry Smith back, and all the men were upset about Lieutenant Binghamton's death. Since I'd apprehended the guy responsible, I pretty much had carte blanche with the 617th.

We'd made our phone calls. I hadn't told MI5 about Bone yet; I needed them to think our pursuit of Crowley was related to the Neville killing, otherwise they'd shut me down in a heartbeat. I asked for background information on Angus Crowley or Angus Wycks, and the whereabouts of Mrs. Wycks. I wanted to know where Angus had been in the years since his mother left Alan Wycks, and why he'd taken so long to exact his revenge. Payne had called Scotland Yard and also left a message for the chief inspector at the Berkshire Constabulary.

I'd spent a restless night, unable to sleep much with my arm aching and my head buzzing. How would Crowley respond? Was that even his real name? And why was he still here? Did he have other victims in mind, or did he think he could stick around given that Angry Smith had been arrested for his crime? It was his home-town, after all. Why not?

"You sure you don't want more firepower, Billy?" Tree asked as he parked the jeep. "I could have a squad up here in no time."

"If the three of us with pistols and a couple of English cops can't take an unarmed man on an army base, then we're all due for a rough awakening in France."

"Don't assume he's unarmed," Kaz said. "The English have restrictive laws regarding firearms, but shotguns in rural areas are quite commonplace."

"I don't know about those pea-shooter revolvers you fellas are carrying," Tree said as we entered the station, "but I know my .45 automatic is going to win any argument with a farmer's shotgun. Especially since I'll be standing behind the two of you."

"Billy is so much larger than I," Kaz said, "I think we both could use him as cover." He and Tree chuckled, which made me wish I took my army rank more seriously so I could chew them out convincingly.

"Morning, gents? Tea." Constable Cook didn't even wait for an answer. Even after months of Yanks swarming over his jurisdiction, he still couldn't imagine any of them passing up a morning cuppa.

"How are you feeling, Inspector?" I asked. Payne was in the easy chair by Cook's desk, his broken leg up on a cushioned stool.

"Tired and irritable," he said. "Leg hurts and I've got a terrible itch I can't get to. Had an argument with the wife about coming in today. Other than that all's dandy. Constable, please fill them in." Payne sighed and leaned back in his chair, eyes half closed.

"Your MI5 blokes were a good deal faster than the Yard," Cook began. "Angus Crowley was born in nineteen-twenty. His birth certificate shows his name as Angus Wycks, although his mother's maiden name was Crowley. You were right about that, Captain. His father, Alan, served in the Great War and was wounded at Passchendaele. Patched up, he was sent back to the front and served until the armistice."

"Lucky, I guess," Tree said.

"Not really," Cook went on, reading from his notes. "He'd been a schoolteacher before the war. He was a sapper at the front, tunneling under no-man's-land. After all that time underground, he couldn't stand being shut up inside when he came home. He took what outdoor work he could and found he had a talent for stone.

One of his mates from the war took him on and taught him the trade. That's how he came here, to make repairs on the manor house at Chilton Foliat.

"Scotland Yard didn't have all the details, but apparently Alan Wycks had a number of minor run-ins with the law. Fights, usually. He was never the same man after the war."

"Few were," I said. I knew that well enough from Dad and Uncle Dan.

"I spoke with the chief inspector at headquarters," Payne said, wincing as he moved his leg. "He checked the files and refreshed my memory on the case. Wycks claimed that Brackmann, who owned the manor house, had given him the shirts, as they were old and worn. Brackmann denied it, but there was also some argument about promised wages. Wycks was owed a fair sum, and there was speculation that Brackmann, who was known to be short on funds, set the whole thing up to discredit him."

"Did that come out in the trial?" Kaz asked.

"Brackmann denied it all. By that time, after a long period of incarceration, Wycks was half crazed. I attended the proceedings when he was sentenced, and I doubt he even understood what was happening to him."

"My God," Tree said. "After all he'd been through, they put him in the nuthouse?"

"Yes," Payne said with a sigh. "At the time, there was little else to do. He'd been accused, had no evidence on his behalf, and could not be let loose in his condition. I testified myself, giving the facts of the case. There was little to say to support his defense, other than his record as a soldier."

"The disappearance of his wife and son couldn't have helped matters," Cook said.

"No, it did raise certain suspicions," Payne said. "But we never found any evidence of foul play. I still think she ran off to protect the child from the father's madness."

"So Broadmoor," I said. "At the pleasure of the King."

"Yes, where he died two years ago, still with his demons." Payne shook his head. "Perhaps Brackmann never intended for it to go that far. He evidently had remorse over something. He was found hanged not long after."

"Was there a note?" I asked.

"Not that I recall," Cook said. "But there were money problems, that much was common knowledge. No family, which is why he left the place to the government. Probably owed taxes on it."

"Where was he found?"

"In the stables. He'd thrown a rope over a rafter."

"Maybe Tom Eastman wasn't the first victim," I said. "Do we know anything about where Angus Crowley—I mean Wycks—was during this time?"

"The mother used her maiden name after she left here," Payne said. "The first record Scotland Yard has of her is in Southampton, on the coast not far from here. Her son was arrested on suspicion of burglary. He was let go on lack of evidence."

"When was that?" I asked.

"In nineteen thirty-four, when he was seventeen years old. More serious offenses were recorded in Weymouth, where they moved next."

"After his father was arrested," I said.

"Likely," Payne went on. "The son visited his father in Broadmoor once, that's from the visitors' logs. That was in nineteen thirty-seven, when the boy would have turned twenty. The mother never did. Brackmann was found two weeks after young Angus's visit."

"He was never questioned?" Tree asked.

"No, there was no apparent connection, especially since he was so young. But he was finally picked up in possession of stolen goods outside of London in thirty-nine. His mother died in nineteen forty of an unspecified illness. Angus was sentenced to five years' imprisonment. He was released less than three months ago."

"I would have pegged him as older," I said, "but that's what five years in the slammer can do to a guy."

"But why didn't he take his revenge sooner?" Tree asked.

"Killing a policeman is a tall order," I said. "He was a young kid. He probably pulled off the Brackmann killing easily enough, one solitary guy in an isolated manor house. Or maybe it was harder than he expected. A copper would have been a lot more difficult."

"Aye," Cook said. "Tom could take care of himself. Young Angus might not have managed it. But then he was incarcerated, and after being schooled for five years by the villains in His Majesty's prisons, he was ready."

"This is sounding more plausible by the minute," Payne said.

"Plausible enough to get Angry sprung?" Tree asked.

"That all depends, Sergeant," Payne said. "There is no direct physical evidence. If Crowley doesn't talk, all he could be guilty of is defrauding the US Army."

"That ought to be enough to get CID to reopen the case," I said.

"Let's bring him in, then," Payne said, rising with a grimace.

"Inspector," Constable Cook said, stepping in front of him. "With respect, sir, you should wait here. Hold down the fort, as it were. With that cast, you're more apt to get in the way than to be of help. Sorry, sir."

"Don't worry, I won't get out of the car, Constable." Payne tried to limp his way past Cook, but the Constable stood his ground.

"We'll still have to watch you, sir. Crowley could give that cast a smash and incapacitate you. You shouldn't go, and I'm certain you know it."

"Damn you, I do!" Payne said, sitting himself down heavily and waving Cook off. "Very well. Take the constable on duty with you. At least I can answer the bloody telephone." I understood Payne's reluctance to miss out on bringing Crowley in. He'd been sidelined yesterday, and as the senior policeman in the investigation, he didn't want to sit this one out either. But Cook was right; he'd be a hindrance, not a help. We left him fidgeting in his chair, eager to leave before he changed his mind.

We decided the best course would be for Tree to drive me in the jeep. Kaz and Cook, with the young Constable Gilbert at the wheel, would give us ten minutes and then follow. The idea was that two

Yanks could blend in and not alert Crowley. The blue-coated constables and Kaz in his tailored British uniform were sure to draw stares. Our job would be to spot him and wait.

We passed over the bridge and took the road to Chilton Foliat. A company of GIs was on the road, doing double-time in two columns, packs on their backs and rifles at the ready. The tromp of boots was deafening as we slowly drove between the men.

"I wouldn't mind settling a score with that MP sergeant," Tree said as we pulled into the Chilton Foliat Jump School. "Like to see if he fights as well as he talks. After we settle this matter, that is."

"I'll be sure to look the other way," I said as we got out of the jeep. "But stick close to me for now. We don't want to get caught up in another boxing event." I surveyed the area. No punishment details digging holes. No sign of Crowley or any familiar faces. We went into the manor house like it was routine business. Sergeant Evans, Sobel's right-hand man, was on duty at his desk.

"Captain, what can I do for you today?" Evans asked, casting a wary eye toward Tree. "You here about that fight?"

"No, Sergeant, I am still investigating a murder on behalf of SHAEF. Just wanted to check in and let Captain Sobel know we're taking another look around."

"He's at the airfield, taking a group up for their first jump," Evans said.

"Is that why no one's digging holes today?" Tree asked. I could've kicked him.

"Don't tell me you're from SHAEF too," Evans said, standing up. This had the makings of another brouhaha.

"Sergeant Jackson is my driver," I said. "I only came in as a courtesy. As you were, Sergeant Evans."

"Yes, sir," Evans said, packing as much disdain for us both as he could into those two words. We left and started toward the stables.

"I ain't your goddamn driver, Billy," Tree whispered as we walked.

"Then who drove the jeep?"

"I gave you a ride. There's a difference."

"Listen, all I want to do is find Crowley, nab him, and get the hell out of here without starting a race riot. Sound like a plan to you?"

"Yes, sir," Tree said, in a dead on imitation of Evans. I tried not to laugh. It would only encourage him. We made a circuit of the manor house, which was high enough for a good view of the surrounding area, stables and all. No sign of Crowley.

"Let's check the stables," I said, glancing at my watch. "Kaz and the others should be here in a few minutes." We rolled open the stable door and six horses gazed at us with their dark, inscrutable eyes. It was quiet, no sound other than the soft exhalations from the horses' nostrils. I pointed to the door leading to Crowley's room. We checked our backs, drew our guns, then trod quietly through the stable, looking for any sign of our man.

We turned at the end of the stalls and with gentle footfalls made our way to Crowley's door. Midway, one of the horses reared and neighed, his head held high, as if he was looking for Crowley as well. We froze, waiting for the door to open, but all was silent. Two GIs passed by outside, not giving a glance our way. I nodded toward the door and we moved forward.

I pointed to the knob and gestured for Tree to open it, then stay put. He laid his hand on it and turned, but nothing happened.

"Locked," he mouthed. I raised my foot and slammed it against the door, right by the lock. Wood splintered and the door swung open. I nearly fell into the room, my .38 revolver pointed ahead of me, looking for a threat.

The room was empty. It was exactly as I'd seen it last time. Except the picture of Alan Wycks looked more sad and tragic, now that I knew his story.

"I'm going to search the place," I said to Tree. "Keep an eye on the door."

"Sure," Tree said, swinging the door on its broken hinge. "What's left of it."

"And here I thought you were a certified criminal."

"Hey, I'm just a driver. You got to explain these things to me," Tree said. He smiled, and it felt like we were kids again, out on some grand adventure. We were about to right a great wrong, free Tree's pal from jail. Everything was going to work out, at least better than it had last time around. I felt good.

I checked under the mattress, went through the bureau, moved the cans and supplies on his shelf around, and satisfied myself there was nothing in any of those spots. Then I sat down at the desk. It was scraped and scarred from years of use, and one of the legs was broken, propped up by a brick. It was like everything in the room, discards from an attic or basement. Which is probably where Crowley got it all from, to create the illusion of a caretaker's room when the army arrived.

The desk held little of interest. Musty paperwork from years ago. Pencil stubs. A photograph of a woman, possibly his mother, folded and shoved in the back of a drawer. Did Crowley despise his mother for leaving his father? It didn't matter. What mattered was what I found in the bottom drawer. A box of shotgun shells, half empty, on top of the newspaper article about the trial of Alan Wycks. I took them out and set them on the desk.

"Bird shot," Tree said from the doorway.

"Can still kill a man," I said. I unfolded the article. The creases were nearly worn through from being opened and closed so many times. It was a different article from the one in the scrapbook. This was from a newspaper in Reading, where the trial was held. It detailed the testimony given by then Detective Sergeant Payne, and mentioned that Wycks had gotten hysterical and had to be removed from the courtroom. The local paper had given Sam Eastman as the arresting officer, but this reporter gave that honor to Payne, either by error or because of the transfer to the headquarters lockup.

"First Brackmann, then Eastman," I said to myself.

"What?" asked Tree.

"Never mind. There's got to be something else here, he wouldn't keep only one article. He was obsessed by his father's imprisonment, so he's bound to have more." I pulled out desk drawers and emptied them on the floor. I dumped out the contents of the bureau, tore the sheets from the bed, looked in every corner of the pathetic little room.

Nothing.

Everything in the room was junk. Everything except the framed photograph of his father. I took it down and removed the cardboard backing. Tucked inside were sheets of paper, covered in writing, words in lines straight across, curving down the margins, filled with underlines, cross-outs, and capital letters. It was addressed to Angus Wycks, "my dear son."

It was nearly incomprehensible. Alan Wycks was no longer a former schoolteacher, ex-soldier, or stonemason. He was a man driven mad by confinement, who felt the demons that pressed in on him from every stone surface that imprisoned him. Four names stood out, each underlined in a fury of ink.

Linus Brackmann
Samuel Eastman
Peter Cook
John Payne

The men who had destroyed his life, cheated him, driven his wife away, torn his son from his grasp, and laid terror upon his soul. Angus had a mission, and he was halfway home.

"Let's go," I said, putting the letter in my pocket. "We have to find Crowley."

"Where's Kaz and the others?" Tree asked as we looked around outside. "They should be here." He was right.

"Maybe they got held up by troops on the road. Listen, we have to find Crowley. I don't like the thought of him loose with a loaded shotgun."

"You think he might have gotten Cook on his way here?" Tree said as we got into the jeep.

"Kaz is pretty good with his Webley revolver," I said. "I'm more worried about Inspector Payne. He's all alone; he wouldn't stand a chance. Let's drive down the lane toward the cemetery, then back up here in case we missed him."

"Wait a minute," Tree said, standing up in the jeep and giving a sharp whistle through his fingers. He waved his arm and I saw Charlie hustle over in our direction.

"Not another fight, Tree."

"Hell no, Billy. Charlie is okay. He didn't want to fight, he's just not smart enough to stand up for himself. If he'd wanted to, he coulda laid me out any time he wanted."

"You didn't mention that before," I said.

"Man's got his pride. Hey Charlie, how you feeling?"

"Okay, Sergeant. Captain," Charlie said, giving a decent salute.

"Hey, it's just Billy and Tree, Charlie, long as there's no other officers around. We're looking for Angus Crowley. You see him around?"

"Yeah, Billy. I saw him this morning. He rode down the road on his bicycle."

"We didn't see him coming in," Tree said.

"No, that road," Charlie said, pointing to the track. "The one that goes to the church. Why do you guys want Crowley?"

"Damn! How long ago?" I asked.

"An hour, tops."

"Was he carrying a shotgun?"

"Not that I saw. He was wearing a raincoat. Doesn't look like rain, now that I think about it." Charlie glanced up at the clear skies, and even he understood.

"Charlie, we need your help," I said. "Get to a telephone and call the police station in Hungerford. Tell Inspector Payne that Crowley is on his way, and he's armed. We're headed back. We'll be there with Constable Cook and the others in ten minutes. Can you do that?"

"Sure. If Sergeant Evans lets me use the telephone."

"Tell him Crowley has been cheating the army, and that I said I'd share the credit for catching him with Sobel."

"He'll love that, Billy," Charlie said, and went off at a run as Tree gunned the jeep, fishtailing in the gravel drive and sending a squad of men flying as we sped away from the base.

I had a bad feeling as we barreled down the road. Crowley had been waiting all this time, and he'd probably heard about Payne and his broken leg, and also assumed Kaz and I would be gone now that the Neville case was wrapped up. No armed soldiers, just a few unarmed English coppers between him and the revenge he sought.

CHAPTER THIRTY-SEVEN

THE POLICE CAR was stuck at the intersection of a sheep crossing and a convoy of army trucks. It was a confusion of khaki green and dirty white wool, and Tree barged through it, horn blaring, as I stood up, grasping the windscreen, waving my arms wildly. Constable Gilbert got the message and backed up, did a hard turn, and followed us into town. Short of the canal we pulled over and I filled in Kaz and the constables as quickly as I could.

"Charlie is trying to get word through to Payne," I said. "But Crowley could already be there."

"Perhaps not," Cook said. "Why would he have waited this long? He could have taken a potshot at either of us anytime."

"Because Kaz and I have been on the scene. Two armed men are quite a deterrent. He probably thinks we're gone now that the Neville killing is wrapped up."

"Yes," Cook said, "that may be. We should split up and cover both entrances. When we get close, Gilbert will go into Doctor Brisbane's office and telephone the inspector from there. The baron and I will go around back, and you take the main door."

"Be careful," I said, looking at Kaz. He already had his Webley out and spun the chamber, checking his load. He shrugged at my warning. Careful wasn't how Kaz operated.

We drove on, parking away from the station. I watched Gilbert go into Doc Brisbane's, but I didn't want to wait on word from him.

Kaz waved as he and Cook scurried around the rear of the station house.

"Let's just take it at a stroll," I said to Tree. "When I go in, you stay outside in case Crowley comes along, okay?" I scanned the street for our quarry, but he wasn't anywhere in sight. There were plenty of bicycles outside of shops, but it was impossible to know if one was his.

"I don't think so, Billy," Tree said. "Nice try, but I'm going in with you. Behind you, yeah, but with you."

"It's not your fight," I said.

"Seems like I heard that one before, when I told you the same thing back in Boston. Didn't stop you then, won't stop me now."

"Okay. Follow my lead," I said, glad to have the extra firepower.

"Sure thing. I'll follow from right behind you. Solid guy like you ought to stop bird shot no problem."

We were in front of the station. Curtains were drawn across the window, which could mean Payne was taking a nap, or Crowley was setting a trap, waiting for Cook to return alone. At the door, I laid my hand on the knob. It was cold. I looked across the street, hoping to see Gilbert emerge from Brisbane's with a look of relief on his face. Nothing.

I drew my .38 Police Special. Tree had his .45 automatic ready and I turned the knob, keeping one hand on it and the other pointing my revolver straight ahead. Cook's office was on the right, his door about ten feet down the hallway the led to the cells, a squad room and the rear entrance. Cook's door was open halfway, but I couldn't see inside. I moved forward, shuffling my feet to keep the sound down.

The telephone rang. No one picked up. After five rings, it stopped. I edged closer to the door.

"Crowley? Are you here?" I asked.

"Come in, one and all," came the answer. I turned to Tree and motioned him to stay where he was. I sidestepped across the open door, glancing inside as I moved. It was Crowley, seated at Cook's desk, his shotgun pointed in the direction of the chair where we'd left Inspector Payne, just out of sight.

"I'm unhurt, Boyle," Payne said. "Mr. Crowley is waiting for Constable Cook to arrive."

"That I am. Come in, Captain Boyle. I've got nothing against you."

"Cook's not coming," I said. "He left for Newbury this morning. Police business."

"Oh, I don't think so. That nice American fellow who called said you'd be here soon with the good constable. Nice try, though. Now come in, come in. I've got a nice collection of shells with me, but none has your name on it." Crowley smiled as if inviting us to a party. For him, it probably was.

"Inspector, are you sure you're all right?" I asked.

"As of this moment, yes. Probably best for you to stay where you are, though."

"Crowley," I said. "There's still time to step back from all this. Why don't you put the shotgun down and we'll talk it over?"

"Step back?" Crowley's voice rose. "No one stepped back when my father was put in this very jail! No one said, let the poor fellow go, he's suffered enough. No one said, step back, it was only three moth-eaten shirts!"

"Okay, I understand," I said, trying to calm the situation down. "I'm going to come in, okay?"

"Not with that pistol, you aren't." Crowley's voice was calmer now, more of a low growl.

"Fine, fine," I said, setting it down on the floor with a clatter before putting it back in the shoulder holster. I hoped Crowley wouldn't notice the bulge, and hadn't noticed Tree behind me. I pointed to myself and then mimicked a left-hand turn, so Tree would know where I'd be in the room. "Coming in."

I stepped into the room, and felt a cold rush of sweat down the small of my back as my heart pounded against my chest. Staring down the black holes of a double-barreled shotgun has a way of focusing your attention, once you overcome the terror of it. I held my hands out at my sides.

"I'm sorry about everything that happened to your family," I said. "My father was in the war too. It took a toll on them all."

"All my dad wanted to do was work out under the sky, earn his wages and come home to us," Crowley said. "But that bastard Brackmann cheated him, and the law drove him crazy. How's that for a heavy toll, Captain?" His face twisted in a grimace of resentment, a generation's worth of hatred.

"But why take revenge on these two men? Why not leave things be, go back to taking care of the horses? It's not too late. I'm sure the inspector understands how upset you are." I didn't think Crowley would buy it, but I wanted to get him talking, keep him distracted, long enough for Tree or Kaz to make a move, if they had one.

"Don't pretend you haven't figured out what happened to Tom Eastman," Crowley said. "It was the next best thing to killing that bastard Samuel. To lay his son's body on his grave. To ruin their family as mine was ruined. That was me who killed him, damn you! You can't take that away from me, especially not by pinning it on that darkie."

"Did Brackmann really hang himself, or was that you as well?" I asked. I glanced at Payne, and saw his hands grip the arms of the chair. The cast on his leg left him nearly immobile in that position, but he was ready to launch himself as best he could.

"Of course that was my doing," Crowley said. "He had no idea who I was. I came by asking for work, and he told me to bugger off. I took a tosh to his head and dragged him to the barn. I only regret he didn't know he was being strangled. Father would have liked him to know, I'm sure."

"This was all for your father, wasn't it?" I said, trying to sound sympathetic.

"Of course," Crowley said, his face softening a touch. "Who wouldn't step into his father's shoes? It was what he wanted, what he taught me to do."

"I know," I said. "We saw the letters. That was a heavy burden to lay on you."

"Go to hell," Crowley said. "You didn't know my father."

"I'm pretty sure your father would think you pathetic," I said, deciding that the sympathetic approach wasn't getting us anywhere.

"He was a veteran, a hero. And what did you amount to? A criminal and a killer. They'll probably send you to Broadmoor too, if they don't hang you." I was working on provoking him, to get him out of that chair and pointing the shotgun someplace other than Payne's chest.

"Stop it! You said you were sorry about my father!" Rage flitted across his face, and then his lips quivered as if he were holding in a torrent of tears.

"I'm sorry he has you for a son, Angus. You didn't even take his name, for God's sake."

That struck a chord. "My name is Angus Wycks!" He stood and shouted again, "Angus Wycks!" He held the shotgun in both hands, waving it wildly between Payne and me, his eyes crazed with pain and memory.

"Now!" I yelled, and dove for the floor, reaching for my pistol.

The door from the squad room crashed open, and Kaz burst in, his Webley searching for a target, finding Crowley and shooting, just as Tree stood in the doorway and fired his .45. The room was filled with sharp thunder, muzzles' flashes, and the hot-metal smell of gunfire. I fumbled for my revolver, rising up on one knee as a final blast rocked the room, the twin booms of both barrels going off as Crowley fell against the wall, his dead hand gripping the shotgun.

"Jesus," Tree said, although it sounded like he was very far away. My ears were ringing, and the room was hazy with smoke. Payne got to his feet, then fell back into his chair. His shoulder was bloody where he'd caught some of the bird shot. Between him and Tree there was a hole in the wall where the shot had hit.

"Jesus," Tree said again, and as I focused on him, I saw he'd caught some as well; his right sleeve was ripped and smoky where the bird shot had hit. Blood dripped down his arm.

"Sit down," I said, taking him by his good arm and leaning him against the desk, away from the sight of Crowley's corpse. "Everyone else okay?" I knew I was yelling, but I wanted to hear myself.

"Everyone but Mr. Crowley," Kaz said, holstering his Webley.

"Mr. Wycks," Tree said. "We ought to at least call him that."

"It will be on his tombstone," Kaz said.

CHAPTER THIRTY-EIGHT

FOUR DAYS, TWO bandages, three depositions, one pauper's funeral, one near knockdown fistfight with the original CID investigating agent, and a visit to Sophia at the Avington School for Girls later, Tree and I were in a jeep heading west to the US Army military prison at Shepton Mallet. We had a thermos of coffee, signed release papers for Private Abraham Smith, a full set of clothes from his footlocker, and sore arms from our respective wounds. I drove.

"I still feel like I got bird shot in my arm," Tree said, rubbing his biceps.

"There were four little pieces of shot in there," I said. "Doc got them out with tweezers."

"What did he call that room we were in?" Tree asked.

"His surgery."

"Well, there you go. I had surgery. You had a little scratch on your arm. You want some more coffee?"

"Sure, if you can manage it." Tree poured, wincing and groaning as he did. We laughed. I sipped the hot java, one hand draped over the steering wheel, the sun behind us and a clear road ahead. I was having fun. The last few days, as we put together the pieces of the case against Angus Crowley, Tree and I had managed to set aside the anger that had been between us the past few years, and get back to the boyhood camaraderie that had bound us together back in

Boston. Tree had medical leave for a week, and I'd gotten permission from Colonel Harding to see the Angry Smith case to its conclusion.

We'd gone to London with depositions from the Berkshire Constabulary detailing what we'd discovered about Crowley, and what witnesses had heard him confess to. The Criminal Investigations Division didn't like hearing it, and we'd been kicked upstairs to a captain who took offense at Tree's race, my Boston accent, and the very idea of letting Smith go free. The argument became heated, and our meeting ended with Tree pulling me out the office, one hand still clinging to the guy's lapel. We found a lawyer from the Judge Advocate General's office who wasn't a complete idiot, and he pushed the release through. Tree sent a letter to the prison, letting Angry know we'd be there soon. We had no idea if it got to him, but we had orders to spring him and a letter from General Eisenhower himself in case we needed an ace in the hole.

"Do you think Angry will really settle here after the war?" I asked Tree as we hummed along the roadway.

"He's serious all right," Tree said. "I think he would even if Rosemary weren't in the picture. He doesn't want to go back to the way he was treated in the States."

"Was it that bad for him?" Tree had had his share of hard times because of his skin color, but I didn't have the sense he was ready to call it quits on his country.

"I'll tell you a story, then you decide," Tree said. "We were doing field exercises outside of Fort Polk—that's in Louisiana. The company exec sent Angry and a corporal into town with a requisition for supplies. They take the jeep into this little cracker town, and Angry goes into the general store while Corporal Jefferson waits outside in the jeep. Before he knows it, there's a crowd of whites around the jeep. Angry starts to go outside, but the storekeeper warns him off and tells him to keep quiet if he values his life. The white boys start beating up on Jefferson, and before long they're dragging him behind the jeep, up and down the street, until he's dead."

"What did Angry do?"

"Went out the back door, ran ten miles back to our bivouac.

Reported to our commanding officer, who went into town to retrieve the jeep."

"That's all?"

"That's all, Billy. The army let one of their own be murdered in broad daylight, and didn't lift a finger. They were afraid white folk across the South would turn against the army if they weren't allowed to murder a Negro soldier now and then. All Angry wants to do is get in combat and prove himself, then be left alone to build a life. Too many people back home don't want either thing to happen. So England looks pretty damn good."

"Can't say I blame him," I managed. Some days I was real clear about why we were fighting this war. Some days I wondered why we weren't fighting other wars. We drove in silence for a while.

"Turn here," Tree said, consulting the map on his lap. We soon came to a sign for the US Military Prison Shepton Mallet. The prison was in the center of town, surrounded by a high grey stone wall. We turned down Goal Street, and I recalled Kaz telling me this place had been a prison since the 1600s. The town had grown up with it, streets and lanes curving around the massive walls like a stream flowing against a rock outcropping. We found the entrance, showed our papers, and were directed to the administrative section. We parked, got out of the jeep, and stared at the gate closing behind us.

It was a sea of stone and barbed wire. The same monotonous grey both underfoot and rising up in every direction. There were interior fences separating the buildings and sentries in the towers that dotted the walls.

"I hope it's as easy getting out as it was getting in," Tree said. He hefted the bag with Angry's Class A uniform, forgetting to complain about his arm. A serious prison drives all trivial thoughts from a man's mind.

They knew we were coming. We presented the papers authorizing the release of Private Abraham Smith, and waited as the warden reviewed them. Ink flowed, rubber stamps were pounded on paper, and soon we were led into the prison proper by a stern-faced MP sergeant. He didn't make small talk.

"What's that?" I asked as we entered a large courtyard. Attached to one of the walls was a two-story brick structure, about as narrow as a row house. Its reddish hue and bright newness were at odds with the weathered grey stone of the prison.

"Execution house," he said. "That's where the hangings are done. The old gallows was falling apart, so we built that to replace it." We didn't talk much after that. I wondered what it was like spending the war guarding your own men and overseeing executions. Most in here probably deserved it, but it would be a helluva thing to explain to your kids when they asked, "What did you do in the war, Daddy?"

The courtyard was empty. From above, faces looked out of barred windows, watching our progress. There were no shouts or insults, no taunts of the guard, Tree, or me. That meant they ran a tight ship here. Respect, fear, or some combination of the two created an eerie silence as our boots echoed on the grey stone beneath our feet.

We followed the MP into one of the buildings. Up two flights, and down a narrow hallway, lit by bare bulbs every ten feet or so. It was damp and cold. The walls were the same greyish stone, and each door was solid wood with iron fastenings. Eyes watched us from thin slits as we passed by. The sergeant finally stopped, took a ring of keys from his belt, searched for the right one, unlocked the door, pushed it open, and stepped back two paces.

"Prisoner Smith, step out!" he shouted. Angry Smith came into the hallway, blinking his eyes against the harsh light. He took one step from the door and stood at attention. He was a big guy, shoulders straining against his denim shirt. Quiet, too. He nodded at Tree as if he'd expected him.

"This is your lucky day, boy," the sergeant said. "Captain Boyle is here to take you back to your unit. You'll make the quartermaster corps proud, now, won't you?"

Angry ignored him. He stood rigid, his fatigues ripped and stained, the letter "P" painted in white on the thighs and back. He was about my size, but it looked to be all muscle. He had a swollen cheek and a cut over one eye about a day old.

"The Six-One-Seven is a combat unit," Tree said.

"Am I talkin' to you, boy?" The MP glared at Tree, then shrugged at me, as if in commiseration.

"Sergeant," I barked, in my best imitation of Harding. "You've unlocked the door. That's all we need you for. Dismissed."

"I gotta escort you out, Captain," he said, spitting out my rank.

"Then do so, without running your mouth."

"Them my clothes?" Angry said to Tree, ignoring the squabble playing out in front of him as he pointed at the canvas bag.

"Yeah," Tree said, watching the sergeant. "Everything you need."

"I'm a free man now, ain't I, Sergeant?" He directed this to the MP, barely acknowledging his presence with the flicker of an eye.

"That's what the orders say," the sergeant said, as if reluctant to see even one of his charges proven innocent.

"Good." With that, he took off his shirt and dropped it at his feet. Trousers, shorts, shoes, and socks followed, a pile of greasy, green, unlaundered clothing not fit for rags. Naked, Angry stepped over the discarded clothes and took the bag from Tree. Old ragged scars showed on his back as he turned.

"Hold on," the sergeant said. "You can't—"

"Yes, he can," I said. "I say so, and General Eisenhower says so, right here in this letter." I tapped my jacket pocket. "Personnel at the Shepton Mallet Military Prison are to provide all necessary assistance, that's what it says. And the nice thing is that I get to decide what's necessary. Understood?"

"Yes, sir," he said, in the neutral tone of a non-com who can't wait to be rid of a troublesome officer.

Angry took his time dressing in his Class As. Tree had figured it would be a morale boost for him to leave the prison in his best uniform. After his time behind bars, the pants were a little loose and there was plenty of shirt to tuck in. He knotted his field scarf, donned his Eisenhower jacket, and finally turned to the sergeant, giving him his full attention. He tapped his own shoulder, where the Tank Destroyer patch was displayed. It was a black panther, crushing a tank in its jaws.

"Combat unit," Angry said. "Not quartermaster." The MP

ignored him, but I could tell by his face he wouldn't forget Angry, either.

Outside in the courtyard, with the MP nearly double-timing it to get rid of us, a rhythmic clapping began. It was a steady, slow clap that built up in speed and volume as we neared the exit. Some white faces peered down impassively at us, while other windows were empty, the prisoners back where they couldn't be seen, sending Angry off with the only salute they could offer. It was a thunderous echo by the time we reached the door.

I don't think I let my breath out until we were in the jeep. I got in and started it up while Tree jumped in the back and told Angry to sit up front. He didn't want to. He and Tree exchanged glares but I didn't care about what was going on between them. I just wanted to get the hell out of the gate.

Once we were on the road, I noticed Tree prodding Angry from the back seat, tapping him on the shoulder, and whispering.

"You guys want to share the secret?" I asked.

"No, sir," said Angry. His voice was deep but coiled, as if tamping down a geyser of words. I was beginning to see where he got the nickname.

"It's only right, Angry," Tree said.

"Okay," Angry said. He seemed to steel himself for a verbal ordeal. "Thank you, Captain Boyle. For getting me out."

"See," Tree said with a laugh, "that wasn't so hard."

"You're welcome, Private," I said. "Tree had something to do with it too, you know. Got himself wounded, if you count bird shot."

"Not where I come from," said Angry, and I thought I detected the faintest of smiles. "I'll thank him later for that. But if you hadn't come along, no one could've helped me. So thank you."

"No problem. What happened to you in there? Someone beat on you?"

"When the release papers and Tree's letter came through. Some of the MPs wanted to rile me, see if I'd hit back. Then they'd be able to file charges."

"But you didn't?"

"Nope. I let four of them work me over till they got tired. Most of the punches were where they wouldn't show. A few landed on my face." He spoke softly, keeping his emotions in check. I didn't ask about the scars on his back. They looked like they were from a long time ago.

"It would have been self-defense," I said. The look from Angry was the only answer I needed. Self-defense for a white man was assault for a Negro. "You need a doctor?" I asked.

"Probably got a coupla broken ribs. But no doctor. I don't want to get separated from the Six-Seventeenth again."

"There's an English doctor in Hungerford," I said. "He's worked on about everyone else involved in this case. One more with no questions asked shouldn't be a burden. Okay?"

"Long as it's off the record, he can tape me up. But we're going to war, Captain, and I gotta be there."

"We all gonna be there," Tree said, clasping Angry's shoulder. "We'll show 'em. The Germans, the rednecks, and our own people."

"Our own is the most important," Angry said. "You understand what we sayin', Captain?"

"I think they call that making history," I said.

"That's right. And we're *gonna* make it, or die trying."

"That's a heavy price to pay," I said.

"No it ain't, Captain. Livin' like a mule, that's a heavy price. You got me out of prison, and I owe you for that. Now I can die like a man or live like one. If I make it through this war, I'll settle down here in England. White people here ain't so crazy, if you know what I mean. No disrespect meant to you, Captain," Angry said.

"I know. Understood," I said. "And Rosemary Adams seems like a good woman. You know her husband is dead?"

"Yeah. Tree wrote that in the letter. They read our mail and I think that got me a few extra lumps, but I didn't care. I feel good now. Goin' home to the Six-Seventeenth, see Rosemary, and go to war. Life looks a damn sight better from where I'm sittin' now."

"Me too," Tree said. "I got the best damn gunner in the battalion back. The Nazis are gonna wish they never heard of the Six-Seventeenth, right, Angry?"

"Damn straight, Tree."

CHAPTER THIRTY-NINE

IT WAS LATE afternoon by the time we pulled into Hungerford. Doc Brisbane was in his surgery and confirmed Angry had two broken ribs but said they weren't the worst he'd seen. He taped up Angry, changed the dressings on Tree's wounds and mine, told us to stop getting injured, and sent us on our way.

We were all hungry, and when I offered to stand for dinner and pints at the Prince of Wales, Angry and Tree didn't need their arms twisted. I found Kaz, and was surprised to see Big Mike waiting in the bar. After introductions, we got a table. Big Mike pulled me aside as we were about to take our seats.

"Billy," he said in a whisper. "I found out Cosgrove is okay, he's going to make it. They got him in that rest home at Saint Albans, but it's all hush-hush. He wants to see you. Just you, alone, was the message. Colonel Harding said the visit would do him good."

"Thanks, Big Mike," I said. "I'll drive up tomorrow." Cosgrove probably wanted details about the case, to be sure nothing about the Millers had been compromised. I wondered if Harding was in on it. I usually complained about the army keeping me in the dark, but this was a secret I'd rather not have been burdened with.

"Billy, you owe us a story," Kaz said as we sat. "You never finished the story of what happened with Basher."

"Yeah, Billy," Big Mike said. "Last we heard Basher dumped a bucket of dirty water on Tree, but doused the boss at the same time."

"Man, seems like months ago we were telling that story, Billy,"
Tree said. "Time to wrap it up."

"We need to bring Angry up to speed?"

"Tree tells that whole damn story every couple of weeks," Angry
said. "Glad you got most of it out of the way. Be a pleasure to hear
someone less long-winded tell it for a change."

"Okay," I said, taking a long drink of ale. Stories are thirsty work.

BASHER HAD KEPT quiet for a week or so after getting chewed
out by Deputy Superintendent Emmons. Tree and I thought it was
over, but that was because we were dumb kids. Basher was watching
us, biding his time, waiting for his revenge. Mr. Jackson warned us
to be careful, and so did Dad. But we thought we were smarter than
them all.

After work I'd head over to Earl's Garage where Tree worked.
We'd talk, and I'd help him so his boss wouldn't get mad. Tree
was a good mechanic, and he taught me a lot about engines that
summer. Basher brought his car in once to get the oil changed,
and he watched Tree the whole time. I thought it was odd that
he did that, since he wasn't a regular customer. I told Dad about
it that night, and the next day I found him down in Mr. Jackson's
office.

"Son, we both think Basher's up to something. You and Tree
need to lay low for a while," Dad said.

"Best if you two don't hang around together so much. White boy
and a Negro boy can only be trouble," Mr. Jackson said. "It's not your
fault, it's just the way things are."

"Is that what you think, Dad?" I wondered if Dad was getting
pressure from his boss, or if he really believed that.

"I think Mr. Jackson knows what he's talking about. It's the smart
move. Let Basher find something else to get all riled up about."

"Okay," I said, not willing to argue with two fathers.

"Billy," Dad said. "Don't soft-soap me."

"No, really, I get it. We make a convenient target. And Tree would get the worst of it, so I understand." They were relieved. The first thing I did after work was to run over to Earl's and tell Tree.

"Yeah, Pop read me the riot act this morning," Tree said. "What are we gonna do?"

"I don't know. I have enough money once I get paid this week to buy the Indian Scout. But it needs work. I thought I could do it here."

"You can," Tree said. "Earl said it was okay, long as you help me out. He's not a bad guy."

"But what if we get caught?"

"They can't stop you being a customer of Earl's, can they? Are that's what you'd be. Sort of." It was with that twisted logic that we began to deceive our fathers, which was not a minor transgression in either of our households.

I bought the Scout, wheeling it in at night to Earl's to avoid any chance of being seen. I'd sounded out my dad about getting a motorcycle, but Mom heard and before he had a chance to give his opinion, she'd weighed in. He went into his study and shut the door on us both. I kind of doubted he'd say yes, but he never said no, either.

Things were going well. Basher was leaving us alone, even on the few times Tree came to see his dad at work. I'd gotten a used oil pump and installed it, and was planning on working on the brakes next. My thinking didn't really go much beyond that.

One day, as I was about to finish up at work, Basher brushed by me, giving me a hard elbow in the ribs. He grinned as he and two other cops made for their squad car. He was happy, and Basher was only happy when other people weren't. I ran to the garage, and found Basher taking a statement from Earl. The place had been robbed, a window broken to gain entry, and a crowbar taken to the cash register. They'd gotten fifty bucks in cash.

And my 1922 Indian Scout.

They had Tree in the squad car, and wouldn't let me near him. Earl swore Tree was a good kid and had had nothing to do with it, but they thanked him for his cooperation and drove away. There was only one thing to do.

Dad was working a homicide down on Fulton Street; he'd been in the station that day and told me to tell Mom he'd be home late. I jumped a streetcar and looked around until I saw the police cars. The coroner's wagon was just taking the body away and Dad was talking to two beat cops. I waved until I got his attention.

It wasn't pretty. Disturbing your dad at work to tell him you've been lying to him is never a good idea. When your dad is a homicide detective with a fresh corpse, it's truly a horrible idea. The fact that he'd warned me about Basher meant that I had to endure the iciest glare ever. When Dad got mad, he got loud and yelled a lot. When he got *really* mad, he got quiet as the veins bulged on his neck.

He dispatched a couple of bluecoats over to Tree's house, telling them to make sure Basher did everything by the book. When I asked him what he meant, his look went from stern and angry to weary, as if he didn't want me to hear what grown men were capable of.

"Son, they're going to find the money and your bike on the Jacksons' property. That's what this is all about. It's what Mr. Jackson and I tried to tell you. This isn't kid stuff. This is real life, the way it happens when you go up against guys like Basher without a plan."

"You mean they're going to arrest Tree?"

"There's no way out of it, Billy. They'll have evidence."

"But you can tell them, Tree wouldn't do this. Earl at the garage even said he was a good kid!"

"Evidence, Billy. They have evidence. It's phony, you and I know that. The judge might even suspect it, but the law is the law. I'm sorry. Best I can do is make sure Basher doesn't pull anything like claiming Tree resisted arrest. My men will keep an eye on him. Now go home, and we'll talk later."

I took the streetcar home to South Boston, wishing it would never stop.

They let Tree out on bail. Mr. Jackson had to put up his house for the bond. The prosecutor argued that the young man was a flight risk, and only the loss of his father's home would serve to keep him around.

Of course, Tree lost his job. Earl said people wouldn't trust the garage if the guy accused of robbing it still worked there. He had a point.

I knew Tree had been planning on going to college in the fall, and I figured that I could sell my bike, once it was out of the evidence impound, to help him out. It was only right, since the whole thing was my fault. We'd both jumped in feet first, but Tree was the one paying the price.

I decided to do some detective work of my own. I canvased the neighborhood, like Dad talked about. But since I was a kid, a lot of people didn't want to be bothered. One old lady didn't mind. Mrs. Mildred Bishop lived in a walk-up apartment overlooking the alley behind Earl's Garage. She stank of cigarette smoke. Her house stank, her cat stank, and two fingers on her right hand were stained yellow with nicotine.

"I wake up coughing sometimes," she said. I tried to hide my surprise. "So I get up and have a smoke. I always stand by the window, it helps me breathe. The other night, when they said the garage was robbed? Well, I was up a lot that night. I had just lit a Pall Mall when I heard a sound outside. It was warm, so the windows were wide open."

"What sort of sound, ma'am?" I asked. I had my notebook out and was scribbling her statement, or what I thought a police statement looked like.

"Breaking glass. I thought maybe a stray cat had knocked some bottles over. People are always leaving bottles stacked in the alleyway. I didn't hear much else, until near the end of my cigarette. A truck pulled up and stopped in back of Earl's. Someone came out and loaded what looked like a motorcycle on it. They had boards out so they could run it up the back."

"Did you see the person, Mrs. Bishop?"

"No, it was too dark to make out faces, dear boy."

"Could you tell if it was a Negro or a white man?"

"Oh, it was a white man. I could see a bit of his face, no details, but I'd certainly say a white man."

"Could you describe the truck?"

"No, sorry, I can't. I don't really know much about cars and trucks." She ground out one Pall Mall and lit another.

"Did the police come by and ask about the robbery?"

"They did come, yes. They had a picture of that nice colored boy who works at the station. They wanted to know if I'd seen him. Of course I had, I told them. When I walk by and he's out, he always waves. Nice young fellow, like you are. Polite."

I wrote everything out, asked her to read and sign it. She did, and invited me back anytime. I coughed a bit myself, thanked her, and left.

What I should have done was go to Dad and give him the story Mrs. Bishop had told me. But I went to Tree first, because I wanted him to know that I was on the case, and that I wouldn't let him be railroaded. I felt bad about everything that had happened, starting with how I got the job, right up to Tree being framed, all because Basher didn't like a white doing a colored job. Also because we'd made Basher look stupid, and he never forgave an offense.

Tree and I figured the best thing to do was take the statement to his public defender. He was a young lawyer who didn't have much experience, but this information seemed like it would give him an edge. Reasonable doubt, that's what we thought. I also knew I wanted to impress Dad, to show him I could fix my own mess without his help.

Shows how dumb I was. The thing I didn't think through was that the public defender had to share evidence with the prosecutor, and the prosecutor works with the police. Meaning Basher. By the time I'd filled in Dad—and gotten a dose of reality, delivered in a long and loud lecture about my lack of brains, judgment, and all-around suitability as a functioning human being—a new public defender had been appointed, the evidence from Mrs. Bishop had been misfiled and lost, and Basher had paid her a visit. She refused to speak to me again, even when I showed up with a pack of Pall Malls.

The fix was in. What we didn't fully understand was how deep and twisted the fix was. At the last minute, the prosecutor offered

Tree a deal. Testify that the theft had been my idea all along, and he'd walk with probation. Then the district attorney would file charges against me. Whether they stuck or not didn't really matter. What mattered to Basher was teaching us a lesson. And he'd have something to hold over my father's head. Dad wasn't exactly an angel when it came to the small stuff. Hell, our kitchen was furnished with a lot of stuff that fell off trucks after a robbery. But Basher was corrupt in a big way, the kind of corruption that led to organized crime and dead bodies floating in the harbor. Dad resisted him every step of the way, but the cop code of silence kept him from doing any more than that. With me coming up for trial, Dad might be tempted to exchange an illegal favor or two to derail the court date.

Tree told the DA to go to hell. Not to save me from trouble, but because he wanted a trial. Probation meant a conviction, and even though he wouldn't serve time, it would kill his chances of college. Pop Jackson had a Negro lawyer, Irwin Dorch, lined up to defend Tree. Dorch was head of the Boston National Association for the Advancement of Colored People, and Mr. Jackson said he'd paid his dollar a year to belong since he came back from the war, and it was time to collect. Dorch took the case pro bono, and he planned to use it not only to exonerate Tree, but to agitate for more Negro police officers.

The whole thing was a far cry from the simple summer job I'd originally signed up for.

Tree and I began to drift apart as rumors swirled about Dorch taking the case. All of a sudden it seemed like it was the whole department, not just Basher, against him and me. It became a case of us and them, with me sitting on the *them* side, since my dad and uncle were both detectives, and being on the force was their whole world.

I tried again with Mrs. Bishop, but she was gone. Took her nest egg and moved to Maine to live with her daughter, the neighbors said. Conveniently outside of the local jurisdiction. Looked to me like any nest egg she had went into buying smokes, and I wondered if Basher had shown up with a wad of cash. No wonder my single pack of coffin nails hadn't opened any doors for me.

I went to see Tree after that. I said I'd talked to the DA, that he'd been to the house a few times, and was what my dad called one of the good guys. Even among lawyers, cops, and robbers there were good guys and bad guys, and you couldn't always count on the uniform or suit coat to tell them apart.

Tree said no, let it go to trial. That way I was in the clear, and he stood a chance of keeping his record clean. I didn't see it that way, but he was in the hot seat, so I told him he was probably right.

But I never said I wouldn't talk to the DA.

I waited outside the courtroom the next afternoon. A big trial was wrapping up, and I knew DA Flanagan would be there for the cameras. He was. As the flashbulbs popped and he puffed out his chest in the August heat, I strolled around the edges of the crowd. Finally I caught his eye, and as the crowd dispersed and he walked to his waiting sedan, he waved me over.

"What are you doing here, Billy?"

"Waiting to talk to you, Mr. Flanagan. About Tree . . . I mean Eugene Jackson," I said.

"Your father know you're here?" He'd stopped and given me his full attention, tapping out a cigarette and firing up a gold lighter.

"No, sir. This isn't his idea, it's all mine."

"And what exactly is it you want?" He drew in smoke and exhaled through his nose. It looked strange, and I unaccountably thought of dragons.

I told him about how Basher had treated us, about Mrs. Bishop and the statement I'd given to the first public defender. "I just want Eugene to get a fair shake. But Basher's got everything lined up against him."

"Billy, the police have presented sufficient evidence for my office to act. If Mrs. Bishop will come forward and give a proper statement, we'll be glad to take it into consideration."

"She's gone. It looked like she didn't have a dime to spare, and now she's moved up to Maine with a nest egg."

"So all I have is your word," Flanagan said.

"Yes, sir."

"It might look very bad for your father if word got out his son tried to influence the prosecution in favor of a defendant," Flanagan said. He moved toward his automobile and the driver hopped to and opened the rear door. He stopped, took a drag, and crushed the cigarette out on the curb. "I wouldn't try this again, young man. You might stir up trouble your family doesn't need."

"Yes, sir," I said to the door as it slammed shut.

I went back to mopping floors as the summer ended. Tree's trial was scheduled for right after Labor Day. The day before the holiday, Dad came home with good news. The prosecutor had offered Tree a deal. A terrific deal. All charges dropped except breaking and entering. And he was given a choice about how to do his time. Take one year in jail, or join the army.

Tree hadn't wanted to take the deal. He was ready for a fight, and thought Dorch could win the case. But Pop Jackson wasn't so sure, and told Tree to take the offer. He wasn't a guy you argued with, whether he was your boss or your father. So Tree took the deal.

I made the mistake of telling Tree that I had been the one to talk to the DA. I was bragging about it, to tell the truth. I thought I'd gambled and won, and I wanted my friend to know. Flanagan had believed me, or at least knew enough about Basher to reconsider his case. I thought Tree would be happy, even thankful. But he was roaring mad. I was the one who'd taken away his chance to prove himself innocent and make his own choices about college or the army. It wasn't my place to decide for him. I wasn't that much better than Basher, when it came down to it. Both of us used the system to get what we wanted, without giving Tree a choice in the matter. We had a big blow-out fight, and Tree told me to never come around again.

I didn't. He chose the army, of course.

"AND HERE WE all are," Tree said. "I thought my life was over. No college, no future. But we didn't see this war coming. I'd be in the army anyway by now. This way, I'm a non-com in a combat outfit.

I don't know if you guys know what that means for a Negro. I'm going to fight for my country, and if I get home, I'm going to fight for myself, and my people."

"You're satisfied how it worked out?" Big Mike asked. "You're not still sore at Billy?"

"I'm not happy I missed Pop's funeral," Tree said. "But that was the Deep South for you. Wasn't Billy's fault. Billy Boyle is a born snoop, but this time around it worked out for me. I got my gunner back." He raised his pint to Angry Smith, and we all drank a toast to the 617th Tank Destroyer Battalion.

Later, as we piled into the jeep to drive Tree and Angry back to their bivouac area, Tree asked Angry why he'd had such a hard time thanking me earlier that day. He took a deep breath, and his answer didn't come right away.

"Because I never thanked a white man before, and meant it. Colored man got to say a lot of things to keep trouble at bay, Captain. Some of those things eat at you, know what I mean? But I can't say no white man ever did me a kindness, until you come along. I know you did it to even things up with Tree, but still, it put me in your debt. I owe you."

CHAPTER FORTY

I MADE THE drive to Saint Albans the next day to see Major Cosgrove. I told Kaz and Big Mike to head back to SHAEF, knowing that Cosgrove wanted to talk to me alone. Saint Albans was a rest home, a hospital for those who held secrets in their heads and sometimes demons as well. It was top secret, staffed by doctors and nurses who had security clearances better than mine.

Saint Albans was reserved mainly for those who had been emotionally damaged but who needed to be patched up, for the greater good, and sent back into the fight. There were SOE agents, commandos, and foreigners from all over Europe. Major Cosgrove of MI5 was important enough to warrant a bed here as well. Or perhaps it was the knowledge he held.

My name was on the list, which got me past the armed guard at the entrance gate. I was taken to the back garden, where I spied Cosgrove seated in a wheelchair, reading a book. He looked up as I approached, and I was surprised at how good he looked, compared to how terrible he had looked the last time I saw him.

"Boyle," he said, standing and extending his hand. "Good of you to come." He was dressed in blue pajamas and a quilted robe. The wheelchair was wicker, and looked built for comfort as opposed to transport. There was color in his face, which had been pallid and pasty after his attack. "Please excuse the casual attire; uniform of the day at Saint Albans."

"Are you supposed to stand, Major?" I asked, pulling a lawn chair closer and taking my seat.

"They have me doing a bit of exercise," he said. "This thing is for moving about the property easily, not because I need it." He slammed his palm down as if to reinforce the point. Charles Cosgrove was not the kind of man who wanted to appear helpless, and I could tell being in the chair bothered him. "But the medicos insist, so here I am."

"You do look pretty good, Major," I said. "I thought I'd find you in a hospital bed, hooked up to some contraption."

"I'm not dead yet, Boyle. It was a heart attack, yes. But they said I was also suffering from exhaustion. I didn't like being taken here, but I must admit the rest has done me wonders. Didn't really understand how tired I was."

"Will you be back on duty, or . . . ?" I let the question linger. *Be put out to pasture?*

"If I have no relapse, and the doctors concur, I expect I will. Desk duty, most likely. No more running about keeping tabs on you, Boyle! That will be a relief for both of us, I wager."

"I don't know, Major. I've almost gotten used to you."

"Well, then I will redouble my efforts to heal from this event. Perhaps you haven't seen the last of me yet. But tell me, your talk with Masterman, what exactly did he tell you?"

"I'm not sure I'm at liberty to say, sir." I waited, feeling the warm breeze on my face. I didn't want to hold out on Cosgrove, but this was beyond top secret, as far as I was concerned.

"Well done. I told Masterman you could be counted upon. Boyle, you must forget what you learned from him. It was necessary to tell you, but it is such a gigantic secret, the most precious of the war so far, I believe."

"It frightens me, knowing," I said in a quiet voice.

"Yes," Cosgrove said. "There are so many things that could go wrong, so many people involved. I think about it nearly every moment of the day. The Millers, they suspect nothing?"

"No," I said. "I visited them this morning, to give them a

report on what we determined about Neville's death. They were relieved."

"You betrayed nothing? Your voice, how you looked at them?"

"Major, I've been a cop long enough to know how to lie with a poker face."

"Very good, Boyle," he said. "I *am* overanxious about this, I know. We've been carrying on this charade for so long it has become a part of me. I'll be glad when it's over."

"When the invasion comes?"

"Yes, and then for some short time beyond, if we're successful. We'll keep Jerry looking in all the wrong places for as long as possible. Then we'll pick up Herr and Frau Miller and deal with them as they deserve."

"What about their daughter, Eva? She can hardly be part of this."

"Likely not. But they are the ones who put her in harm's way, not us. She may be lucky, if that term applies. If she had stayed in Germany in any one of their cities, she could have been long dead by now. Every night we bomb and burn them, Boyle. It is a terrible business all around."

We sat for a while, thoughts of burning cities mingling with the visions of crippled men and women all around us, enjoying the sunshine while night reigned supreme in their minds. After a few minutes, I gave him all the details of the investigation, everything that happened after he was taken away. He asked a few questions until once again we lapsed into silence. The quiet and the clear blue skies were deceptively calming.

"Can you tell me anything about Diana?" I finally asked. "Where she was sent?"

"She angered some very powerful people, Boyle. Politics and passion are not a good mix. But rest assured, she was not sent on a suicide mission. She is probably quite bored where she is."

"Here in England?"

"In Great Britain, yes. A training facility. Sealed tight. A dilapidated country estate surrounded by barbed wire. I hope to find out about getting her back to London soon."

"Sounds like she's safer there."

"Yes, but the Diana Seaton we know would not be satisfied with mere safety, eh Boyle?"

"No, sir. Is there anything you need? Anything I can get you?"

"No, thank you. You've done enough by telling me about the Neville case. Justice was served, official secrets kept. Well done."

"Thank you, Major."

"And your Negro friend, that case was concluded to your satisfaction?"

"Yes, the real killer was found and Private Smith was released. He's back with his unit, and they're ready for action."

"I wish them well. And you too, Boyle. I hope our paths cross again, but if not . . ." This time, he was the one to let the sentence hang. He rose and we shook hands. For two guys who started out not liking each other much, it was a helluva goodbye.

"See you in the funny papers, Major."

Cosgrove laughed and shook his head, settling back down into his wicker wheelchair. It's always good to leave them laughing.

DRIVING OUT OF Saint Albans, I wondered why Cosgrove had really sent for me. Was it to hear a first-hand report about the Millers and the murder investigation, or was it something else? Cosgrove was a military man through and through, a pal of Winston Churchill's from the Boer War. If this was the end of his career, or perhaps his life, maybe he wanted one more taste of the hunt. Couldn't blame him one bit.

I had nothing to do until I had to report back to SHAEF tomorrow, so I decided to go back to Hungerford for a final visit with Tree. All this talk of the unknown future had gotten to me. And I wanted to see Angry Smith back with his crew, in his element as a gunner. I headed south, navigating my way through heavy traffic, hundreds of trucks, flatbeds, jeeps, and every conceivable vehicle the army owned, it seemed. All heading in the same direction, south. Toward the invasion ports. Someday soon, a huge fleet would set sail. Me, I was probably sitting it out. Not a lot of crime in the middle of an amphibious invasion. But the 617th could be in on it. If not the first to hit the beach, then among the follow-up units once the initial landings were successful.

I hit Hungerford in the late afternoon, and drove out to the Common where they were bivouacked. The roads were choked with vehicles, and as I maneuvered the jeep closer, I saw a dozen or so flatbed trucks, the same kind I'd seen on the road with tanks chained down on them. I was just in time; they were moving out.

I drew closer, and could see that the tents had been struck and that men were drawn up in platoons, some of them already boarding trucks. Officers—all of them white—stood by the flatbeds and directed the men who'd driven the TDs up onto them back to their platoons. The officers were laughing, the enlisted men were quiet. The privilege of rank.

I asked for Tree's platoon and was directed down the line by a sullen corporal. I spotted him as his crew moved to board their truck.

"Tree," I yelled, running over to him. "You're shipping out?"

"Yeah, we're shipping out," he said, not meeting my eyes.

"What's the matter? What happened?" I looked around to get a clue as to what the problem was. It looked like the 617th was joining the long march to the sea, along with everyone else.

"They took our TDs away," Angry Smith said, his voice a low growl. "They make us drive them up those flatbeds and they're going to take them away."

"What? Are you getting tanks? Where are you going?"

"We're not getting tanks, Billy!" Tree shouted, exploding in a fury I hadn't seen since we parted in Boston. "They're giving our TDs to a new battalion, a *white* battalion! All the officers are going, all of them except the one Negro officer we have."

"But what's happening to you?" It didn't make any sense.

"Plymouth," Tree said, spitting out the word as if it were foul and rotten. "We've been designated a quartermaster battalion. Lots of ships to unload in Plymouth. Supplies for the invasion. So they take a well-trained unit like ours and turn us into stevedores, then give our TDs to white boys who don't know them. It ain't right, Billy." He was up against me, his anguish paralyzing, his agony awful to see.

"Don't bother, Tree," Angry said, taking him by the arm. "Don't give them an excuse." A squad of white MPs stood at the ready near the knot of white officers. Just in case.

Tree took a breath and calmed himself, turning back into a US Army sergeant. "Okay men, grab your duffles and board the truck. Let's go!"

"I'm sorry, Tree," was all I could get out. It was pathetic. He brushed by me, unable to look at me. His hand squeezed my arm, briefly, a sign from the depths of a childhood friendship, and then he was gone, swallowed up by the shaded darkness of the truck.

Angry was the last to board. He leaned over the tailgate, and beckoned me closer.

"What I said last night? It don't hold no more. I don't owe you a damn thing."

The truck lurched forward, dust rising from the road as it followed the rest of the battalion, six hundred strong. They passed by their Tank Destroyers, loaded on the flatbeds. Most looked away. One man saluted.

I stood to attention and returned the salute, keeping my hand to the brim of my cap until the last of the trucks passed.

AUTHOR'S NOTE

THE SEGREGATION OF American armed forces during the
Second World War was not only morally wrong, it was an inexcus-
able misuse of manpower and scarce resources. The government
and military could have chosen this national emergency to signal a
change in race relations on the basis of wartime necessity. Instead,
segregation resulted in wasteful duplication by creating separate
and unequal facilities so the races would be kept apart. Shipping,
transportation, post exchanges, and every aspect of military life
had to be provided independently for white and black usage.
Perhaps racist attitudes were too ingrained to change when
America entered the war in 1941, but in doing research for this
book I was struck by the extent to which the separation of the
races hampered the war effort and gave the enemy a gift of pro-
paganda, pointing out the dichotomy between the American war
aims and the treatment of minorities.

Each incident of racial conflict and violence described in this
work actually occurred; from the smashing of glassware in pubs
frequented by black soldiers to the dragging to death of a black GI
in the Deep South. These encounters are true, if fictionalized for the
purpose of this narrative. The sign on the Three Crowns Pub in
Hungerford stating "This place is for the exclusive use of Englishmen
and American Negro soldiers" was observed by George Orwell and
reported in the *London Tribune* in 1943.

Black soldiers training in camps in the southern US were subject to harsh treatment by civilian authorities when they ventured off base. In 1941, a black soldier named Felix Hall was found lynched in the woods outside Fort Benning, Georgia. Even though his hands were tied behind his back, the army listed the official cause of death as suicide, eliminating the necessity of an investigation that would have involved local white authorities.

Similar bias existed within American bases in England as well. At the US Army prison in Shepton Mallet, eighteen military executions were carried out. Of those, ten were black soldiers, even though blacks accounted for only eight percent of Army personnel. One black GI did escape the death penalty thanks to the outrage expressed by the British public. Leroy Henry was sentenced to death for raping a white woman in the village of Combe Down. Local residents were aware that Leroy Henry had been engaged in an ongoing relationship with the woman and tended to believe his story that she accused him of rape after an argument over the price of her services. The British public were also appalled at how he had been beaten by the military police during questioning. As the result of newspaper publicity, over 33,000 people signed a petition calling for Leroy Henry to be reprieved. It was sent to General Eisenhower, who agreed to grant the soldier his freedom.

The deactivation of black combat units and reassignment of personnel into service units, as experienced by Tree and the fictional 617th Tank Destroyer Battalion, was routine. The 9th and 10th Cavalry Regiments (known historically as Buffalo Soldiers) along with the entire 2nd Cavalry Division were all disbanded and their combat-trained men assigned to non-combat units.

Independent Tank Destroyer and Tank battalions were one of the routes for blacks to serve in combat. The 761st Tank Battalion was the first black armored unit committed to combat, assigned to the Third Army under General George Patton, who famously welcomed them with this speech: "I don't care what color you are, so long as you go up there and kill those Kraut sonsabitches. Everyone has their eyes on you and is expecting great things from you. Most of all, your race is looking to you. Don't let them down, don't let me down." They didn't, serving 183 days in combat and receiving commendations from every unit they were assigned to.

THE BRITISH COUNTERINTELLIGENCE service MI5 was charged with apprehending German agents in England. Operations were overseen by the Twenty Committee, chaired by John Cecil Masterman. The name of the committee came from the number twenty in Roman numerals: XX, or double cross.

MI5 was quite successful in catching Nazi agents who reached British shores. Many turned themselves in to the authorities as soon as they landed. Others were captured soon after coming ashore. As the war progressed, German spies were instructed to contact agents already established in Great Britain. But by then, those spies were controlled by the British. As explained by Masterman in this book, the greatest fear the Twenty Committee had was one German agent slipping through their hands, thus revealing to the Nazis that none of the information coming from their agents was be trusted. With D-Day approaching, this could make the difference between a successful landing and a disaster. After the war it was determined that every agent sent by Germany to Great Britain had given themselves up or had been captured, with the possible exception of one who committed suicide. The work of the Twenty Committee is one of the great success stories in the history of counterintelligence and deception campaigns.

ACKNOWLEDGMENTS

I AM SUPERBLY supported and assisted by the diligence and keen eye of my wife Deborah Mandel, my first reader and editor. As in all things, her work improves mine. Michael Gordon continues to provide a close read; his comments and edits are valued, even though we don't always agree on comma usage. Juliet Grames, Senior Editor at Soho Press, provides a clear guiding hand as the manuscript undergoes her expert scrutiny. Her dedication is extraordinary.